HIGHLAND WEDDING

Running his fingers down the laced front of her gown, he murmured, "This is lovely, but I think I like the other better."

"The other isnae a lady's night rail."

"'Tis simpler." He began to slowly undo her lacings.

"Ye didnae drink your wine," she squeaked.

"Why so tremulous, lass?" He brushed light kisses over the delicate lines of her face. "Ye are a maiden no longer."

"Aye, but last eve was, weel, different. We just went about it. T'was not so planned."

"Lovemaking is planned more oft than otherwise, especially atween a mon and his wife."

"T'will take a wee bit of time to get used to it, though."

She trembled when he gently removed her gown, then tossed it away. When he pulled her body close to his, she moaned softly. The feel of their skin touching set her blood running hot. She smoothed her hands over his broad back, loving the feel of smooth skin stretched tautly over muscle.

When he kissed her, she clung to him and her lips parted willingly.

"Ye are a verra fast learner, lass," he rasped.

"And is that good?" she asked in a husky whisper.

"Ye willnae hear me complain," he murmured against her throat . . .

Books by Hannah Howell

Only for You
My Valiant Knight
Unconquered
Wild Roses
A Taste of Fire
Highland Destiny
Highland Honor
Highland Promise
A Stockingful of Joy
Highland Vow
Highland Knight
Highland Hearts
Highland Bride
Highland Angel
Highland Groom
Highland Warrior
Reckless
Highland Conqueror
Highland Champion
Highland Lover
Highland Vampire
Conqueror's Kiss
Highland Barbarian
Beauty and the Beast
Highland Savage
Highland Thirst
Highland Wedding
Highland Wolf

Published by Zebra Books

HIGHLAND WEDDING

HANNAH HOWELL

ZEBRA BOOKS
Kensington Publishing Corp.
www.kensingtonbooks.com

ZEBRA BOOKS are published by

Kensington Publishing Corp.
850 Third Avenue
New York, NY 10022

All Kensington titles, imprints, and distributed lines are available at
special quantity discounts for bulk purchases for sales promotion,
premiums, fund-raising, educational, or institutional use.

Special book excerpts or customized printings can also be created to
fit specific needs. For details, write or phone the office of the Kensington Special Sales Manager: Attn. Special Sales Department. Kensington Publishing Corp., 850 Third Avenue, New York, NY 10022.
Phone: 1-800-221-2647.

Zebra and the Z logo Reg. U.S. Pat. & TM Off.

ISBN-13: 978-0-8217-8002-2
ISBN-10: 0-8217-8002-6

This book was previously published by Leisure Books under the title
Promised Passion.

First Zebra Books Printing: November 2007
First Leisure Books Printing: November 1988

10 9 8 7 6 5 4 3 2 1

Printed in the United States of America

Chapter One

She turned the corner and he was there, sitting and staring at the roses as if they could talk and would at any moment. That sad, lost look was on his scarred face again. Sometimes she would allow herself to pretend that he revealed that side of himself to her willingly, then savored the glow that gave her. It never lasted long for she was too practical. Soon she would tartly remind herself that the only reason she had seen it was because she was lurking around, catching him when he thought he was alone.

This night she would be presented at court. She had been brought in hopes of forming an alliance through marriage, preferably one that would further the family's favor with the king. From the moment she had laid eyes on the man she had fought against hoping that he would be the one chosen for her. He had all the right qualifications, but her luck had never been that good. Instead of a man her heart ached for, she would no doubt get some mincing courtier or even a man past his prime and probably past all else.

At nineteen years she was late in wedding but her father had held off finding her a husband hoping that she would fill out to look more like a woman than a child. It was not to be. She was small and no amount of potions and porridge would change that. Only she and Meg knew that she was perhaps not as unwomanly as she appeared. All that, however, did not alter the fact that she thought she was not comely. She had been told that often enough to know it was so. With so little to offer a man, one like Iain MacLagan was not for her.

Her hair was the color of claret wine, such a deep red that many swore it ran with a purple hue despite her adament denials of such an oddity. It was of such thickness with a strong tendency to curl that it was always slipping its bonds, looking untidy. Her eyes were a deep brown with flecks of gold set beneath finely arched dark brows and ringed with such long, curled dark lashes that she was always denying accusations of their being unnatural. Though she knew her skin was lovely and pale, she had been cursed with freckles which, though faint and few, would not be removed. She sighed.

Whether it was that soft sigh or just a sense of being watched she was not sure but Iain MacLagan suddenly looked her way. She stood like a terrified hare, pinned to the spot by turquoise eyes that shone bright yet emotionless in his harsh dark face. At any moment she expected him to verbally flay her with his cold, remote voice, so well-known in court, for being so insolent as to invade his privacy.

Iain had thought to lash her with words but she looked so much like a frightened child that he could not. She was sadly disheveled with a vast amount of wine red hair easing free of her headdress. Her eyes were huge dark pools in her small ivory face, a dainty visage that wavered between being heart-shaped and triangular. Perfect white teeth worried the bottom lip of her full mouth. There were few curves to indicate she was a grown woman, but he could see she was at least past her first flux. She was also rather lacking in height and flesh elsewhere on her body for her neck and arms were slender nearly to frailty.

He wondered what fool let her wander about unattended. Her youth was no protection. Although he himself felt it abhorrent to lust after and bed a girl barely past her first flux, he could think of others who did not. There were also those men who would care little that she was obviously well-born and innocent. For all her daintiness, she was rather pretty.

"There is no need to quail so, mistress."

"I didnae mean to disturb your privacy, Sir MacLagan." She willed her body to disappear but it did not happen.

"The garden is to be enjoyed by all. Come, sit. Ye ken my name but I ken not yours. Come."

Tentatively, she did so, sitting beside him as if she expected the bench to singe her backside. "I am Islaen MacRoth."

"Islaen. 'Tis fitting," he murmured for her voice was soft, low and slightly husky with the attraction of fine music. "I have not seen ye here before. Newly arrived?"

"Aye. I am to be put forward this eve." She saw his winged dark brows quirk and knew he thought her too young. "I am newly turned nineteen. Fither kept me at home in hopes I would grow. He gave up."

A smile ghosted over Iain's face for even with her head-dress and painfully straight posture she barely rose to his shoulder. The hands that plucked at her skirts were small, delicate and long-fingered. Except for the huge dark eyes that stared up at him everything about Islaen MacRoth was small, including her lightly freckled modestly upturned nose. He could not help but wonder how she would find a husband, which was undoubtedly the reason she had been brought to court.

"I have a sizeable purse, some verra sweet property near the border and an excellent bloodline."

"Ye read minds, do ye? 'Tis a verra uncomplimentary thought ye put in my head."

Guilt gave his voice the sternness he sought in order to sound convincing. It was an insult to a woman to think her unweddable and he had no real wish to insult her. She looked a sweet child.

Inwardly he cursed for his body was reacting to her as a man's did when in the presence of a lovely woman. His loins did not doubt her age. It was a feeling he fought, although he found it not as easy as it had become since Catalina's death. That troubled him deeply for he felt it vital that he keep his passion under firm control.

"Nay, only the truth and 'tis your look I read for oft have I seen it. 'Tis the ones who gape or snicker that I consider rude."

"So ye should." His face hardened suddenly. "T'would be wrong for any mon to wed ye and make ye bear his bairn."

Unaware of what prompted his statement or put the harshness in his voice, she drew herself up to her full, inconsiderable height. "And just why do ye say that? I am a woman and ye wed women and get them with bairn. I can do it as weel as any other."

"Nay, ye cannae. Ye havenae got any hips, ye foolish wee lass."

"Pray tell me then what it is I am sitting on?"

"Your backside and cursed little there is of it."

"My mither looked much as I do and she bore a dozen bairns, healthy bairns. She didnae die bearing them either. Went fishing for salmon when I was five and drowned. If she could then I can."

"Ye cannae recall your mither exact, child." He stood up to glare at her. "Ye are a wee thing not made for childbearing."

To counter the effects of his towering over her, she stood on the bench. "Then what did God put me here for?"

"Only He kens. Aye, and only He kens how I got into this discussion. Ye would be wise to join a nunnery and forget the bairns."

"Ye be a mon. What do ye ken about it?" she asked scornfully and squeaked when he roughly grasped her shoulders.

He did not really frighten her with his sudden fierce intensity. She found that she had a deep, abiding trust in him. What she did not understand was why he was so fierce. Their conversation had taken a strange turn that left her confused. It was certainly not like any she had dreamt they would have when she finally got to talk to him. 'Although,' she mused with an inner smile over her own foolishness, 'it is no stranger than if he began to spout flowery phrases of undying love as I have so often imagined him doing.' In truth, next to that fantasy, this strange discussion seemed quite reasonable.

"I ken more than I like, little one. To get a wee lass like ye with bairn is much as cutting her throat. Aye, she will do naught but scream while day fades into night and back again, only to spill out a dead bairn and her life's blood. I ken all too weel."

She staggered when he released her abruptly. "That fate can visit a woman with hips as wide as a loch," she said calmly, knowing from the brief glance she had had of remembered horror in his eyes that he spoke of something very personal.

"Suit yourself, lass," he said coldly, his calm restored.

"Aye, I will. I will wed and by a year's end I will have me a bairn. Nay, I will have twins and ye can come to the christening, Sir MacLagan," she retorted with a mixture of confidence and childish defiance.

That haughty declaration almost made him smile. She looked belligerent and confident. That made him feel certain that she had little idea of what she spoke of. Some women could be kept very sheltered, knowing little or nothing of life until they found themselves wed and thrust from their family home.

"'Tis your life, mistress. Toss it away as ye please."

The reply forming on her lips was never made for she spotted a familiar shape in the distance. "I must go now, Sir MacLagan."

With that she was off and running even as a farewell formed on his tongue. Her skirts were well hiked up and, even as he noted that her legs were slim as well, he deemed them very fine legs indeed. He then looked to see what had sent her off.

Marching down the path was a tall, thin woman adorned wholly in black. Her hawkish features made him think of a carrion bird. The impression was not lessened when she paused before him, fixing him with a cold, grey stare.

The woman was so completely the opposite of the woman-child that Iain almost smiled. He mused with a touch of humour that they made a strange pair. Then again, he mused, such a stern guardian was probably just what the minx needed to keep her from getting completely out of hand.

"Did ye see a wee lass aboot, m'laird? Most like she was disheveled and without an escort."

In a courtly manner that never failed to impress, Iain replied that he had indeed seen just such a lass. In the same way he politely sent the woman in the wrong direction. As he strolled back to the castle he wondered why he had done that.

After just a few moments of conversation with the girl he was already acting strangely. Since she was going to be around often now, he decided that was something he had to watch out for. His cold, hard pose had been hard won and he had no intention of losing it to some tiny lady with wild, wine-red hair. It had worked and no knight worth his armor gave up a successful defense.

He fought down his emotions as he saw her in his mind's eye. She was daintier and smaller than Catalina had been. The only reason he could find for speaking out so bluntly was that he could see her meeting the same fate. She would go to her marriage bed, get with child and die to be buried beside her babe, two innocents lost in one stroke. Iain shook his head wishing there could be some sort of law against letting such tiny, frail ladies wed. It was tantamount to a death sentence.

Islaen suffered no concerns about childbirth once she left Iain. Her only worry was surviving Meg's scolding which had duly fallen on her moments after she had reached her room. A distant cousin of her father's, Meg had been hired to raise her after the death of her mother. The woman set about her job with admirable vigor. Making use of the tender spot her father and eleven brothers had for her did not deter her at all.

Each of the men in Islaen's family treated the girl with amused and loving tolerance. Sometimes Meg suspected they forgot Islaen was a girl. She had dragged the girl from wrestling matches, riding contests, knife hurlings. That Islaen seemed ill-equipped to be a fine lady was no help either. Not only ill-equipped but none too interested either, Meg feared, as was illustrated by an incident just a week past. Fine ladies did not get on their hands and knees to join in a dice game.

Meg had no sense of failing with the girl. Improvements had been made. When the laird had first brought her to care for Islaen, the girl had been as wild as any lad. With determination Meg had smoothed away many a rough edge.

"Is he not the bonniest mon ye have e'er seen?" Islaen sighed after Meg soundly denounced Iain MacLagan's trick.

Meg's sharp eyes grew even sharper as they rested upon her charge sprawled somewhat ungracefully in her bath. "He is scarred."

"'Tis just a wee one," Islaen retorted defensively. "Ye hardly e'en see it."

Thinking of the scar that ran from the man's right temple nearly to his lip, Meg drawled, "Oh, aye, barely visible. A wee nick in the skin."

With no trouble at all, Islaen ignored Meg's sarcasm. She had never found it hard to do that. Long before Meg had arrived Islaen had learned that, as well as how to return it in equal measure, for her family had sharp tongues.

"I wonder how he came by it. Something gallant, I wager. A duel o'er a fair lady's honour or heart." She let her imagination take hold of her.

The noise Meg made was highly derisive. "Or bed. 'Tis the

sort o' thing that puts most men in a lather. They wield one
sword and hack aboot at each other just tae win the chance to
wield their other sword. Men have but twa thoughts in their
heads."

"Aye," Islaen sighed, "fighting and wenching, blood and
flesh, violence and lust, swords and seduction, rampaging and
rutting . . ."

"I ken that covers it, ye wicked girl." Meg met Islaen's
dancing gaze without expression. "Out o' the bath ere ye
wrinkle."

"Heaven forbid that I should add wrinkles to the freckles,"
Islaen murmured as she stood up and stepped out of the bath.
"I wish I could have such a husband as Sir Iain. Would we not
have bonnie wee ones? And strong, like my brothers and
fither. T'would be verra nice."

As instructed by her kin, Meg took note of Islaen's stated
preference. At the first opportunity she would tell the laird. It
would be nice if the child could have a husband she fancied,
but none of them hoped too hard. She was a wee lass that
many a man would fear to break. It had been the same when
the laird had married the lass's mother only to have everyone
proven very wrong indeed. The trouble was that few recalled
the girl's mother, so few would believe that Islaen could prove
as strong or as prolific. Then too, Islaen was a bit more delicate and not quite as lovely, her mother having been highly
praised for her beauty.

Meg could not help but wonder if she had erred in keeping
Islaen's true looks a secret from her family. There was no
chance that a husband could remain ignorant. She had only
tried to insure that the girl did not become an object of
ridicule and looked her loveliest. Perhaps that would be
enough to gain forgiveness for the deception she had practiced, and forced Islaen to, when the truth was finally revealed. As she began to help Islaen dress she hoped the girl
would not suffer from her own husband the very scorn and

ridicule she had tried so hard to protect the girl from. It would cut the child deeply, inflict a wound that might never heal.

Islaen was dressed in her finest. Her father was a wealthy man and no expense had been spared. Her chemise was of the finest silk, as were the braes she insisted upon wearing. The corset was a rich brown velvet with elaborate embroidery on the sleeves that matched the gold surcote. Shoes of the finest gold velvet adorned her small feet. The houppelande that was becoming more and more popular was left off for Islaen had not yet mastered wearing the voluminous robe with any grace, having difficulty with the draping sleeves and the way it trailed on the ground. After placing the fine couverchef upon Islaen's head, Meg surveyed the results with a very critical eye.

After a final check to make sure that there were no lumps, bumps or wrinkles and that the errant hair was still neatly contained, Meg declared Islaen ready. She then took her charge to join the men in the great hall where the search for a husband would begin and Islaen would meet the king.

Islaen fought to control her nerves. She did not want to do anything silly or stupid. Her pride quailed at the very thought of it.

She did not like the situation but had decided to forbear. It was far past time she had a husband. Coming to court allowed a greater choice. She simply wished the choice would be more in her hands than it would be.

The resentment that tried to gnaw at her was fairly easily put aside. This was the way such matters were settled. She was grateful she had not been betrothed at cradleside. There had been the opportunity for her to find a man and there were plenty to choose from around home. When she had reached the age of nineteen still unattached, it was no surprise that her father would take matters into his own hands. She could not blame him for that. Even if she did not really agree with his methods, she knew he was doing it out of love, because he wanted to see her happy. The political, defensive or monetary arrangements that could come out of her betrothal were only pleasant additions, not necessities. Glancing towards her father, who was talking to Meg, she hoped he would give her some pleasant surprise in his choice of groom that would ease the sting of not having Iain MacLagan.

"The lass has an eye for Sir Iain MacLagan," Meg informed Alaistair MacRoth at the very first opportunity. "Do ye ken the mon?"

"Aye." Alaistair adjusted his long, broad-shouldered frame more comfortably upon the bench. "Widowed for o'er a year. Said he is still grieving sore as he doesnae pursue the lasses, doesnae show an interest in them at all. Said he is cold, that his emotions lie with his late wife. Be a good match, for the land Islaen would bring him lies near his kin, but I cannae think there will be any move made there." He frowned at his cousin. "Are ye sure? 'tis a hard face on the mon that isnae helped by that gruesome scar etched upon his cheek."

"The lass claims ye hardly see it, 'tis a mere nick. Cast an eye on your wee daughter, cousin, and watch where her eyes linger."

It was an easy thing to confirm, for Islaen's whole face radiated her admiration for the man who sat at the king's table. She would seem to come to her senses, conceal the look and act nonchalant, but it did not last long. Within moments her control slipped again.

"Och, weel, I will give it a try but I cannae think it will lead anywhere. 'Tis said that a murderer stalks him, a mon who blames him for the death of Catalina, his late wife. Some old lover, I would wager. Could be he takes no wife for fear she will soon be made a widow." He shook his head and ran a hand through his graying auburn hair. "Still, best she be happy for a short while than unhappy for a long while. If ye can, turn her eye to Ronald MacDubh. That mon is godson to the king and he has expressed an interest in our Islaen."

"Ye mean in her purse. Coin flows through his hands like water, hands that cannae keep off o' the lasses."

"He is young and nay hard to look upon. He is also close to the king. After him they grow older and less fair to the eye. There are too many full-bodied women about. The young men want a wife that willnae be lost beneath the covers, some curves to hold."

Alaistair wished his words were not true but, though Islaen's dowry put many men to thinking, there was money and land to be found in other places. So too would there be some flesh to hold onto and make a soft bed with. Delicacy of looks only aroused brotherly feelings when it was unaccompanied by full breasts and well-rounded hips. Their eyes would light up over the dowry, only to flicker and die when they closely observed what went with it. What interest could be stirred was not held long. A little less dowry for a lot more woman was a sacrifice most of the young men were willing to make.

Islaen had not expected much interest, so was not disappointed when there was so little. Her menfolk did all the work while she entertained herself watching Iain MacLagan. Assuming that her family would soon find her a husband, she decided that she should soak up as much about the man as she could. A multitude of memories could come in handy later. It was highly possible that her marriage could use a great deal of imagination and dreaming to make it tolerable.

She knew that few men could equal the image she had of Iain MacLagan. It was going to be difficult not to constantly compare others, whatever husband she gained, to him. That was something she was going to have to try very hard not to do. It would be very foolish indeed to ruin her chances for happiness with another man because she was unable to let go of a dream. It would also be unfair to her husband.

That was true, of course, only if she was blessed with a husband who was also willing to try for the best marriage possible, full, rich and lasting. There was, however, far too great a chance that she would not get a husband like that, no matter how carefully her father chose for her. She knew enough of the world to know that not all men considered marriage a sacred trust or a wife of any importance save that of a breeder of legitimate heirs. With a husband like that, memories of Iain MacLagan might well be her only source of joy aside from whatever children she might have.

Despite her admirable reasoning for her steady perusal of Iain MacLagan, she admitted that she simply liked to look at him. He was a feast for her eyes. Even when she knew she was being too blatant and fought to turn her attentions elsewhere, her gaze was drawn back to him and she was yet again lost in the pleasure of watching him.

He was dressed in dark blue and maroon. Long, well-shaped muscular legs were snugly encased in maroon hose. The tight sleeves of his deep blue jupon revealed strong arms. Broad shoulders, a trim waist and slim hips completed what was a fine figure of a man. He was taller than most yet moved with a lithe grace that belied his strength and size. Many a woman's eye touched upon him in approval. It did not seem to matter all that much that he returned neither inviting looks nor friendly smiles, remaining impervious to all ploys and flirtations.

Facially he was somewhat daunting. His was a lean face with harsh lines not enhanced by either the jagged white scar or remote expression he wore. Grief had made his high cheekbones more prominent, the hollows in his smooth shaven cheeks deeper. His mouth was well formed although his lips were on the thin side, something made more noticeable by their grim set. A long straight nose and proud jaw were more delineated than on other men. A dark complexion only added to what seemed a formidable and constant darkness of expression. Rich brown hair was cut neatly, framing the remarkable face. It was also shot with strands of white, unusual in a man of only four and thirty.

It was all food for her imagination. She wondered at his loss, the grief that had left such a mark upon him. From there it was easy to imagine herself as the one who could return love and laughter to his life. As she dreamed, there were more people than she knew working towards giving her dream a chance.

Chapter Two

"MacRoth searches hard for a husband for his daughter," the king observed dryly. "Has he aproached you yet, MacLagan?"

"Aye. He did." Iain suddenly wished himself elsewhere for there was a gleam in the king's eye that unsettled him.

"And ye said no, I presume." MacLagan nodded somewhat curtly. "Might we inquire why? Dowry's quite impressive."

"I have had my turn at marriage, your majesty. Let some other fellow have a chance. Tavis has secured our line weel enough."

"True, and there is Sholto left to wed. Howbeit, the Bible tells us to go forth and multiply. A man cannot do that upon his own."

"That too I have tried but 'tis not to be."

"We think you have given up too easily. Have you met the lass? She watches you, if you have not noticed as yet."

Iain looked to where Islaen talked with her twin brothers, Calum and Donald. They were one and twenty, tall, lean and handsome with fiery red hair and brown eyes. Although she appeared to be totally attentive to her brothers, Iain could see that she was indeed watching him. He scowled but noticed that it did nothing to deter her. Absently, he also noticed that with her tall, broad-shouldered brothers flanking her, she looked even smaller than ever. Remembering the king, Iain shrugged nonchalantly.

"Mayhaps she does. 'Tis hard to be sure, but it matters not." Iain said the last three words with as much firmness as he dared.

The king caught Islaen's eye and beckoned her. To his amusement she looked around, looked back at him and pointed to herself mouthing the word 'me.' The king nodded just as her brothers nudged her in his direction. His amusement grew when she somehow managed to trod on each brothers' foot before she approached. He noted that, although she curtsied and said all that was required, most of her attention was on the tall, solemn man at his side.

Islaen felt tight with nerves, yet it was not because she met with the king, a man who held the power of life and death over them all. It was because of the man who sat at the king's side. She only wished that there was the barest hint of warmth in the gaze Iain fixed upon her. With an effort she forced her attention to the king so that, even if she could stir no interest in Sir Iain, she would at least do nothing to make herself look the fool before him. There would be no way she could stay in court if that happened.

"You have much the look of your mother, child. We knew her when your father was courting her. A lovely woman. Your father has not brought all your brothers, has he?" He smiled. "How many are there? 'Tis hard to keep accounts."

"Eleven. He only brought seven. The eldest four stayed at home, your majesty. Their wives are with child and cannae travel."

"Imagine that, MacLagan. Eleven strong sons. MacRoth needs no army. He breeds his own. Grandsons?"

"Aye, sire. Six of them at last count. Only twa lasses. Angus, the next to the eldest, has one as does Colin, one of the twins."

They talked a while longer about her prolific family. Islaen was slightly confused but decided it was simply a matter of curiosity on the king's part. Iain was not so naive. He had the sinking feeling he knew exactly what his sovereign was about, why he had had the girl talk about her prolific family. A sense of helpless rage grew in him as he saw what was coming. But he saw no way to stop it. One did not go against the king's wishes, nor even his gentle suggestions.

He had taken up the place near the king not only because the king wished it and for the prestige it gave. It kept him out of the tangle of flirtations that ran rampant in court, away from the machinations of women. He had been without a woman so long that a pretty, willing one could well be too much temptation. Now, seeing the danger headed his way, he wished he had not sought a somewhat cowardly way to avoid it. He was caught in the trap about to close tightly about him.

It was ironic in a way, almost funny, although he felt no urge to laugh. He had fled Caraidland for the court to avoid the temptation of a woman. Each day had drawn him nearer to succumbing to her lures, but he had seen clearly that she sought no brief pleasurable interlude, but marriage. Now the very thing he had fled to court to avoid was about to be pushed down his throat.

"A lovely girl. Well mannered yet not reticent. A man could do worse, or so think my godson and Lord Donald Fraser."

No matter how he tried, Iain could not completely repress a look of distaste. Lord Donald Fraser was two and forty. He had buried two wives already. Wine, wenches and gaming dominated his life. Iain did not want to picture what would happen to the girl.

"Do not think poorly of MacRoth. The man is little at court and does not know Fraser as we do. Nor does he know our godson. We cannot refuse a match there but we would prefer it not be made." The king sipped his wine. "The MacRoths are as loyal to the crown as the MacLagans. A bond between two such families would be viewed with great favour."

"I have no need of a wife," Iain said as pleasantly as possible.

"Or a woman. Or so you would have all believe. It is not right to bury yourself with your wife. A man needs a woman's softening touch ere he grows too hard, for a hard man cares for naught and his loyalties thin."

"Does his majesty feel I can no longer be trusted?"

"Do not get stiff, MacLagan. We merely make an observation. The land she holds is in a line with MacLagan land."

"I hadnae realized that, sire."

"To have it in MacLagan hands, with MacRoths bound to its defense through marriage would strengthen that length of the border. To have it go to Fraser or my godson could well mean keep fighting with little eye kept upon the English. There are enough feuds along there as it is. We would like to have one less area to fret over. Our mind would be greatly eased to know it is held firm and peaceful by the bonding of two loyal clans. To wed a man's only daughter, one he cares for," the king nodded to where Alaistair stood with Islaen, his affection clear to see, "is a bond as strong as any. You have proof of that in Tavis's marriage."

Iain nodded, his jaw clenched. His marriage to Catalina had assuaged the MacBroths' ill feelings over Tavis's not wedding another of their daughters, although he had had her as a mistress. Due to the girl's lack of chastity it had not broken the alliance, but it had strained it for hopes had been disappointed. Tavis's marriage to Storm Eldon meant that at least one point along the border the English were anxious to keep the peace, for to raise sword against a MacLagan meant endangering the only daughter of an English marcher lord.

Short of a direct order the king could not have made his wishes any clearer. A look into his sire's eyes told Iain that the direct order would come if it was necessary. The border was a source of aggravation to the kings on both sides of it, quite often a law unto itself. Two loyal clans bound by blood standing shoulder to shoulder at one point along that area of unrest was a temptation the king could not resist. It would mean that at one point the king's orders would be obeyed and he could be assured of support in the troubled area.

He could easily see the wisdom of it, understood the king's desire for it. That did little to ease his tension and anger over the noose slipped so gently around his neck. Even the fact that it would better his position at court, enrich his purse and undoubtedly please his father did not console him.

Deciding he could not escape, Iain said, "An I may beg your leave for a while, sire, I will seek out and speak to Lord MacRoth."

Iain cautiously approached Alaistair MacRoth. That man astutely guessed that it was all in the manner of a royal command. Even as he agreed to the match and discussed settlements in vague terms, Alaistair wondered if it was for the best. It was true that the girl had an eye for the man, although Alaistair thought him the antithesis of a maiden's dream, being dark and formidable in looks. He could also see that the young man did not want to wed Islaen, perhaps any woman. Also, there was the man's coldness to consider. Islaen was used to affection, be it rough, teasing or gentle. There seemed to be little chance of any to be found in Iain MacLagan.

Reading the concern in the man's eyes, Iain said, "I will be a good husband to the child. I willnae beat her nor go wenching. She will want for naught, Lord MacRoth."

"Save love," Alaistair thought but said nothing. The others held no love for the girl either. In his prejudiced eyes she was eminently loveable, and he could not understand how it was that the men around could not see past her lack of curves to discover that.

Inwardly, he sighed. Iain MacLagan may hold no love for Islaen, may not even be capable of such an emotion, but the girl wanted him. That was far more than she did feel about any of the others put forward. Perhaps that could be enough to keep her happy and he truly wanted her to find happiness. The things the man had just sworn to were far more than the others had promised.

"'Tis a comfort to hear ye say that. T'would be a greater comfort if ye could act a little less like ye are headed for a hanging," he growled.

"I understand your sense of outrage, m'lord. Forgive me my surliness but ye ken I have buried one young wife. T'was not my wish to take anither and maychance stand o'er her grave as weel." Iain sighed but he felt the man was due total honesty.

"She is a great deal stronger than she looks, laddie. Many thought marriage would send her mither to an early grave, but Meghan proved them very wrong. Islaen's nay been treated like some doll by her brithers and come through the better for it." He could see his words were being politely heeded but not believed, so he changed the subject. "The land's a sweet bit of property, but the keep needs tending to."

"'Tis no worry, m'lord. My kin live near to it. My wife and I may reside with them until matters are set straight. My eldest brither has a wife. T'will be company for Islaen. Aye, Storm will be glad of some female company."

The soft look that flickered over the man's harsh face at the mention of his sister by marriage eased Alaistair's worried mind. There were softer feelings in the man. If anyone could rescue them from permanent burial it was wee Islaen.

"Weel, come speak to the lass then. I ken she willnae refuse you. Nay, nor need much persuasion."

He watched in silent amusement as Alaistair edged him into the group of redheaded MacRoths and then dragged away his four youngest sons with a total lack of subtlety.

He then looked at the girl. She was a pretty little thing who made no effort to hide her appreciation of him even now. He could not fully subdue the good feelings that stirred within him. This worried him. If he lost the hard, cold emotional

armour he had donned since Catalina's death, he could all too
easily find himself reaching for all he had tried for before, all
that his brother had found with Storm, and that could kill the
girl smiling at him so sweetly. He would fight that with every
ounce of willpower he had.

"May I sit down, mistress?" he asked and joined her on the
small window seat when she nodded.

Islaen studied him. Her father had made it rather clear as
to why Iain wished to speak to her, though she dared not believe it. The closed look upon his face was hardly encourag-
ing. If he was about to propose marriage, she felt sure it was
not by choice. That left her in a quandary, for she wanted to
be his wife above all things but would like him to feel at least
amiable to the idea.

However, if he had no choice then she probably did not
either. Even if she did she realized that she would much rather
be the one he had to wed than to watch him wed another. Although he was so clearly reluctant, there was the chance for
her to make something good out of it, but, if she refused,
there was no chance at all. He would be lost to her forever and
that, she decided, would be harder to bear than anything else.

"Do ye ken what I wish to speak to ye about?"

"An I read my fither right 'tis marriage, yet your face doesnae look much like that of a suitor."

"Aye, 'tis marriage I wish to speak to ye about. The king
feels a match between us would be a verra good thing."

''Tis hardly the proposal of a young girl's dreams,' she
mused silently but aloud she said, "Then I ken 'tis set."

Iain looked at his hands, then glanced at her. "Aye, that it
is. Can ye stomach it, lass?"

"Of course. Why should I not be able to?" She saw his
hand feint to the scar upon his face. "Wheesht, that is naught.
It doesnae pull your face about into a horrid grimace or some
such. Might I ask how ye got it? Ye need not say."

Iain almost smiled. He had never thought himself vain, but

some of the reactions to his scarring had cut him deeply, almost as deeply as the knife that had marred his features. In her lovely eyes he could read the truth of her words. A familiar, if long ignored, knot formed in his loins and he inwardly cursed.

"T'was an attack at my wife's graveside by a mon who felt I had stolen, then murdered, the lass he loved."

"Oh. Did ye steal her from him?"

"Nay. T'was a marriage sought by her family and mine. I kenned naught of him until t'was done." He frowned at her. "I dinnae ken why I speak so freely to ye, lass."

"I shall tell nary a soul and 'tis it not right that I, as your wife, should ken if there be some mon creeping about ready to plunge a dirk into ye? 'Tis a bit of information that could be useful."

Amusement flickered through his eyes. "Aye, that it could."

Dangerous, Iain mused. She had an impish sense of humor as well as a directness of speech. Both were things he admired. In their two brief meetings she had affected him more than the most practiced of flirts, drawing him out despite himself. He would have to be more wary. She could chip away at his wall until it crumbled.

"Did ye have someone ye loved?" she asked softly.

"Aye but she was given to anither ere I became betrothed."

"Is she still wed?"

"Nay," he answered slowly, beginning to see where her questions were leading. "I dinnae love her still either."

Color tinged her cheeks. "I am sorry. My tongue oftimes outruns my mind and my good manners."

"'Tis no matter, lass. I will be honest though it be far from polite. I dinnae want to take a wife. One buried is enough for me. The king doesnae want ye to wed either of your other suitors, doesnae want them with land upon the troublesome border. Our families are both loyal and obedient to the king.

He wants our forces joined and that land to be held in loyal hands."

So romantic, Islaen mused wryly, but she had expected little else. Something had to drive such a man to do what he so clearly did not want to do. It was no surprise that the king was the prod. It also told her that, as she had suspected, she had as little choice in the matter as Iain did.

"Ah, a bulwark against unrest, one place along the border that he need not worry about. In the end, three loyal houses."

Iain nodded. "All that doesnae mean I will be a poor husband. As I told your fither, I dinnae beat women nor wench."

"That is nice. Such things could cause strife within a household," she drawled, her eyes dancing, and was pleased to see a brief laughing light flare in Iain's remarkable eyes. "I suspicion that Lord Fraser is a wencher."

"Aye? How did ye espy that in him?"

"Ye will laugh, but t'was because he licked his lips and his palm was sweaty."

"Sure signs of a wencher," Iain said in a choked voice and, to the amazement of all, he did laugh, although softly.

The pair became of great interest to all as the news of the betrothal seeped through the hall. An official announcement would be made after they had all dined, but by the time the feast was laid out, it was not really necessary. Neither was it much of a secret that it was a match urged by the king. Islaen did not know whether to be embarrassed, angry or amused as she was seated next to Iain at the king's table. She was certainly unaccustomed to being paid such a great deal of attention.

Some of the attention was far from favourable. Many a woman thought and whispered spiteful things about her. It did not matter that the king had urged the match. All the women saw was that a tiny girl with little figure and none too spectacular looks had what they had tried so hard to get. To be outdone by a border wench of no great standing was a bitter potion to swallow. The king's part in it was a salve of sorts, but inadequate. Many of them decided to increase their efforts to draw Iain into a liaison. They felt sure that, once he had become reaquainted with loving and his wife proved sorely lacking, his eyes would turn elsewhere. Knowing that her new husband was romping with another would put Islaen MacRoth in her place.

Islaen sensed all that, could read it in a number of fair faces. It both pleased and worried her. She found pride in the fact that she would soon be wife to a man so many wanted. She worried that she might not be wife enough. Although he had said that he was no wencher she doubted he knew just how great a challenge to resist temptation would now be tossed at his head. Islaen could read the threat to trespass in far too many female eyes.

It also annoyed her that they could not leave well enough alone, plotted to do to her as she would never dream of doing to them. The sanctified bonds and vows of matrimony clearly meant little to them. Their vanity needed appeasing, she supposed, and she felt ashamed for them. There was to be a fight ahead and she dreaded it, for she could not feel sure of victory.

Dissatisfaction was in two male breasts as well. Ronald MacDubh and Lord Fraser were hard put to hide their anger. In each case the money Islaen would have brought them was sorely needed. The lives they led, remarkably similar, were costly. Debts were owed and to people who would not wait patiently for repayment. The chance of getting a well-dowered bride were few and far between for men who were of an increasingly unsavory reputation. MacRoth had been blissfully ignorant of their full characters. It grated to see such a prize go to a man who neither needed it nor wanted it. Such a thing hit them in the purse, where all their sensitivity rested.

They also resented the property MacLagan would get. Opportunity for gain could be found upon the border. The king's

mailed fist was unable to fully control the area. Loyalties
thinned in that area making it ideal for a man whose loyalty
was only to himself. The chances of anyone outside of the
clans or their allies marrying into them and gaining land that
way were small. To watch such an opportunity slip into the
hands of another man, himself from a border clan, was too
much to tolerate. Resentment boiled and fermented in their
breasts, aimed itself at Iain MacLagan and gave rise to plots,
vague but growing clearer, of satisfactory revenge.

Iain was not oblivious to all the undercurrents. He was uninterested in any female plots, just as he had been more or
less unaware of women for a long time. His attention was on
the disgruntled suitors. Money and land could stir emotions
as easily and as deeply as love when lost to another. The fact
that both rejected suitors were in sore need of both only increased the chance of possible trouble.

What was frustrating was that he could not be sure how they
would react to their loss. At the moment they looked close to
uniting in their anger over losing such a prize. A union like
that could be deadly. It was not really for himself that he worried either. Although Islaen was the prize the men sought, she
could all too easily be hurt in whatever plan they might form.
He was going to have to keep a close eye on both men.

It occurred to Iain that, for such a tiny thing, Islaen
MacRoth was towing a lot of complications behind her. Several of her brothers had hinted that any hurt done to their
sister would be repaid in full. Iain wondered if the king knew
how easily the strong alliance he sought could become the
bloodiest feud the borders had seen in a long time. Added to
that was the resentment of two men not known for their even
temperament or good sense. There could easily be swords
drawn from that direction.

When he recalled that he already had a sword hanging over
his head like Damocles, Iain nearly laughed. While he fretted
over Islaen possibly getting with child, he was ringed with

people who could easily make her a widow before any seed of his could take root. He knew his sense of humour might be thought rather twisted, but such thoughts caused him to smile rather openly when the king called for a toast to the betrothal.

Bemused by Iain's smile, Islaen responded to the congratulations absently. She did wonder, with a touch of bitterness, why they congratulated her. She had not won the man's hand nor heart; he had been shoved her way by the king himself, ensnared into marriage by a king who wished to lessen a few of his troubles.

Very firmly Islaen pushed aside that bitterness. It was a feeling that only brought trouble or grief. She had seen the proof of that more often than she had cared to. That was not a poison she wished to seep into her life and marriage. Ruefully, she admitted that she would probably find more than enough trouble in her marriage than she could handle anyways. When Iain's smile faded she wondered if he had suddenly seen all the difficulties that lurked ahead for them.

Iain's smile was gone when the king proceeded to announce that he would be seeing to the wedding himself. It meant that the wedding night would take place within the palace, thus killing any hope Iain had of leaving the union unconsummated. His protest that his family would be unable to attend only brought sympathy, no change of plans. Now he would have to exercise one of the various methods used to prevent conception and hope that Islaen would not feel it was a personal affront.

After the king's announcement Islaen could feel Iain retreating. It surprised her that she seemed to so easily sense his moods. She hoped she was not fooling herself, seeing what was not there or misreading what was. Despite warning herself that she could be, she still felt sure that he was retreating, pulling back into his hard, cold shell, and she felt helpless to stop it. It was something she had no experience with, for her family was the open sort, hiding little of what they felt or thought. She also saw how hard it would be to establish any sort of true bond with him when he could so neatly pull away from her as he was doing now.

She realized her path was going to be strewn with stones. Love was what she sought but her ever-present practicality reared its head. To hope for that was to invite pain. She would instead aim for a congenial relationship. In the ways only a wife could, she would make herself important to him. Watching her brothers' wives, she had seen how that could be done, how a man could find himself turning to that woman without thought whether there was love there or not. Habit could serve almost as well. Depending upon how demanding he was in the bedroom, whether or not his reputed celibacy came from lack of interest or rigid control, she would learn to give him all he could want until there too no other woman could do as well. She might not attain the perfect marriage, but she was determined to have as near to it as she could get.

Chapter Three

Cursing softly, Islaen struggled to keep pace with the men. Iain and the king were several strides ahead of her. Her three brothers, Calum, Nathan and Donald, kept pausing so as not to leave her behind. She wished fervently that she had not tried to be so fashionable. The houppelande she wore badly hindered her usual lithe, nimble stride.

Vanity, she mused, was a troublesome thing. She had wanted Iain to see that she could be as well dressed as any of the other women in court, women who were making obvious and strenuous efforts to catch his eye. Instead she was stumbling along like an awkward babe taking its first unsure steps. She might be fashionable but she was far from graceful.

"Why did ye wear the cursed thing if ye cannae walk in it?"

She glared at Nathan. "I can walk fine in my chambers. The ground isnae even here."

Calum snorted in scorn at her excuses. "Ye walk with less skill than Colin's youngest."

Annoyed beyond caution, Islaen started to angrily stride away from her brothers. Her foot caught in the long garment and, with a soft cry, she started to fall. Nathan tried to catch her, but she took him down with her. Being on the very edge of a small rise they started to roll. She tried to get out of

Nathan's way but he tumbled over her, then she over him. When they came to rest at the base of the rise, Nathan landed on top of her. It was a full moment before Islaen was able to catch her breath. Then she began to curse a laughing Nathan and struggled to push him off of her.

When he finally moved, it was only to lie at her side still laughing. She could hear her other brothers laughing too, their laughter growing louder as they approached. Hearing Iain call her, she closed her eyes and wished heartily that, by some great miracle, she could simply disappear. It was a shame, she mused, that intense embarrassment could not be immediately fatal.

Iain was unaware of any trouble until the king, his voice trembling with amusement, pointed it out. He gaped at the sight of his betrothed tumbling down the small hill, her slim stockinged legs well displayed. By the time her brother got off of her, Iain was hurrying to Islaen's side. He had to fight the urge to laugh, something made very difficult by the king's amusement and Islaen's brothers' hilarity. For one brief instant her stillness bothered him, but then he saw how tightly her eyes were shut and how she had clenched her hands into small fists. He reached down and gently grasped her by the arm, ready to help her stand.

"Come along, Islaen, ye dinnae appear hurt."

Hearing the laughter he could not fully keep out of his voice, Islaen was very reluctant to look at him. "Nay, I think I will but lie here until I disappear."

"I ken how ye feel, lass, but it willnae happen."

"Nay, I wager not," she murmured and opened her eyes.

As he helped her to her feet she decided that his eyes, when touched with laughter, were beautiful. She stood quietly letting him tidy her up as if she were a small child as she wondered if she could bring that light to his eyes more often, preferably without having to embarrass herself.

"How did ye come to have such a tumble?" he asked.

"Wearing that cursed houppelande," Nathan answered as he handed her one of her shoes that had fallen off.

"An it causes ye trouble why do ye wear it?"

After glaring at Nathan, Islaen put her shoe back on with Iain's support and answered softly, "I wore it for ye."

"For me?"

"Aye. 'Tis the fashion and I wished to show ye that I can be as fashionable as all the ladies dancing after ye."

"Weel, I havenae noticed so many but ye need not go to such reckless lengths, wee Islaen," he teased and started to remove her now disheveled houppelande. "I care little about such foolish trappings."

"Oh. Ye mean I near broke my neck for naught?" She flushed with embarrassment when the king himself laughed, for she had thought her words soft enough to be private.

Iain restrained his own laughter with an effort. She flattered him with her attempt to appear the most fashionable of ladies and he did not wish to reward that with laughter, a laughter she could wrongly interpret as mockery. It also amused him that she so openly admitted her ploy, harmless as it was. She was honest almost to a fault.

When they returned to the castle, Iain watched Islaen hurried away by Meg and sighed. Everything about the girl seemed to tug at him. She seemed to promise all he had ever wanted in a mate. It was going to prove to be a severe trial to maintain any distance between them but he would have to. Wondering why that thought should depress him, Iain suddenly realized that he had been neatly encircled by her brothers.

After pondering seven shades of red hair for a moment, he asked, "Did ye wish to speak with me?"

Duncan, the eldest of the seven at seven and twenty, growled, "Aye, about our wee sister."

"That is a surprise."

"We havenae much to say," Duncan continued, ignoring Iain's sarcasm, "but say it we will."

"Aye," Malcolm, an astoundingly handsome young man of just four and twenty, agreed. "Ye ken that we are muckle fond of wee Islaen."

"I had noticed that, aye."

"Ye be a cold mon, Iain MacLagan," the twenty-six-year-old Robert said with no real criticism shading his voice, "and Islaen isnae accustomed to that. We will be ill-pleased if ye hurt her with your hard nature."

"Or elsewise," Duncan growled.

All the brothers nodded one by one and slowly left. Iain soon found himself standing alone. As he moved to go to his chambers he contemplated the warning he had just been given. They had not said exactly what form their retribution would take, but he decided it mattered little. Neither had they said that they would be watching him all the time, but the implication that they would was clear. One needed little imagination to sort out the various particulars of the threat. Any hurt he dealt Islaen would come back upon him twelve-fold, for he was certain that the absent brothers and the father would also stand behind the threat.

As he made his way to his chambers, he saw the many signs of the preparations for his wedding. For a brief instant he felt the natural resentment of a man caught in a trap but he forced it aside. Such feeling could easily turn itself upon Islaen, and she did not deserve it. She was as trapped as he. He wondered how she felt about it.

"Why did ye wear this fool thing when ye ken how poorly ye move in it?" Meg grumbled as she tried to clean the grass-stained houppelande.

"I wished to impress Sir Iain."

"He's nay courting ye, lass. The marriage is set firm."

"Aye and it must feel like a noose about his neck. I just thought to ease the rub of the hemp by showing him that I could be as fine as all those other ladies that eye him so."

"Whores. Ye neednae fash yourself o'er them. Ye will be the mon's wife and none can be changing that."

Islaen decided there was little point in trying to explain her thoughts and feelings to Meg. When it came to men and matters of the heart they would never really agree.

What Islaen put her mind to was yet another way to show Iain that he was not getting such a bad bargain. By the next morning she felt she had one. As she stood impatiently while being fitted for her wedding gown she decided to show him that he could speak to her about most anything, that she could be the best and most trusted of confidants. She was fairly certain he could count upon his brothers for such a thing, but they had their own very full lives and might not always be there for Iain. A wife would ever be at hand.

Iain politely greeted Islaen when she joined him for dinner, but inwardly he frowned. There was a glint in her lovely eyes that he was already beginning to recognize. Her attempts to impress him were clearly not at an end despite the blunder with high fashion.

As they ate he began to see her game. It was a dangerous one although he knew she did not see that. If he allowed her to be his confidant she would soon be far more. All he could do was fight this newest lure she held out and hope he did not hurt her too much by doing so.

Silently cursing, Islaen decided that Iain was not being very cooperative at all. She felt as if she were banging her head against a stone wall. While he was never rude nor cutting, neither did he tell her anything. By the time they separated she had a terrible headache. Retiring to a bench removed from the rather large crowd of people in the hall she tried to soothe her aching head even as she wondered what it was she was doing wrong, if perhaps she was being too subtle.

"All alone, Mistress MacRoth?"

Biting back a curse, Islaen looked up at her unwanted intruder. Lord Donald Fraser was a man whose body and face revealed his tendency to excess. His attempt at high fashion only showed that his stocky figure was becoming more fat than muscle. What really unsettled her about the man was the look in his rather small grey eyes. They revealed his lusts. When he took a seat beside her, uninvited, she quickly became aware of the fact that the man was none too fond of soap and water.

"I had but sought a moment of quiet." She was not surprised when he did not acknowledge her hint to be left alone.

"Aye, there are far too many at court. Your wedding will be well attended, much witnessed."

She nodded and struggled to be courteous. "'Tis a pity that Sir MacLagan's family cannae be here."

"What is a pity is that the king has sacrificed ye to a mon with no heart."

"Ye speak unfairly about a mon who is soon to be my husband," she said coldly.

"Ah, lass, ye act brave and 'tis honourable that ye strive to defend the mon, but all ken the truth."

"I cannae guess what truth they think they ken," she snapped and edged away from him, wondering how he could keep getting closer yet not appear to move. "They trouble themselves with that which isnae their concern."

"None can help but be concerned when they see a young lass with your beauty given o'er to a mon who cares naught for any woman. 'Tis well kent his heart was buried with his first wife. Aye and the warmth a wife needs. There is many a mon here who aches to give ye what a cold mon like Mac-Lagan ne'er can. I am but one of many, but I pray that ye will see me more clearly than all the others," he said huskily, his gaze fixed upon her partially agape mouth.

When his arm had slipped around her she had stiffened in

surprise. As his words became understandable to her she gaped slightly. She could not believe the man would be so utterly audacious as to woo her before all the court, her betrothed and her brothers but feet away. When she realized he was actually attempting to kiss her she gave a soft cry of revulsion and leapt to her feet even as she shoved him away from her.

Taken by surprise by her abrupt retreat, Lord Fraser was unseated by her push. Islaen spared only one brief glance for her vilely cursing erstwhile lover before fleeing. Intending to seek the safety of the nearest of her protectors, she was pleased to see that that was Iain. Politely greeting the three people he spoke with, she hooked her arm through his and stood close by his side. By the time she spared another glance for Lord Fraser, the man was on his feet. He sent her a look that chilled her blood before striding away, and Islaen huddled even closer to Iain.

For a moment she bemoaned her cowardice, then told herself not to let pride make her a fool. Her brothers had once admitted to her that only a fool felt no fear, that men simply hid it well most of the time. It would also be foolish to think she could face one such as Lord Fraser alone. A person of her small stature was wise to accept her limitations. If Fraser got a hold of her, only luck would save her then. She certainly did not have the strength to fight a full-grown man. Wit and swiftness of foot were her best weapons and they only went so far. She would not, however, tell Iain all that had happened just yet, for she wished to avoid the trouble that could bring.

Her thoughts on Lord Fraser were abruptly ended when her attention was drawn by one of the two women talking to Iain. Lady Constance was fulsome and lovely. She was also brazenly flirting with Iain. A quick glance at Iain told Islaen nothing. If he noticed the woman's attentions, he was concealing it very well. Islaen found the attentions annoying. Her glare, however, only brought a condescending look from the older woman.

Islaen wished she could think of a way to extract Iain from the others. When the woman used the slimmest of excuses to caressingly touch Iain, Islaen resisted the urge to slap her hand and decided to use the first opportunity to get Iain away from the woman.

Feeling Islaen's grip tighten slightly, Iain glanced down at her. "Ye are looking somewhat flushed, wee Islaen."

Considering how furious she was with the fawning Lady Constance, Islaen was not surprised. She also saw her chance to separate Iain from the small group. Resting her cheek against his arm, she gazed up at him from beneath her lashes.

"I feel so. Do ye think ye can walk me back to my chambers, Sir MacLagan?" she asked in what she hoped was an appealing faintness. "I should like to lie down for a wee while, I believe."

"Of course, sweeting."

The endearment startled her but Islaen struggled to hide that as he politely excused them. She saw that Lady Constance had noted it and did not want the woman to think it was anything unusual.

In but a moment, Iain was escorting her to her chambers. Unused to subterfuge, Islaen forgot that she was supposed to be ailing and strolled along with her usual liveliness. She suddenly became aware of Iain's steady look and glanced up at him, musing silently that it was easy to understand why Lady Constance so avidly sought him.

"I thought ye were ailing," he murmured, wondering idly if she had any idea how lovely her eyes were.

He had not really thought her ill. When she had first reached his side, he had not only sensed her agitation, but also that she had rushed to him. Although her humour had drastically altered, he still wondered why she had originally hurried to his side. Something had clearly upset her and he wondered if he could get her to tell him what. He suspected

Lord Fraser had something to do with it for he had seen the man approach her.

"Oh, aye." She sighed. "Weel, nay. I just grew verra tired of Lady Constance slavering all o'er ye and wished to be away 'tis all." She frowned when she thought she saw laughter in his eyes, but it came and went too quickly for her to be sure.

Iain fought to keep the laughter out of his voice. "Slavering, eh?"

"Now, I willnae believe ye didnae notice the woman eyeing ye. Ye had to."

"Weel, I did ken that she was flirting a wee bit."

"Oh, aye, a wee bit," she grumbled. "She near to tore her clothes off and threw herself upon ye."

"Ah now that I would have noticed."

"Ye jest but 'tis true." She shook her head. "I cannae understand it."

"Thank ye," he murmured.

"Now her setting after ye I do understand. What puzzles me is that she would do so right afore me verra eyes. The ways of the court are a puzzle to me. Do they obey no laws?"

"The ones they wish to. Was it the ways of the court that sent ye hieing to my side?"

Islaen looked away hoping that, if she had to lie, he would not be able to read it upon her face. She did not really want to lie but neither did she want any confrontation between Iain and Lord Fraser. In a fair fight she knew Iain would win easily, but instinct told her that Lord Fraser would never fight fairly. Lord Fraser seemed to her to be the type to slip a dagger between a man's shoulder blades in the dark of night.

"Weel, aye, mayhaps. 'Tis my first time here, ye ken."

She was easy to read, he thought with some amusement. "Ye didnae understand something Lord Fraser said? Or did?" he added quietly.

Cursing viciously but silently over his obviously keen

sight, she answered with a false calm, "I am but unused to the
ways of the courtier. 'Tis naught."

"I had the feeling ye were most upset."

"That doesnae mean that there was aught to be upset
about."

It was clear to Iain that she was not going to tell him what
had occurred between herself and Lord Fraser. He wondered
why for only a moment. She was no coward, he knew that instinctively, so what had sent her rushing to his side, trembling
slightly, had to have been serious. He was certain she said
nothing because she wished to avoid any trouble.

The mere thought of Lord Fraser forcing even the slightest
of unwanted attention upon her infuriated Iain. He almost
laughed, for he had not wanted the marriage yet he was already strongly possessive. Her actions might have been
enough to deter Lord Fraser from trying anything else but
Iain decided to keep a close watch upon the man.

Breathing a sigh of relief, Islaen hurried inside her chambers when Iain stopped before her door. She knew she had not
fooled him for a moment with her elusive answers concerning what had happened between herself and Lord Fraser, but
fortunately he had not pressed the matter. If he kept a closer
eye on the man that could only be for the best. She decided to
forget Lord Fraser and concentrate on her faltering campaign
to impress Sir Iain MacLagan with her worthiness as a bride.

Contemplating the move that would checkmate Iain, Islaen
wondered if she should make it. She had clearly impressed
him with her ability at chess, a game he evidently liked very
well, but she wondered if beating him at the game was going
too far. Her brothers had never liked it. The last thing she
wished to do was hurt his pride.

"Islaen, I swear I shallnae sulk."

Hearing the laughter in his voice, she grimaced and made her move, muttering, "Checkmate."

Seeing her pained look Iain could not restrain a soft laugh. "I think that hurt ye more than it did me, lass."

"Aye, she does look pained," said a deep seductive voice.

Glancing up as Iain rose to greet the man, Islaen gaped. Never had she seen such a beautiful man. From his thick golden hair to his long, elegant and graceful body there appeared no flaw. It no longer surprised her that a voice could send shivers down her spine. As Iain introduced her to Alexander MacDubh, Islaen decided that such a voice suited a man like Alexander to perfection.

Subtly watching Islaen's reaction to Alexander, Iain suddenly understood why his brother Tavis, even after ten years of marriage to Storm, hated to have the man within feet of his wife. Islaen watched Alexander as if the man fascinated her. It struck Iain as highly contradictory that he did not want to be wed yet he did not want her to be drawn to any other man. Ignoring Alexander's amusement, Iain rather hastily agreed with Meg when the woman arrived to say that Islaen ought to take some time to view the preparations for the wedding.

"I hear the king arranged the marriage," Alexander remarked as soon as Islaen had left.

"As he neatly arranged yours."

"True, but I think ye got a better bargain. Howbeit, I hear that many wish the bond broken ere it is e'en made."

"Ye have heard a lot for a mon who has but now arrived at court."

"Ah, weel, I had a talk with the Lady Constance."

"A talk, hmmm?"

"A short one followed by a kind lady's consolation for a lonely widower."

"Ye have been a widower for twa years. Ye bleed that ploy dry."

"And ye tell me naught. Have ye no words about the wedding or the wee sweet child to be your wife?"

"That child is nineteen." He almost smiled at Alexander's surprise. "Lord Fraser and your cousin Ronald MacDubh wished to gain her hand. Neither is pleased that I now gain the dowry they hungered for. Aye and the lass. She has eleven brothers and a fither who would kill me in an instant if I cannae keep her weel and happy. Aye, I am to be wed but best ye not raise your tankard in salute unless 'tis to wish me the luck to live 'til the year's end."

"Especially with MacLennon still lurking about. Ye have stepped into a mire, have ye not."

"Aye and I am sinking fast."

"She seems a sweet lass. There could be some good to be found."

"Aye there could be, but I willnae seek it. She could wake up to find herself a widow but hours after she has become a bride. T'would be most cruel to play with her affections in any way when my life is in such danger."

"True and mayhaps ye run from the wrong things, Iain, my friend."

"I ken weel what I flee, Alexander."

"Do ye ken what ye can lose? I had no chance in my brief marriage. I wed a woman whose heart belonged to none, but whose body was given to all. The only good I gained was my wee daughter. Ye deny yourself all opportunity for some happiness. Aye and the lass."

"All I deny her is pain," Iain said coldly, then abruptly changed the subject.

He did not think on Alexander's words again until he escorted Islaen into the hall for the last repast of the day. The way he planned to direct their lives was indeed unfair to Islaen, but he could think of no way to alter that. He was almost glad of Alexander's company as they dined, for the man kept Islaen from being too troubled by his remoteness.

It was an appreciation that warred with something even he recognized as jealousy, as Alexander kept Islaen well amused, flattered her and flirted with her. By the time Iain escorted Islaen back to her chambers, he was not sure whether he considered Alexander a blessing or a curse.

"And what do ye think of Alexander?" he asked abruptly as they stopped outside her chamber's door.

A little startled by his question, as well as the fact that he had suddenly broken what had been an almost complete silence during the evening, Islaen answered, "He is verra nice."

"Verra nice, hmmm? An accomplished wooer of the lasses."

"Oh, aye, of course. A mon like that would take to wooing like a bairn to the breast of its mither. Do ye ken what makes him so good? He can do it and ye dinnae feel nervous or foolish or naught."

Smiling crookedly, he asked, "Nervous or foolish?"

"Aye. 'Tis that voice of his, I am thinking. 'Tis as soothing as a nurse's lullaby. He must get verra tired of people staring at him."

"Do ye think so?" Iain was finding her candid observations about Alexander amusing.

"Oh, aye. The mon kens how fine he looks but I dinnae think he is vain. An he lost his beauty I think he might regret that the ladies didnae fall into his arms as they did, but not much else. He might e'en be glad of it for then people would cease seeing naught but his beauty and look at the mon he is. I should not like to be so beautiful."

"Ah, but Islaen, ye are lovely."

"Nay," she demurred, coloring slightly over his soft flattery. "I have freckles and my hair is too bold a color."

"I dinnae find it too bold."

"Ah, weel, ye may do so when ye see it loose." She blushed when she realized when that would happen. "Ye have just seen a few locks slipping free, disobedient as my hair can be at times."

"Islaen, sometimes ye try too hard to be honest."

Her subsequent good night was subdued. Once inside of her chambers she leaned against the door and sighed. She felt riddled with guilt. She was not honest at all although she had tried to be on several occasions. The words stuck in her throat, however. There was a confession she had to make to Iain and time was running out. If she did not make it soon he would find out rather shockingly just how big a liar she could be.

Chapter Four

Frowning as she did so, Meg helped Islaen into bed. "T'will be the last night for that nightshift, lass."

Islaen looked at her attire, a sleeveless linen shift that only reached to mid-thigh. "I ken ye are right. 'Tis no lady's wear."

"Aye. I have a few lovely ones sewn for ye. Now ye get your rest, for 'tis a wondrous busy day for ye on the morrow."

Reminding her of that was not the way to insure that she would get any sleep, Islaen thought, as Meg left. Ever fair, Islaen then admitted that she did not really need Meg's reminders, for there was little else upon her mind. On the morrow she would marry Iain MacLagan and she was afraid, although not of marriage and all it entailed. She was afraid she would fail him and herself.

Now and again he had slipped in his aloof pose but it always returned, sometimes stronger than before. She feared the pose would become the man, that she would never reach the person he tried so hard to hide from everyone. That failure would leave her wed to a distant stranger who held prisoner the man she wanted.

Then too there was her secret. There would be no hiding it in the intimacy of marriage. Several times she had gotten up the courage to speak to him only to lose it when she looked upon his face. For a while she had thought it best to leave it as a surprise but now she doubted the wisdom of that. Not only was it unfair to Iain but she would not be able to bear his disgust when he found out. It would wound her sorely to have him turn from her on their wedding night, the very night he should be making her his.

Coming to a decision, she rose and searched out her houppelande. It was best to undeceive him now, before they had exchanged any vows. Somehow the wedding could be stopped if it was necessary. Even as she made a final check upon the fit of her houppelande she hoped Iain would, at the worst, insist that the candle stay snuffed for it might not feel as bad as it looked. Telling herself that exposure now was the only way, the only fair thing to do, she slipped into the hall and set out for Iain's chambers.

Though late at night, the way was not clear. Islaen was amazed at the number of people wandering about. It did not take many guesses to know that liaisons were plentiful. The fact that none of those about wished to be seen either made Islaen's way easier. Her first and only difficulty came when she was but two doors away from her goal. A woman she knew was wed met a man who was equally tied causing her to press herself into a shadowed niche from where, to her increasing discomfort, she could both see and hear the couple's rendezvous, a meeting that proved beds were not necessary.

When she finally reached Iain's door, she paused with her hand raised to knock. It might be the right thing to do but it was far from easy. No one liked to expose a fault or shame. Nevertheless, Iain had a right to know about her shames and faults before he was irrevocably tied to them, she told herself firmly. Her resolve strengthened, she rapped upon his door sure that her heart could be heard all along the hallway.

* * *

Iain lay sprawled upon his bed. He was trying very hard to get drunk, blind drunk, but was failing miserably. He was certainly not sober, but he had failed to achieve the soddened oblivion he was seeking. Very colorfully he cursed Fate which seemed against him at every turn. He did feel that depriving him of the ability to get stinking drunk was an exceedingly cruel trick. It was also a sad waste of some fine wine.

Admitting that it solved nothing to get drunk, Iain took another long pull of wine. Nothing had gone his way of late. He had felt like a good sulk, a thorough wallow in self-pity. However, even that was not working out.

The king had thwarted his plan to wed Islaen away from the court, so that he could avoid the consummation. The maids in the castle would quickly report the lack of virgin's blood. Since he could not explain that in any satisfactory way, Iain knew he would have to truly bed the girl. Even if he was very careful, there was ever the chance she could conceive, especially coming from as prolific a clan as she did.

Briefly, he wondered if that made a difference. He had been deluged with tales of her tiny mother and seen seven of the healthy brood of sons the woman had produced. Just possibly Islaen could do the same.

He then shook his head. It was something he could not chance. He freely admitted to cowardice. No matter what her heritage he could not gamble with another woman's life.

He groaned and poured another tankard of wine. As clearly as if it was occurring before him, Iain could see Islaen writhing upon her childbed, her screams filling the halls for long hellish hours until he feared to go mad from it. When it was over there would be nothing but a blood-soaked bed, a gruesome bier for her and their child. He could see Islaen and Catalina blended into one woman, the small lovely face still etched with agony, the pale lifeless body surrounded with blood and the bairn still wet from the womb,

blue from the lack of air that killed him and the cord that had
kept life going now wrapped around the tiny neck to end it.

Catalina had been right to curse him as she lay wracked
with pain. He should never had bedded her, wife or not. She
had not enjoyed the act at all, blessing the pregnancy that
killed her in the end, for it had allowed her to ban him from
her bed. Her shrill agonized voice still haunted his dreams,
rightly blaming him for her cruel and far too early death. She
had been but twenty, much too young to seek a cold grave or
be pushed into one as he had pushed her. Islaen was but nineteen he recalled and felt like weeping.

"Oh God," he moaned softly, "have mercy upon me. Make
the lass barren. God, dinnae put me through it all again. I
cannae bear it."

A soft knock broke into his morbid thoughts. When he
flung open the door his first thought was to slam it shut again.
Realizing that Islaen was no vision of a mind drunker than he
had thought, he yanked her into the room, made a hasty check
of the hallway to assure himself of the absence of people, and
then slammed the door.

He then cursed the lust that tightened his drink-weakened
body. Despite appearances to the contrary, he felt sure she had
not come to his room for a tryst. If nothing else, she looked
too solemn, even a little frightened.

Islaen looked at his dark scowling face and nearly winced.
It was going to be hard enough without him being furious
before she even started. Although it was an effort, she re-
frained from looking around his chambers to see if his anger
stemmed from her interrupting a last bachelor frolic. It would
not surprise her, despite the rumours of his monkish lifestyle,
for he did not want the marriage, but was simply obeying his
king.

Another cause of her embarrassment was his attire, or
rather its absence. He wore only his hose. The lack of covering on his torso made her very aware of how broad of

shoulder and muscular he was. A modest pelt of dark hair covered his chest, tapering to a thin line that dissected his taut stomach to disappear into his snug hose. She had seen many a man partly clothed, even naked, for it was unavoidable living with so many brothers, but she had never felt so warm before. Neither had she suffered such an urge to touch a man's chest. She forced her gaze upwards to his face.

Iain was just drunk enough not to care about his lack of attire before his young bride. "Be ye mad, lass? Why are ye here?"

"I had to talk with ye," she replied, following him as he strode to the table by his bed to retrieve his drink.

Sitting down on the bed he took a long drink before looking at her. "Could it not have waited until the morrow? What if ye had been seen?"

"I wasnae and what folk I saw about wouldnae have wanted me to see them. What I have to tell ye couldnae wait any longer."

He reacted to that statement with increased alertness. Perhaps the girl meant to tell him she had a lover, was carrying some man's seed. Even as he decided that was impossible he realized that the thought did not cheer him despite the fact that the king would not make him wed her under such circumstances. Shaking his head over his own vagaries, he waited for her to speak.

"There is something ye maun be told ere we wed. Weel, shown actually. I am not as I seem, Sir MacLagan."

"Deformed?" he thought and could not believe it. "I can hardly reject ye for some mark or scar, child," he said dryly and touched his cheek.

"'Tis nay a mark or a scar, sir." She began to shed her houppelande. "I cannae deceive ye any longer. 'Tis unfair and dishonest to do so."

After watching the houppelande fall around her pretty feet he studied her. Her night rail was no more than a short shift, revealing a great deal of her lovely legs. There was also something vaguely different about her but he could not pinpoint it. It did not help him to think when he was so attracted, his loins tightened painfully and his hands itched to bury themselves in her thick, hip-length hair.

For such a tiny girl she had a real skill for heating his blood. It was going to be very hard to keep that in control. Even harder for a large part of him did not want to control it, wanted to savor it to its fullest. The need for a woman, any woman, indiscriminate as it was, had been easy enough to control. What Islaen instilled in him was all mixed up with who she was, her looks, her character, even her smell. It was not easy to dispel it. In truth, it was beginning to prove impossible.

"I ken that my night rail isnae fitting for a lady, but Meg has made some more suitable ones," she murmured as she fumbled to unlace her shift and felt color flood her cheeks even as her heart beat against the wall of her chest in growing agitation.

Realizing the girl was about to strip before his very eyes, Iain croaked, "'Tis no matter, lass. We can keep the candle snuffed."

He felt close to panic and actually thought of bolting from the room no matter how foolish that would look. Unfortunately, his body was not obeying his mind's frantic urgings to get away. It intended to stay where it was, intended that he should see if her image fit the one that had recently haunted his dreams.

"That willnae help, sir. Ye will still be aware of my deceit. Dinnae fear to hurt my feelings. I will understand if ye cannae bear it. Ye see, I am weel aware of my ugliness. 'Tis why I have hidden it. I couldnae bear to reveal my oddness to the world."

She let her shift fall, her folded arms all that kept her from complete exposure as the loosened top draped over them. Iain stared speechless at the full ivory breasts she revealed, the pink tips hardening as he watched. Forcing his hungry gaze from such beauty, he searched for the defect she spoke of. He almost hoped for some startling mar so as to divert his mind from the lushness within reach of his lips. Aside from noting that the rest of her was still very tiny, he found nothing. His gaze returned to her breasts although he had intended to look at her face. Other than a few faint freckles that he found delightfully alluring, she was perfection. Groaning, his hand found its way to one of those full firm breasts that almost seemed too much for her slight frame as if it had a mind of its own.

His mind screamed its warning of the danger he now faced but he heeded it not. He felt spellbound. It seemed as if there was no part of his body that did not ache for her.

The feel of her warm silken breast beneath his hand made him shake with want. He knew he could not pull back now, could not grab at some semblance of sanity. All he could do was touch her, savor the feel of her and pray that she would stop him, even flee. A small part of his passion-fogged mind reluctantly admitted that there was little chance of that. She did not seem to see the danger she was in.

Trying to speak even though his touch was sending pure fire shooting through her veins, Islaen croaked, "Ye see? I grew all out of proportion. There is nay a need to pretend; I will truly understand if ye cannae abide such an oddity for a wife."

"Oh, God," was all Iain managed to say as he dropped the tankard in his other hand and reached out to cup her other breast.

Whatever reaction she had anticipated, it was not this. Touching them as he was, his fingers toying with the hard tips, seemed to indicate that he was not repulsed. Nonetheless, there was an odd look upon his face, a strange fire in his eyes that turned them green, and a tic in his cheek that she was having trouble deciphering, especially with a mind that was rapidly disfunctioning as the heat in her body increased.

"Iain," she gasped as one of his hands moved down to her stomach, pushing her folded arms down as well. "Will ye say naught? Are we still to be wed?"

In the grip of a force he could not fight, Iain simply reiterated, "Oh God."

His mouth was drawn to her and his tongue flicked over each taut nipple. Islaen's hands jerked up to grasp his shoulders in a natural reaction to the shaft of desire that careened through her. That action pulled them free of the light shift which quickly joined the houppelande at her feet. Diverted for an instant, Iain's gaze moved over her in pure white hot greed. He was swamped with desire as he noted her tiny waist, slim gently rounded hips, slender well-formed legs and the wine red triangle at the juncture of her beautiful thighs. His hands gripped her small waist and he tugged her closer.

"M'God, Islaen," he groaned before his mouth closed over the beckoning tip of one full breast.

Islaen's knees buckled as waves of pleasure melted her. She made no sound as he tossed her down on the bed and partly covered her body with his own. He kissed her hungrily, his tongue ravishing her untried mouth. The hair upon his chest further excited her breasts while his hands searched out every curve and hollow. Her hands moved over his back feeling the tensed muscles as she fell beneath the power of his fierce uncontrollable passion. A flicker of sanity came when she felt him probing for entry but it did not gain strength fast enough to stop him. Crying out softly, she gave him her innocence. In payment he gave her ecstasy, swiftly taking her to the heights where he met her in the delirious fall into desire's abyss.

For several moments they lay silently entwined, their breathing growing less harsh and their rapid heartbeats slowing to normal. Islaen was surprised to find that the weight of him felt quite nice, not light by any means but nothing she would not gladly bear, even enjoy. A tiny voice in her head murmured something about sin but she easily ignored it. This was the man she would marry in hours or, at least, she hoped so. She wondered if she were being presumptuous by assuming he did not find her odd shape repulsive just because of what had occurred. According to Meg and a good many others, a man was not overly choosey about what he lay with if the urge was strong enough.

Iain was mortified. He had gone half mad. The problem was, he was feeling so inclined again. Worse, he had spilled his seed into her and he had the feeling that that would be hard to control as well. With that dismal thought he eased their embrace slightly and looked at her unaware of the tortured look in his eyes, a look that made Islaen think all her fears confirmed.

Islaen stared at him feeling her heart contract. "Ye cannae really abide it, can ye. I had feared as much."

Silently cursing herself and fighting tears, Islaen wished she had not come to his room. She had not saved herself anything. He had shown her what they could have together and would now take it away. The very worst of her fears had become reality. Shifting beneath him, she moved to flee but he held her still.

With a sigh, Iain put aside his own fears. Someone had done a very good job of giving the girl the ridiculous idea that she was ill-formed. It was important to rid her of that yet he was not at all sure how he could.

"Islaen, ye are not odd and certainly not ugly. Where did ye come by such an idea?"

"But I am all out of proportion. 'Tis not right to be fat in one place yet so skinny everywhere else."

"Ye are small, not skinny." His hand touched her thigh and lingered. "There is flesh enough to draw a mon's touch. Who has given ye the idea that ye look odd or ugly?"

"Meg says I look a cow, all udder and little else," she replied in a small voice.

"I wouldnae hurl a cow to the bed and leap upon it. Aye. 'Tis true that ye carry more than t'would be thought right for such a wee lass but 'tis far from ugly." His hand moved to her breasts.

"Oh," she breathed as his touch restoked the banked fires within her. "I dinnae mind them when ye do that, Sir MacLagan."

He bit down a laugh. "I think ye can call me Iain now. Little one, every mon here would love to be where I am now, touching such perfection. Aye, they are full but not too much despite the slightness they adorn. To then come down and clasp a waist that I can span with my hands is a true delight." His hands moved along with his words. "This gently rounded backside feels exquisite in my hands as do these slim hips. Och, lass, these slim thighs leave a gap at their top that fair begs a mon to move in. Meg is a jealous cow."

She stared at him in speechless wonder. There was no hint that he did not mean exactly what he said. For reasons that eluded her he seemed to find the body she had kept hidden so long of interest. Doubt still lingered, however, for she could think of no reason for Meg to lie to her. Then again she could think of no reason for Iain to lie to her either. She wanted to believe he found her fair to look upon, but for too long she had been thinking otherwise. Islaen found her thoughts growing decidedly confused and decided to get back to the matter at hand.

"Weel, I cannae believe I have suddenly become a beauty, but does all that mean that we will still be wed?"

"Aye." He hid his dislike of the match for the first time. "I have just had of ye what should have been saved for your wedding night."

"That doesnae matter, Iain," she gasped, her voice failing

as his lips caressed her breasts. "I will understand if ye cannae abide it."

"Sweet, stupid, Islaen, I cannae keep my hands nor my mouth from ye. Would it be so if ye were at all repulsive to my eyes?"

"Nay, mayhaps not. Oh," she breathed as his mouth closed over the tip of one breast and his hand caressed her taut belly, edging ever closer to the wine red treasure that he was aching to possess again. "How do ye do that? Make me go all hot and melting?"

A shudder tore through him at her words and he eased his hand between her thighs. "I dinnae ken, lass. How do ye make me crave this when I ken 'tis the last thing I should seek? How can ye make me break all my vows to myself?"

Her initial shy tension gone, Islaen was turning to fire in his hands. "What vow was that?" she moaned, arching to his touch.

"That I wouldnae touch the women. Ah, ye have a muckle fine touch, lass," he groaned as her hands moved over his backside. "I vowed I would be careful when we wed for ye maun ne'er get with child. I willnae kill anither woman." He moved her hand to the proof of his strong, uncontrollable desire for her. "Touch me here, lass. Ken what ye do to a mon."

Her long fingers curled around him, then stroked and explored. She astutely understood his meaning but knew no way to dispel his errant opinions. There was really only one way to prove him wrong. It was soon evident to Islaen that Iain had no intention of letting her get with child, so that she could show him that he was wrong.

It was difficult to speak as her small hand lightly stroked him. Iain wanted to simply give into the strong, exquisite feelings she was able to stir in him but he fought that temptation. Later, when he had made her understand, when she had given him the promise he needed, he would let his passion run wild and free.

Forcing himself to think, he tried to gather the words needed to explain himself, yet not offend her. To tell a woman that she could have the marriage but not the children was not the easiest thing to do. Some women would be very grateful, but Iain sensed that Islaen was not one of those. She certainly had not sounded so on that day they had argued in the gardens.

Looking into her eyes he found that he also had to convince himself again. All he could think of was a sweet, lively girl child with Islaen's pretty eyes. He ached for a family but he tried to fight that weakness. Those thoughts put him into such a state of confusion that he decided not to explain himself. He would simply tell her what she would do. It was, after all, his right as her husband.

"I can at least try to keep my vow that I willnae get ye with child. For me to spill my seed outside is one way," he gasped as her naturally skillful fingers toyed with the holders of that seed, "but I ken that will be verra hard so I will have ye do this for me." Ignoring her blushes, he explained the sponge method to her. "Promise me, lass." He was suddenly fierce as he stared at her. "Promise or we will ne'er lie this way again, I swear it."

Islaen stared at him for a moment. She could not believe what he was asking of her. For only one brief moment did she think he was joking when he threatened to stay out of her bed. That hope faded when she looked into his eyes. He meant every word he said.

It was a sin, both what he asked and what she decided she had to do. Then again he had no right to ask her to commit the sin of preventing conception. So too did he have no right to deny her the child she had every right to as his wife and in the eyes of God. She threw out a hasty prayer for forgiveness and asked that, in the end, she did not simply add to his anguish and guilt. With that done, she looked him straight in the eyes, her hands clutching his hips to pull him closer and proceeded to lie through her teeth.

"Aye, I promise, Iain, an it is what ye wish."

"It is," he growled and then took her mouth in a hungry kiss.

His response to her promise was all that she could wish. Her guilt was pushed aside as they made their rapid climb to the heights and made the dizzying fall into passion's abyss as one. Sated, they lay in each other's arms. Iain knew he should send her back to her chambers but, instead, he let her rest a while before making love to her again. It was dawn before they both succumbed to exhaustion, Iain's head nestled comfortably on the full breasts that had so long been only a burden to their owner.

Chapter Five

Cold steel prodding one's side makes for a rude awakening. Iain felt the cold of the blade seep through his veins. When he slowly lifted his head from the sleeping Islaen's breasts, he knew a mixture of relief and consternation. For a moment he had feared that Catalina's lover had found him, which could well have meant Islaen's death along with his. The eight MacRoths surrounding his bed looked far from friendly, but they would at least not harm Islaen. They would also be appeased by the wedding.

"If ye be wondering why your squire didnae stop us 'tis because he is tied up for the moment."

The iciness in Alaistair MacRoth's voice made Iain wince inwardly. It was hardly wise to antagonize one's father by marriage. Neither was it wise to get on the bad side of your wife's brothers especially when there were eleven of them.

"Ye best start explaining this and fast, laddie."

"Fither?" mumbled Islaen as she opened sleep-clogged eyes and began to realize that she and Iain were no longer alone.

That brought all eyes of the MacRoths to fix upon her. Iain watched those eyes widen with disbelief and followed the direction of their gazes. Islaen's lovely full breasts were bared to view. Seeing the stunned looks upon her kin's gaze, Islaen colored deeply. Her blooming had been kept a secret from a lot of people. He almost laughed when the MacRoths looked at him again, accusation in their faces.

Islaen hurriedly pulled up the linen to cover herself. It had been her intention to talk to her father, tell him of what she had kept hidden. This was a terrible way for him to find out that his own daughter had deceived him for years.

"What did ye do to the lass?" Alaistair demanded, his angry gaze turning back to Iain.

"Sir, I think if ye will but stop to consider for a moment, ye will ken that I had naught to do with that. What occurred here might have changed the lass but not to such an extent. 'Tis not a mon's work ye view."

"Aye, aye, I am not thinking clear." He ran a hand through his hair and frowned at Islaen. "When did ye grow those, lass? Ye have hidden the change from me and I cannae understand the why of it."

Embarrassed that such an intimate part of her body was being discussed so openly, Islaen nevertheless did her best to answer her father honestly. "I changed not long after I, weel, became a woman."

"When ye were but thirteen?" he croaked, totally astonished over the longevity of her deception.

"Aye," she admitted reluctantly, afraid that she might have wounded her father with her secrecy.

"For six years I have waited for ye to grow and ye had grown apace already. Why hide it?"

Seeing her family look at her as if she were totally mad annoyed Islaen and she snapped, "Why not when all ye wished for was to set me out to market like a prized sow?"

"Here now, lass," Alaistair blustered, puffing up in preparation of arguing with his daughter.

Before the argument could gain any strength, Iain gently interrupted, "An I might have a word with ye?"

"I have more than a word or twa I wish to say to ye," Alaistair hissed, his fury directed at Iain again. "If ye mean to claim her unchaste now and flee the wedding that way, ye best think again."

"Papa," Islaen protested, feeling it unfair to be so insulting when Iain had not even been given a chance to speak yet.

"I mean to wed her, sir. Naught has changed," Iain said quietly but with a firmness none could doubt.

Seeing how all the MacRoths immediately eased their fighting stances, Iain moved to don his braes. He then handed Islaen her night rail. Giving her a reassuring smile, he turned to face Alaistair.

"Could we speak o'er here for a moment, sir?" Iain moved to the far corner of his chambers.

When Islaen made to follow, Alaistair growled, "Ye stay right where ye are, lass, and ye lads see that she does."

Islaen sat down reluctantly. She wondered what Iain and her father would talk about but knew she had no chance of hearing the conversation. Her brothers were clearly intent upon being very vigilant.

"I dinnae think I need say that I am ill pleased by what I have found here," Alaistair growled softly once he and Iain were secluded on the far side of the room.

"That I can understand, sir. There is no explaining it or excusing it. I went mad," he said with a strong hint of self-disgust in his voice. "She came to me to reveal this secret she has kept for so long."

"Reveal it?" Alaistair's eyes widened as he began to get an idea of just what had happened.

"Aye, just that, sir. I havenae had a woman for near to twa years. 'Tis no real excuse, I ken it, but when she set such lovely bounty afore my eyes. . . ." Iain shook his head. "I had been drinking as weel."

"Did ye hurt her?" Alaistair asked tightly, his hand going to his sword in a clearly threatening gesture.

"Nay, I feel sure I didnae. In all honesty I cannae say exactly for, as I have said, I went mad."

"The truth tell, I can understand what has happened here. A mon can only take so much temptation ere he grabs it, especially when 'tis the fleshly sort and he has been without for a verra long time. I will trust to the fact that ye would have left the lass be had she fought ye or cried nay."

"Aye but to be fully honest, I think she didnae only because she didnae really ken what was about until t'was all over"

"Mayhaps. What I cannae understand is why she has hidden her form, why she has left me to think her form more that of a child than a woman. I ne'er thought she was unhappy to be a female though she did have a few complaints about it."

"'Tis not that, sir. She thinks she is ugly in her shape."

"The lass is daft. She could ne'er have gained such an idea from me and the lads."

"Nay. That woman, Meg, felt Islaen had grown all out of proportion and the lass believes her. She came to me because she truly believed I would find her deformed and turn her away. She wished it done ere the vows were spoken."

"She must ken otherwise now," Alaistair drawled. "Men dinnae go mad, as ye call it, o'er an ugly lass."

"She kens that I find no fault, but I am nay sure she has lost the idea that her form is odd, unseemly."

"I will kill that udderless cow Meg."

"'Tis my thought that love directed the woman, sir. She didnae want the lass ridiculed."

"Aye," Alaistair agreed after a moment. "Islaen's the bairn Meg ne'er had. She would ne'er hurt the lass apurpose. I will speak to the foolish woman though. There must be a way we can explain the sudden change in the lass. She cannae go back to what she was," he mused aloud, frowning in the direction of his daughter.

"She could until we leave for Caraidland. Few from here would see her then. Later, when they do see her again, they would think that they had recalled her wrongly or that marriage had matured her."

"Aye, or childbirth."

Iain could not meet the man's gaze when he nodded in agreement. "Aye, or that."

"And now we come to the next trouble that needs sorting out. She is a maid no longer."

"The proof of her chastity is clear to read upon the linen." With a wave of his hand Iain invited the man to look but Alaistair did not move.

"Which will be changed this day, and unless 'tis seen by the right eyes, t'will be ignored. Robert, ye must go and fetch the king. He must be shown that all was as it should be, e'en if the wedding night was had ere the vows were said. I dinnae want this matter talked about, but better this than talk of my lass going to her marriage bed unchaste. The king arranged this match so let him bear witness now and mayhaps advise us."

Islaen softly groaned in embarrassment, earning sympathetic looks from her brothers. She had foolishly hoped to keep her fall from grace a family secret. The very involvement of the king in the arrangement of her marriage made her chastity a matter of great importance. He must know exactly what was going on. Islaen understood all that but that did not make her like it very much.

The fact that it was the day of the wedding he so wanted brought the king to Iain's chambers quickly. He wanted nothing to go wrong, yet a summons from Alaistair now could only mean trouble. When the king entered Iain's chambers, saw the disheveled bed, the undressed state of the betrothed couple and the gathering of armed MacRoths, he easily guessed what had happened and relaxed. It looked to be something easily solved; thus saving the union he sought.

"This is most unexpected," the king murmured looking at Iain with mild condemnation.

"Aye, I surprised meself," Iain grumbled, running a hand through his hair.

"Och, weel, Robbie, it isnae fully the lad's fault. My lass tempted him sorely."

The way Alaistair so familiarly addressed the king shocked Iain. When the king made no protest, accepted it as natural, Iain felt stunned. He had not realized just how close to the throne the MacRoths were. Iain could not help but wonder if he must now add the king himself to the growing list of ones who would be displeased if he made Islaen unhappy.

"Wee Islaen?" the king asked in total surprise. "Nay, the lass is no temptress, Alaistair."

"Weel, not by intent. Islaen, come here," Alaistair commanded, looking at her sternly when she briefly hesitated.

Feeling color heat her cheeks, Islaen reluctantly obeyed her father. When her father directed the king's attention to her breasts and the king's face clearly showed his growing surprise, she felt like melting with embarrassment. Unable to stand such close scrutiny any longer she stepped behind Iain, using his tall body as a shield.

"Surely the change in the lass did not occur over the night," the king muttered, his confusion clear.

"Nay, she hid the change. Her nurse convinced her t'was unseemly, odd, e'en ugly. The lass felt she had to tell Iain this secret, let him judge her shape for himself, so crept to his chambers last eve and showed the lad all she had hidden."

"Showed him?" The king's voice shook with laughter and he looked at Iain in sympathy. "Has a man e'er been so tried? So ye are human after all, Iain lad. Many have wondered."

"For Islaen's sake I would hope that they dinnae ken my weakness. She came to me in all innocence. That she no longer enjoys that state is my fault alone."

"Are ye saying ye forced her, laddie?"

"He would be dead if he had," growled Alaistair.

At the same time Islaen peered at the king from around Iain. "Nay, sire. I ne'er once protested."

"Not once?" he teased, grinning when even Iain looked slightly disconcerted.

Islaen groaned and hid behind Iain again, pressing her hot face against his back. She felt this was more embarrassment than any soul should have to suffer. It was her fervent hope that they would hurry up and solve the problem her impetuosity had made so that she could retire to her chambers and try to compose herself. Perhaps in the rush of activity and celebration that her wedding would bring she could forget the whole trying morning.

"So the marriage has been consummated ere the vows were said," the king mused aloud. "'Tis not the first time this has occurred. Many a betrothed couple tastes the joys of the marriage bed ere they speak the vows."

"Aye but I fear the tale that might go the rounds is that my Islaen wasnae chaste when Sir Iain took her to his bed as wife."

"Ah and it could be hinted that Iain was not the first. I see the trouble weel now. Robert, fetch the queen. She will be expecting word from me. Bring her and her woman here. Aye and this Meg woman. They will help us in smoothing over this trouble. You may cease your scowling, Alaistair. 'Tis not such a big problem."

When the women arrived Islaen saw that she could suffer even more embarrassment than she had already. The linen was inspected, her chastity confirmed and the discussion about what to do next began. Islaen tried to distance herself from it all by watching her father and Meg, the former quite clearly chastizing the latter. She tried to discern just how much trouble Meg was in.

It was decided that the bedding ceremony and the morning visit to the bride and groom would be done by the royal couple, the queen's handmaiden, Meg and two of Islaen's brothers as weel as Alexander MacDubh to represent Iain's absent family. That settled, Islaen was hurried back to her chambers by her family.

Once assured that his squire was unharmed, Iain sent the man to locate Alexander MacDubh. When Alexander joined him, Iain rather crossly explained what had happened. He also told Alexander what part he was to play now. His humour was not at all improved by Alexander's bursts of hilarity. He was glad that strenuous efforts were being made to keep the whole matter secret. Iain had no wish to become the object of court jests.

"Come, Iain, you must see the humour of it," Alexander said when he finally controlled his laughter.

"Mayhaps I will when I am certain we have all escaped unscathed," he said.

"Though distant, the MacRoths are kin to the king and he is fond of them in his way. He will let nothing sully their name."

"Am I the only one who didnae ken the relationship there?"

"Weel, you are the first of your clan to linger much at court and t'was before your time that the real bond was formed and easily seen by all. If ye cocked an ear to the gossip more ye would have kenned it ere now."

"I thought ye came to court for other than talk."

"'Tis true that I come for the ladies but they do talk upon occasion. Men should pay more heed to the lasses. 'Tis astounding what they ken, e'en if they dinnae always ken the importance of the knowledge they have gained."

"I will keep that in mind. Come, I best don my finery. They will soon wish access to my chambers."

"My friend, ye should show more cheer. Ye gain a fine lass." Seeing little comfort in Iain's face, Alexander sighed. "Ah, weel, at least your bed will no longer be empty and mayhaps this lass can change your mind about some things."

"Right now I suspicion she has more than enough to think on without fashing herself o'er me or my thoughts."

Islaen grimaced as Meg scrubbed her back. The woman was being far more vigorous than usual. She suspected that her father had severely chastized Meg. After another moment Islaen decided she did not need to suffer for the argument her father and Meg had had. She snatched the sponge from Meg and wondered how such a soft thing could be made to feel so hard.

"I will have no skin left upon my back if ye dinnae cease," she complained, glaring at Meg who glared right back at her.

"Dinnae fash yourself. That mon will still bed ye," Meg grumbled and angrily moved to sort out the clothes Islaen would wear.

"Wheesht, ye have got a burr in your braes, havenae ye," Islaen murmured as she started to bathe herself. "I had to tell the mon, Meg. I couldnae leave it 'til the wedding night. T'wasnae right, not right at all."

"T'wasnae right to jump into the mon's bed neither."

"Weel, I didnae really jump. Rather, I fell. I didnae think he would react in that way." A continued surprise tinted Islaen's voice.

"A lass goes waving her body parts afore a mon and 'tis just how he will act," Meg said with hearty conviction.

Biting back a laugh over the image Meg's cross words invoked, Islaen said calmly, "I ken that now. He still weds me."

"So he should. Here, ye have washed enough." Meg held out a drying cloth. "Do ye try to wash his touch away?"

"Nay," Islaen said firmly as she stepped out of her bath. "I like his touch and I am nay ashamed to say so. There is something that troubles me and I speak of this expecting it to be kept the greatest of secrets atween us."

"Secret e'en from your fither?"

"Aye, sad to say, e'en from him."

"Aye then. Secret e'en from him."

"Do ye ken that Iain's first wife died in childbirth?" Meg nodded. "T'was a long, painful birth and the bairn died too. Iain has a fear of it now, a deep abiding fear. E'en though his brother's wife keeps having bairns and all is weel, Iain sees childbirth as a death sentence upon a woman. I cannae make him see elsewise. He willnae let me bear a bairn."

"How can he stop ye unless he keeps himself out o' your bed. 'Tis God's decision, not his."

"There is a way for him to stay in my bed yet not leave me with bairn—sponges."

"'Tis a sin," Meg gasped.

"'Tis a sin to keep me from e'er having a bairn, aye, but I think the trick he speaks of could have its uses. 'Tis not good for a woman to bear a bairn every year. Such a thing could give a woman time to grow strong again. I cannae help but think that my mither used them for we are all nearly or little more than two years apart. Seems too coincidental."

Meg frowned thoughtfully as she began to help Islaen dress. "Aye, I think ye may be right. If that is a sin, 'tis a little one. Go on, child. I ken ye have more to say. Has he demanded that ye use such things?"

"Aye. In truth, he threatened to ne'er lie with me again an I refused. I couldnae abide that, Meg. Agree with me or nay as ye please but I mean to grasp for as full a marriage as I can. That cannae come an he and I dinnae e'en share a bed."

"Nay. Ye would soon grow to be mair strangers than ye are e'en now. Muckle a marriage is saved or lost in the bed-chamber."

"So I thought, so I promised to use those things."

"Then ye mean to be barren, to ne'er hold a bairn o' your own?" Meg asked, her shock and anger clear to hear in her voice and see in her face. "Ye would wither in sic a marriage."

"I ken it. I want bairns. I love them and dearly wish to hold my own. Truth, I think I would grow to hate Iain for denying me, yet I understand his fear. I lied, Meg. I looked him straight in the eye and lied."

Hearing the pain and guilt in Islaen's voice, Meg awkwardly patted her cheek. "'Tis nay sic a big sin, lass."

"'Tis not the way I mean to go in my marriage but I felt I had to do it. I will tell him the truth eventually. I mean to have my bairn, Meg, and, in doing so, I mean to put an end to Iain's fears. I tell ye all this for I may need your aid in this deception. Aye, especially an I get with bairn. I just pray that I dinnae add to his fears."

"Ye willnae. 'Tis the way o' the women in your family to be fruitful and nay suffer too much o'er it. Why maun ye keep the lie to yourself e'er ye get with bairn? Could ye nay tell him the truth once ye are sure?"

"Nay. He fears it, Meg. For a man to deny himself an heir, weel, he must fear it verra much. The longer I can keep my being with bairn a secret the less time he will have to fash himself o'er my fate. Once I am delivered of a healthy bairn and prove to him that not all women need die in childbirth, I will tell him of my lie. An I feel something amiss I will tell him for I willnae add to his guilt and pain."

"Och, lass, I think ye have a rough road ahead o'ye. Ye will have tae tread muckle carefully with nary a misstep."

"Aye, I ken it. I aim to cure yet I could make matters worse. Yet, I cannae feel that death upon a childbed is to be my fate. I cannae claim to have the sight, yet the feeling is strong that I will do as weel as me mither and me kin afore her. Do ye think 'tis a false hope that I cling to? I really cannae risk being wrong."

"Ye are nay wrong."

"Good, 'tis a shame that Iain hasnae any of his kin here," she continued, "I should like to have met them ere I am made their kin. In truth, I dinnae e'en ken when I am to finally meet them. I ken little about the MacLagans. They are a small clan like ours, I think."

"I ken little mair than that. There is little bad that I have heard, which be good. I wouldnae fash yourself, lass."

Easier said than done, Islaen mused as Meg vigorously brushed her hair. Unless she somehow broke through the wall Iain had built around his heart she would be facing a lot of strangers more or less upon her own when they went to his home. She had rarely left her father's strong keep and certainly never without some of her seemingly vast family at her side. Only Meg would be with her at Caraidland. She decided she had best try to get Iain to tell her something about his family and Caraidland. Perhaps then she would not feel so lost when she arrived there. It might also give her enough knowledge to stop her from stepping wrong. Her bid to win Iain's affections could never be successful if she offended any of his kin, even through ignorance. Instinct told her that he was very close to his family.

When Meg was finished, Islaen reluctantly let the woman pull her towards a mirror, an item she felt there were far too many of at court. Warily she looked at herself. She strongly wished to look beautiful upon her wedding day and, with surprise widening her eyes, decided that Meg had come very close to fulfilling that wish. In fact, Islaen was not sure that anyone would recognize her but then she smiled. Her hair would give her away.

Glancing briefly at the bodice of her deep gold gown she wondered how she would look if her breasts were not bound, then grimaced. Iain may claim that her fullness did not truly bother him but she was far from ready to reveal her true figure to all. She was certain there would be far more stares than she would ever be able to tolerate. Islaen was glad that Iain felt it best if she waited until they went to Caraidland before she ceased to wear her binding. Looking closely, she suspected that Meg had not done her bindings as tightly as she usually did, however.

"Weel, 'tis time to join the queen, lass. Do ye wish a bracing sip o' wine first?" Meg asked gently and Islaen nodded.

After quickly downing the drink, Islaen took a deep, long breath in a further attempt to quell a sudden bout of nerves. "I cannae understand why I am all atremble. I have had my wedding night."

"Aye but soon ye truly leave the hame of your father, soon ye truly belong to Sir Iain MacLagan and no other."

"I just pray that he will let me belong to him."

Chapter Six

Iain was hard put not to gape when Islaen was brought to him in the crowded hall. Her thick glorious hair hung in waves almost to her knees and the occasional sparkle of a jewel was hardly noticeable in its depths. As she reached his side he saw that the gold of her gown brought forth the gold flecks in her lovely eyes. His loins tightened as he thought of the additonal beauty that lay hidden beneath her gown and the bindings. As he took her hand, he covertly glanced around and saw that others were now fully aware of Islaen's special beauty, something he suspected would cause him some trouble for a while. Despite that, he could not fully suppress an inner glow of pride as he led her to the priest.

Islaen was only partly aware of the priest's words. She had always thought Iain a splendid figure of a man but in his black and silver wedding finery he left her speechless and more than a little afraid. No matter how she tried to dispel the thought she could not help but wonder how she could ever expect to hold onto such a man.

When they finished their vows they rose and he gently kissed her. Islaen found that she had to fight the urge to press for a fuller kiss. She mused, with a great deal of mockery directed at herself, that she had certainly learned quickly to crave that sort of thing. From total innocence she had rapidly become quite the wanton. When the look in Iain's fine eyes told her that he had recognized her reaction to his brief kiss, she sent him a very stern look but it only made him smile.

The feasting had barely begun when Islaen found herself growing annoyed. Even though it was her wedding day the women still tried to catch Iain's eye. Their flirtations and invitations were far from subtle. There was one spot of humour in it for her, however, and that was found in Lady Constance's actions. The woman seemed to be in great turmoil over which man she really wished to draw to her side, Alexander Mac-Dubh or Iain. Alexander sat on Islaen's left while Iain sat upon her right. Islaen was almost able to laugh as she mused that the woman was apt to do herself an injury with the way she kept turning her face from right to left and back again.

"Come, Lady MacLagan," Alexander said quietly, "'tis not right for a bride to scowl so at her own wedding feast."

"Weel, ye would think they would give it a rest today of all days," Islaen grumbled and took a drink.

"Give what a rest, sweeting?" Iain asked and signaled a page to refill her now empty goblet.

Quickly shaking free of the bemusement his use of an endearment always sent her into, Islaen replied, "The women should cease leering at you. 'Tis nay right for them to leer at the groom at the wedding feast."

"Leering at me?" Iain croaked, rather flattered by what appeared to be jealousy upon Islaen's part. "Cease cackling, Alex."

"Och, weel, 'tis no matter an he laughs." Islaen fleetingly grinned at a still chuckling Alexander. "People will think I am the greatest of wits. Aye, Iain," she belatedly replied, "leering at you. 'Tis quite clear to see if ye would but look."

"I dinnae care to look."

"Weel, mayhaps ye ought to tell Lady Constance that for the

poor woman is near to twisting her head off o' her shoulders trying to share her smiles atween ye and Sir Alexander. I have set him to laughing again."

"Pay the fool no heed." Iain felt extremely high spirited and decided to do nothing to hide or stop it. "Ah, the musicians begin to play." Iain stood up and took Islaen by the hand. "Come, we must lead the dancing."

"God's teeth," Islaen gasped, then flushed and covered her mouth with her hand. "Forgive me. It slipped free."

"I heard nothing."

"Nor I," declared Alexander.

"Weel then ye are both as deaf as posts but thank ye. Iain, I am nay verra good at this dance."

Tugging her to her feet, he smiled. "As long as ye keep upright, t'will do fine enough."

"Weel, an I fall just pay me no heed," she said on a sigh as he towed her out onto the area cleared for dancing.

"As you wish. I will merely take care not to step upon ye."

"So gallant," she managed to murmur before forced to concentrate upon the steps of the elegant dance.

At the end of the dance, Iain kissed her, a kiss far less chaste than the one before the priest. Islaen was oblivious to the rowdy cheers of their audience. She felt her insides melt as she tasted the promise in his kiss. When he lifted his head, she gazed up at him from beneath her eyelashes feeling quite bemused by the way he could make her feel.

"Ye do that verra weel," she said, surprised at the soft huskiness of her voice.

"Dancing?"

"Aye. That too." She grinned.

Before they were able to return to their seats, Islaen was whirled away by her brother Robert. Iain sprawled in his seat and watched her. She revealed no uncertainty or reluctance in the less courtly forms of dance. Glancing around, he caught

the king and Alaistair MacRoth watching him and raised his
tankard in a cocky salute. This day he knew they would find
little to criticize.

Breathless from dancing and laughing with her brothers,
Islaen hurried back to Iain's side. She returned his welcoming smile with a bright one of her own. He was acting almost
carefree but she did not let her hopes rise for she knew it
could be due to the celebration. Good food, plentiful wine
and gaiety could soften the hardest of men. For the duration
of the wedding and the wedding night he may have decided
to ease the aloof stance he usually clung to. While it was a
very good chance for her to try to grasp at a little of his affection before he shut it all away again, she would not let herself
hope that her fight was so soon over.

Taking a refreshing drink of wine she leaned against Iain.
Inwardly she smiled when he began to idly toy with her hair.
The man was not totally uninterested. Such small touches,
ones he seemed unaware of making, did give her hope as did
the occasional endearments that seemed to slip free without
his knowing it. They were signs that she was slipping beneath
his guard, making some chinks in his wall.

Iain found that he was swiftly growing very weary of the
celebrations. He buried his hand deep within her thick hair,
savoring its silken fullness, and wished to be within their
chambers wrapped as fully in her arms as his hand was in her
hair. It was more than a lengthy celibacy that made him so
greedy and he knew it. There was a weakness that could cause
him a great deal of trouble.

Espying a youth with a boyish face and unruly chestnut
hair hastening towards her, Islaen groaned softly and closed
her eyes. "Tell Dugald I have fainted from exhaustion from
dancing."

"Dugald?" Iain murmured.

"Aye, my cousin now hieing o'er here to us."

A moment later the youth stood beside them, introduced himself and looked at Islaen. "Cousin?"

"She has fainted from exhaustion from dancing," Iain dutifully repeated.

"Och, has she now. Ah weel, I but meant to tell her that Nathan is sniffing about that Douglas wench again."

Shocked that her brother would return to a lass who had caused him nothing but trouble, Islaen sat up quickly and stared at her cousin. "Nathan wouldnae be such a fool, would he?"

"Nay, though the lass is chasing him. Now that ye have recovered, ye can dance with me," he drawled.

"A cruel trick to play. Weel, Dugald, I have done a muckle lot of dancing already," she demurred.

He studied his fingernails and murmured, "I have had some lessons, ye ken."

"Truly?"

"Aye, truly."

Still wary, she let him take her by the hand and help her stand. "An I get one sore toe or one bruise, ye will pay dearly, cousin."

"I am all atremble, cousin," he said cheerfully as he towed her towards the other dancers.

Iain watched her until she disappeared into the crowd of dancers. Although he did not know Dugald personally, he knew of the youth's rather powerful, wealthy father and the size of the family. Each new revelation about the family he was now connected to by marriage was a startling one and not necessarily pleasing. It did not surprise him that the MacRoths got on well with their kin, nor that they did not boast about what were some rather illustrious connections. He wished they would, though, for he was not fond of surprises. It would suit him to know far more than he did about the MacRoths. They were a small clan but it was becoming clear that they reached far in their relations.

"Why the frown now, Iain?" Alexander asked quietly.

"I begin to wonder just how far and wide this family reaches that I have wed into."

Alexander laughed softly. "Very far, my friend. On Alaistair's side many of his forebears married well. The women were well-known for their beauty and the families were large. His wife's family was much akin to that. The ties of blood grow thin but they ne'er seem to break. There have been some rogues and traitors, few families escape having those, but it ne'er seems to end the ties amongst all the rest. I wouldnae be surprised if, for a righteous cause, Alaistair could pull near half of Scotland to his side. The ones that are caught up in a feud might e'en call a truce to ride to his side."

"Has he e'er done it?"

"Nay, nor have any of them, I think. 'Tis not their way to ask any to shed blood in a fight that is theirs alone."

"The king kens all this, does he?"

"Aye, there is little our sire misses or used to miss. His love for Alaistair is not just politic, however."

"Nay, I kenned that. I have been flung into what could be the greatest of mires."

"Or the best of alliances. Come, Iain, ye look for trouble where there is none. I have said all I mean to upon that. I am nay one to bang my head against a wall. Here comes your wee, fair bride and, by the look upon her bonnie face, I am thinking Dugald best take a few more lessons."

"I will ne'er walk again," Islaen groaned as she sat down. "I wish I kenned who gave Dugald lessons. I would beat him."

"Should it not be Dugald that ye beat?" Iain asked, amusement tinting his voice.

"Aye but he is hard to catch. The lad's e'er been quicker on his feet than I. I have to trick him when I want revenge. Last time I tipped him into the water when we went fishing. That was for dancing all o'er my toes at my brother Colin's wedding."

Gently and as subtly as he could, Iain coaxed her to talk about her family. As he had suspected there was no boasting of ties with rich or noted kin. If the names had not been familiar to him her manner of speaking of them would have told him nothing except that she knew them and, occasionally, that she might not be as fond of them as of others.

Islaen was feeling mildly drunk when the women managed to subtly lead her away to Iain's chambers. She heard enough, however, as she left to know that Iain's assistants cared little about being subtle. When she finally reached Iain's chambers she had to smile. She was not so sure that Iain would be that appreciative about the rose petals strewn over his bed. In fact, she mused as she took a deep breath, it might prove too much for her and she was rather fond of roses.

"How could you have borne it for so long?" the queen asked as Islaen's binding was revealed.

Coloring slightly, Islaen murmured, "I have ne'er been without it. Nay," she protested as they prepared to help her into her lacy night rail, "let me wash up first."

"But ye bathed ere ye dressed."

"I ken it, Meg," Islaen said as she hurriedly washed up, "but I have danced a lot and t'was most warm."

"'Tis a pity we could not find you chambers more suited to a wedded couple," the queen remarked, glancing around.

"It doesnae matter," Islaen demurred as she dried off and the women started to dress her. "Sir Alexander and my kin surround us and we are very near the married quarters. I am nay sure when we travel to Caraidland but I think it will not be long from now." She sat still as Meg brushed her hair. "I hear Caraidland is a verra fine keep, strong yet comfortable to live in."

Although that prompted the queen and her lady to chat quite amiably, Islaen gained little real information about her husband's home and kin. Like many ladies of the court, their interest was in gossip about things that Islaen felt were unimportant or not really her business at all. It was somewhat disappointing.

"Here come the men," the queen announced and giggled much like a young girl.

Despite the fact that the men were kin, her husband and ones she knew, Islaen blushed deeply when they made their somewhat rowdy entrance. As she and Iain were placed side by side in the bed and given goblets of wine, Islaen thought crossly that her brothers Duncan and Robert were the worst of the lot. The more she blushed the worse they got. As soon as she and Iain were alone she downed half her wine in an attempt to ease her embarrassment.

She was distracted from thoughts of revenge against her brothers when Iain left the bed. When he presented her with a supply of sponges she blushed and finished off her wine. Now the lie she had to live would truly begin.

Without saying a word she went behind the screen that had been brought to supply her some form of privacy. Grimacing, she did as Iain had instructed. This once she would do exactly as he had said. It would aid her in her deception to know as much as possible about the whole matter. From what Meg had found out for her Iain would not really know whether she was using the sponges or not, but Islaen wished to be sure. Still blushing, she slipped back into bed unable to look at Iain.

Feeling guilty for what he asked of her, Iain sighed and pulled her into his arms. "Islaen," he began.

"Nay, dinnae speak on it." She feared she would reveal the deceit she plotted if they talked on the matter too much.

Running his fingers down the laced front of her gown he murmured, "This is lovely but I think I like the other better."

"The other isnae a lady's night rail."

"'Tis simpler." He began to slowly undo her lacings.

"Ye didnae drink your wine," she squeaked.

"Why so tremulous, lass?" He brushed light kisses over the delicate lines of her face. "Ye are a maiden no longer."

"Aye but last eve was, weel, different. We just went about it. T'was not so planned."

"Lovemaking is planned more oft than otherwise especially atween a mon and his wife."

"I ken it. Life and work and all get in the way. T'will take a wee bit of time to get used to it though."

She trembled when he gently removed her gown, then rather callously tossed it away. When he pulled her body close to his she moaned softly. The feel of their skin touching set her blood running hot. She smoothed her hands over his broad back, loving the feel of smooth skin stretched tautly over firm muscle.

When he kissed her, she clung to him. Her lips parted willingly when his tongue nudged at them, begging for entry. Daringly she parried the thrust of his tongue. His soft growl was so clearly one of approval that she grew even more bold. She quickly discovered that joining in the lovemaking was very exciting. When Iain suddenly pulled away she stared up at him a little groggily, astounded at the power of a mere kiss.

"Ye are a verra fast learner, lass," he rasped as he fought to retain some control over the desire she stirred in him.

"And is that good?" she asked in a husky whisper, moving her hands slowly over his slim hips.

"Ye willnae hear me complain," he murmured against her throat as his stroking hands sought her breasts.

"How nice," she managed to say before she found it impossible to talk clearly.

A little saner than he had been the first time, Iain was able to appreciate the desire he stirred in her. He was able to fully realize what a passionate woman she was, unrestrained and more than willing to give as well as take. Simply thinking of all he could teach her for their mutual enjoyment sent his passions soaring. She was a treasure and he knew he had only begun to discover her full worth as a lover.

Islaen cried out softly when his tongue flicked over the aching tip of her breast. She bore the teasing strokes of his tongue for as long as she could, then buried her hands in his thick hair and pressed his face closer, silently urging him to end his game. When he finally answered her plea, drawing the swollen tip of her breast deep into his mouth, her soft cry of delight held a note of relief. Her body arched against his as each draw upon her breast seemed to send heat straight to her loins.

She welcomed the touch of his hand when it slid between her thighs. It was not really enough, however, even though she suddenly realized that his skilled touch could bring her body the release it ached for. Islaen sought to break the control she sensed he exercised, her hands moving over him in an impassioned search for a place where her touch would end that control. A small part of her passion-fogged mind expressed shock over her wantonness but she easily ignored it.

Iain shuddered and groaned when her long delicate fingers trailed up his inner thigh, then curled slowly around his engorged manhood. He buried his face in her breasts and trembled as she stroked him, but knew he had waited too long to enjoy her touch. Pulling her hand away a moment later, he drove into her. Feeling her body shudder beneath him he gritted his teeth and gathered up a few shreds of his tattered control, holding himself still as he looked down at her.

"Did I hurt ye, lass?" he rasped, drawing in a shaky breath as her gaze met his and he saw how passion made the gold in her lovely eyes sparkle, the brown turning nearly black and accentuating the golden flecks.

"Nay," she replied on a husky sigh, her hands sliding down his back to cup his taut, smooth buttocks. "Can ye feel it?" she whispered, hoping he would not guess the reason for her query.

"It?"

"The sponge."

"Oh. Nay. Ye did put one in, didnae ye?"

"Oh, aye, 'tis there." Wrapping her legs around his waist, she arched her body even as her hands pushed against his backside forcing him deeper. "Now?"

It took Iain a moment to catch his breath. "Nay, not even now. All I can feel is the moist, tight welcome of ye."

"And 'tis verra welcome ye are, Sir MacLagan."

"'Tis verra glad I am to hear it, wee Islaen, for I think I shall often be tirling at the pin."

"Knock and the door shall open," she whispered and her last word ended on a soft gasp for he began to move.

For just a little while their movements were slow, each of them savoring the feel of the joining of their bodies. Neither of them really had the patience for such leisurely lovemaking, however. Iain's movements soon grew fiercer and Islaen welcomed the change, her body greedy for the release that hovered just beyond her reach.

Iain was only able to watch the first glow of her release transform her face before her inner shudders forced him to join her in the fall into passion's abyss. When he felt her body greedily accept the gift of his passion he clung tightly to her and felt a brief but strong touch of sorrow for the fact that the seed he poured into her welcoming body was denied any chance of taking root. It seemed unspeakably unfair that God should make him desire children, then show him how easily and horribly that desire could bring about death.

Determinedly he shook away that thought and simply enjoyed the feel of a soft, willing woman beneath him. Catalina had always made him feel little better than a rapist, nothing he did raising her response above that of a grudgingly endured duty. Islaen gave freely of her passion, turned to fire beneath him, and he reveled in it. She even likes the aftertime, he mused with an inner self-satisfied smile, as he felt her body move beneath his, her hands moving over him in a sign of lethargic satisfaction.

When Iain finally moved off of her, Islaen eluded his attempt to pull her close. Mumbling something vague about a need to wash up, she slid out of bed, cursing the fact that she had nothing at hand to slip on. Moving quickly and blushing deeply, she hurried behind the screen and extracted the sponge, then washed up.

She felt confident that he would make love to her again before morning. Although he had said he had felt nothing she had to make sure. Being so new to the game she was sure he would accept the excuse that she had forgotten to replace it after washing up and would give her another chance. She prayed that he would not notice for she did not know what to do if he did.

Before dashing back to the bed she took careful note of how the sponge looked after use. She doubted he would go so far in assuring himself that she obeyed his demands but she would take no chances. Every time they made love she would make sure that everything indicated that she had obeyed him. So too did she pray that she did not take too long to accomplish what she planned, for she did not want to have to bear the strain of such deception for too long.

Taking a deep breath, she hurried back to bed. She colored deeply when she saw that Iain watched her every step. Slipping beneath the covers she saw him grin, then he reached for her and she pressed her flushed face against his chest.

"Ye bounce," he murmured, a tremor of laughter in his voice as he nuzzled her thick hair. "'Tis lovely to watch," he said when she groaned softly. "So lovely I am sore tempted to ask ye to run about the room a few times so that I might just watch."

"Och, ye wouldnae," she gasped, lifting her head to stare at him, not sure if he was teasing her or not.

"Weel, I will wait until ye arenae so shy about your nakedness. 'Tis a lovely shape ye have, lass. Ye should be proud of it."

"Ye are muckle bonnie yourself, Iain."

"I have no more nor less than any other mon."

"Mayhaps but 'tis put together most pleasingly."

"Weel, if ye are pleased 'tis all that matters."

"Ye really dinnae see it, do ye."

"See what?" He idly began to trace the gentle curves of her body with his hands.

"How the women look at ye. They wouldnae eye an ugly mon so eagerly nor invite him so boldly."

"Weel, I have ne'er thought myself ugly. I have little interest in whores, lass. They can tempt when a mon has naught in his bed, but I have more than enough for any mon now. I think t'will take near all my strength to handle ye."

Smiling with unconscious seductiveness, Islaen rubbed her body lightly against his, an invitation he was quick to answer. Her passion was checked slightly when he entered her but when he said nothing, seemed to notice nothing, she was quickly caught in her desire for him again. She did not think of it again until she laid sprawled beneath his sated body enjoying the tingle his lovemaking induced in her.

"Do ye need to go, er, wash up?" he asked as he slowly eased the intimacy of their embrace.

It was hard not to cheer with relief at this proof that he had noticed no change. "It willnae hurt if I wait a wee while, will it?"

"Nay," he answered and turned onto his back, pulling her into his arms and smiling at the way she cuddled up to him.

"Good. I am feeling too nicely weary to trouble with it."

"Ah, weel, and here was I eager to see ye bounce again."

"Ye are a rogue."

"Aye, mayhaps."

"Anither time."

"Aye, we have years." He suddenly thought of Duncan MacLennon as he spoke and inwardly grimaced.

Islaen heard an odd note in his voice but instinct told her she would find out nothing if she asked about it. Suddenly she recalled him speaking of a man set upon killing him and she pressed closer to him. She was going to have to do something, she decided firmly, to remove that shadow from their lives.

Chapter Seven

Glancing over her shoulder to make sure neither Ronald nor Lord Fraser was watching, Islaen hurried to a secluded corner. With a relieved sigh she sat down upon the chest there. It was not as out of sight of the others in the hall as she would have liked but she prayed it was enough of a hiding place to give her some respite from the two men who seemed so determined to pursue her. She was growing very tired of their constant fawning and rather bold attentions, attentions not at all curbed by her marriage.

Searching the hall for some sight of her husband, she scowled when she finally espied him. It was not only Ronald and Lord Fraser who ignored the sanctified boundaries of marriage. As far as she was concerned too many women did too. Lady Constance never failed to corner Iain whenever they came to the hall or any other place the woman could find him. She was not the only one either, Islaen thought crossly, just the most persistent.

"Her husband will soon arrive."

Islaen jumped, then frowned at Alexander as he sat down beside her. "Ye startled me. Her husband is coming here?"

"Aye and our fair whore will become as demure as a nun."

"Does it really fool the mon? 'Tis sure he must hear talk of how she behaves when he isnae about."

"He hears but seems to care little as long as she behaves when he is near. He acts no better when out of her sight."

"Is that why ye now avoid her, because her husband soon comes?"

"Aye, the mon sore hates me. He would challenge me but isnae as good with a sword as he thinks. I have no wish to kill a mon simply because his wife is a whore. Ye need not fear that Iain will e'er pay her invites heed. He doesnae like her."

"I hadnae realized that that mattered," she drawled and Alexander grinned.

"With most men, nay, not much. Iain prefers to at least like the woman. In that he was e'er a bit different from his brothers."

"Aye? I ken little of his kin."

"Weel, Tavis, ere he found Storm, just cared that they were somewhat clean and nay too hard to look upon."

"Most important," she murmured sarcastically and he laughed softly.

"Now, Sholto is a rogue. Mayhaps e'en more so than Tavis was. He can charm most any lass and I am sure the men in France, where he has gone to fight, would as lief he came home."

"And the men here hope he stays there."

Alexander laughed and nodded. "Aye, most like. They all want what Tavis has found, though, lass."

"A Sassanach lass?" she said pertly and met his grin with one of her own then grew serious. "Ye are sure of that?"

"Verra. Each has said as much at least once. Sholto still searches. Ah, but Iain, now he has had the dream scarred by that bitch Catalina."

"Many a woman has died upon her childbed."

"True. Sad but true. But did they curse and accuse their man with every birth pain and with their dying breath?"

"Is that what she did?"

"Aye. His guilt was added to because he didnae love her though he was willing to try. She ne'er was. She loved another, treated Iain's every touch or soft word as if it were poison, a torment she had to bear out of duty to her family. She e'en made Tavis feel guilty for t'was his romp with another MacBroth lass whom he cast aside that brought about the wedding. Katerine MacBroth was and still is a whore but they had hoped Tavis would wed her. Iain's wedding Catalina soothed those disappointed hopes and strengthened an old alliance. I think Iain paid a high cost, though, mayhaps too high."

"Ye would think such things would show people that arranging or forcing marriages is not right. It only brings grief."

"Is that how ye feel about yours?"

"Nay but there are some odd twists to this arranged mating. I ken I willnae surprise ye by saying I wanted Iain." She blushed slightly when he grinned. "It wasnae me he objected to but taking any lass as wife. Weel, I feel certain ye ken all of that."

"Aye, ye have a rough road ahead of ye, lass," he said quietly and, seeing the direction of her gaze, added, "but 'tis not other women ye need fash yourself o'er. None of the Mac-Lagans are saints, 'tis true, but they dinnae take their vows lightly."

Islaen tried very hard to remember that assurance. The fact that Iain was never absent from their bed, not even when, to her extreme disappointment, she had her woman's time, was also reassuring. Most nights they even retired to their chambers at the same time. There was also the fact that he was never really out of her sight. Nevertheless, she found it a trial to watch how the women flirted with him. She was heartily relieved when her father told her of the plans to leave for home.

"T'will be soon?"

"Aye, lass, there is but a little business to finish. Do ye grow weary of court?"

"Aye, verra weary," she muttered as she watched a fulsome woman give Iain a blatantly inviting smile.

"Aye, that is a nuisance and ye have one or twa sniffing at your heels. Do they give ye much trouble?"

"Nay, neither the ones after me nor the ones hunting him. They but grow verra tiresome."

"And ye have enough problems, eh?"

"I am not unhappy, Fither."

"But are ye happy?"

"Aye."

"Weel, I have caught ye looking wistful a time or twa."

"Wistful isnae the same."

"Islaen, lass, I ask ye to speak honestly with me. I wanted ye wed, aye, but I wanted ye happy too."

"Fither, I am happy. Aye, I willnae lie and say naught is wrong. There are problems. The mon's been most honest with me. I ken weel what might lay ahead. Aye, I may feel muckle sad at times, e'en hurt, but I will tell ye true, Fither, t'will be naught to what I would feel an I ne'er had the mon. I wanted him and I have what I wanted. Now, if there is to be some bitter with the sweet, 'tis what I chose so I will swallow it and nay complain. Weel, not too much," she added with a half smile.

He laughed softly and briefly hugged her. "I ken what ye mean, lass. My prayers are with ye."

Islaen was glad of her father's prayers but she soon wished she had accepted the silent offer he had made to help rid her of the unwanted attentions of Ronald MacDubh and Lord Fraser. She found herself neatly cornered by Ronald after an evening meal and looked around for some assistance in ridding herself of him but saw none. Iain was deep in conversation with the king and none of her kin was near enough to really see her or notice that she was trying to secure their attention. She resigned herself to trying to diplomatically get away from him, but it was getting harder and harder to be polite. While she did not want to insult the king's godson she was beginning to think that it would be the only way to stop his attentions. Polite refusals of his rather blatant bid for her favours were not working.

"I find it hard to believe your husband would leave ye unattended for so long."

"He has business with the king," she said a little testily, trying to avoid his attempts to pin her against the wall.

"And so he leaves his bonnie wife all alone with naught to do. I could help ye pass the time," he murmured huskily as he finally succeeded in getting her trapped between him and the wall.

Shock held Islaen still for a moment. She could not believe the man meant to kiss her or more right there in the crowded hall, yet it was clear that that was exactly what he meant to do. When he pressed his body close to hers, she shivered with revulsion and prepared to shove him away only to have him yanked free of her.

She saw that her rescuer was Alexander and was a little disappointed. It also surprised her that such a beautiful man could look so hard and threatening. Alexander held a now frightened Ronald by the back of the neck of his jupon and Islaen's eyes widened a little when she saw that Ronald's feet were several inches off the floor.

"I believe the lass has made it verra clear that she doesnae wish ye to help her pass the time."

"Rescuing my wife?"

Islaen wondered how Iain had reached her side so quickly, then realized that he was not as unawares of where she was and what she was doing as she had thought.

"I wasnae sure that ye had seen that she was in need of it."

"I could have managed," she said defensively but neither man paid her any heed.

"I saw. The king wishes to speak to that." Iain nodded towards Ronald.

Although she would not have thought it possible, Ronald went even paler and Alexander smiled coldly as he dragged the younger man off. She peered around Iain and watched the king signal Alexander and Ronald to follow him. It then came to Islaen's attention that everyone was avidly watching them and she blushed deeply.

Iain stared at her and fought to control his anger before he spoke. Despite the whispered slurs of some of the women he knew Islaen had done nothing to draw Ronald's attentions nor to make the man think they would be welcome. Many times he had wanted to step in when he saw the man or any other pursuing Islaen but he had held back. He believed it was best if she learned how to handle such matters on her own.

When Ronald had cornered her, Iain had not hesitated an instant. Even as he had leapt to his feet he had informed the king almost casually that he was going to kill his godson. Iain knew he would have, too, if not for Alexander's presence. He could not help but wonder if Alexander had sensed it, and that was why the man had been that one step ahead of him. Such was Iain's rage that he could not be sure he would even have given Ronald a chance to defend himself.

That rage bothered him. He realized he was failing in keeping a distance between himself and Islaen but he could see no way to do more than he was already doing. The girl was a witch, he decided crossly, effortlessly pulling him closer to her, bewitching him without seeming to even try. It was a dangerous bewitchment for he could see no way to successfully fight it.

Troubled by that thought his voice was almost accusing as he said, "Ye should have told me he was growing so troublesome."

Hearing that accusation in his voice, Islaen grew angry. She saw no reason for her to be scolded just because some fool did not know how to heed a no. It struck her as being the very height of unfairness.

"I have been managing the fool verra weel on my own, thank ye," she snapped.

"Oh, aye, so weel that he traps ye against the wall and paws ye with half a hall full of people looking on."

Her hands clenching into fists, she glared at him. "He didnae paw me and I was just about to push the oaf away. The hall full of people werenae paying me any heed either, not until ye and Alexander made it all such a grand show. Aye and 'tis a fine show ye give them now as ye stand here and curse at me for what was none of my doing, nor my fault. Weel, I shallnae abide it. Nay, by God's beard, I willnae."

She kicked him firmly in the shins. His hissed curse of pain was music to her ears as she strode away. She headed straight for their chambers deciding she had had more than enough of the court and of men in particular.

Just about to follow his wife, Iain was confronted by her father who drawled, "Roused her temper, did ye?"

Still a little stunned by the quickness and strength of her anger, Iain said calmly, "A wee difference of opinion is all."

"Of course," Alaistair murmured. "I would wait a wee while ere ye go to her. Let her finish her bath."

"She had a bath this morning," Iain growled, not sure he appreciated the man telling him how to handle his wife.

"The lass always has a bath when she's in a temper. She will be more pliable afterwards."

Islaen paused in brushing her drying hair when Iain entered their chambers. Although she had not gone to their chambers expecting him to run after her, she did wonder why he had stayed away. Her bath had soothed her temper some but she found that she still felt somewhat insulted. He had acted as if she had welcomed Ronald's loathsome attentions.

Iain saw her glance at him, then look away. Seeing her seated upon the bed, her luxurious hair hanging free and her slim legs well exposed by the simple shift she wore, he felt his lust stir but fought it. He owed her an apology and he did not need anyone's advice to tell him it would be best to give her one before he tried anything else.

When he started to undress and snuff the candles, she put her brush aside and crawled beneath the covers, her back to him. Iain mused that he would probably not be able to do anything else anyways until he soothed her sense of insult. It occurred to him that it was a perfect opportunity to put some distance between them. All he had to do was nothing or possibly worse, demand his husbandly rights without even the faintest murmur of apology. Sighing as he crawled into bed beside her, he knew he would do neither if only because he did not want to be reduced to asserting his husbandly rights, he wanted them to make love.

When his arm slipped around her waist, Islaen tensed. She knew he could easily stir her passion despite her continued outrage but hoped that he would not.

"Islaen," he murmured, kissing the back of her neck and feeling her tremble at his touch.

That sign of her susceptibility to his touch pleased him. She was clearly not one of those who could give or withhold her passion as she willed. If he wanted to, he could make love to her, taste her passion and not offer a word of apology. For reasons he did not really understand, that made it far easier to give her the apology she both wanted and deserved.

"Islaen, I am sorry. I was angry that he would dare paw ye, but he was taken out of reach of my anger so I turned it upon ye. I ken weel that ye didnae encourage the fool."

Turning to face him, she said quietly, "Ye didnae really have to say it, ye ken."

"Aye, I ken it. T'was why it was so easy to say, daft as that sounds."

She laughed softly, then teased, "Ye said it because ye mean to do some pawing yourself, eh?"

"Pawing?" he growled in mock outrage and briefly tussled playfully with her as he removed her shift. "I ne'er paw."

"And what do ye call it then?"

"Stroking."

"Wheesht, there isnae a muckle lot of difference."

"Nay? Weel, let me show ye. By morning ye will ken the difference weel, lass."

Stretching langorously, Islaen watched her husband dress. He had fulfilled his threat, she thought with a softly lecherous smile. She knew well the difference between pawing and stroking as well as the subtleties of most any other sort of touch anyone wished to mention. When he came to give her a brief kiss, she twined her arms about his neck and persuaded him to give her a longer, fuller one.

"Do ye mean to linger abed all day?" he asked huskily, a little astonished at how easily she could arouse him especially when he should be well sated, even in need of a rest.

"Weel, I am nay sure I am quite clear on a word or twa," she murmured.

Almost grinning and wondering how she could look seductive and impish at the same time, he drawled, "Weel, I could take a moment to teach ye one more thing. This is a pat," he said as he neatly flipped her over and gently patted her on her backside, "and this is a wee spank." He gave her one not too hard slap and, laughing, loped out of the door.

"Wretch," Islaen cried but by the time she had the pillow in her hands to throw at him the door was shutting behind him.

She sighed and got out of bed. Islaen felt no real eagerness to leave her chambers. In the night and often first thing in the morning, Iain was far from aloof and cool. He was passionate, talkative and sometimes teasing. Yet, by the time she joined him outside of their chambers in the morning, the mask was back in place and all his shields were up.

With a shrug of her shoulders she thrust away that wistfulness. She had seen what could be, saw it each time they lay in their bed shut away from the world. He was content then, she had no doubts about that. It was a start, a base she could build from. It bothered her a little to use her body and the passion they shared to break down his walls, but it worked and she was in no position to quibble over what methods she used.

Iain barely restrained himself from smiling at Islaen when she joined him at the table in the hall. Grinning at one's bride like some besotted groom was not the way to keep her at a distance, he thought wryly. It was hard, though, to act aloof when his mind was still filled with clear and delicious memories of a passion-filled night. He knew he should try to hold himself apart even in their bed at night just as he knew he would never do that. As he had each night since their wedding he would find himself drawn to their bed by the promise of her passion and would find himself softening inside as she held him. He sometimes felt as if he were two men and could not help but wonder if he were equally confusing her. Iain thought a little wryly that that might be the way to keep her feelings for him from deepening.

Deciding Iain was going to be especially withdrawn today, Islaen allowed the queen to tow her off to where some of the women gathered. She collected her needlework and sat down with the others only to soon realize that needlework was not the real purpose of the gathering—gossip was. Some of the tales told shocked Islaen although she tried to hide that fact. It was difficult not to leap to the defense of some of the people whose names were being so completely blackened even if she did not know them at all. She began to get a headache as she tried to sort truth from rumour or lie.

"And here is something that will interest ye, Lady MacLagan."

Resisting the childish urge to stick her tongue out at Lady Constance for the way the woman sneered her name, Islaen asked, "And what would that be?"

"Lady Mary Cameron arrived at court today. She used to be Mary Chisolm, ye ken."

"Nay, I dinnae ken. The name means naught to me."

"Weel, ye best learn it then."

"Had I?"

"Aye, she is the woman Iain loved."

"Ah, that one. He told me about her."

"Did he tell ye she was a widow now?"

A chill ran down Islaen's spine but she maintained her pose of calm disinterest. "Nay. It really doesnae concern us."

Before Lady Constance could make the jeering remark that so clearly hovered upon her lips the queen changed the subject. Islaen breathed a silent sigh of relief.

As soon as she could do so without raising any suspicion that she was retreating, Islaen left the women. Once in her chambers she sprawled on the bed and quelled the sudden urge to scream in frustration. The last thing she needed was another problem. She knew Iain had told her that he did not love his old love anymore but she also knew that he could be mistaken. The flames of love could simply have been tamped down and, once confronted with the woman, flare back up again. The very thought of that hurt and Islaen gasped from the sharpness of it.

She was in love with the man, she decided a little sadly. It had been something she had suspected from the moment she had set eyes upon him, but she had tried, and succeeded, to not think about it too much. This very real threat made her face it squarely. None of the other problems had really threatened her with the loss of Iain's love. She simply did not have it and had to fight to gain it. Now she faced the possibility that all she fought for could be handed to another.

Shaking her head in vigorous denial Islaen stood up. That

might happen but it did not have to. She certainly would not simply stand back and let it happen, she decided firmly as she started for the hall, hoping she would get there before Lady Mary Cameron presented herself.

Iain looked around for his wife, frowning faintly when he was unable to spot her. He was just about to give into the urge to see if she had retired to their chambers when a hand tugged at his sleeve. When he saw who vied for his attention he almost gaped.

"Mary."

"I wondered if ye would remember me. It has been four years."

"Ye havenae changed at all," he said quietly and felt a twinge of resentment over that fact.

When she had been given to another he had been devastated. It was then that he had started to close off his heart, determined never to feel that sort of pain again. He knew that had left its mark upon him. Mary did not look as if she had suffered at all despite being taken away from him, a man she had claimed to love more than life.

Mary studied the man she had once thought to wed until the richer more powerful Lord Cameron had asked for her hand. Age and the trials of life had added to Iain's exciting looks. She felt her pulse quicken. The one thing she had really regretted was that she had never had Iain for a lover. At first she had had to save her maidenhead for her husband, and Iain had always treated her like the greatest of virgins. After her marriage he had been out of reach. She had never stopped wondering how he would be as a lover, however, and she intended to find out.

"Ye flatter me."

"Nay, ye look the same as ye did when we parted. I have changed, though."

She reached out to trail her finger over the scar upon his face. "It makes ye look attractively dangerous, Iain. Ye are wed?"

"Aye, but a fortnight ago. I was just about to seek her out."

Islaen paused just inside the hall and frowned as she began to look for Iain. Despite his height it was not always easy to find him when the crowd thickened. It was at its thickest now for there was food in the offering.

"Looking for someone, love?"

Sparing a brief welcoming look for Alexander, Islaen nodded. "Iain, and should ye really be calling me love?"

"Mayhaps not but I think I will."

"It may cause talk."

"Aye, we will set the gossips' tongues to wagging at both ends. T'will be most amusing."

"Ye have a strange idea of fun, Alexander MacDubh."

When she finally spotted Iain she tensed. A fulsome blonde stood very close to him. She was on the tall side for a woman, her shape one that Islaen was sure men desired, and she was both elegant and graceful. What truly frightened Islaen was the softening she could see in Iain's face as he looked at the woman.

"Alexander, who is that woman with Iain?" she asked even though she felt sure she knew.

"What woman?" he asked with an overdone innocence.

"Ye ken what woman," she said sternly.

"Lady Mary Cameron. Ye dinnae ken the woman."

"Aye, I am afraid I do." She looked at him after watching the woman stroke Iain's face and smiled crookedly. "Weel, are ye going to tell me again that I neednae fash myself about the women?"

Chapter Eight

It was one of the hardest things she had ever done but Islaen did not ask Iain about Mary. She decided the best way to handle the matter was to trust Iain and, in truth, she did.

Mary, however, she did not trust one little bit. The woman would push until Iain fell. She was already doing it. Islaen wished she knew how far the woman intended to go. Depending on how ruthless one was, a wife was not an insurmountable obstacle. Islaen had the feeling that Lady Mary could be very ruthless indeed.

Taking a long drink of wine, Islaen fought to keep her temper just as she had for the three nights since Lady Mary had arrived. She sat next to her husband but could have been miles away for all the notice he took. Mary had managed to usurp Lady Constance's seat, and thus practically all of Iain's attention. He seemed quite willing to give it too, she thought crossly. She told herself firmly that attention was all he was giving the woman and she ought to be grateful for that instead of sulking.

"Och, Iain, we are sorely neglecting your wee wife."

Islaen wondered how big a scandal would be raised if she poured her wine over Mary's elegantly coiffed head and sweetly said, "Iain's wee wife is doing fine, thank ye."

Iain looked at his wife thinking her voice just a little too sweet and was surprised at how flat and hard her eyes were. He knew he was neglecting her, lavishing far too much attention upon Mary, yet he could not seem to help himself. Neither the growing withdrawl of Islaen nor the increasingly belligerent glances of her brothers was enough to stop him. Mary was from a happier time, a time before his life had soured. He knew he could never really go back, yet he could not resist the urge to try to recapture a part of it.

"Aye, ye have Alexander, dinnae ye," Lady Mary purred, then drew Iain into a discussion of a mutual acquaintance.

Frowning slightly, Islaen looked at Alexander and saw that he held the same suspicions she did about why Mary had said what she had. "Do ye really think that she would try that game?"

"Aye, the conniving slut."

"Is she?"

"She is and she was. Aye and most like ever will be a slut. Iain ne'er saw it."

"And ye ne'er told him."

"Nay, I had already been through that with Tavis. Odd, her name was Mary too."

"Near half the woman in the country are named Mary."

"Och, weel, to be direct, and pardon an I offend, Mary did keep her maidenhead intact but t'was all that was untouched. To Iain, all was virgin. He didnae see it and she didnae let him. She kenned more tricks than the finest courtesan," he muttered and took a deep drink of wine.

Although she blushed over his direct talk Islaen was also curious. She also felt sure that Alexander was a little less than sober and that that roughened his tongue. There was the slightest flush to his lovely skin and a shine to his beautiful eyes.

"Did Tavis hate ye then?"

"Nay, but until he found Storm our relationship suffered. It took a lot of healing and the lass wasnae really worth it. O' course, he still bridles like a dog protecting its bitch whene'er I talk to Storm."

"Tried to steal her once, did ye?"

"Aye, I did, but before she was his wife. I seem fated to lust after MacLagan women."

The implication of his words and the way he looked at her made Islaen blush. That such a man would want her was quite flattering. Then she had to smile. He looked remarkably like a sulky little boy.

"There is a lass out there for ye, Alexander MacDubh."

"Weel, she is hiding herself verra weel. I mark two and thirty years next week."

"Wheesht, so verra old ye are. Bent with age."

"Ye are a wretched wee lass."

"I ken it. Ye will find a lass. Of course, ye will most like not see it at first and ye being such a bonnie rogue, it willnae go too smoothly at first, I am thinking."

"A bonnie rogue, am I?"

"Aye and the poor lass will fash herself woefully o'er it, I am certain."

"Poor wee lass. Weel, I will have to console her a lot."

"Aye, a muckle lot."

"I dinnae suppose ye need any consoling."

"Nay, not the sort ye speak of."

"A shame. Will ye settle for a wee dance then?"

She laughed and nodded letting him tow her out to mingle with the dancers. Many looked at them with knowing expressions and Islaen sighed. Clearly they thought there was only one reason a woman would have anything to do with Alexander, or he with a woman. When she caught a glance from Iain, Islaen could tell that he wondered the same thing as the others. It annoyed her as well as hurt. She was offended by his mistrust, yet could not help but wonder why, if he thought she and Alexander were having a liaison, he did nothing to stop it.

For the first time since Mary's arrival, Iain found that he was easily distracted from her. The sight of Alexander and Islaen enjoying each other's company thoroughly troubled him. He trusted Islaen but knew how easily Alexander could seduce most any woman. Iain knew he had shamefully neglected Islaen for another woman and now worried that she would be vulnerable to Alexander's charm.

Inwardly he grimaced, a little ashamed at the way he wanted to violently stop her from having a lover while he was thinking of taking one himself. Mary's hints that she was willing to take him to her bed were subtle but clear. Iain was finding it a temptation too strong to resist. As the evening wore on, Mary's invitations grew stronger and he grew weaker.

Islaen heard the soft murmur of voices as she returned from visiting the garderobe. When she recognized the man's voice, she slipped into the shadows, her heart beating furiously as it anticipated the pain it might soon have to endure. The couple hesitated before her hiding place and Islaen pressed deeper into the shadowed niche, her hands clenched into painfully tight fists as she fought the urge to dart out and scream her anger and hurt at the adulterous pair.

Mary frowned when Iain hesitated. She had thought her success at hand. Already she had begun to lay her plans for ridding him of his wife so that he might be free to wed her. In the four years they had been apart he had gained more of the riches and power she craved. Even better was his closeness to the king which promised even more money and power.

"Why do ye hold back, my love?"

"Mary, I am a wedded mon."

"Had I only come to court sooner I could have stopped that folly," she breathed as she twined her arms around his neck and then kissed him with all the seductive skill she possessed, a skill she had begun to hone shortly after her first flux. "We were torn from each other's arms," she said huskily, pleased with his apparent bemusement, as she subtly urged him towards her chambers, "and forced to take others as our mates. Come, my love, let us not shy again from taking what is our right due to the love we share."

Iain let her lead him along. He was bemused after her kiss, unable to think clearly, because it had not gone as he had expected it to. His passion had not flared to life despite the somewhat unsettling skill Mary had displayed. It had stirred slightly in response to sweet memory but nothing more. He found himself thinking of how easily Islaen could set him aflame and began to wonder if anything he could share with Mary was worth risking what he had with Islaen.

The pain that had begun to sear through Islaen's insides when she had watched the pair kiss seemed to double when they continued on, Iain saying nothing else in protest. Giving a convulsive sob, she covered her face with her hands and began to weep. Just as she began to sag against the wall two strong arms encircled her. Islaen spared one startled glance to affirm the identity of who held her before collapsing against Alexander's broad chest and giving herself over completely to her misery.

"What are ye doing here?" she rasped when she finally calmed down.

"I kenned ye were down this hall and wished to stop ye from seeing just what ye have seen."

"Here, what are ye doing with our sister?" Malcolm's easily recognizable bellow echoed through the hall an instant before Alexander was forcefully yanked away from Islaen.

"He wasnae doing anything wrong," Islaen hastened to say as she saw how belligerently her brothers were eyeing Alexander.

"I but tried to console the lass."

"Aye, and I ken how ye do that, Alexander MacDubh. Ye would console her right into your bed," Malcolm growled.

"Islaen would never use me that way, sir." Alexander then winked at her. "Howbeit, I am at her disposal if she wishes . . ."

"That be enough out of ye," Robert said shortly, then placed an arm around Islaen's shoulders in a gesture of consolation. "Ah, ye have been weeping. So ye saw the black scoundrel, did ye. Weel, dinnae fash yourself, sweeting. We go now to make him pay."

"That was the other reason for my being here, lass," Alexander said quietly. "I had a wish to stop a killing."

"Nay, ye wouldnae," she gasped, pushing away from Robert and looking at all her brothers, seeing the truth of their intentions in their taut, hard faces. "Ye cannae do it."

"Lass, he has shamed ye. Aye, and hurt ye."

"'Tis not your concern, Donald."

"Ye be our sister and we willnae let him treat ye so," Nathan hissed.

"I dinnae care."

"Of course ye do. 'Tis clear to read upon your face."

"Of course I care but nay enough to want him dead. Aye, there was a moment there when I did and a wee part of me is telling me I should urge ye to go after him, impale him and his whore to their adulterous bed. I cannae let ye do it, though. Ye would cut me far more than he e'er could. T'would not only be him that would bleed ere your swords touched him."

Seeing that her words had drastically dimmed her brothers' ferocity, Alexander gently urged, "Go to your chambers, lass."

After a close look at her brothers' faces, Islaen did as Alexander suggested. She felt a need to hide away for at least a while. Islaen just wished she could go somewhere besides the chambers she shared with Iain.

As soon as Islaen had left, Alexander looked at her brothers. They were an impressive array of tall, strong and handsome young men, even more impressive when one recalled

that there were four more like them at home. Iain would be
well matched in a fight with any one of them. Alexander
knew it would not only be Iain's blood that could flow, however, if they came to sword point. He was fond of Islaen, more
fond than he knew he should be, and wanted to spare her the
pain that would surely come if her brothers fought Iain.

"Ye cannae take up sword against the mon," he said quietly.

"Ye defend him because the mon is your friend," Malcolm
growled.

"Aye, and because Islaen is my friend."

"I am nay sure I want ye sniffing about our sister," Nathan
said coldly.

Alexander shrugged. "I care little. She will continue to
hold my friendship no matter how ye snarl about it. Islaen
does me the honour of liking me. Few women have."

Duncan snorted in disgust. "They all like ye and far too
much."

"Nay, they like my face and form but pay little heed to
what lies beneath. That is not the question in debate now,
howsomever. Islaen has made it clear exactly why ye cannae
take up sword aginst Iain. She loves the fool. She also loves
all of ye. No matter how the battle fared the one whose hurt
ye are so eager to avenge would be hurt e'en more. There is
no sense to that."

"He is right for all I hate to admit it," Robert said quietly.

"So we let the dog pay naught for his crime against our
only sister?" hissed Nathan.

"Weel, I didnae say that," Alexander drawled. "A good
beating might put some sense into his head. Aye, and I might
just join ye."

"Are ye sure ye are his friend?" Robert asked with a faint
smile.

"Aye, but that doesnae mean I need approve of what he
does. Nay, especially not when he turns his back on a good
fine lass who loves him and trots after a whore. Mayhaps a

good thrashing when the time is right will make him see that he reaches for dross and turns his back upon what is truly of value."

Iain tore his mouth from Mary's very eager one and stared at her. Her hands moved over him, undoing his laces with a speed and nimbleness that startled him. There was a greediness to her actions that almost repulsed him. It certainly did nothing to rouse his passion. He finally admitted that he did not want to be there. The freedom to enjoy her skill was not there. "I am no wencher," he heard himself say to Islaen, yet here he was doing just that.

He pulled out of her hold and began to redo his loosened clothing.

He knew Mary could stir him, that he could have an enjoyable tussle with the woman if he could but forget Islaen. That was what he now knew he could not do. Islaen and the promises he had made to her stood between him and the woman who now stared at him with a mixture of astonishment and growing anger.

"What are you doing?" Mary squeaked as she watched Iain straighten his clothes.

"Leaving. I ne'er should have come here. I am a wedded mon."

"Ye would desert me for that child ye were forced to wed?"

"I made promises to her. I willnae break them. She has done naught to deserve that." His eyes widened when she started to scream at him.

"Do ye ken what ye toss aside? I have refused better men than ye my favors. Can ye no see what we could have together? Combine our power and riches and we would be nearly kings! Can that udderless child give ye that? Ye are a fool, Iain."

For a moment Iain said nothing, simply looked at her. The

eyes he had thought so lovely were hard. Suddenly he knew he was seeing the Mary that had always been there. The one he had held and spoken of love to four years ago had never existed. Mary was a woman using any means, including her body, to gain power and coin. Four years ago Lord Cameron had had more than he so she had married him. Now she looked to him to satisfy her greed.

"Nay, not for leaving. I was a fool to think I could regain what had never been." He started towards the door.

A little desperate, she grabbed him by the arm. "What of the love we shared? How can ye turn away from this chance to regain all we lost?"

"We lost nothing." He somewhat roughly loosened her grip and opened the door. "I begin to see that old Cameron actually saved me from making a great mistake. I but pray that I havenae just committed a greater one."

Upon reaching her chambers, Islaen washed up, undressed and donned her night rail. Snuffing all the candles save the one on Iain's side of the bed, she crawled beneath the heavy covers. Bed had always been a nice place to huddle when she had felt sad or hurt but it did not work now. She was all too aware of how often and how passionately she had shared the same bed with Iain. There was a strong urge to go to the pair, to confront them, but she fought it. Pride helped. She had no wish to appear the fool before him and especially before Lady Mary.

The sound of the door opening abruptly stopped her tears. She could not believe Iain would come to her bed directly from Mary's, yet it was clear that he had returned even though she did not look at him. When he reached out and touched her after silently getting into bed, she felt herself pull away although she did not really move. She could not stomach the idea of his touching her with those hands that had so recently caressed Mary.

Iain felt her skin recoil beneath his touch and felt pained. He had known that she had discovered he had gone to Mary's chambers from the moment he had stepped into the room. Despite her obvious efforts to hide it she had been weeping. A little wryly he decided he could not have felt much worse had he actually bedded the woman. Feeling the way his usually welcoming Islaen retreated from his touch gave him the urge to get down upon his hands and knees and beg forgiveness. Here was the proof of what he had already suspected, that no matter how much he wanted to keep a distance between them, he could not abide actually hurting her.

"I couldnae do it," he said softly and felt her tense.

"Ye didnae bed the woman?" Islaen whispered.

"Nay, I couldnae. I willnae lie to ye, lass. I went to Mary's chambers intending to bed the woman."

Turning onto her side, Islaen looked at him, wondering if he knew how very important his honesty was to her. "I ken it. I saw ye in the hall that leads to her chambers."

He grimanced, recalling the deep kiss Mary had given him. "Aye, I hesitated but not for long, eh? I wanted to go back to that time four years ago when she and I were in love."

"But ne'er lovers."

"Nay, ne'er lovers. I was that curious to ken what it would be like to bed her."

"I can understand that, Iain," she said quietly and she could for, although she would never admit it and would never follow through, she had felt that curiosity about Alexander.

"I think ye may be more understanding than I could be."

"Weel, 'tis easy enough for ye didnae bed her."

"Nay. I made promises to ye but I will admit that that wasnae the only reason I left her. T'was there but not the only one. I was seeking the past and I suddenly kenned that I wouldnae find it in her bed. Something told me that what I thought was the past, what I thought had been, was a lie. In truth the Mary I thought I loved ne'er really existed.

"There was something I saw in her eyes, something I have seen in the eyes of women from the past, the women I used to still a mon's hunger, whores parading as fine ladies. When she kenned that I was turning away from her, she condemned herself with her own lips. She was ne'er a sweet lass forced to wed an old mon, but a grasping woman who chose the richest and most powerful of her suitors. Now widowed, she saw my rise in fortunes as reason enough to reach out for me. I dinnae think I care to ken how she meant to deal with ye. What little regret I had, and there was some, was ended when she showed me what she really was."

It hurt a little that he did not say he turned from Mary out of love for her but Islaen told herself not to be a fool. For now it was enough that he had turned aside a beautiful skilled woman, one he had long thought he had loved, in honor of the vows they had exchanged. She might not have all she wanted from him but he had shown that he would see his vows as important and binding. Islaen knew well how many men never did.

She then found herself feeling bad for him. He had suffered a deep disappointment, the hint of it in his voice. Once he had loved a woman named Mary only to discover, after he had suffered the pain of losing her, that she had never existed.

Silently she began to make love to him. She kissed him, improving a little upon the skill he had taught her. When he tried to hold her, to take control of the lovemaking, she neatly eluded him. As she caressed his strong throat with soft kisses, her hands slowly stroked his body. She was emboldened to continue by the way his body began to tighten with passion beneath her touch, the way he trembled slightly as her kisses moved over his broad chest.

Tentatively she flicked her tongue over his flat nipple. His hands tightened their grip in her hair just as hers so often did when he did the same to her. Encouraged by that sign of approval, she began to lathe and suckle until he was squirming gently beneath her. She noted with some fascination that his nipples grew taut just like hers.

"Did ye like that?" she whispered huskily, knowing he had and made bold by that knowledge.

"Do ye e'en need to ask?" he croaked as her tongue flickered over his abdomen

"Weel, ye could just be being gallant." She darted her tongue into his navel and felt him buck gently.

He just groaned as her kisses moved to his thighs. Her warm breath and soft hair caressed his loins and he felt as if he was on fire. A little wildly he recalled how slowly he had been introducing her to the intricacies of lovemaking. He almost laughed. It was clear that she did not really need to be treated so delicately.

"Iain?" she called in a passion-thickened, singsong voice as she gently nipped his thigh, then soothed the sting of her lovebite with slow strokes of her tongue. "Do ye ken the first night I came to your chambers?"

"Aye," he answered a little groggily, feeling himself tremble as her soft lips brushed daringly close to an area that ached for their touch. "Our wedding eve."

"Aye. I saw a couple in the hall. They made love."

"Shameless."

"Och, aye, verra shameless. The woman did something to the mon that I have oft wondered about when we lie together."

"What was that?"

"Weel, I am nay sure how to explain it. It may be a whore's trick."

It took him a moment to catch his breath when she kissed the patch of skin directly above the tip of his shaft. "Then show me."

"Ye will tell me if 'tis a thing I shouldnae do."

"Oh, aye, I will tell ye."

When she ran her tongue down the heated length of him he bucked rather violently and she cried out. "Iain?"

"Nay, dinnae stop. God's teeth, dinnae stop," he rasped, urging her mouth back to the spot it had abruptly abandoned.

He closed his eyes and reveled in the pleasure she gave him. When she took him into the moist warmth of her mouth he shuddered. Gritting his teeth, he fought to control a passion swiftly racing out of his control. He wanted to enjoy the pleasure of her intimate caress for as long as he could.

Islaen could sense that he was close to reaching his peak. She moved back up his body, straddling his hips. As she kissed him, enjoying the fierce edge of his passion, she slowly joined their bodies. When she sat up, she eased off her shift, excited by the way he watched her, then she tossed it aside. It surprised her a little that she could feel so hungry for him, so abandoned, when he had hardly reciprocated her caresses at all.

Iain felt the moist welcome of her body and shuddered. It was clear that her passions had been fully aroused by making love to him and the knowledge further frayed his tottering control. He watched her remove her simple shift with a seductiveness few practiced women achieved and, gripped her hips tightly, preventing her from moving. Iain was sure that if her body began to stroke his, his control would snap completely, bringing too swift an ending to their loveplay.

With a soft growl, he sat up, his knees coming up slightly to help support her as, placing an arm around her, he arched her back away from him. The way she squirmed against him as he hungrily assaulted her breasts was enough of a movement to bring him to the very edge of release. When his hand moved to her hip and gently urged her to a more rhythmic movement her release came quickly. He pressed his face against her breasts as she clung to him and let her pull him along with her as she tumbled into the brief-lived but exquisite oblivion of passion's apex. It was a long while before, still holding her close, he eased the intimacy of their embrace and laid back down.

"Does this mean that I am forgiven?"

Smiling sleepily as her body curled around his, Islaen drawled, "Weel, mayhaps. I will have to think on it a wee bit longer."

"Let me rest a while e'er ye really forgive, if that wasnae it. I am nay sure I could live through the true forgiving."

She joined in his soft laughter.

Chapter Nine

A frown touched Islaen's face as she found herself awake. She did not usually wake until Iain began to stir but he was still sleeping soundly. The hairs on the back of her neck felt as if they were standing on end and, without moving or opening her eyes very wide, she searched the shadowed room for the reason for her tense wakefulness.

Suddenly a movement by Iain's side of the bed caught her eye. Even as she admired the silent stealth of whoever approached them she grew taut with a readiness to act. No one came to a person's chambers in such a stealthy way unless they intended some ill. She recalled Iain speaking of an assassin who stalked him and her blood ran cold. When she caught the glint of a blade in the moonlight she gave Iain's inert body one mighty shove even as the blade lowered, then leapt up to light a candle knowing it would be impossible to battle the threat successfully in such darkness.

Iain gave a startled howl as he felt himself roughly thrust from the warm bed but was instantly alert. He knew who the softly cursing man was who tried to squirm free, kicking savagely at his restricting weight. In one clean move Iain rolled away and leapt to his feet. At that moment Islaen lit the candle and Iain was not surprised to find himself facing Duncan

MacLennon. He simply wished he was not doing so naked and unarmed, the bed and MacLennon between him and his sword.

"Ye will die this time, MacLagan, and after ye, your wee whore of a wife."

"Your vengeance is with me, MacLennon. Islaen has naught to do with ye."

"She is yours. That is enough. Mayhaps I willnae kill ye too quickly. T'would be justice for ye to watch me take your woman as ye took mine. Aye, as ye lie dying ye can watch me force her to lie with me as ye forced Catalina."

"I ne'er forced her."

"Catalina would ne'er have lain with ye willingly," MacLennon nearly screamed.

"She was willing to do her duty by her family."

"She would have come to me out of love. Ye stole that from me."

Islaen shivered as the man talked, unsettled by Duncan MacLennon's insanity, but she wasted little time watching the two men stalk each other. Iain was unarmed and that was her main concern. Yanking on her shift she dashed to the chest where his sword lay, gleaming and useless on the top. When she turned back to face the men, plotting a way to get the sword to Iain, she did find a moment to appreciate the sight of her husband. Taut and wary, ready to repel the attack that was sure to come, the grace of his trim well-muscled shape was clearly displayed. She forced her gaze to MacLennon, however, watching him closely as she edged towards Iain, ready to toss Iain his sword at the first opportune moment.

She saw that moment when MacLennon became aware of her and cried, "Iain, your sword," even as she tossed it to him.

The weapon had barely left her hand when MacLennon swung towards her. She whirled out of the reach of his sword but was not quite quick enough. A soft cry of pain escaped her as the blade scored the soft flesh of her outer thigh on its downswing. She hurried to get further out of his way but realized there was no real need. His attention had already returned to Iain. Careful not to draw the man's attention again, she began to circle around the man in an attempt to get to the door and call for aid.

Even as Iain grasped his sword he had to put it to use, blocking MacLennon's savage swing. He could not concentrate completely on his foe, however, for he had heard Islaen's cry. Taking a moment to glance her way he saw her trying to get to the door and, although there was a lot of blood on her leg, the smoothness of her movements indicated that the wound was a slight one. Giving into the urge to see to her welfare cost him, however. He poorly dodged a deadly strike of MacLennon's and felt the man's blade take a piece out of his side. The wound was not incapacitating but Iain knew the slow loss of needed blood could soon make it so. He took the offensive hoping to even the score or cut the man down before his loss of blood made him weaker than MacLennon.

Seeing that Iain was keeping MacLennon too occupied to bother with her, Islaen raced for the door and, flinging it open, screamed, "Murder! Fither, Robert, the rest of ye, come quickly. A mon is trying to murder Iain."

A vile curse escaped MacLennon as he heard the swift response to her cries. He made a lunge at Iain's loins, Iain leapt back, all too aware of his vulnerability. In that instant, MacLennon bolted for the window. He was disappearing through it as Iain dashed after him and Islaen's kin tumbled into the room dressed only in their braes, their swords ready and barely in time to catch a brief glimpse of Duncan MacLennon.

"He went out the window. After him," Islaen ordered a little hysterically, desperate to end the threat to Iain.

His sons immediately obeyed but Alaistair hesitated a moment, seeing the blood on her leg. "Ye are hurt, lass."

"'Tis not bad, Fither."

"Aye, but the lad is hurt too." Alaistair decided he was needed more where he was and set his sword aside.

Islaen saw how Iain leaned against the window clutching his bleeding side and rushed to help him. She had been too intent upon the need to get help to see clearly how the fight had progressed. As her father helped her get Iain to the bed and insisted that she too lie down, Islaen wondered how much of Iain's collapse was due to sheer disappointment that MacLennon had escaped yet again. Then a nearly frantic Meg, roused by one of her brothers, arrived to help her father tend their wounds.

Despite her protests, Meg, her father and Iain insisted that she drink a potion. Islaen was already succumbing to the sleep it imposed upon her when the first of her brothers returned. She heard just enough to know that Iain's assassin was still free to strike again before she fell asleep.

"I thought the mon sought only ye," Alaistair growled, noting with interest how his daughter clung to Iain even in sleep.

"So did I. He struck out at her when she tossed me my sword. Howbeit, he did speak on killing her too."

"Then the mon must be killed and swiftly," Malcolm growled.

"Fine words," Nathan said wearily as he entered, the last brother to return, "when we cannae find the mon."

"Faded into the morning mists like some wraith," Donald muttered as he nudged Meg out of the way and sat down by Islaen's side, gently brushing a few strands of hair from her face. "I was sore eager to gain hold o' him." He looked at Iain and said coldly, "'Tis a wonder he found ye here at all. He might have found our Islaen alone and unprotected."

Iain bit back a curse as he sat up and reached for his braes. Islaen had not told him that her brothers also knew of his going to Mary, but it was clear that they did. He decided now was not the time to discuss that. Flushing slightly beneath the condemning gazes of Islaen's kin, he sought to change the subject.

"I wasnae much protection at first," he admitted as he struggled to get dressed with Nathan's somewhat grudging help. "T'was Islaen's quick action that saved me from being murdered as I slept." He told them all what had happened.

By the time he was dressed, they had decided that there was little that they could do. A more watchful guard would be kept and a search begun. It satisfied none of them but it was all that could be done. As the MacRoths started to return to their rooms, Iain went in search of Alexander. Later he would seek an audience with the king. He doubted that either man could do much, but now Islaen's life was also in danger and Iain wished to leave no possibility for her increased safety unexamined.

Islaen woke to find her brother Nathan sprawled at her side. "Where has Iain gone? He was hurt."

Nathan rose and poured her some wine. "'Tis surprising he was here at all. That mad mon could weel have found ye alone had your husband nay crawled back here from his whore's bed."

After taking a refreshing drink of wine, Islaen said, "He didnae bed her."

"Lass," he sat down by her side, "we all saw him leave with the woman."

"Aye, but he didnae bed her. He told me."

"And ye believe him?"

"Aye. I willnae tell ye all he said for 'tis not really your concern but t'was enough for me to ken that he spoke true."

"He meant to."

"Aye. He said as much. He stayed true to me, though. 'Tis no small thing."

"Nay, I can see that," Nathan agreed reluctantly.

She could see that he would be slower to forgive than she would, though, so she adroitly changed the subject. After finding out what would be done about MacLennon she sent Nathan after Meg. Firmly ignoring the woman's disapproval, Islaen got dressed and went in search of Iain. She wanted to be sure that he was not pushing himself beyond his strength.

To her dismay, she found Lady Mary. Seeing the beauty of the woman Islaen felt a pang of doubt, then shook it away. She had no reason at all to doubt Iain's words. She would not let her fears make her mistrust him. Whatever Lady Mary said, Islaen would choose to believe Iain. Islaen did wish, however, that the woman had not towed Lady Constance along to witness whatever the confrontation resulted in.

"Have ye lost your husband," Lady Mary smiled coldly, "again?"

"'Tis a big place. I presume ye havenae seen him."

"Not since last night—in my chambers."

"Och, weel, I am after more than a quick keek at his backside as he leaves me."

"Ah, so he told you that we did naught and ye, like a dutiful wife, believed him."

"Aye, I believe him and, an I didnae have more important business to attend to, I would look close at why ye wish me to think otherwise. Adultery is a thing to hide as the shameful sin it is, not something to boast about."

"Iain said he didnae bed this woman?" Lady Constance demanded.

Even as Islaen wondered of what possible concern it could be to Lady Constance, Lady Mary laughed shortly, "She but says that to save face. And what husband would not lie? Iain but decided that t'was too early to tell her about me, 'tis all."

"M'lady, an he took ye t'was but the briefest of tussles, nay more than a quick toss up of your skirts and a hasty rut. 'Tis all he had time for atween the time I saw him walk away with ye to your chambers and when he returned to me. I think I will believe what Iain said, that he couldnae bed ye. Iain has his faults, as does any mon, but he doesnae lie." Thoroughly disgusted, Islaen started to walk away.

"Nay, MacLagan doesnae lie," Lady Constance said coldly. "Ye do, though, m'lady Mary. Ye didnae win the wager. I will have my coin back."

"Ye will believe that scrawny fool?" Lady Mary screeched.

Islean hurried away from the resultant squabble. She felt sickened by the women. It seemed distastefully cold to her that they would turn the destruction of a marriage into a matter for a wager. Islaen felt a real need to leave the court and all its leeches and sycophants. She wondered if she could convince Iain to speed up their departure.

Inwardly, she grimaced as she had to accept the fact that even though she might convince him to leave now, they would be back. Iain was his clan's representative at court, their ear to all the intrigues and possible benefits. She would just have to become hardened to the ways of the court as she did not intend to let him travel to such a pit of immorality without her. Islaen wondered how some of the men could look their wives in the eyes when they arrived home after the debauched way they had carried on.

Meg finally caught up with her and forced her to go and rest. Since she had just discovered that Iain was closeted with the king and her leg was throbbing some, she let Meg bully her into a rest. She was dismayed, however, when she not only fell asleep but did not wake until very late, the sun having clearly set a while ago.

Dressing quickly, she started towards the hall, sure that she would find Iain there. Concentrating upon getting there as quickly as possible she did not see Lord Fraser until she nearly bumped into him. Hastily taking several steps backward she noticed several things that filled her with dismay. There was no one about and Lord Fraser looked decidedly drunk.

"All alone? No hulking protectors about?" He began to advance upon her. "I have been waiting for just such a moment. I am nay as great a fool as young Ronald MacDubh. Attacking ye afore all in court was madness. They have banished him, ye ken."

"Nay, I gave no more thought to the rogue after Alexander took him away." She tried to elude his advance but was finding it difficult, the corridor being too narrow for any good evasive movements. "Now, if ye will but move aside. . . ."

"Alexander, is it?" he growled, ignoring her request. "Have ye been gifting that pretty fellow with your favors then?"

"Ye are insulting. Ye are also drunk. I think ye would be wise to let me pass and then seek your bed."

"An I go to my bed this night, lass, t'will be with ye beneath me."

He lunged for her and she tried to avoid him but the train on her gown, small though it was, made her falter. She stumbled up against the wall and he took quick advantage of that, using his bulky frame to pin her there. Islaen struggled against his hold but realized with a growing panic that, drunk though he was, the man could hold her easily.

"My kin and my husband will see ye dead for this," she gasped as he wrestled her to the ground.

"Such petty lordlings willnae be allowed to draw my blood. I will have the fair Lady Mary on my side as weel. She does hate ye, lass. She seems to think," he panted as he struggled to pin her thrashing form firmly beneath him, "that, an I possess ye, young Iain will turn to her." He tore open the front of her gown and frowned when, instead of the bared breasts he had expected, he saw a cloth wrapping. "What is this?" he muttered as he drew his dagger.

Islaen struggled to free her hands but he had her wrists pinned beneath his knees so firmly that she feared they could easily break. Trying to buck him off only wearied her, robbing her of breath. When he began to cut away her binding, she cried out softly for several times his dagger pricked her tender skin. He stared at her in open-mouthed astonishment when he finally cut away her binding and the look in his eyes made her skin crawl with revulsion.

"God's beard, lass, why should ye try to hide such bounty?" he rasped as his hands greedily mauled her breasts.

He shifted his position, freeing her hands. In that brief moment that she was free, Islaen struck at his face but the weight upon her wrists had cut off the flow of blood to her hands. She was unable to curl her fingers into the dangerous claws she had intended, her swipe at his face barely breaking the skin. It was enough to earn her a stunning slap, however, even as he pinned her wrists over her head with one meaty hand.

The moment his mouth touched her breasts she felt bile sting the back of her throat. She fought the urge to vomit as hard as she did the urge to weep knowing that neither action would gain her anything. Cursing him fluently and occasionally crying out as his teeth scored her soft skin, she continued to try and break free of him. To her horror all she accomplished was to further arouse him by the rubbing of her body against his.

Feeling his hand tearing at her braies, Islaen briefly gave into helplessness. As he tore her skirts in his nearly frantic attempt to get them out of his way, she realized there was one last weapon she had. The corridor they were in was dark and little used but sound carried far. There could be someone nearby and the fear of being seen in such an ignominious position now paled next to what she felt about what Lord Fraser was about to do to her. Opening her mouth, Islaen managed to get out several hearty screams of her husband's name before a swearing Lord Fraser stuffed a handkerchief in her mouth, nearly choking her in his effort to silence her. She could only pray that someone was near enough to have heard her.

* * *

Iain hesitated, frowning as he decided which way to go. There was a little-used passageway just ahead that would save him a few minutes and, pressing his hand to his throbbing side, he decided he would use it. He glanced at Alexander who strolled companionably at his side carrying a well-ladened tray of food.

"I can take that from here," Iain said, not sure he wanted Alexander along, especially if Islaen was in their chambers.

"Nay, ye cannae. Your poor wee wife will get naught if hands as unsteady as yours are carry this."

"I didnae say it was for Islaen," Iain muttered and wondered if he sounded as much like a sulky child as he thought he did.

"Nay, ye didnae. I had just hoped ye might be taking an interest in your wee wife at last, 'tis all."

"Ye are far too concerned with my wife, Alexander Mac-Dubh."

"'Tis hard for a mon not to be when he has held the poor weeping lass as her husband pants after a whore. Aye, and when he has been the one she has had to talk with because her husband is rolling his eyes at that whore and nay speaking a word to her."

"Shall we just forget Lady Mary?"

"Aye, if ye have."

"I have."

"Just when did ye start to forget her, an I may be so curious?"

"'Tis nay your concern but t'was moments after I entered her chambers." Iain looked sternly at his friend. "So, there is no wife for ye to take to your bed for a wee bit of consoling ere her husband starts to look about for her again."

"An I took your wife to my bed, friend," Alexander said softly, "t'would not be but to console her and ye could look about all ye liked after your wenching paled, I wouldnae be giving her back."

Before a stunned Iain could make any response to that a

scream ended the tense silence between them. Even as Iain recognized his name in that desperate cry he recognized the voice that delivered it. He raced towards the sound only dimly aware of the sound of Alexander tossing the tray aside and following him.

The sight that met his eyes blinded him with a rage that burned away all aches and weariness. With a feral growl he lunged for the man sprawled on top of Islaen. He pulled Lord Fraser off of Islaen and threw the man against the wall, then leapt upon the man.

Islaen was stunned by her abrupt rescue. One moment she was braced for the horrifying completion of her rape and the next an enraged Iain was hurling a far heavier Lord Fraser through the air. She met Alexander's concerned gaze blankly as he crouched over her. With an odd detachment she realized she was beginning to shake.

Taking the gag from her mouth, Alexander took one startled look at her bruised breasts and then began to tidy her tattered clothing as well as he could. "Ye have been keeping secrets, lass."

"They are too big," she said dazedly.

Helping her sit up, he gently kissed her on the forehead. "What a great fool ye are for such a wee lass. Now, set here for I feel I must stop your husband from killing Lord Fraser. The mon deserves it, but t'would cause a great scandal."

Not fully taking in what she saw, Islaen watched Alexander forcefully restrain Iain from delivering any more blows to a badly battered Lord Fraser. When Iain finally stopped, Lord Fraser slid to the floor and did not move again. Wrapping her arms about herself in a vain attempt to stop her shaking, Islaen stared up at her husband when he crouched before her.

"Is he dead?" she whispered.

"Nay, I think not. Did he rape ye?"

"Almost." She felt the tears she had held back begin to flow. "I want a bath," she said shakily.

When Iain reached for her Alexander stopped him. "Ye opened your wound when ye were tossing yon scum about. I will carry the lass." He helped Iain stand, then gently picked Islaen up in his arms. "Dinnae scowl so, Iain. Ye would most like drop her. Ye will need what strength ye have left just to get yourself back to your chambers. What about him?"

Glancing at Lord Fraser Iain needed a moment to resist the urge to rouse the unconscious man so that he could hit him again. "Leave him. Someone will find him an he doesnae crawl back into his hole of his own accord."

As they hurried to Iain's chambers both men tried to get Islaen to stop crying. She had gained some semblance of control by the time Meg, fetched by Iain's squire, arrived. As Meg took her behind the screen to help her scrub herself clean and tend to her small wounds, Alexander tended to a distracted Iain.

"Did ye see what that animal did to her?" Iain growled. "I should kill him."

"And have all the world ask the reason? Do ye wish the lass to suffer that shame? Ye ken weel that none will believe he didnae possess her and many will think her to have been willing, that she cried rape to save herself from your wrath."

His wound cleaned and reclosed, Iain took a deep drink of ale to still the throbbing. He recognized the truth of Alexander's words but cursed the unfairness of it. The silence that would be necessary to save Islaen from the blackening of her name especially galled him when Meg tucked her up in bed at his side and he saw the bruises Fraser had inflicted. Somehow he would make the man pay even if he had to wait years to do it.

Islaen said little as Alexander and Meg said their goodnights. She lay stiff and silent at Iain's side even after they were alone. The bath had helped calm her but she still felt defiled. Although she knew she was not at fault, had done nothing to invite the attack, she could not help but fear that Iain would now be repulsed by her, see her body as soiled by Fraser's mauling. From what she had dared to view of her sore body, there did not seem to be any part of her that Iain could view without being reminded of Fraser's brutal attack.

Iain gently pulled her into his arms, felt her tension and felt a renewed anger at Lord Fraser. "Dinnae come to fear me too, lass."

"I dinnae fear ye, Iain. I dinnae ken how ye can bear to touch me."

"Wheesht, lass, it wasnae your fault. If we werenae so battered that t'would cause us more pain than pleasure I would love ye thoroughly right now to let ye see clearly how weel I can bear to touch ye, aye, want to touch ye still."

After lying in the comfort of his arms for a while, Islaen began to believe him and relaxed. Once her fear of his rejection was eased she felt weariness overtake her. The day had been long and too full of danger. Despite her aches and pains she cuddled up to Iain and knew she would soon be asleep.

"Better, lass?" he asked softly, caressing her hair.

"Aye, better, but, Iain?"

"Aye, lass?"

"Can we go home?" she whispered, not wishing to push but desperate now to leave court.

"Aye, lass. On the morrow an I can manage it, but by the next day for certain," he swore and soon felt her relax in sleep.

Chapter Ten

"Are ye sure ye can ride all the way?" Iain asked as he helped Islaen mount what he thought was far too much horse for her.

"Aye, Iain, I will be fine. Beltraine brought me all the way here. He can take me back too. Can ye not, me fine beastie?" she softly cooed, patting the stallion's strong neck. "Do ye think your mares will be pleased with this new blood in your stables, Iain?"

"The horse is yours?" he asked in some surprise even as he began to mentally pair the fine stallion with several mares at Caraidland.

"Aye," replied Alaistair as he rode up beside his daughter. "He took to her, so as he grew I decided she might as weel have the great brute. She is a muckle fine rider, lad, and can handle such a horse."

When they started on their way she did not even look back. Glancing at Iain she was glad she had overcome her lingering terror from the attack enough to insist that they remain at court two extra days so that his wound closed properly. He had been ready to leave as he had promised, having worked hard to clear away all his remaining business, but she had seen that he was not quite ready for the long ride home.

Despite her near retreat from court society and her pre-occupation with Iain, she had noted two changes in court. Lord Fraser had simply and abruptly disappeared. Considering the beating Iain had given the man Islaen was not sure how Lord Fraser had managed to leave but, since a few of his kin and all his men had also vanished, she suspected the family had managed his swift but quiet exodus to avoid scandal. Lady Mary had also disappeared and Islaen was sure the woman had fled out of fear that Lord Fraser would implicate her in his reprehensible act. Islaen had never mentioned Lady Mary's part in the attack to Iain and was not sure she should. It was enough for her that the woman and Lord Fraser were gone. She fervently hoped she would never have to set eyes upon either of them again.

By the time they stopped for the night, Islaen felt exhausted and ached as if all her fading bruises had been renewed. Even the wound upon her leg throbbed a little. She realized that Iain was also suffering when he grumpily apologized for not having a tent for them, sulkily adding that he had not anticipated towing a wife back to Caraidland. Iain was not a cross-tempered man and she knew instantly that his wound troubled him.

She suspected there was an added reason for his gruffness when they bedded down for the night. When her backside came up against his loins as he held her close there was no ignoring his arousal, an arousal that would have to go unsatisfied. With her kin, Alexander (and she still puzzled over his sudden desire to leave court) and all their men-at-arms ever near there would be no chance of finding the privacy needed to satisfy Iain's needs. Or her own, she mused with a sigh. She doubted they would be able to do anything about those particular desires until they reached Caraidland, and that was several days away.

On the third day of their journey, she and Alexander, with Meg's concurrence, removed Iain's stitches. His wound had healed nicely, Islaen decided as she helped him with his tunic, although MacLennon had succeeded in leaving yet another scar upon him. She then became aware of the fact that her brothers had gathered round.

"What do ye want?" she asked suspiciously.

"We mean to have us a wee talk with your husband," Nathan replied.

One sharp glance at their faces told her it was not talking they had in mind. Her suspicions were strengthened by the way Iain's men were bristling. They sensed the threat facing Iain.

"Weel, ye arenae going to do any talking." She sneered the last word. "Get away from here."

"Islaen," Iain said quietly as he stood, "I think ye best stay out of this."

He was idly amused by the way she stood before her much larger brothers, with her hands upon her slim hips. She looked like a small hen ready to defend her chick. This time, however, it would indeed be best if she stayed out of it even though he knew it was going to make her furious.

Silently signaling his men that he would take care of the matter alone, Iain prepared to leave with Islaen's brothers. He knew they intended to do their talking with their fists and that he would undoubtedly be nursing many a bruise for the rest of the journey to Caraidland. However, he understood why they were intent on doing it. He knew he would do the same if he had a sister. There had also been a tension between him and Islaen's kin since the night he had gone off with Lady Mary. Iain knew this confrontation would put them back on a more companionable footing, something he was eager for. He did, however, feel a little slighted when he saw that Alexander was aligned with Islaen's brothers.

"Ye as weel, Alex?"

"Aye. Me as well."

"Now wait just a minute," Islaen snapped as they started to

move away, but when she reached out to restrain Iain her father caught her up in a hold that was gentle but very firm. "This is the greatest of foolishness, Fither."

"Weel, most women think that of a mon's business. No harm in ye lads having a look," he said to the hovering men-at-arms who immediately hurried after the others. "Now, lass, will ye set here an I release ye?"

"Aye," she answered with cross reluctance, "for I ken I will do no good chasing after them. They willnae hurt Iain badly, will they?"

"Nay, lass. Truth is, I will be muckle surprised if some of the lads dinnae come back a mite bashed themselves."

Iain fully intended to give as good as he got when Islaen's brothers halted and Nathan murmured, "This looks as good a spot as any to have our wee talk."

"She willnae be pleased by this," Iain said calmly as he took off his tunic and handed it to one of his men.

Doing the same, Robert drawled, "Nay, I suspicion she will burn our ears a wee bit as she should have burned yours."

"Aye, but she is an understanding lass."

"We arenae and we did warn ye," growled Nathan.

"Aye, ye did. So how is it to be then? All of you?"

"Nay, that wouldnae be quite fair," murmured Robert.

"Weel, then, two at a go. Alexander makes it even."

"Wheesht, ye are a boaster, are ye not?" muttered Duncan.

Glancing at all the bared chests of his opponents and seeing that, despite the slender build of some, they were a strong collection, Iain thought he was too, but drawled, "T'will get the business done faster. I havenae supped yet, ye ken."

"Me and Alex will have at ye first," growled Duncan as he advanced. "I mean to knock ye on your arse, MacLagan."

He did just that but Iain quickly recovered. His main

objective was to down his opponents as quickly as possible in order to have enough strength to get through all of them without too many injuries. Duncan was good but his method was easily guessed and Iain soon sent him down. Alexander went down an instant later and, although he was fully able to get up and continue, simply began to laugh.

"I had forgotten how cursed quick ye are, Iain."

"Had enough then?"

"Aye. I just wanted a wee knock or two."

Malcolm and Leith were next. Iain saw that the MacRoths were indeed fighting men. They had clearly watched him closely, learning his manner of fighting. It was a lot harder to bring them down.

By the time he faced the twins, the last pair of opponents, Iain was surprised that he was still standing. He knew he had done himself proud, something aided by the fact that his opponents were considering a good knock down enough to end it, even if they were still conscious. If he had had to fight each one until they were totally incapacitated he felt sure he would never have gotten past the first four.

He knew he had been right about what the fight would accomplish when he heard Calum say, "Mayhaps we ought to let him catch his breath first."

"Dinnae be daft. If we do that he will knock us on our arses," Donald said cheerfully, then charged Iain.

Iain sidestepped Donald's charge and booted the youth in the backside much to the amusement of his men. He was not quick enough to elude Calum's charge, however, and hit the ground hard. Donald was quick to join in and Iain was not really able to discern who was doing what to whom in the ensuing melee. He was barely conscious when the fighting ended, the twins collapsing beside him upon the ground. Wincing as he partly raised himself up on his elbows, Iain saw that neither was unconscious, that they had simply quit, deciding that they had had enough.

"Who won then?" he rasped and everyone laughed.

"Weel," Robert said as he helped a groggy Leith to stand, "we best get back so that Islaen can glare and mutter."

"Mutter?" Iain mumbled as two of his men helped him to his feet.

"Aye, mutter." Nathan shook his head. "She mutters when she is too angry to think of what she really wants to say or to get the words out clear and all."

When the men finally staggered back into camp, Islaen glared at them. Iain looked terrible but she had seen the results of too many fights and knew that he was not nearly as bad as he looked. She also noted fleetingly that he had indeed given as good as he had gotten. When she heard them jesting and talking about the battle as if it was something wonderful, she was sorely tempted to leave them all to wallow in their own blood and grime.

Muttering about the incomprehensible foolishness of men, Islaen gathered up what she needed to tend to Iain. Stalking over to where his men had helped him to lie down, she gave him one fierce glare and then set about tending his bruises and abrasions, muttering all the while about the silliness of grown men. She wondered crossly why he kept smiling.

Glancing around she decided her help was not really needed elsewhere. Since she had already eaten and Iain refused her grumbled offer of food, she decided she might as well turn in for the night. Still grumbling, she prepared for bed and then joined him beneath the blankets. When he laughed softly she turned to glare at him.

"Just what do ye find so amusing? Do ye enjoy the pain of being bashed about?"

"Nay, though it was a good fight. Nathan's right," he said with a smile. "Ye do mutter. I will be fine come morning, little one."

"Humph. Ye will be as stiff as a wet cloth put out of a winter's frosty morn."

"Aye, most like but t'will pass. It was a thing that had to be done."

"So ye all tell me but I dinnae understand it."

"Nay, I didnae think ye would. Truth tell, I cannae really explain it. There was anger sitting atween me and your brothers, lass, an anger I earned, I ken that weel. We beat it out of us 'tis all. Ye will see. T'will be there no longer."

In the morning as her brothers, Alexander and Iain mounted their horses with a great deal of groaning and gritting of teeth, Islaen watched them closely. It did not take her long to see that Iain was right. The tension that had existed between her husband and her brothers, one that had deeply troubled her, was gone. She was glad of it although she still did not really understand the whole business.

By the time everyone's bruises were starting to heal they had reached the point in their journey where her kin would leave them. Islaen knew it was foolish but she could not fully repress the fear their leaving instilled within her. She could not stop them for Colin had sent word that the English had raided. Her family was needed at home and could not continue on to Caraidland as had originally been planned. Since she loved Iain it puzzled her that her family's leaving should make her feel so all alone. She had to fight tears as she kissed each brother farewell.

"We will come to meet with Iain's family as soon as we can, lass," Alaistair promised.

"I ken it, Fither." She returned his kiss and then hugged him for a moment.

"Dinnae look so dowie, lass. Ye said this was what ye wanted, that he made ye happy."

"Aye, 'tis. He does. I just wish I could have ye both, him and all of ye."

"Wheesht, lass, ye will always have us. There isnae a place upon God's green earth ye could go to be rid of us. T'will just take a wee bit longer to get to ye if ye need us."

Islaen kept repeating that as she watched them ride away. She also told herself that she was a grown woman now and beyond tears simply because her family was no longer right at hand. None of it helped. The tears still flowed. As soon as her family was out of sight she huddled close to her horse and stared at her feet in a vain attempt to hide her tears as she fought to compose herself. She did not want the men remaining, especially Iain, to think her a child.

Iain sighed, dismounted and went over to her. He had suspected that the parting would be hard for her. Eventually she would be able to find contentment in the knowledge that they were not very far away but, for now, he suspected that she felt lost. With a twinge of guilt, he admitted that some of that could well be because he was not really giving her anything to replace all that love her family had given her.

"Islaen," he said gently as he put his arm around her.

"I am sorry, Iain. I am acting the wee bairn."

"Nay." He pulled her into his arms. "I ken weel the pull of family. They arenae too far away, lass."

"I ken it." She sniffed and gave him a watery smile. "And now that ye have beat each other bloody and are great friends mayhaps we will see them oft enough."

"Aye, I ken that we will. If they but come one at a time we can see your kin all the year round," he teased. She laughed softly and a moment later he helped her to mount her horse.

"We will be at Caraidland ere the sun sets tomorrow," Iain announced as they stopped for the night.

Sighing as she attended to her horse, Islaen tried not to get nervous. Iain and his men certainly looked happy about it. Even Alexander and his men looked pleased. That surely indicated that Caraidland was a good place, she told herself. She sighed again and wished she knew at least one person there besides Iain. The reminder that she knew the five men that rode with him cheered her only a little. This would be the first time she had ever met anyone without some of her family along for support.

"Lass, they are good people," Alexander said quietly as he moved to her side.

"My face is so easy to read?"

"Nay, not truly. 'Tis but clear that ye dinnae really share our delight o'er the nearness of our destination."

"Weel, it has ne'er been so important that I find approval," she admitted softly and unconsciously touched her breasts freed from their bonds from their first night upon the road.

Alexander smiled and shook his head. "Lass, ye are bonnie, but I ken how hard it must be for one who has long thought otherwise to believe it. All his kin need to approve of ye is to ken that ye love their son. Ye do and they will."

"I have ne'er said so," she mumbled, coloring deeply.

"Mayhaps 'tis best that ye dinnae. Not yet."

"Aye. He would hie to the hills," she grumbled.

He laughed softly and nodded. "Ye wouldnae see him for the dust."

"Alexander? Just why have ye come along?"

"Weel, lass, I ken that Iain will simply tell his kin that ye are his wife and ye will say little more than 'Aye, I am.' T'would be best if there is another there they can speak to and I am kenning more than I ought."

"Are ye sure ye ought to?"

He shrugged. "It cannae hurt."

"Nay, I suppose not."

"Dinnae ye have anything to do, Alex?" Iain demanded as he walked over to them and a grinning Alexander strolled away. "That mon smiles too much," Iain grumbled, then looked crossly at Islaen. "Why are ye always talking with him?"

"Because he is my friend. Iain, I ken that he is a beautiful mon who can seduce a woman with but one soft word but we are only friends."

"He would be more."

"Mayhaps but only until he finds what he seeks."

"He thinks he has found it in you."

"What he sees is that I see the beauty, aye, but I see the rest too. That is what he wants, a lass who will see past his face and form. Once another lass does that he will ne'er e'en passingly think of me as more than a friend and a body can ne'er have enough good friends. He is your friend too, Iain," she added quietly.

Iain nodded, understanding all that she said and inferred. If he tossed Islaen aside as he had almost done when he had gone with Mary, Alexander would be right there for her, but otherwise he would be no more than a friend. It was, nevertheless, a little unsettling to have such a mon ready and willing to take over his wife if the chance arose. Suddenly, he felt a greater understanding of Tavis's feelings. He supposed that Alexander would find it amusing to have two MacLagans scowling his way and hovering over their wives.

He thought of that again as Caraidland came into view the next day, and looked at Alexander who rode at his side. "Tavis will be so verra pleased to see you," he drawled.

Alexander laughed. "Aye. I always get a warm greeting at Caraidland."

A wild cry broke the relative quiet of the countryside. Islaen stared wide-eyed at the rider charging towards them. Surely one man would never try to attack all of them, she thought, and then saw Iain grin. A moment later the youth came to an impressively neat halt before them and grinned back at Iain.

Despite the brightness of her own family's hair, Islaen found the youth's orange hair a wonder. She knew he could not be kin to the MacLagans for she had heard enough about them to know that they were dark. He looked at her and she nearly gasped. His eyes were beautiful, vaguely slanted, thickly lashed and a warm rich amber in color.

"Phelan, ye will be killed one day for someone will think ye some attacking madman," Iain drawled."

"Sure'n are ye certain I am not?" Phelan grinned, then nodded towards Islaen. "And this fair maid is your wife?"

"Aye. Islaen MacRoth ere she became a MacLagan. Islaen, this wild mon is Sir Phelan O'Connor."

When he kissed her hand with all the grace of a skilled courtier, Islaen felt his long hair brush her hand and was bemused to find that it felt as soft and sun-kissed as the marigolds it resembled. She blushed when he looked at her. For all the sweet boyishness of his face, his eyes held the warm appreciation of a man who was no stranger to passion.

"M'lady," he murmured in a soft, rich voice she could not help but compare to Alexander's.

"Oh, Islaen, will do."

He smiled. "And I am but Phelan. The sir but means that I was in the right place at the right time."

A glance at Iain told her the young man was being modest. That and the fact that he looked too young to carry the accolade of sir told her that he shrugged away an act that probably made for an exciting tale. She knew instinctively, however, that she would not get the whole story from him, that he really did believe it all a simple piece of luck. There was something about the young man that made her relax just a little concerning her impending meeting with Iain's family.

"Your father has a feast in the making. Caraidland has been a mad whirl since your squire arrived yester morn."

"And that is why ye are out riding o'er the hills, Phelan?"

"Aye, Iain. They kept trying to put me to work. T'was not easy escaping Storm's keen eye either." Phelan grinned impishly at Alexander. "Mayhaps I should hie back to warn Tavis that this pretty mon rides along with ye. Sure 'n he will be so pleased."

"Nay, let it be a surprise. 'Tis why I told Murdo to say

naught," Iain drawled. "Mayhaps Alexander will tell Tavis why he blesses us with his charming company."

"Can a mon not travel to see his friends without his reasons being suspect?" Alexander asked soulfully.

Islaen realized with surprise that Alexander had yet to explain himself to Iain. Although Iain might not appreciate Alexander's reasons for joining them, an explanation would ease the suspicions Iain so clearly held. It was evident that Alexander found it amusing to let Iain puzzle over it. Islaen decided a little crossly that Alexander's idea of fun could get quite annoying at times.

"Nay, not when he sets a mon's wife to sighing," Iain said dryly.

"Are ye sighing, m'lady?" Alexander asked Islaen.

She met his grin with a mildly disgusted look, then, closing her eyes, placed one hand upon her breast and the back of the other across her forehead. "Aye. Wheesht, I am near to swooning upon the ground at your feet."

"Ye will be upon the ground soon if ye dinnae keep the reins in your hand," Iain muttered as the men laughed.

"Nay. He willnae move. I told him to be still." Islaen hugged her stallion's neck. "He is a verra good lad, arenae ye boy?" she cooed.

"'Tis a stallion ye have there, m'lady, not a lap dog," Iain said with mock disgust. "Weel, shall we cease sitting here and finish this journey?" Iain asked and there was a round of hearty agreement from the men.

Sighing inwardly, Islaen urged her mount onward, staying close to Iain. She could sense his eagerness to see his family. He did not seem at all aware of the fact that she was not quite so eager.

As they rode through the gates she tried to divert herself from her growing apprehension by studying Caraidland. Here was no simple tower house. It was large, strong and well run, if the orderliness about her was any indication. The Mac-

Lagans might be a small clan, but they looked strong and there was the air of wealth to the place. Islaen could easily understand the pride that colored Iain's voice every time he spoke of Caraidland.

Iain helped her dismount and felt her tension. He suddenly realized that she might not share his delight in coming to Caraidland. He was coming home but she was riding into a nest of strangers.

"Come, love, t'will not be so bad," he said gently. "Ye are at least not a complete surprise. They do expect you."

She managed a weak smile for him as they moved towards the keep. There waited a huge group of people. Islaen found herself caught up in a dizzying round of introductions. While everyone seemed friendly she sensed a wariness in them. They were as unsure about her as she was about them. Islaen prayed that in the trial period to come she did not step too far wrong.

Chapter Eleven

"She is a bonnie lass but a wee one," Colin MacLagan said to his sons when they had a moment alone.

Iain sighed and nodded. He had been tempted to linger in the chambers he and Islaen had been given, waiting for her to join him, so that he could avoid any time alone with his family. That, he knew, would only postpone the inevitable. They naturally had a lot of questions and he decided it might just help Islaen's settling in if he answered them as soon as possible.

"Aye, she is a good lass. Do ye ken the MacRoths?"

"Nay, not weel. Good people and the mon has a lot of sons."

Inwardly, Iain grimaced, knowing that his father wanted him to have sons, and answered reluctantly, "Eleven."

"Wheesht, there's a brood to be proud of. The lass is the only daughter?"

"Aye. The youngest child too."

Tavis grinned and winked at his wife who sat at his side, also a cherished only daughter. "Her kin have a heavy hand, do they?"

"'Tis nay too bad, though," he half-smiled as he touched a fading bruise near his eye, "they guard her weel."

"I was going to ask ye about that," growled Colin. "Ye arenae still at odds with them, are ye?"

"Nay, that settled it all."

"Men," Storm grumbled in disgust. "Knock each other about, then shake hands. 'Tis foolish."

"So Islaen said," Iain drawled and Storm shook her head as the men laughed. "T'was a good fight. Her brothers are good."

"But ye are better."

"Aye, Tavis, but I willnae be if there is a next time. They watch and, if it works, they learn it."

"Why didnae they come here with ye?"

"The English had raided, Fither. They got word of it halfway through our journey."

"Bad?"

"Bad enough so they felt they had best get back home and see to things ere they came here."

As Iain continued to answer questions he realized that his knowledge of Islaen, her life and her kin was still somewhat vague. He also saw that he needed to be evasive. While his family would never intrude too deeply into his private affairs they were quite naturally interested in how his marriage was working. Finally, he muttered the excuse that Islaen might need his help in finding her way to the feast and left what had begun to feel like an inquisiton, though he knew it had not been.

"The lad is being verra coy," Colin muttered. "Do ye have naught to say, Alex?"

Alexander straightened up from where he lounged against the wall, having eavesdropped upon the family conference in the ever filling hall. "Me? Now what would I have to say about Iain's marriage?"

Tavis's bright blue eyes sparkled with laughter although his voice was stern. "Ye always ken more than ye ought about other men's wives. I also ken that this time ye didnae come just to annoy me by flirting with Storm."

"How ye wound me, Tavis," Alexander murmured, winking at Storm, who smiled and shook her head.

"Come, Alex, enough teasing. Tell us what ye know," Storm urged gently. "Is it a good match? Will it work?"

"Despite Iain's effort, aye, I think it will. She is a good lass, Storm, a very good lass and she loves him though she willnae say it. She kens weel that Iain would flee that. Aye, the lass kens her mon very weel indeed."

"He clings to his fears," Colin said with a sigh.

"Aye, he does but 'tis not only her death upon a childbed that he fears. Death stalks him."

"MacLennon," Tavis growled.

Nodding, Alexander told them of the attack upon Iain. So too did he tell them of Lady Mary's games. By the time he finished relating all that had happened in court the MacLagans were both dismayed and angry.

"It sounds as if they should have left court weeks ago," murmured Storm.

"Most of that happened in the last few days but, aye, it will be better for them here. Is Maura still about?"

Thinking of the woman who had so avidly pursued Iain before he had gone to court, Storm grimaced. "Aye, though I believe she has set her aim at another. She is not wed yet, though, and not too far away either."

"Ah, weel, at least she is but one and not many as there were at court."

"Do ye really think the lass can pull him from himself? Stop him from being the cold mon he fights to be?"

"Aye, Colin, but it would help if MacLennon was dead. Until then," Alexander shrugged. "Watch them when they come down to indulge in the feasting. Ye will see what I mean. If the matter werenae such a sad one t'would be funny. Iain catches himself softening and pulls back whilst poor, wee

Islaen struggles to stop that retreat, wavering between sadness and anger."

"Well, what matters most this night," Storm said firmly, "is that the girl is very nervous and we must put her at ease."

Islaen stared at herself in the mirror and then cursed softly, bringing a muttered reprimand from a harrassed Meg. She knew she was being a nuisance and perhaps foolish but she was desperate to look her best. Not used to her breasts being unbound she could only see a rather vast amount of bosom when she donned her fine gowns.

"I look the veriest whore," she said sulkily, glaring at the soft rise of her full breasts.

"Ochane, ye will drive me mad," hissed Meg. "Do ye mean to change again?"

"Nay, she doesnae."

Iain grinned when both women turned abruptly to gape at him. He had stood in the doorway watching Islaen fret for several minutes. It was rather amusing to watch her struggle to hide what most other women would flaunt. She would clearly need a while yet before she was used to seeing herself unbound.

"But, Iain, I . . ."

"Ye look fine, lass," he said sincerely as he moved to stand before her.

"Are ye sure? I wouldnae want your kin to think me shameless."

"That they would ne'er think. Ye best come with me, lass, or t'will be little there is for us to eat."

She smiled weakly and let him pull her along with him. Her gown was lovely and well made, of the finest materials, but she was certain she was showing far too much of herself. She colored with nervousness and embarrassment when she entered the hall at Iain's side and all eyes turned towards her. It was not the best time, as far as she was concerned, to wear such a gown. As a stranger, and Iain's new wife, all eyes were upon her anyways. Now was the time to be extremely demure.

Seated at the laird's left, it did not take Islaen long to feel she had been given the best of seats. Colin was an open, friendly man and reminded her of her father in many ways. Within moments, she was feeling at ease.

It took a little longer to be sure she wished to be opposite Tavis's lovely wife, Storm. Never had she been so close to a Sassanach although there had been times when some more or less friendly contact had been made with England. That Storm was not only accepted by the MacLagans but loved helped ease the awkwardness as did Storm's friendly manner. It seemed as if Storm was more than willing to accept a new lady at Caraidland, even seemed genuinely glad of it. Tentatively, Islaen eased her wary stance, reaching for the friendship Storm seemed to offer.

It would be nice to have a woman friend, Islaen decided. She had Meg but Meg was more like a mother than a friend. Meg also had no experience with marriage and little with men. A woman to discuss things with, to confide in, could be very beneficial. Sometimes, Islaen mused, she felt very much alone as she struggled to adjust to marriage and being away from her home and her large family. Neither would it hurt to have some advice, she thought wryly. In her position, mistakes were costly. Storm had had ten years with the MacLagans, and Islaen grew more and more eager to discuss that, to ask questions.

Soon after the food began to disappear, musicians began to play. Islaen mused that Colin had managed quite an impressive feast despite the short notice he had received of their arrival. She wondered if the man had started planning it when he had been sent word of his son's marriage. It was something he was obviously delighted about, if somewhat cautiously.

Islaen decided that Colin's wariness was not directed at her.

Colin evidently knew of his son's fears and problems. She wondered just how much Colin had done to try to change his son's opinions and attitudes. A faint smile touched her face as she envisioned the two strong, stubborn men in such a confrontation. Having seen many such confrontations amongst her brothers and father she had a very good idea of what it would have been like.

When the dancing began, Islaen found herself much in demand. It was a long while before she was able to retreat to a modestly quiet corner to catch her breath. As she finished a long refreshing draught of ale, she looked up to find Storm taking a seat upon the bench next to her.

"Do not look so wary, Islaen," Storm said gently and smiled. "Might I call ye Islaen?"

"Oh, aye. T'would be most confusing if we called each other m'lady all the day long."

Storm laughed softly and said teasingly, "We shall save it for when we are annoyed with each other."

"Do ye think there will come such a time?"

"But of course. I have a fierce temper and I would wager that ye do as well."

"Aye, I fear 'tis so."

"And it passes quickly."

"Aye, fairly so. I dinnae hold fast to it and pout."

"Good, then we shall go along fine. Tempers are a common thing here. They ne'er last and spite is rare. Iain has the calmest nature of all the MacLagan men, though Sholto is the more jolly. We all expect to be able to show our tempers, let free with them and not have to pay for days because we have done so."

"'Tis the way of it with my family." She felt a pinch of pain over the still fresh separation.

Patting her hand in a gesture of sympathy, Storm said quietly, "T'will pass. Ye must find comfort in the knowledge that ye can see them when ye wish."

"It must be verra hard for ye to see your kin."

"Not as difficult as ye may think. We have grown very good at visiting without danger or suspicion. In truth, 'tis the bandits, rogues of no country, who are the biggest threat. Phelan was very nearly murdered last year by the freebooters."

"I would think that he soon made them sorry that they had attacked him."

"Aye, most sorry, though he took a wound that kept him at Papa's all winter."

"Phelan resides here?"

"He does. Being Irish, he was wanted by few when it was time for him to begin his training. As soon as I was wed and came to abide here, Phelan joined me. Colin took him in hand and has oft expressed his pleasure in having done so." Storm smiled when she caught the way Islaen watched her husband. "Alex is right. Ye do love Iain."

"Alexander talks too much," Islaen grumbled as she blushed but she made no effort to deny Storm's assumption.

"At times, aye, but he spoke out this time for he recognized our need to know how matters stood."

"And Iain would say naught."

"Quite. Ye have a hard battle afore ye. I do not envy you it. Alex said ye knew all about Iain?"

"Weel, not all. I ken that he is afraid of childbirth."

"Aye, he is that."

"Why doesnae it help that he can see how weel ye do?"

"I truly do not know. Of course, it was very bad with Catalina. He was beset with guilt. I think you can cure him though, Islaen. Ye do not fear, do ye."

"Nay. All the women in my family are wee lasses but they have braw bairns and little trouble in the birthing of them."

For one brief moment Islaen was tempted to confide in Storm about what Iain had made her promise, and how she worked to deceive him. She resisted the temptation, however.

Storm was offering friendship but Islaen felt it far too early to test that with such a secret.

"He also fears leaving you a widow."

Startled out of her thoughts by that quiet statement, Islaen stared at Storm. "What?"

"MacLennon."

"Ah, aye."

"The man haunts Iain and none can seem to find him so that the threat may be ended for all time. So many eyes seek the murderer out that I oft think he must turn to mist, gathering into the form of a man whene'er a chance to strike at Iain arises."

"I cannae believe Iain fears him. Weel, no more than any mon fears a knife at his back."

"'Tis not really MacLennon nor death Iain has fear of but of causing ye grief. He is a man with death ever at his heels. Iain thinks t'would be cruel to woo ye and win ye when MacLennon could strike at any time and succeed. Death is not often so clear to see, so near at hand. He sees it as unfair to bind your heart to him when he knows of this threat."

It was so logical Islaen could see the truth of it. She could also see the stupidity of it. The more she thought on it the angrier she got. She also felt the fury of helplessness. MacLennon could be haunting Iain for a long time. Unless Iain saw the man die he would always use that specter to hold her away from him.

"Sometimes I think that mon is half mad or a fool," she muttered and Storm laughed softly.

"Ah, well, mayhaps. His intentions are good."

When Islaen succinctly said what Iain could do with his good intentions Storm laughed heartily. The woman was still laughing when Tavis collected her for a dance. Islaen sighed as she watched the couple leave her. There had been a look in Tavis's eyes when he had gazed at his wife that Islaen feared she would never stir in Iain's gaze.

Thinking again on what Storm had said about that threat of
MacLennon, Islaen sighed with some exasperation. She
began to wonder why she bothered. The wise thing to do
might be to just go about the business of life and let her
much-muddled husband sort himself out. If Storm was right
there was a battle it was nearly impossible to fight. Only
MacLennon's death would end Iain's reticence and Islaen
knew she could not manage that on her own.

Inwardly, she grimaced. She knew she would not stop
trying to reach Iain's heavily armoured heart. Common sense
had very little to do with the matter. She loved and she ached
to have that feeling returned. The love she felt for Iain constantly fought to be set free, to fully express itself and find
some reward, some welcome. At times she had to bite her
tongue to hold the words back. She badly wanted to know the
full glory of love, one shared and returned.

Her frustration turned upon Duncan MacLennon. The man
had no real right to a vengeance. Iain had done no wrong. If
the man felt a need to blame someone for the loss of his love
he should look to Catalina's family. They had been the ones
who had taken her from him and forced her to wed another.
Iain had but agreed to an arrangement between the families.
From what she had heard and could easily guess, Iain had
treated the bitter woman far better than any other man might.

She sighed again. All that made wonderful sense, but even
if she ever had a chance to speak to MacLennon, the man
would never heed it. His grief had turned him mad. Islaen
suspected that he sought his own death as avidly as he sought
Iain's. She could understand the man's madness, but she
knew that would not help her find any forgiveness if he succeeded in murdering Iain. It could well be herself that next
became some wild-eyed assassin for she knew her grief
would run far deeper than she could ever anticipate or want
to. Although it upset her to think it, she knew she would
crave the man's death.

The irony of it all made her laugh bitterly. Iain sought to protect her from grief, yet that had been a lost cause almost from the moment she had seen him. Telling him was no good. She was sure he would then do whatever he could to kill the feelings he stirred in her. The way his mind worked she could almost guarantee it. To him it would probably seem the kindest thing to do. He would see the grief he caused her now as necessary to save her from a greater one later.

When he approached her she glared at him. She wanted to call him a fool, tell him of the pain he caused her now as he held himself away from her. It would gain her nothing, she was sure of it, but she thought it might make her feel better if only for a little while. She had swallowed so many words now, her belly ached from it.

"Someone has angered you?" Iain asked cautiously, noticing the glitter in her lovely eyes.

It was a supreme effort not to tell him just who but she mumbled, "My head throbs. It makes my mood sour."

He smoothed his hand over her forehead. "Ye have had a long day. Mayhaps we should seek our bed."

"How can ye do that?" she thought with an inner sad sigh, as she stared up at him. "How can ye stroke me with one hand, yet push me away with the other?" but only said, "Aye, t'would be best, if ye dinnae mind."

"Nay, 'tis late and I feel weary myself. I will no doubt soon join ye."

Nodding she quietly retreated to her bedchamber, leaving Iain to make her excuses. It had been a long exacting journey from the court to Caraidland and she was weary. The two had little to do with each other but she did not feel guilty about letting Iain tell that lie. It was better than telling the truth. She did not think it would endear her to her new kin by marriage if she told them she was retreating to her chambers before she gave into the strong urge to throttle Iain.

"Wheesht, didnae it go well, lass?" Meg asked as Islaen entered her chambers.

"If ye had joined the festivities ye could have seen for yourself," Islaen answered crossly as she ungracefully flung herself upon the bed.

"T'wasnae my place."

Islaen made a very rude noise and ignored Meg's scolding look. With little cooperation she let Meg undress her. She knew she was being awkward, even sulking, but she made no effort to shake free of her mood. A little petulantly, she told herself that she had earned a good sulk.

"Och, lass, it maun have been verra bad for ye. 'Tis a rare mood ye are in," Meg muttered as she started to brush Islaen's hair.

"Meg, can ye hate a person e'en as ye love him?" Islaen asked quietly as she sat still beneath Meg's ministrations.

"Of course ye can. I love ye, lass, and weel ye ken it, but there have been times when I was muckle pleased to strike ye. I ken little of the ways of men and women but I suspicion 'tis much the same. Loving a mon doesnae mean ye like all he does or says."

"Nay, that would most like be impossible. Love just means that the bad things willnae drive ye away, willnae make ye leave."

"What has the lad done now? 'Tis no wench, is it? Wheesht, I had thought we had left that trouble behind us when we left that brothel called court."

"Nay, 'tis not a wench. I would be little surprised an one is about, one that might cause me a worry, but she hasnae shown herself yet. I am hopeful that whatever wenches there may have been have turned their eyes elsewhere whilst Iain was at court and that they arenae the sort to ignore the boundaries of a lawful marriage. I am most weary of that sort of trouble."

"Then what ails ye?"

"Oh, 'tis Iain. Ye are right in thinking that."

"Ye cannot expect a locked heart to spring open with but one smile, lass."

"I ken it. Such a thing takes work. I have come across another problem or so I think. Iain has not spoken of it to me, 'tis Storm who spoke of it, so mayhaps it doesnae exist. It seems Iain feels it would be cruel to try and win my heart."

"Cruel? How so? Though I have little trust in men, I cannae feel he would abuse such a gift, not purposely."

"Nay, he wouldnae, not e'en an he didnae return the love offered. He has too kind a heart, e'en an he does keep it well secured. In truth, what Storm said confirms that. She said he will ne'er woo me nor try to win my heart as long as death stalks him."

"That madmon MacLennon."

"Aye, him."

"Death stalks us all, lass. A mon usually kens that weel. I dinnae understand this."

"Neither do I. I would think 'tis because he cannae fight this, not weel. The mon is as hard to catch as smoke. He lurks in the shadows, e'er at the ready to strike without warning. 'Tis different than the normal way of things."

"How can ye fight such a thing?"

"I cannae, can I, and therein lies the reason for my anger with the mon. He seeks to save me from grief. I cannae tell him 'tis too late for he would most like try all the harder to push me away, denying me e'en the little I can pull from him now. That I could not bear."

Meg had little comfort or advice to offer, and was wise enough to know that she could do no more than be there in case she was needed.

When Iain entered their chambers Islaen only briefly thought of pretending to be asleep. She would not play his game, pulling into herself, turning cold and withdrawn. Islaen suspected she could not do so even if she really wanted to. It was against her nature. Simply not speaking of the love she had for him was as much as she could manage. Words she could swallow, even though they sometimes choked her, but all the other signs of her love she could not restrain. They came easily, without thought and denying any control.

When he pulled her close, his hands lightly stroking her she placed her hand over his heart and felt its quickening beat. It beat with the thrill of desire but she wanted it to beat with love. She wished she could reach beneath his taut skin and tear away the wall there. As the strength of her desire disrupted her thoughts she prayed that someday Iain would give as freely of his love as he did his passion.

Chapter Twelve

A little out of breath, Islaen struggled to keep up with a preoccupied Iain's long strides. She had thought that journeying with him to survey the estate her dowry had brought would be a good chance to be alone, would provide them with needed time together. Instead, she had tramped or, more exactly, trotted over the tower house and now the land, hurrying along after a man who only occasionally tossed a remark her way concerning something that needed repair. While she had as great an interest in their future home as he seemed to have she was starting to wish she had stayed home. Her feet certainly wished she had.

Iain frowned and stopped to stare at a crofter's hut. They too could use some work. His father had always stressed the need to see that the crofters were well housed and content. If nothing else, it gave the people something they would fight to keep, enhanced their loyalty. When a laird took good care of even the lowest of his people, they fought to keep him as their laird.

Turning to tell Islaen this wisdom, he frowned even more. She was leaning against a tree, one hand upon her breast and breathing heavily. Although she looked delightfully disheveled and flushed, he felt a twinge of concern.

"If ye were feeling poorly mayhaps ye should have stayed behind," he said as he moved nearer to her.

Islaen wondered if she had the strength left to bloody his nose. "I am not feeling poorly."

"Are ye certain? Ye feel most warm," he murmured as he felt her forehead.

"Running oft heats up a body."

"Come now, I havenae made ye run."

"Iain," she said with a strong hint of exasperation as she sat down and tugged off her boot, "for each step ye take I must take at least two." She stared at her foot, amazed that it was not coated heel to toe with blisters.

Biting back a smile, he knelt before her, his gaze fixed greedily upon the slim leg her raised skirts revealed. "I will remember to walk more slowly, sweeting. We wouldnae want ye to wear these lovely limbs down to the bone."

"Iain," she squeaked in protest when he began to slide his hand up her leg. "We are out in the open," she gasped in shock, leaping to her feet, her back against the tree.

When he only grinned and reached for her, she took a hasty step to the side. Their playing was brought to an abrupt halt by the soft, deadly hiss of an approaching arrow. There was the sound of tearing cloth as the arrow cut through the sleeve of her gown, scoring the soft skin of her upper arm before it buried itself in the tree.

"Iain," she rasped as she realized that, had the arrow arrived an instant earlier, it would have pinned her to the tree.

Cursing viciously, Iain grasped her by the ankles and roughly tumbled her to the ground even as a second arrow was sent at them. It sliced harmlessly through the space Islaen had occupied but a second before. Islaen said nothing as she was hurriedly and roughly yanked along, held close to the ground and Iain until they were sheltered behind two large trees growing close together.

"Ye cannae hide from justice forever, MacLagan."

"Murdering this innocent lass isnae justice, MacLennon."

"Aye, 'tis. I will take from ye as ye took from me."

"Come out from hiding, MacLennon; face me mon to mon and let us have done with this."

"Nay, a woman-killer deserves no such honour as a fair fight."

Islaen pressed closer to Iain, trying in vain to soothe the sting of what Duncan MacLennon called him. She knew nothing she could do would shield Iain from MacLennon's accusations, for Iain believed them. He would probably take little notice of the fact that she did not believe him guilty of the crime MacLennon sought to execute him for.

She shivered when an arrow slammed into the trees they huddled behind. The man had them at his mercy and his chilling laughter told them that he knew it. Just as she wondered why no one came to their aid, wondered if no one had had the wisdom to keep a close watch upon Iain, the sound of hoofbeats reached her ears. She was almost able to smile when she heard Phelan's wild cry but her jubilation was dimmed by the sounds of hoofbeats rapidly retreating. MacLennon was yet again escaping. Islaen wanted to scream her frustration and could only guess at what Iain must feel.

Iain leapt to his feet. After one burning but thorough look at Islaen, he left her. Just as Phelan, Tavis and Iain's squire, Murdo, reined in, Iain reached them. He dragged his brother from his horse and hurled himself into the saddle.

"Watch my wife," he snarled as he spurred the horse into a gallop.

Islaen watched warily as Tavis stood up and brushed himself off. As he neared her she saw anger glittering in his eyes, but she had the feeling that none of it was directed at Iain's abrupt handling. His gaze settled upon her arm and he hurriedly knelt at her side. It was only then that Islaen was aware of the sharp burning there and looked to see that she was bleeding.

"'Tis but a flesh wound," she murmured as Tavis took the small water bag from his belt and dampened a handkerchief.

Glancing over her before concentrating on washing her wound, he asked, "Are ye sure?"

Gritting her teeth against the sting as he washed her cut, Islaen looked at herself, noticed the sad state of her gown and almost smiled. "Most of this damage was done when Iain dragged me to safety. His concern was for speed not gentleness. I willnae be surprised an I find a few bruises in the morn but naught else is wrong."

"This was verra close, verra close," Tavis muttered, then flashed her a brief smile before helping himself to a piece of her petticoat to use as a bandage. "I hadnae realized that he now stalks ye as weel."

"He has taunted Iain with the promise of killing me but he has yet to attack me unless I am with Iain." She frowned slightly. "'Tis true that he shot at me first though Iain was a clear target but methinks 'tis really only to taunt Iain. He wants Iain to see me murdered is what he says." She decided there was no need to mention the threat of rape. "I began to fear that Iain wasnae watched and t'would be too late ere anyone came to aid us."

"Iain has been closely watched since the first attack though I think he doesnae oft notice."

As she thought about that her eyes widened. It only took a short search of her memory to see the truth of Tavis's claim. Although never intrusive there had always been an armed man near Iain. The moment he was not in the company of others he was shadowed by Murdo or one of his men-at-arms. She had thought it by Iain's orders but now suspected otherwise. MacLennon had reached Iain at court, but only by coming in through a window so high up and treacherous it had been thought inaccessible. To a sane man it would have been so.

"Look out your window or chamber door some time in the middle of the night and ye will find well-armed mon."

"They are muckle quiet about it."

"Aye. We wish no complaint from Iain. After this day, ye too will acquire an extra shadow."

"T'would be nice if they catch that madman so that there would be no need." Her voice held little hope of that and she found none at all in Tavis's solemn expression.

Iain studied the tracks at the edge of the gorge for the fifth time but there was no denying the message they relayed. "He leapt the gorge," he muttered, amazement tinting his voice.

Phelan shook his head. "The man is quite mad. Do ye think he made it?"

"The only way to be sure is to go and look upon the other side."

"Aye and by the time we ride around to that side it will matter little for he will be an hour gone."

"Ye could always try the jump yourself."

"I may lack some sense at times, my friend, but I am ne'er that great a fool."

"He had a dead mon's courage," grumbled Murdo.

"Aye." Iain shook his head. "He cares naught for life so laughs in death's face as no sane mon would."

"An' he did not clear the gorge then he died in the waters below."

"'T'would be cause for celebration if that is what happened, Phelan."

"I will take the ride round to gain the answer. T'would be best if we can know one way or t'other. Best ye get back to your wife, Iain." Phelan grinned faintly. "I should think she would prefer you to nurse her hurts."

After watching Phelan ride off, Iain took one last look at the gorge and shivered faintly. How did one deal with a man

mad enough to try such a jump? If he made it to the other side
he did so upon the wings of luck alone. There would be no
reasoning with a man who so clearly lacked all reason and
fear. This could only end when one of them died.

When he reached Tavis and Islaen, Iain sighed. He could
read the hope upon their faces. So too could he see that Islaen
did not like to hope for a man's death and cursed MacLennon
for causing her that turmoil.

"He leapt the gorge," Iain reported flatly. "Phelan goes now
to see an he made it across or fell into the waters below."

Tavis said nothing, simply shook his head. When Iain
moved to dismount, Tavis shook his head again, silently
urging Iain to stay where he was. After helping Islaen to
mount in front of Iain, Tavis swung himself up behind Murdo.

Once back at their future home, Islaen and Iain mounted
their own horses. Little was said as they headed back to
Caraidland. Islaen was a little hurt by the way Iain ignored
her. He had not even inquired about her wound, slight though
it was. She understood what had put him into such a dark
silent mood but it still pinched at her heart.

It also frightened her. She could almost hear the gates to
his heart locking tighter than ever before. This attack would
add weight to his beliefs.

Meg hurried her off to her chambers when they arrived at
Caraidland. Partly she wished to join the others in the hall to
hear all that was said or planned concerning MacLennon, but
she was also more than willing to seek her bed and be cod-
dled by a fretting Meg.

"'Tis but a scratch, lass," Meg said as she tucked her in.
"I dinnae think t'will e'en scar ye."

"Ah, weel, if 'tis but a wee scar my freckles will hide it,"
Islaen jested weakly.

"I dinnae understand why he seeks your death. Ye have
done naught to the madmon. Ye didnae e'en ken that lass."

"I am wed to Iain. 'Tis enough of a crime in that mon's

eyes. In truth, I am but something by which he can further hurt Iain. I hope he died in that gorge, may God forgive me." She snuggled down beneath the covers. "Either that or those who now talk of him come up with a way to end his murderous attacks."

Iain finished off his wine and refilled his tankard. He knew getting drunk was no solution but he needed to wash away the bitter taste of frustration. When Phelan entered the hall he tensed, only to curse viciously when the young man shook his head. He had not realized how badly he had wished to hear that the man had died at the bottom of the gorge. It would have denied him the pleasure of killing him, but it would also have put an end to the whole problem.

"I stared at the tracks for near to half an hour but there was no denying their message," Phelan said wearily as he sat down and accepted a tankard of wine from Storm. "He made the jump."

"Ye should have told us that he sought to kill the lass too."

"Aye, I should have, Fither, but I didnae really believe it. I thought it but a taunt he used to make me act foolishly that night he attacked us. Aye, he cut her, but only when she sought to get my sword to me."

"This time t'was no mere taunt."

"Nay. Had she not suddenly moved he would have pinned her to the tree. The second arrow was also aimed at her but I pulled her out of the way. Both times I was a target it took no skill to hit. She is my wife and that is enough to draw his hate. He wants me to watch her die. He feels that will be fair payment for Catalina."

"And then you."

"Aye, and then me." After a moment's thought Iain decided to be completely honest. "He has also mentioned taking her before my eyes, preferably as I lay dying. That too would be to pay for Catalina, for bedding her."

"There can be no softness towards the mon now," Tavis said coldly.

"Nay. I have none. He cut all understanding from my heart when he cut Islaen that night, e'en though I had not yet come to see that he wanted her dead too. There is no reason for him to strike at her."

"There is no reason for him to strike at ye either," Storm snapped. "Ye take upon yourself a guilt that was ne'er yours."

Iain smiled wearily. "We shall ne'er agree upon that. What matters here is that MacLennon blames me, seeks to kill me out of revenge for Catalina's death and, most important, now includes Islaen in that vengence."

"She will be watched," Tavis stated firmly.

"As I have been?"

"I wasnae certain ye noticed."

"I nay stumble o'er them all the time but 'tis hard not to see a constant shadow," Iain drawled, then sighed, running a hand through his hair. "I best send word to her kin. They would cut the mon down e'en now ere they caught sight of him simply because he drew her blood, but 'tis important they know that he seeks her death. There will be e'en more eyes searching the shadows for the mon. It cannae hurt, though t'will no doubt anger her kin that I have brought such a danger upon her."

"Did ye not say anything to them that night at court?"

"Aye, Storm, I did but then there was a reason for him to strike, as I have said."

"I will go to them, Iain," Phelan offered. "Ere the sun rises tomorrow, I will set out."

"Go warily, Phelan. The English have raided there and may yet be causing trouble. Ye dinnae wish to find yourself in the midst of that sort of difficulty."

"Nay, although," he smiled faintly, "there are one or two English I should not grieve to cross swords with. But, aye, I will watch. Best ye give me something to identify me without any doubt. I am not a Scot, do not sound one, and, if trouble is still brewing, it could be costly for me."

"We will send one of the men with ye as weel," Tavis said. "Take who ye please, if we have any that can keep pace with ye, that is. And best an he speaks first. As ye said, ye are no Scot."

"Ye are certain Islaen was not badly hurt?" Storm asked. "Mayhaps I should go and see her."

"Nay, that old corbie, Meg, is with her. Islaen wasnae badly hurt."

"Not that ye would have noticed, brother," murmured Tavis.

"I noticed."

"Went black-faced and silent, did he?"

"Aye, Storm. Sat glowering and sulking upon his horse with nary a word to the lass. Tossed me at her to chase after MacLennon, e'en though she sat there awash in her own blood."

"She wasnae awash in blood. 'T'was naught but a flesh wound."

At that moment, Alexander arrived. "How is Islaen?"

"Fine," snapped Iain, irritated even more by Alexander's interest.

"Where have ye been all day, Alex?"

"Just visiting a few friends, Storm."

"Ye have some, do ye?" Iain muttered.

Alexander grinned and strolled over to the table to help himself to some wine. "Mayhaps I should visit with the lass."

"Meg most like has her abed."

"All the better."

"Alex, behave yourself," Storm ordered, biting back a smile.

"For ye, Storm, anything." He then grew serious. "Ye are certain the lass is all right?"

"Aye and it seems to me ye are muckle concerned about anither mon's wife," Iain growled. "My wife."

"Tsk, such a black mood. I fear I have news that willnae lighten it."

"What news?" Iain demanded impatiently when Alexander did not elaborate, simply sat down. "Where have ye been?"

"That matters not."

"With a lass," Storm said firmly.

Ignoring that, Alexander continued, "Lord Fraser didnae die from the beating ye gave him, my friend."

"Ye are right. 'Tis not good news."

"It seems he is, howsomever, scarred and crippled."

"Crippled?" Iain struggled to remember what he had done to Fraser but could only recall his intense murderous rage.

"Aye. Ye busted his leg when ye threw him up against the wall."

"But he stood up."

"Fear most like gave him the strength. He was trying to run, broken leg and all. It didnae break clean."

"So he will have a limp."

"Aye, Storm, there is little doubt of it. His kin see it as a just payment."

"So there willnae be a lawing done." Colin's voice held a note of relief.

"Nay, there willnae be a feud, but Lord Fraser cries out for vengeance and none can silence him."

Iain indulged in a long, colorful bout of cursing, ending with a muttered apology to a wide-eyed Storm. "Anither knife aimed at my back. Lord Fraser willnae face me square. He has e'er been a coward."

"Aye, ye have the measure of him. Best ye have the full measure."

"What do ye mean?"

"'Tis not just ye he claims must pay." His gaze never leaving Iain's face Alexander reported flatly, "He claims Islaen is to blame too. He says she lured him, taunted him and tempted him, then cried rape when ye caught her at her games." Alexander barely saved his tankard of wine when, with one swift sweep of his arm, Iain cleared a wide arc of the table off. "He cries her a whore and claims ye tried to kill him to keep him from telling the truth about her," Alexander continued doggedly, viewing Iain's rage with interest. "He is talking loud and long for the tale has e'en reached here."

"No one will believe it," Iain rasped.

"None that ken her, nay," Alexander said quietly.

"But not that many do," Iain ground out.

"Nay. I am sorry, my friend. I should not have stopped ye from killing the mon. It hasnae stopped the talk."

"He has cut his own throat."

"Ye can do naught until he is up and about. Nay, not until he strikes at ye."

"Why not?"

"Ye cannae kill a mon in his bed. That would bring about a feud and the death of many. Neither can ye strike at a cripple. I fear ye have your hands tied and cannae loosen them until he strikes at ye."

"Or Islaen."

"Aye, or Islaen. The least ye would bring upon yourself is the whisper of cowardice, the worst is outlawry. Only if ye cut him down in the act of fighting for your life or Islaen's can ye come away clean."

"Shall I tell the MacRoths this news too?" Phelan asked quietly.

"Aye, tell them. I will seek my bed now," Iain said as he abruptly stood up. "There seems little else I can do."

Iain wondered blackly what Islaen had done to deserve being burdened with a husband who seemed doomed to bring about her destruction. She had been safe and content with her family. Now she had two men eager to see her pay for crimes she had not committed. Worse, she had a husband who was unable to really protect her, could only wait for the enemy to strike and pray that she was not killed before he could end the threat to her life.

Finding her asleep, he undressed quietly, then carefully eased into bed. Despite his better intentions, he reached for her. She murmured his name and cuddled up to him. He fought to clear his mind of worries and prayed that all the wine he had drunk would help him sleep. A bitter laugh echoed in his mind when he realized how much holding her close helped him in that aim.

Islaen woke with a start, then cursed herself for being a foolish child. A nightmare had frightened her awake, one she clearly recognized as having been inspired by the day's events. Letting that fear rob her of needed sleep was the worst thing she could do, she thought crossly. It would insure that she was not alert enough to protect herself if she had to. She would not let that madman defeat her in that way, especially not when he only meant to use her to deepen the hurt he dealt Iain.

Slipping out from beneath the arm Iain had draped over her waist, she moved towards the window. Below she spotted the guard, alert yet strangely unobtrusive. She did not bother to peer outside of the chamber door. Tavis had said there would be one there too and she did not doubt it.

"He has made us prisoners in our own home, upon our own lands," she thought with a touch of bitterness. "We cannae e'en feel safe within our own chambers. I begin to think ye a sorcerer, Duncan MacLennon. If ye would but turn that skill and hatred against the English, Scotland would ne'er have to fash herself about that country again."

"Islaen."

She turned quickly, hearing a note of fear in that husky call. "Here, Iain. By the window."

"Best ye get back into bed ere ye catch a chill and take ill."

Biting back a smile, she dutifully returned to bed. Despite her confusion and doubts about how he felt for her she was confident that he held an honest concern for her safety. She had heard that hint of fear in his voice and knew men well enough to know that his grumpiness now was because he feared she had. She had been in no danger and he now felt foolish about worrying.

"God's teeth, woman, your feet are like ice," he growled as he pulled her close. "Did ye have a need for fresh air?" he muttered.

"Weel, Iain, I have been meaning to speak to ye about your feet," she began, grinning against his chest, then squeaking with outrage when he gave her hair a gentle punitive yank.

"Pert wench." He grew serious. "How fares your wound?"

"'Tis naught, Iain. Aye, it pinches, but 'tis so shallow t'will soon heal."

"I should have asked ere now."

"Ye had other matters upon your mind."

"Aye—murder. The sight of your blood made me hunger for his. I raced away thinking only of how eager I was to kill him."

"Ye could see that I wasnae hurt badly. There really was little reason for ye to stay."

"Ye had been badly frightened. 'Tis reason enough. I should have stayed to see that your fright was eased, your wound tended."

"Tavis managed both verra weel. Iain, t'was more important that ye try to catch that mon. Aye, I was frightened and I did wish ye near but those are wee things, easily soothed later. 'Tis far more important that that madman be stopped. Aye, and e'en then I understood weel your need to be the one that stopped him. I too want him stopped though it troubles me to want a mon's death."

Before resting his head against her breasts, he gave each one a kiss, then nuzzled against them and yawned. "Dinnae fash yourself o'er it, dearling," he murmured sleepily. "He gives us no choice."

Chapter Thirteen

Islaen stumbled to the washbowl, splashed cold water on her face and rinsed out her mouth. The door opened and, for an instant, she felt panicked, then saw that it was Meg. She smiled weakly as the woman hurried over to her.

"Ye have been ill." Meg felt Islaen's forehead for signs of fever.

"Aye, for the sixth morn. I am a wee bit slow this morn or ye wouldnae have discovered it."

"Why do ye wish to hide it, ye foolish lass? I maun look ye o'er and think of how to physic ye."

"Ye cannae physic this, Meg. Come, think. What makes a woman empty her belly every morn?"

"Ye are with child," Meg gasped and hurried over to the bed to place a cool cloth upon Islaen's forehead. "Are ye certain?"

"My woman's time hasnae come since a fortnight after I was wed."

"Och, aye, there is a sure sign. Ye were e'er verra regular. And now this sickness of a morn."

"Aye, for near to a week. For a week afore that I felt it but didnae empty my belly. 'Tis a pity that has changed."

"Weel, it doesnae last long. Does the lad ken?"

"Nay, and I mean to keep him from kenning for as long as I can."

Meg nodded. "The months can move by verra slowly for one who is afraid of it all. 'Tis a pity ye cannae share this."

"That is my penance for the lies I have told," she said quietly as she carefully stood up.

"God wouldnae expect a penance. Ye are doing as He commands. 'Tis proper that ye choose His will o'er that of your husband's."

"Only this once, Meg. I swore to obey my husband and to honour him."

"Ye will honour him by giving the young gowk a bairn. A lass can do a mon no greater honour."

"Mayhaps. Help me dress. I need to eat something."

"Are ye certain?"

"Aye, 'tis the only way to end this illness." Although she had to eat it carefully food did settle Islaen's stomach. She then wandered through Storm's garden somewhat aimlessly. Iain was gone, as he often was, claiming a need to be at Muircraig, their future home. There was little for her to do. Storm only occasionally needed help in keeping Caraidland running smoothly.

"Such a dark look on such a lovely late summer's morn."

Startled from her thoughts, Islaen managed a smile for Storm. She found herself growing closer to the woman. Islaen just wished she could feel sure enough about the friendship to confide in the woman. They had talked about a lot of private things but there were still a few things Islaen kept secret.

"I was but feeling too idle."

"Then come with me." Storm linked her arm with Islaen's. "'Tis my time to romp with my children."

"Are ye certain ye wish me to intrude?"

"Most certain. There are five of the little dears and only

one of me. Extra hands are ever welcome. Tavis sometimes comes, whene'er he is about, but he is off with Iain."

"Aye. At Muircraig."

Storm laughed softly upon hearing the crossness in Islaen's voice. "He readies your home."

"I ken it. I also ken that he hides."

"Sadly that is undoubtedly true. Still, he cannot seem to stay away too long."

"Nay," Islaen grumbled, "every few days he feels a need to come to me for a good rutting."

"Islaen," Storm gasped, torn between laughter and worry. "Is it truly that bad?"

"Weel, mayhaps not. I am but too sensitive, mayhaps. It does seem, though, that he stays no longer than is necessary to sate his body's hungers. The last time he didnae e'en arrive in time to dine with me and he always leaves ere I waken in the morn."

Wincing slightly, Storm murmured, "It does sound a bit, well, cold."

"Aye. I begin to feel like a whore."

"Ye must not think so, Islaen. I know he would ne'er want ye to think that. Instead, take hope in the fact that he cannot keep away from you. Aye, it seems as if 'tis but a lusting, but he does not really need you to sate that. I am certain there is a wench or two about Muircraig that would gladly become the leman of the new laird, yet he rides for hours to seek your bed."

"I do think it. 'Tis all that of times keeps me from striking him." She smiled crookedly when Storm laughed. "'Tis just that he gives me no chance to win him, to woo him. I had hoped that, once away from court, we would have time together, time for me to weaken his efforts at keeping us strangers. I feel sure that, an I can make a break in that cursed wall he built around his heart, t'will crumble. I cannae do it when he stays out of reach. That keeps us strangers."

"It makes it harder, aye, but do not ignore the importance of that time in the night."

"Och, I dinnae. 'Tis just that I grow a wee bit weary of only seeing him soften in the night. Weel, at least this way I need-nae face that stranger each dawning. 'Tis a blessing of a sort. That did grow muckle tiring."

Their talk was abruptly ended when they entered the nursery. Although the twins, Aingeal and Taran, were nine and beginning their training, they too were there. With so much to do, their time together with their mother was considered more important than any training, for it was too rare. Islaen recalled her mother doing the same and then her father until they were all of an age to dine together.

She smiled as the youngest, two-year-old Blythe, toddled her way. Soon they were all involved in a game. It went slowly for each child had a great deal he or she wished to tell Storm, but none complained. The game was merely used to keep them seated in a companionable circle as the children took greedy advantage of having their mother's undivided attention. As she watched the group, helping to keep Blythe from chewing on the game pieces, Islaen felt that Iain would not, indeed could not, fault her for refusing to let him deny them a family.

Iain frowned as he entered the hall. Having not found Islaen in their chambers, he had paused only long enough to wash up before seeking her in the hall. She was not there either and he was not sure about where else to look.

"Looking for Islaen?"

"Aye, Tavis. Have ye seen her?"

"I was told she was with Storm. Since that is where I am bound right now, ye may as weel come along."

"With the bairns?" Iain asked as they strode along and he recognized where they were heading.

"Aye, 'tis their time with Storm. Can ye no hear them?" Tavis asked, grinning as the sounds of rowdy children grew louder. "Here now," Tavis growled with mock sternness as he paused in the doorway, then waded into the tangle of laughing children and women. "Here is a muckle great noise."

Iain watched his laughing wife sit up, a giggling Blythe clinging to her. Islaen was flushed and disheveled but looked happy and content. It was obvious to anyone who cared to look that she thoroughly enjoyed being with the children. It was also obvious that the children had accepted her quickly and completely.

He felt swamped with guilt. Because of the fears he could not conquer, he was denying her all of that. However, each time he held Islaen close, his fear grew stronger. Even the guilt he felt now did not really ease that fear.

As she approached him, trying vainly to tidy her appearance, Islaen wondered about the look upon Iain's face. His expression was remote but his eyes were clouded with troubled thoughts.

"Ye have returned early this time," she said quietly, smiling her welcome. "Is there any trouble?"

"Nay." He absently tidied her hair. "I but need extra time here to gather supplies. Where is Alex?"

"He left for home early this morn. He said he had been too long away from his daughter."

"Weel, I shallnae miss his unasked advice."

"Why did ye not tell me about Lord Fraser?"

Iain's step faltered slightly and he eyed her warily. He could easily see her annoyance and understood it even as he cursed Alexander for having too busy a mouth. Iain was not really sure why he had said nothing to her. He did not want to hurt her by repeating the man's loathsome insults but that was not really reason enough to keep her ignorant about a danger that lurked around her.

"I am nay too sure why. He spoke most unkindly about ye," he said quietly as they entered the nearly deserted hall.

"Aye. I ken it. He calls me a whore, a temptress, mind ye. Wheesht, what a fool. Me, a temptress." She shook her head.

Smiling with a soft lechery as he sat her at the table and poured them each some wine, Iain murmured, "Ye surely tempt me, sweeting. Can ye fetch us some bread and cheese, David?" he asked a young page as he sat down.

"That is most convenient since we are wed," she retorted softly, even though she blushed over his words.

"Aye, true enough." He grew serious. "As I said, I am nay sure why I didnae tell ye. I have e'er thought 'tis best to ken a threat e'en if the kenning brings some pain. Ye need to ken a threat if ye are to protect yourself from it."

"Do ye really think he will do it? Mayhaps he but boasts and rattles an empty scabbard."

"He is a mon to do that, but we cannae just assume that he will this time."

She reached across the table and patted his hand. "We are troubled by a madman and a fool. They see wrongs where there were none and wish to blame someone for what wasnae their fault. Ye didnae hurl Fraser on top of me and I didnae lure the fool on. Ye must cease to blame yourself for what isnae your doing and what ye have no control o'er. I put no blame upon ye."

He took her hand in his and kissed her palm, smiling faintly when she trembled. "Ye are of a verra forgiving nature."

She smiled and shook her head in silent denial. "What do we do about Fraser?"

"Naught, curse the fool's eyes," growled a voice from the doorway.

Islaen gasped when she saw her brother Robert standing beside Phelan. Giving a soft cry of delight, she raced over to him and was caught up in his arms. She flung her arms around his neck and kissed his cheek, then giggled as he strode over to the table still holding her, then set her down back in her seat.

For a while she was allowed to dominate Robert, plaguing him with questions. As she did so, the page, David, arrived with Iain's bread and cheese. The boy then hastily left to get some more as well as some more wine.

"Now, lass, if ye are satisfied that we have all managed to survive without ye," Robert drawled, winking at Islaen, "I would be pleased to pass a word or twa with your husband."

"Weel, I will leave ye to it," she said as she stood up, "and see that ye have a place to bed down for the night."

"I will be here for more than a night, lass. Fither says I am to set here until I can tell him that both Fraser and Mac-Lennon feed the worms. T'would be worth me verra life an I return afore that."

Nodding in understanding, Islaen hurried away to find Storm. She hoped that Robert's presence and his insistence upon staying would not anger Iain.

"Ye think I cannae take care of her?" Iain growled as soon as Islaen was gone.

Robert shook his head. "Nay. Doubt of your ability isnae what brings me here. 'Tis worry. When so many swords point at one who is so dear to ye, ye want to be there e'en if ye ken weel that ye arenae needed."

Iain relaxed and smiled faintly. "Anither sword on our side cannae hurt. Nay, nor anither pair of eyes watching the shadows."

"T'was sore tempting to end the threat of that fool Fraser with a dirk in the night."

Phelan laughed. "Alex was right about the roar. Phew, Iain, I ne'er saw such a display of tempers."

Grinning, Robert nodded. "We were all ready to ride straight to Fraser and cut the dog to pieces but the women blocked the door out o' the hall. Is Alex still here?"

"Nay, he left this morning."

"'Tis best. I wasnae too certain I liked that mon sniffing round my sister."

"I wasnae too certain I liked him sniffing round my wife," Iain drawled and Robert laughed.

"Come, tell me what ye are doing, though by God's toe-nails it seems we arenae allowed to do much."

Discussing the danger he and Islaen faced and what little could be done about it was the last thing Iain wanted to do. He had used the excuse of needing supplies to come to Caraidland but what he really sought was time alone with Islaen, in their chambers, naked. However, there was no way he could say that to her brother so, with an inner grimace of frustration, he entered into a rather fruitless discussion with Robert and tried very hard not to think of Islaen.

As the day wore on into the night, Iain began to wonder if he would ever get time alone with Islaen. His family soon gathered to meet this representative of Islaen's large family. As always, they wished to hear any news Robert might have that they had not heard yet. The food was good and the company enjoyable, but it was not what he needed or wanted. He found himself watching Islaen more often than he liked and grew a little angry at the way she seemed to pull him to her despite what he thought best for both of them.

"There, ye see?" Storm murmured, leaning close to Islaen. "Iain was home early this day and did not rush ye off to bed."

"He had no time. Robert arrived and wished to talk. Iain couldnae say, 'Excuse me, Robert, but I really must go and bed your sister. 'Tis why I came home.'"

"Oh Islaen."

"Look at how he stares at me and tell me that that is not what he thinks on." When Storm looked, then blushed, Islaen asked, "What troubles ye? I have seen Tavis look at ye thus. Are ye no used to it?"

"Well, Tavis does not look at me just so."

"Aye, there is the love to soften the lusting in his eyes. There is none of that in Iain's look."

Storm was not so sure of that, but decided it would probably only cause difficulty if she stated her opinion, so held her tongue. "That was not what I referred to. I know what it is," she breathed in sudden realization. "Well, well."

"Weel, weel, what?" Islaen pressed when Storm fell silent.

"Beneath the hunger lurks a touch of anger."

"Aye, that is oft there," Islaen said dismissively, and wondered if she had had enough wine as she had her goblet refilled.

"Do ye not wonder why 'tis there?"

"I assumed I had done something to annoy him."

"Aye and I think I know what it is ye do. Ye make him want you."

"That doesnae make much sense."

"I think ye have drunk too much wine to think clear. We agree that Iain wishes to keep his heart locked away?"

"Aye."

"Well, he wants you. He mayhaps wants you far more than he wishes to. So, he comes to you because he is unable to stay away but with a man's twisted logic he blames ye for that. Aye, he most like accuses ye of bewitching him."

"Because he wants a lass?"

"Not just any lass but ye, his wife, the one he tries to hold at a distance."

"Weel, if 'tis true, aye, that would annoy him. It could also just be lusting."

"An it was just lusting, he would not be so particular. Nay, nor would he find aught in it to be annoyed about."

"I ken what ye are saying, Storm, but I am thinking t'would be best an I didnae think on it. 'Tis the sort of thinking that could bring me some pain. Ye could be wrong, ye ken. He could just be feeling in a black mood but nay black enough to still the lusts that brought him home. Nay, 'tis best for me an I just wait, wait for more than a look in his eyes and a hearty tumble atween the sheets. Aye, that be the supplies he has come for."

"Islaen, ye sound a little bitter."

"Och, weel, I do get so now and again. 'Tis naught and passes quickly."

"I am glad. It may not seem as if ye have much now, and how well I know the pain of holding back all the love ye ache to give the fool who does not want it, but t'will change. I am certain of it. All I felt I had from Tavis in the beginning was his lust. Many times he hurt me because he did not want to love me. I too tasted the bitterness and anger that brings, but I ne'er stopped loving him. When I was with him, I gave him all I could save the words. That is what ye must do. Tavis had his scars too, deep bitter ones, but they healed. I am certain that Iain's will too."

"Weel, I just hope that when they do heal 'tis me he reaches for."

At the very first chance that came his way, Iain caught hold of Islaen and hurried her off to their chambers. He ached with wanting and did not really care if anyone guessed exactly why he had hurried his wife out of the hall. However, he could not fully repress a grin over the way Islaen blushed as he towed her along to their chambers.

"Iain," Islaen gasped as they entered their chambers and he sent a dozing Meg scurrying out by just one fierce glance. "Poor Meg."

"She best get accustomed to it. God's teeth, woman," he growled as he tumbled her onto the bed, "I have sat for what seems like a lifetime just thinking about ye under me, naked and aching as badly as I am."

"Ah, is that why ye have been sending me such black looks."

Even as her passion was stirred she was a little amazed at the speed with which he disrobed them. She was sure she would find a tear or two in her clothing in the morning. It was also a little surprising that such haste would arouse her. Islaen suspected that his powerful need invaded her body too.

"The black looks were because ye werenae trying too verra hard to creep away with me." He sighed with near relief when the last of their clothing was tossed aside and their flesh met. "Och, lass, this is what I needed," he murmured as he pressed his body close to hers, savoring the feel of her warm soft skin.

"Only this?" she purred as she ran her hands over his back.

"Nay, ye greedy wench," he growled just before kissing her hungrily.

As Islaen returned his kiss with a hunger that was swiftly equalling his she mused that, if passion was all Iain was going to give her, he was certainly giving her the best. She knew she had nothing to compare it with, but she was certain that no other man could make her feel as good, make her soar as high. The way he could stir her had to be unique.

She cried out softly as his lips touched her breasts. Although she would have thought it impossible, she seemed more sensitive to his touch. When he began to suckle with a gentle greed, she nearly grew frantic with the desire flowing through her. She was almost relieved when his kisses moved from there to caress her abdomen, then her thighs.

That sense of near calm, when she sought to gain some control over her passion, faded instantly when he kissed the bright curls that adorned her womanhood. She went still with shock, then tried to move away. Although she felt no qualms about caressing him so intimately, she was not sure it was a caress that was meant to be so fully returned, nor that she wanted it to be despite what her body was beginning to tell her. Her attempt to draw away was easily thwarted by Iain.

"Be still, dearling. Ye will like it as much as I do, I promise ye."

With a few strokes of his tongue he filled that promise. All resistance Islaen had felt fell away, passion smothering her modesty. She made no further attempt to elude the intimacy until she felt her desire about to crest. Even as she called his name he was over her, joining their bodies almost roughly. She clung to him with near desperation, as they sought and found passion's goal together.

Once her mind began to clear of desire's haze, Islaen no longer felt so sanguine about it. She was sorely embarrassed by the wantonness she had displayed. It was a little difficult to face him after he had caressed her so intimately. When he eased away from her, she tried to roll out of his reach but he laughed softly and pulled her close.

"Such modesty from a woman who has tasted every inch of me," he murmured and kissed the top of her head when she pressed her face against his chest.

"Weel, that is different," she mumbled and wondered if that sounded as foolish to him as it did to her.

"Nay and weel ye ken it." He combed his fingers through her thick hair. "I thought on it this past fortnight."

"Thought on it?"

"Aye, thought on it often, wondering why I had been so slow to enjoy that pleasure with you. I was certain t'would be nectar and I was right. Ne'er have I tasted such sweetness," he whispered, then laughed huskily when she groaned softly, clearly embarrassed by such direct talk. "Islaen?" he asked after a moment of companionable silence.

"Aye?"

"Were ye ready?" he asked hesitantly, thinking upon the swiftness with which he had bedded her.

'Was I ready?' she mused incredulously. 'Surely he can tell such things? How much more ready does he want me? I near to impaled myself upon him in my greed for him.' Then she grimaced, suddenly realizing that he referred to the sponges she was supposed to be wearing and wondered idly what had prompted him to ask when he had not done so since their wedding night.

"Aye, I was ready soon after ye arrived," she replied and felt his sigh of relief and was both angered and hurt by it.

It was an effort to keep her hand from drifting to her stomach. There now rested the cure for Iain's fears. She would present him with a healthy child and rise unharmed from her childbed. Islaen just prayed that God would grant her that.

Chapter Fourteen

Reaching out, Islaen's hand met only cold linen. She sighed, then hurriedly moved to get her chamberpot as her stomach rolled and heaved. Weak but no longer nauseous, she hurried to clean up. With a cold compress held to her forehead she crawled back into bed for a moment's rest and decided it was probably for the best that Iain left her side so early in the morning. Men could be slow to guess that a woman was with child, but she suspected even the slowest of them would begin to suspect when the woman emptied her belly every morning.

Still, she mused, it was disheartening to find him gone. She was lost in thought on that problem when she suddenly realized someone had entered the room. Expecting Meg she was startled to find Storm at her side.

"Meg was feeling a little poorly so I came to see if ye needed anything. Are ye feeling poorly too?"

"Just a headache."

"Ah, they are a nuisance. Let me freshen that compress for you."

It was not until Storm had stepped behind the screen placed before the chamberpot and washing utensils that Islaen realized she had erred. She winced when she heard

Storm gasp softly. When Storm reappeared, Islaen did not really need to look to know that the woman had found the sponges. They were left out for Iain's benefit. She was, however, discomforted by the anger upon Storm's face. For a moment Islaen cursed Iain. It was, after all, his fault that she found herself in such an uncomfortable situation. Islaen knew that she could no longer keep the truth from Storm and hoped that the woman would understand as well as help her keep her secrets.

"Islaen, I would ne'er have thought this of you. I find it hard to believe e'en now though I hold the proof. Is this why you can say you do not fear childbirth, because ye know you are safe from that? How does this help Iain?"

"Come and sit down, Storm. 'Tis a long and complicated tale."

Hesitantly Storm did so after putting the sponge back and handing Islaen the compress. "I hope 'tis one to ease my temper. We are friends and I wish us to stay so, yet I love Iain as my own brother and feel as if this is a betrayal of him."

"Iain was the one who wanted the sponges used. He insisted upon it."

"Oh, but, well, that did not mean ye had to."

"I had to or he would not share my bed." Being as discreet as possible, Islaen told Storm of the wedding eve and the wedding night.

"He obviously feels damning your soul is better than risking your life upon a childbed," Storm said crossly.

"So ye feel 'tis a mortal sin too."

"Aye, I also feel 'tis a sin against you. I will not believe you if ye tell me ye do not wish to bear his children."

"I would not mouth such a lie though I fear I am not clear of the sin of lying. He gave me no choice, Storm."

"I know and I do not think he realizes how cruel that is. He thinks only to protect you. Oh, this is a disaster. How can ye show Iain that not every woman need die upon a childbed, that ye can do it, if he forces you to use those things?"

"By not using them," Islaen said quietly and smiled faintly when Storm's eyes slowly widened. "I used them once on our wedding night. That was enough to tell me that he doesnae really notice their presence, though it puzzles me that he doesnae."

"His passion runs too hot, Islaen. He notices little save the sating of it, I wager. Ah, poor Islaen, he forces you to deceive him and I can tell that that pains you. I should dearly hate to be caught in such a snare."

"Something else pains me and that is that I must ask ye to keep my deception a secret, to share my lie."

"Of course I will."

"Ye agree most readily."

"Aye. Ye do intend to tell him yourself eventually, do ye not?"

"Aye, when the bairn comes."

"It will."

"I ken it will." Islaen grinned. "In about six months, mayhaps seven. 'Tis hard to tell exactly."

"So quickly."

"Nay as quick as I should have liked. I wished for it to be blamed upon the first night we laid together."

"The sponges are not without fault. I use them and was using them when I found myself carrying Blythe."

"Ah, I had wondered. She is so close in age to Moran. Barely a year younger. I can see their use in such control. In truth, I begin to think my mother made use of them and Meg agrees. We are nearly all twa years apart in my family. I mean to do that."

"Good. I had thought to speak to ye about it. Bearing a child takes a great deal from a woman, before, during and after. She needs time to recover, to regain her full strength and 'tis not only for her sake. The babe needs that too. I truly believe that resting between babes is why both I and all my children survive. So, Colin will have his grandchild," Storm murmured with a smile.

"The mon has five already."

"Aye but he wishes all his sons to know that joy. He is in the winter of his life and wishes to see his sons happy. Colin also knows that Iain needs that, though he would deny himself."

"I must keep my condition secret for as long as possible."

"We-ell, with the first 'tis oft a long while ere it shows, but why do ye wish it kept hidden?"

"Because of Iain's fears."

"Ah, of course. He will worry himself sick when he knows."

Islaen nodded. "Whate'er else I fash myself o'er, I ken that he has a strong need to keep me safe, worries o'er me. In his eyes my being with child is much akin to putting a knife to my throat. The less time he is troubled by that image, the better."

"Are ye afraid, Islaen? Many women are. I was a little."

"I am a little. An anything goes wrong . . ."

"I pray God it does not."

"So do I but an it does, I shall tell Iain of my deception. I willnae let him add to his guilt. He will be told that I willingly took the risk upon myself, disobeyed him. He cannae blame himself when 'tis kenned that I deceived him."

"I will help ye in that, but I feel there will be no need. Ye and the child ye carry will be fine. Now, 'tis my thought to visit the crofters today. Winter draws nigh and I must be sure that they need naught more to face it."

"Iain has left again?" Islaen asked even though she knew in her heart that he had.

"Aye. Phelan went with him. Come, I shall keep ye busy enough to help ease that loss."

Storm was true to her word and Islaen was torn between

chagrin, thankfulness and amusement. Despite the concessions made for her condition, she crawled to bed exhausted every night.

One night as she wearily washed up she realized it had been a full week since she had seen Iain. She had never stopped missing him but she realized that hard work had made her days too full to linger on it much. One day melted into the next with work taking up every waking hour. The loneliness she might have felt in the night was deadened by exhaustion. Her body demanded sleep and nothing could forestall it getting what it needed. Sighing as she crawled into bed and almost immediately started to fall asleep, she wondered if hard work was what Iain used to stay away from her, exhausting his body so that the hunger he never hid from her was vanquished.

Iain sighed as he ate the bread and cheese a sleepy page had fetched for him. Phelan had sought bed, too weary to think of food. After a week of hard work the night ride to Caraidland had taxed the strength of both of them.

Shaking his head, he wondered how long he could continue and stay sane. He was back at Caraidland for one reason and one reason alone—Islaen. No matter how hard he worked he could not completely vanquish his need for her. Eventually, the need to see her, to speak to her, to hold her, grew too strong to ignore. Finally he rose from the table and headed for his chambers.

Islaen woke to passion. So afire with need was she that she barely had enough presence of mind to know that it was no dream that Iain had come home. When they lay sated in each other's arms she wondered sadly how long he would stay this time, then shook away that distressing thought.

"That ye, Iain?" she asked sleepily, grinning when she felt him jerk in her arms.

Seeing her grin, he nipped her shoulder in gentle reprimand. "Wretch. Who did ye think it was?"

"Weel, it being dark and your manner of waking me leaving little time for clear thought . . ." she shrugged.

"Islaen, 'tis a verra dangerous sort of teasing ye indulge
in," he growled as he eased the intimacy of their embrace but
stayed wrapped in her slim arms.

"Aye? And what can ye do about it?"

"'Tis a husband's right to beat his errant wife."

"Errant am I?" She watched him rise, then fetch a damp
cloth to wash them with.

"Verra errant," he murmured as he cleaned himself off then
gently tended to her. "Pert too and impertinent."

"My, my, I am weighted down with faults," she said softly
welcoming him back into her arms.

"Aye but I strive to overlook them." He nuzzled her breasts.

"How gallant ye are."

"I ken it."

"And vain."

"Vain am I? I should punish ye for such harsh words."

"And what form shall this punishment take?"

"An ye stay awake for a wee while, I will show ye."

She found it easy to stay awake as she reveled in the passion he gave so freely.

When she woke in the morning to find him still in her arms
she was both delighted and dismayed. It would be nice to
spend a little time with him but she feared he would discover
her pregnancy before she was ready to reveal it to him. Her
sickness in the morning had become erratic, a sign that it was
leaving her, according to Storm. She could not be sure, however that she would be fine each and every morning. There
was, she realized, some advantage to his absence.

"Iain," she gasped, startled when the man she had thought
asleep suddenly acquired some very busy hands, "I thought
ye were sleeping."

"I am," he growled against her neck. "I am dreaming."

"Ye have some verra lively dreams then."

"Lass," he murmured as he moved to crouch over her, "ye dinnae ken the half of it."

The day was half over before they left their bed. Islaen quickly sought out Storm. She felt guilty for not being there to help the woman with all the work that needed doing.

"Not to worry, Islaen. Ye have helped immensely and I know you will again. Take time with Iain. 'Tis important."

"I just feel guilty leaving ye to do it all alone."

"Do not. I have done it these past ten years and will do so again when ye move to Muircraig. Best I do not get too accustomed to your help. Does Iain stay long?"

"Nay, I think not. He gathers supplies now. He suddenly recalled that that was his excuse for coming here," she drawled.

Storm laughed but then said carefully, "Islaen . . ."

"Nay, ye dinnae need to say it. I ken that seemed a wee bit bitter, but I didnae lie when I said it passes quickly. I have promised myself that in the hours he is with me he will ne'er find an excuse for his neglect in my behavior. I fear that means I swallow so many words that they but spill out on occasion. Please be patient with me."

"I understand completely. Ye are not the one who needs patience. The more I see of Iain's actions the more I am amazed at your tolerance. I should sorely have bruised Tavis by now for such hurtful nonsense. If ye feel a need to spit out the bile that builds up whilst ye must hold your tongue, I am willing to hear it. I think I would have choked on it by now."

"'Tis a near thing. If ye hear a crash in the night, dinnae fash yourself. 'Tis but me giving into the urge to kick him out of bed."

Laughing softly, Storm shook her head. "'Tis not truly funny. Come, soon winter closes in and he must stay home. Travel is treacherous and no work can be done at Muircraig. How fared ye this morning?"

"I wasnae sick. Mayhaps I shall be lucky and not be all the while he is here. 'Tis too soon for him to ken that I carry his child. I suddenly kenned this morn that, for all it pains me, there are advantages to his staying away so much."

"Aye. He is not there to see all the changes."

"And, because he believes I work to remain barren, my being with child isnae the first thought in his mind." She sighed and shook her head. "I but hope that I willnae be adding to his burdens."

"Enough of that. Do not let his fears taint ye. There is fear in all women with child but ye must not let the ones that Iain carries draw your own out. They could do ye much harm and I think ye know it."

"Ye are right, of course. I mean to take the darkness from his heart, not take it into my own. I must work to remember that. As ye say winter comes. Soon there will be no hiding my condition from him and then I fear t'will be a verra great battle."

"Aye, his fears will be strong then. Ah, there, he looks for you. Go on now."

"Are ye certain, Storm?" Islaen asked as she watched her husband from the granary door.

"Aye, very certain."

Islaen spent most of the day with Iain and began to wonder why she bothered. He seemed to want her with him yet he was aloof. The way he worked so diligently preparing to leave her again was rather painful to watch. Finally she gave up and used the excuse of needing a bath before the evening meal to leave him. She felt she needed time away from his coolness, away from fruitlessly trying to break through it, if she was going to be able to welcome him into their bed later.

Iain watched her walk away and cursed himself. He held onto her tightly with one hand and pushed her away with the other. It was not only mad, it was cruel, but he could not seem to stop acting so contrarily.

"Such a dark face. My wee sister raise your ire?"

Managing a smile for Robert who leaned inside the stable doors, watching him, Iain asked, "Any luck today?"

"Nay, curse MacLennon's eyes. He is about."

"Always. He doesnae wish to miss any chance at me."

"So he watches closely, aye. I catch a glimpse of him or find his trail, but he e'er slips away. Are ye sure the mon isnae a spirit?"

"Nay, he lives though many seek to end that life. 'Tis uncanny the way he can elude us all. Unnatural almost."

"His time will come. He will taunt death once too often. I fear I have more bad news for ye. 'Tis about Fraser."

"Does the loudmouthed worm finally crawl our way?"

"I think so. His own family sent warning. They search for him, him and twelve of his men."

"They arenae sure he heads this way?"

"Nay, though they think 'tis most likely. They want no feud with your family or mine, so, though he is kin, they sent warning. T'was hinted that they are done with the fool, feel no more need to protect him from his own folly."

"Yet they search for him."

"The bond of kinship is hard to sever. I think they dinnae wish it said that they did naught. Whate'er befalls the fool now, their hands are clean. Do ye tell Islaen what might ride this way?"

"I think not. 'Tis yet only a possibility. She is well watched now because of MacLennon. There is no need to add to that."

"Aye and because of MacLennon, she is alert to danger," Robert mused aloud. "Weel, I must wash the dust off. Do ye run again to Muircraig?"

Iain muttered an affirmative response, then watched Robert leave. Run was the right word he supposed but it was discomforting to think that others might see it as that.

Islaen woke to an empty bed and felt little surprise. Iain had kept her awake most of the night with his lovemaking.

She wondered a little crossly how long he felt that sensual gluttony would last him. Considering how busy he had kept her during the night, she decided it would not surprise her at all if he stayed away a full fortnight. Sighing and scolding herself for her bitterness, she rose. Storm had said that there was still a lot of work to do and she hoped the woman was right.

For nearly three weeks, Islaen worked hard. She filled every minute of the day, needing the busyness more and more as each day passed and Iain did not return. It worked to keep her from lying awake at night but as the third week drew to a close, she found herself pausing more and more to stare off towards Muircraig as if she could will Iain to return.

"Are ye tired, Islaen?" Storm asked as she moved to where Islaen stood just outside the door of the smokehouse.

"Nay, not truly. I couldnae stomach working with the meat any longer. My stomach began to turn on me, I fear."

"Come, we will go and sit for a time. I could do with a rest from it all myself. Aye, and a drink. Here, what happens now?"

Both women watched as a small ragged boy eluded the men and raced towards them. When the men tried to give chase, Storm held up a hand to halt their pursuit. The boy was so small he could be little danger to them even if he was armed. Islaen listened as the boy frantically told his tale to Storm. She did not know the Gaelic well enough to understand what was happening however.

"I must go, Islaen. I am needed," Storm said even as she hurried off to her chambers to collect what she would need.

"What is wrong?" Islaen asked as she followed close on Storm's heels. "I could not understand it all."

"Oh, aye, 'tis a waning language, I am sorry to say. I wondered why ye did not look more upset."

"'Tis Iain?" Islaen felt her heart stop with fear as Storm hurriedly collected her medicinals.

"Nay, but mayhaps as bad. 'Tis Robert. He has been hurt."

"Badly?"

"The boy was not clear. He does need physicking though."

"I will come with ye."

"Are ye sure ye should? The ride and all . . ."

"Willnae harm me. We can take Beltraine. He is strong and fast."

When they went to have the horse saddled one of the men insisted upon going with them. It was only then that Islaen recalled the threat of MacLennon. She wondered frantically if Robert had fallen victim to the man's madness.

"Do not look so fretful, Islaen," Storm said as she mounted behind Islaen. "Robert will be fine."

"I pray so. If there is a favorite in our family, 'tis he. Where do we head to, Storm?"

"To old Sorcha's croft. He was taken there. Recall? We went there but three days past to settle a squabble o'er the gleaning."

Islaen nodded and urged her mount forward. She was only barely aware of the well-armed man that rode by their side. Since her marriage such a guard had become so common as to be unnoticeable. A small voice in her mind reminded her that, if Robert's injury was due to MacLennon, they would have need of the man with them but she was too worried about Robert's well-being to think on that. If there was trouble in getting to Robert she would face it when it came and not fret on it beforehand.

When they slowed as they approached the croft they sought, Islaen frowned. The hairs on the back of her neck tickled a warning and she halted her mount. Leaning forward in the saddle, she stared hard at the place wondering what made her sense danger. She scolded herself for her foolishness, told herself Robert could be dying while she sat but feet away, yet she hesitated. Something was just not right.

"Why do ye wait, Islaen?"

Islaen's eyes widened as she saw one thing wrong with the scene before them. "Robert's horse isnae there, Storm."

Frowning, Storm demurred, "Mayhaps the beast ran off, became frightened and inexperienced hands could not hold him."

"Would we not have seen the beast then as he ran back to his stall?"

"Aye, mayhaps. Does all look well to you Robbie?"

The man frowned as he stared at the croft. "'Tis muckle still."

"Aye, mayhaps too still yet . . ."

"Robert could be there."

"Aye, Islaen, so I keep thinking."

"Yet here I sit thinking this all wrong somehow."

"Mayhaps we should return for more men?"

"That could take time and Robert might have very little. Where did the lad go?"

"I have not seen him since I spoke to him," Storm replied slowly.

"'Tis most odd, is it not? Yet naught has happened as we sit here."

Just as she decided she might as well go to the croft, Robbie cried out. The sound that preceded his cry chilled Islaen's blood. As she and Storm turned to look at the man he slumped and began to fall from his saddle. She was not really surprised to see the shaft of an arrow protruding from his back. The sound she had heard had warned her. When she moved to go to his aid, Storm's grip on her tightened, halting her.

"We can do little for him. They will not allow it. Behind us, Islaen."

Looking over her shoulder, Islaen gasped. Six armed men rode towards them. She did not hesitate any longer but urged Beltraine into a gallop. The men were between them and Caraidland so she headed towards Muircraig although she found little hope within her that she and Storm could escape.

"They move to encircle us," Storm yelled. "There were more than six."

Cursing viciously, Islaen tried several evasive maneuvers but the men were good. Although a good rider, she had little skill in playing and winning such a dangerous game. With little hope of success as the circle around them tightened, Islaen tried to break through. She cried out as the reins were torn from her hands, burning them. In his fright, Beltraine nearly flung her and Storm from his back. Gritting her teeth Islaen hung on knowing that, if she went, so too would Storm. By the time Beltraine settled down she was dazed and stared blindly at the men encircling them.

"Curse it," muttered Storm. "A trap. But whose and why?"

"I believe he is about to tell us," Islaen murmured as one of the men moved to face them. "'Tisnae MacLennon. Too fat and short."

"Ah, two lovely damsels in one net."

"Who are ye and what do ye want?" Islaen demanded, fighting to sound unafraid.

"When ye ken who I am, m'lady, ye will ken weel what I want."

Something about the man's voice chilled Islaen's blood. She sat tensely as he removed his helmet then she gasped. Despite the now crooked nose and two disfiguring scars there was little mistaking the man that now faced her.

"Fraser."

"Ah, so ye remember me, do ye, sweeting? Weel, no more to say?"

"Ye are mad, Fraser," Storm snapped. "Ye harm either of us and ye will soon be so full of swords ye will look like a hedgehog."

"Ah, Tavis's Sassanach bitch."

"She is naught to you, Fraser. Let her go," Islaen demanded. "Your quarrel is with me, not her."

"So she can raise the clan? I think not. Come along," he said and signaled one of his men to take Beltraine's reins.

"Where are ye taking us?"

"To Hell, m'lady. Aye, to Hell." Fraser laughed and Islaen shuddered, feeling Storm echo it. "And, with the bait I hold, t'will not be long ere your husband joins us there."

Chapter Fifteen

The anger Iain felt for giving into the need to see Islaen was forgotten when he stepped into the hall and found Tavis throttling a man while a glowering Robert watched. "What goes on here?"

Tavis flung the man he held away from him. "Fraser."

Iain felt his blood run cold with fear. "Islaen?"

"He has her. Her and Storm," Tavis snarled. "That is what this dog says."

"T'was all he managed to say ere your brother proceeded to strangle him," Robert drawled but fury made his voice harsh.

"Aye, Tavis," Colin said as he gripped his eldest son's shoulder in a gesture of sympathy and understanding. "That willnae help. Has the mon got his breath back yet?" he asked the men guarding Fraser's messenger. "I ken there is more to the message he brought us."

When his guards yanked him to his feet, Fraser's messenger wheezed, "Wants Iain. Trade lasses for Iain MacLagan. Sorcha's croft."

Robert grabbed hold of Iain when he turned to leave. "Where do ye think ye are going?"

"Ye heard the terms."

"I heard a trap."

"Do ye think I didnae? There is no choice. We cannae leave Storm and Islaen in his hands."

"And we cannae put ye into his hands. That will just give him three to kill."

"How he thinks to get away with this madness, I cannae guess," Tavis growled, then looked at Fraser's messenger, smiled coldly and pulled out his knife. "Mayhaps this coward will tell us. 'Tis nay too hard to make such a dog howl." He looked to his father. "We cannae plan until we ken what Fraser plans. E'en his ravings could be of use."

"An I go . . ." Iain began.

"If ye go to him ye die," Tavis said flatly, "then the lasses die. Mayhaps he will keep Storm alive to bargain for his own life but I wouldnae wager on it. Sending ye willnae e'en buy us time."

Colin went to shut the hall doors, then turned. "Do it, Tavis."

It was not to Iain's liking to torture a man and he knew Tavis had no stomach for it either, but their need was desperate. The man would not talk unless he knew they would sink lower and hurt him more than his master. To Iain's relief the man broke quickly. It took great restraint to keep from killing the man, however, when he spoke of all Fraser had threatened or planned for his twisted revenge.

"He hadnae planned on the second lass," the man finished. "He will use her to ransom his life an he's attacked."

"Ye would have Storm back an I went to him, Tavis."

"Aye and she would most like cut my throat an I bought her back with the lives of ye and Islaen. Iain, the mon must be mad to think he can do this and live. Ye cannae deal with such as he. We will have to rescue the women."

"That could be verra dangerous," he said even though he knew Tavis was right.

"Aye, but we havenae any other choice. An any harm

comes to those lasses, ye slinking dog," Tavis growled at his prisoner, "and ye will be hung by the thumbs from the walls of Caraidland and provide a living feast for the corbies. Secure him weel."

"Now that we have all that what do we do with it?" Robert drawled.

"Go after the women and, if we are lucky, get them back alive and unharmed," Colin answered quietly.

Islaen barely swallowed a screech when Fraser roughly shoved her and Storm off of the back of Beltraine. She knew she was lucky to land without seriously injuring herself. Turning to look at Storm she found the woman groggy but unhurt. Even as she reached to help Storm, Fraser grabbed her by the hair and yanked her to her feet.

"I should have worn my coif," she muttered. "Storm?"

"I am fine, Islaen. Just hit my head, 'tis all," Storm answered as one of Fraser's men roughly yanked her to her feet. "Where's Sorcha?"

"Ye mean the old slut that lived here?" Fraser shoved Islaen inside the crofter's hut. "She is dead."

"You whoreson," Storm hissed as she was shoved into Islaen, making them both stumble and fall.

"She wouldnae have lasted the winter."

"M'lord?" Another of Fraser's men stood in the doorway. "The mon we shot is gone."

"It doesnae matter. An he lives to reach anyone, he cannae tell them any more than I did in my message."

"Iain is no fool, Fraser. He willnae walk to ye like some heathen sacrifice," Islaen said coldly as she and Storm stood up.

"Oh, I think he will. Aye, for his wee wife, he will. And we have Tavis's little Sassanach too." He stroked Storm's cheek.

Storm slapped his hand away. "Keep your filthy hands off of me, ye swine."

Snarling a curse, Fraser backhanded her across the mouth. "Sassanach bitch. There are few in Scotland that would fault me for killing the spawn of a marcher lord."

As she knelt by the fallen Storm, Islaen glared at Fraser. "There are many who will kill ye if ye harm her. Every one of the MacLagan clan to begin with. Ye are the greatest of fools if ye think ye will live after this."

"I have a right to my vengeance."

"Vengeance? For what? Because a mon stopped ye from raping his wife?"

"He isnae here to stop me now, is he. But first, I must place my men." He turned sharply and left with his men.

"Are ye all right, Storm?" Islaen asked as she sat down by the woman.

"Aye, I have had worse. Curse it, I see no way out of this."

"Ye dinnae think Iain will come, do ye?"

"I cannot say. His first thought will be to do as he is told, but 'tis hoped that wiser heads will prevail. They have to know that that will not help us, that they deal with a madman. He must be mad to do this."

"Aye, he cannae win e'en an he gains the blood he seeks. He isnae crafty like MacLennon so there is hope."

Clasping Islaen's hand in hers, Storm hesitantly said, "Islaen, he means to . . ."

"Aye, I ken it. At least he doesnae threaten ye."

"That does not mean he will let me be."

"Nay, I ken that too. We must pray for a speedy rescue or something to divert him."

"Mayhaps if we fight him together. I have my dagger. The fools did not check for weapons."

"Let us hope he is so stupid as to face us together."

"He has shown little intelligence thus far. Although he did

know Robert was there, that he could safely use your brother as bait."

"That would take little to find out. Robert is much about looking for MacLennon and making no secret of it."

"Then he could also know that Iain may not be at Caraidland but at Muircraig," Storm said quietly, her worried gaze upon Islaen.

Islaen nodded. "I thought on that. We are on our own and must act accordingly until 'tis proven elsewise."

"Aye. That pig will not find it easy to defile us. Mayhaps we can find some comfort in that."

Despite the fact that there was no way of leaving the croft unseen, they searched for one. They found a weak spot in one wall that could be utilized with some work. It would be of no use until dark, however, when they would have some chance to elude Fraser's men. Both women tried not to think too much about all that could happen to them in the hours until dark.

When Fraser returned, Islaen and Storm stood hand in hand to face him. He was neither as tall nor as strong as either of their husbands, but they both knew he could easily beat them unless Storm could make use of her dagger. For all his weaknesses he was a man of battle and they were two small women. Luck would be needed to defeat him before he could harm them.

To Islaen's horror, Fraser did not even give them a chance. With a surprising swiftness he struck out at Storm, hitting her on the jaw. Storm crumpled unconscious to the ground with barely a whimper. Islaen stared at Fraser, torn between outrage and terror.

"Now, ye shall pay for what your husband did to me."

Backing away from him, Islaen wished the hut was not so small. "He did as any mon would when what is his is threatened."

"He near killed me."

"He wanted to. Aye and ye deserved no better. Ye are lucky he didnae do more, but let ye leave."

"Lucky?" he hissed as his arm darted out and he grabbed her by the hair. "Ye bitch, he scarred me, crippled me."

Islaen bit back a cry as he slammed her up against the wall. His grip on her hair brought tears to her eyes. When he tore the front of her gown and chemise she felt terror grip her but fought it. She needed a clear head if she was to fight him at all. That calm was nearly impossible to gain when he began to maul her breasts, cuffing her soundly when she scratched his hands.

"Do ye ken what else he did to me? He unmanned me," Fraser hissed. "The whoreson unmanned me. Aye, but his fair wife will be my cure. By Christ's foot, ye will stir the life in me again or die trying." He started to unlace his braes.

His grip loosened as he struggled to expose himself and Islaen took quick advantage of that. Her fingers curled like talons, she slashed at his face. When he screamed and his hands instinctively went to his face, she darted away. The injury was not severe enough nor was she quick enough. With a savage growl he grasped at her skirts. They tore as he yanked and she fell. Before she could scramble to her feet, he was upon her.

Pinning her arms over her head, he rubbed his flacid organ against her breasts. Islaen choked on the bile of revulsion. She tried desperately to buck him off but he laughed at her efforts. Islaen felt a chilling fear for the child she carried, certain that it could never survive much of the ordeal he so clearly planned to put her through.

Seeing a slight movement to the side, Islaen felt a brief flare of hope. Unfortunately, Fraser, despite his distraction, also sensed danger. Even as Storm stuck him with her dagger, he turned to deflect her blow.

"Bitch. Sassanach bitch," Fraser hissed as he caught

Storm's wrist in a bruising grip, then slapped her. "Ye will pay for this."

Storm cried out softly as Fraser twisted her wrist. Islaen watched the dagger fall from Storm's hand. Fraser then threw Storm to the floor and leapt upon her. Islaen watched in shock as he put his hands around Storm's slim throat. He seemed oblivious to the way Storm clawed at his hands as he choked the life from her, cursing her all the while.

Terrified that he would kill Storm before she could stop him, Islaen scrambled for the dagger. Without any thought of what she was doing save that she needed to stop him, she plunged the dagger into his back. He bellowed and swung at her, sending her slamming into the wall, knocking the breath from her body, and leaving her groggy.

She nearly wept when she saw him stand up and turn towards her. Struggling to her feet, she prepared to meet him but then, still glaring at her, he fell to his knees. She knew a moment of sheer terror when he grasped her skirts but then his eyes rolled back until only the whites showed. Then he sprawled facedown upon the dirt floor and did not move. Islaen looked to Storm who was on her hands and knees gasping for air. Carefully avoiding Fraser's body and tearing off the piece of skirt he still clutched, Islaen rushed to Storm's side.

"Is he dead?" Storm rasped as she collapsed in Islaen's arms.

"I think so. I have ne'er . . ." Islaen began in a shaking voice.

"I know what ye are feeling but t'will pass as soon as ye are o'er the shock enough to recall what he planned to do to us." Storm shook her head. "My fault. I did not plan my strike. I woke up, saw what he was doing to ye and simply went for him. I wanted to stop him before he could perform that final indignity."

"I dinnae think he can. Seems Iain did something to him when they fought."

"Ah, aye. Considering what the man was trying to do, Iain could well have delivered a damaging blow or two. There lies the seed of his madness."

"So I thought. What do we do now? If his men discover this they could weel kill us. They might actually be loyal."

"I doubt it, but best we not take any chances. Come, we will work at that weak place on the back wall. Did ye hear something?"

"Aye, I . . ." Islaen's words strangled to a halt as she looked to see Fraser standing up. "God's teeth, he isnae dead."

At that moment one of Fraser's men burst into the hut. "The MacLagans have come. They killed five men e'er we e'en kenned they were about. Best ye flee now, m'lord. The game is lost."

"Nay, not completely. Kill these bitches."

The young man looked at Storm and Islaen in horror. He not only seemed shocked by the order but by the clear evidence of their having been roughly handled. Islaen wondered if the lad had not listened to Fraser, who had undoubtedly made his plans very clear, or, perhaps, simply had not believed any of it. She knew in her heart that he would not kill them, could read it in his light grey eyes.

"I cannae," the youth croaked. "Ye ne'er said . . . what have ye done to them? They are but lasses, wee lasses. I will-nae do it."

"Fine. Then die with them."

Islaen cried out when Fraser thrust his sword into the youth. The man stumbled back a few steps staring at Fraser in surprise, then crumpled to the floor. She and Storm tensed, readied for Fraser's attack but he just laughed and went out the door. When Islaen heard him bar the door from the outside she thought a little wildly that he had at least planned well for keeping them captive, then hurried along with Storm to see if Fraser had killed the youth.

"He isnae dead," Islaen said with relief when she felt the youth's heartbeat.

"I do not know why we fret so. He is one of Fraser's men."

"He is but a lad and he wouldnae kill us."

"Aye, I know it. Fear makes me sharp. Let us bind his wound." They each tore strips from their petticoats although Islaen's was so badly torn she suspected her contribution would only serve as padding. "The sword thrust pierced his side cleanly."

"Do we try to escape now or wait for Iain and Tavis?" Islaen frowned, sniffed the air, then froze. "Smoke," she whispered.

"That filthy dog. Come on, help me drag this fool boy nearer the back. We must get out. We cannae wait for our men now."

Iain stared down at the small crofter's hut and fought the urge to ride down there, sword swinging. He noticed Tavis looking as taut as he felt and suspected his brother suffered a like urge. They had to go slowly but he felt it was the hardest thing he had ever done. He tensed when he saw Fraser come out of the hut. Iain wished he could be sure that Fraser had no men there with him for then he could simply kill the man and collect Islaen and Storm.

"Fraser," he bellowed. "Give it up. Ye have lost."

"Aye, but so have ye, Iain MacLagan," Fraser cried, grabbed a stick from the fire before the hut and darted around the side.

"What is that madman doing?" Tavis grumbled and signaled his archers to be ready.

Fraser darted back to the fire, laughing in a way that made Iain shiver. "Aye, MacLagan, ye have lost too."

"Nay," Iain screamed when he saw what the man meant to do with the burning stick he pulled from the fire.

Even as Fraser tossed the stick at the thatched roof the MacLagan archers fired. An instant later his body bristled with arrows. With a maddened bellow echoed by Tavis, Iain charged towards the hut but, by the time he reached it, flames engulfed the place. When he and Tavis tried to get closer, a white-faced Colin ordered the men to hold them back. The hut was burning so fast that even if the men got inside they would never come out alive. They could not even use the water that was near for there was nothing to carry it with.

"'Tis nay so bad at the back," one man cried and they all raced to where he led.

Islaen did not think she had ever been so scared. She and Storm were breaking through the wall but it seemed to go so slowly. The place was filling with smoke. Her eyes streamed and she felt as if she was choking. She noticed that Storm was no better. Burning pieces of the roof were falling in by the time they felt the hole was big enough to get through.

"Ye go first, Islaen," Storm ordered. "Do not argue. Ye carry a babe. Get out there and then pull the lad through."

She knew she would only waste precious seconds by arguing so Islaen wriggled through the hole. Reaching back through she grasped the youth under the arms and was pulling him out when suddenly she was yanked away. Roughly set down away from the rapidly burning hut, she watched dumbfounded as Iain and Tavis yanked the youth out, then Tavis pulled Storm out. Seconds later the roof collapsed in a shower of sparks and Tavis, the nearest to the conflagaration, had several sparks land on him. She heard him curse when too many hands roughly slapped out the embers. It was not until Iain yanked off his tunic and put it on her that she came out of her stupor. She then realized she had been sitting there almost naked while the MacLagan men stood around.

Iain saw her torn clothes and her bruises and felt like weeping. "We had to wait, lass, to go slow for fear he would kill ye."

Still blushing over how she had sat so exposed before his men, Islaen only nodded as he helped her stand, then whispered, "'Tis all right."

"An I had come to him as he had asked, I could have saved you from this."

"I am alive, Iain. 'Tis all that matters."

"I feel the same, Islaen. Believe that. No matter what that whoreson did to ye, I care only that ye have survived it all."

Suddenly realizing what he thought had happened, Islaen whispered, "He didnae rape me, Iain."

Gently grasping her by the shoulders, he said, "Islaen, there is no need to lie. It doesnae matter. Ye arenae at fault."

"But I tell ye, he didnae . . ."

"Sometimes," Robert interrupted softly, "they say the shock is so great the woman puts it from her mind. Best we get her back to Caraidland."

"Aye," Iain agreed. "Meg can tend to her."

"Iain, will ye just listen . . ." she began.

"Come, Islaen, we will take ye to Meg. Ye will learn to accept this," he said softly, "and understand that it doesnae matter to me."

"Iain," she ground out, "I wasnae raped."

"Islaen, we can all see the truth," he said sadly.

Following his gaze she did not need to see beneath the tunic that hung on her. She knew all too well how badly torn her gown was. It was not, however, proof that she had been raped. Then she glanced at Storm but the woman could not speak, her voice finally taken due to the abuse her throat had suffered. Storm nodded towards Islaen's legs, however, and when Islaen looked she gasped for there was blood there, a small trail of blood from her thighs to her calves. For one hor-

rified moment she thought she was losing the child but then
became aware of the stinging in her thighs and relaxed.
Sometime in her fight with Fraser he had cut her or she had
hurt herself in her rush to escape the fire.

Over her head Iain and Robert discussed her as if she were
simple. She began to feel furious. No matter what state she
was in, no matter how she looked, she should know better
than anyone else whether or not she had been raped. She
knew her fury was easily stirred because her emotions were
raw from her ordeal, but when Iain spoke to her as if she were
a small, frightened and somewhat stupid child and the men
gathered there looked at her so sympathetically as he reas-
sured her, she cursed and slapped his consoling hands away.

"I hate to prick your noble understanding, Iain MacLagan,
but there is no need of it." She punctuated her words by jab-
bing a finger into his chest. "Now listen to me, ye wooden-
headed fool, I ought to ken what was done to me. Aye, he
tried but he couldnae. Fraser couldnae rape a hole in the mud.
Ye see, ye great gowk, when ye beat him that day at court ye
mashed his cullions to pudding and the bastard couldnae get
his pintle stiff if ye put a rod in it." The look of astonishment
upon Iain's face as well as the sudden silence around them
caused Islaen to realize what she had been saying. "Oh, God's
beard, what did I say?" she groaned, one hand covering her
mouth as she stared at Iain in growing horror.

"Weel," he said in a choked voice, "ye certainly made it all
verra clear."

When he burst out laughing and all his men and kin joined
in, Islaen thought she would die of embarrassment. She put
her hands over her flush hot face and wished she could disappear. No lady would have used such coarse language, Islaen
was sure of it.

"Lass," Iain murmured, his voice shaking with laughter,
"ye can stand there 'til the final reckoning and it willnae
happen. Ye willnae disappear."

That seemed to amuse the men even more, which made Islaen forget her embarrassment and glare at them. "Oafs. I am going home."

"Wait, sweeting," Iain gasped as he moved after her and struggled to subdue his laughter. "I will get my horse."

"Nay, thank ye kindly, I will get my own," she said haughtily, then put her fingers in her mouth and whistled loudly for Beltraine, who quickly appeared from the wood and trotted towards her.

She was just wondering how to mount without exposing too much of her legs when she heard someone mention the wounded youth. One man pointed out that the lad was one of Fraser's men and several voices offered some very chilling suggestions as to what should be done with him. Seeing that Storm was trying to speak up for the youth but was still nearly mute, Islaen hurried back to where the young man lay. She was partly aware of how Iain continued to stay at her side.

"Nay, ye must not hurt the lad."

"Did he help ye?"

"Weel, Iain, when Fraser asked him to kill us the boy refused. Fraser cut him down."

"He was part of it though, sweeting. He didnae stop it."

Looking at her husband she said quietly, "When he came to tell Fraser that ye had come, he looked horrified at what had been done to Storm and me. He was shocked to his soul when Fraser ordered us killed. I think he is just a lad who was tempted by an adventure and had no idea of the mire he had stepped into. Nay, nor of the mon he rode with. He could have killed us but he didnae and, if Fraser hadnae been weakened by a wound, the lad could have died for that. Can ye nay give him a chance? 'Tis a small reward."

"Aye, it is."

Islaen began to feel very weary as Iain saw to the youth's transport back to Caraidland. She did not try to ride off by herself but waited for Iain. He mounted and had Robert hand her to him. Once she was settled on Iain's lap, she let her weariness conquer her.

"The blood upon your legs, Islaen?" Iain asked softly.

"Cut myself somehow. Either in fighting Fraser or in crawling out through the hole in the wall," she replied tiredly. "Did ye find Robbie?"

"Aye, he was trying to get back to Caraidland. He will be fine."

"Fraser?"

"Dead."

"There is one threat gone then. A shame MacLennon's madness cannae make him as foolish as Fraser."

"Aye, a shame," Iain agreed softly, then realized that she had fallen asleep and he tightened his hold upon her a little.

He stared down at the sleeping woman in his arms. From the moment he had heard that she was in Fraser's hands he had been fighting panic. He had kept thinking of all the days he had stayed away from her, days that could never be regained. The depth of his fear for her told him something he did not really want to know. She was not pulling at him any longer—she had him.

Chapter Sixteen

Holding back a smile Islaen fought not to look at Storm knowing she would see laughter in the woman's eyes and lose her control on her own. Gamel Brodie, the youth she and Storm had rescued, was vowing his undying devotion, swearing to sacrifice all in their service. Islaen decided the youth had listened to too many minstrel's tales of knights and chivalry. Worse, he had taken it all to heart.

As soon as they could, she and Storm left him. When they felt they were far enough away so that he could not hear them, they gave into their laughter. They were still giggling over the matter when they entered the hall where Tavis and Iain awaited them. They told their husbands, who exchanged rueful glances, what they found so amusing, for it was clear that neither Tavis nor Iain saw the humor of it. That lack became clearer as the days passed and Gamel healed enough to start trying to prove his devotion.

Iain glared at young Gamel when he found the youth singing love songs to Islaen as Islaen sat by the fire in the hall doing her mending. He sat next to Islaen and continued to glower at the youth but Gamel paid him no heed. It was not only the way Gamel paid such attention to Islaen, for the youth paid equal attention to Storm, but the handsome young man made Iain all too aware of the years that separated himself from his young bride. He could not stop himself wondering if Gamel would make Islaen aware of it too.

"Storm is having a wee bit of trouble settling her bairns for the night," he lied smoothly. "Mayhaps ye can soothe them with your singing, Gamel." He smiled with satisfaction when Gamel left.

"I was enjoying that, Iain."

"That drivel?"

"Aye, Gamel has a sweet voice. I also ken that Storm ne'er has trouble settling her bairns."

"Are ye saying that I lied?"

Looking at him in wide-eyed innocence, Islaen said sweetly, "Nay, merely that ye may have been mistaken. I also feel sure that ye but forgot Tavis's threat to make Gamel eat his lute an he doesnae cease singing love songs to Storm."

Sprawling more comfortably on the settle, Iain smiled faintly, "Nay, I didnae."

"The boy means weel, Iain."

"Islaen, that boy is near one and twenty."

"Aye but he is a boy still in many ways."

"Nay in the ones I think on."

"Gamel doesnae think on that. To him, Storm and I are the ladies of his songs. He plays at the old courtly love, love pure and from afar."

"Hah. I have seen courtly love. So have ye, in the halls e'en. T'was neither pure nor from afar."

"Ah, aye, weel, I did say the 'old' sort of courtly love." She sighed for, while it was nice to see this jealousy in Iain, it was not something she wished to go on for too long nor to worsen. "I admit he can be tiresome but he means weel. He feels he owes us his life."

"He does."

"Aye, I suppose. He has no one, Iain. I cannot toss him out."

"He has kin."

"Iain, ye ken weel that they tossed him out."

"Aye, for nearly causing a bloody feud by singing love songs to anither mon's wife. The lad didnae learn by it, 'tis clear."

"Actually, I think t'was more that he challenged the mon because the mon had raised his voice to the lady." She giggled when Iain cursed softly. "So, ye best not yell at me, Iain."

"I ne'er yell at ye," he bellowed.

"Nay, of course not," she murmured, then laughed.

His lips twitched with suppressed laughter. "Ye are a brat and that lad is fast becoming a nuisance beyond bearing."

She nodded and frowned in thought. Soon the humor would vanish from the situation. Since she could not simply throw the youth out she had to think of somewhere to send him. Her eyes widened as she suddenly saw the perfect solution to it all.

"Iain," she cried, dropping her mending to throw her arms about his neck, "I have the answer. We will send him to my kin."

Lightly putting his arms around her, he smiled crookedly. "I would be glad to see the back of him, but I think your brothers may object to having him underfoot. They too have wives he can swear vows to and sing to."

"Aye, but such has happened before and they ken the way to cure the lad of his fancies. We had a cousin afflicted with such fancies and they soon set him aright, yet didnae kill all that makes it so sweet. Do ye ken what I mean?"

"Aye, the ideals remain but the foolishness is gone. 'Tis the best way for, aye, there is good in the fancies the boy holds. Do ye ask first?"

"I best do so." She pulled out of his arms and stood up. "I will ask Robert to send his mon to our father. I dinnae think Fither will refuse the boy."

Iain watched her hurry away and sighed. He was letting his

jealousy show but he could not help it. His only comfort came in the fact that Tavis acted much the same. It was a hint of his feelings, however, that he would be wise to hide. Shrugging, he decided a man did not have to love to be possessive. Islaen had an excellent understanding of men, a rather uncomfortable one at times, and he could console himself with the thought that she would not read too much into his jealousy over the youth.

As soon as the youth was gone, Iain decided he would go to Muircraig. He had lingered at Caraidland to see that Islaen had healed completely, in mind and body, after Fraser's attack. Once sure of that he had lingered because he had not wanted to leave her alone with the young, ardent and handsome Gamel. Soon that reason would be gone for Iain was also sure that Alaistair would accept Gamel.

Heading out of the hall he decided to go soak in a hot bath. He was restless and he knew why. Islaen was healed enough to make love to and he ached to do so. With his emotions still in such a turmoil, Iain knew it would be dangerous to hold her close and make love to her, just as he knew he would surely do so before he fled to Muircraig.

Watching her brother, Duncan, ride away with Gamel, Islaen looked over her shoulder at Iain. "The thorn has been plucked out."

"Verra amusing. T'was not only my side that thorn pricked."

"Nay. I noticed Tavis was in high spirits today."

"I swear, the lad was more annoying than Alexander," Iain grumbled as he escorted Islaen back inside.

She laughed softly, then frowned as she realized they were headed to their chambers. "Why do we go here?"

Gently pushing her into the room, then shutting the door, he murmured, "Ye are all healed from that attack, are ye not?"

Beginning to grow suspicious, Islaen answered, "Aye, I have been for a few days. I thought ye kenned that."

"Aye, I did, but I was being gallant."

"Ah," she watched him start shedding his clothes and knew she was going to go along with what he so clearly planned, "and ye arenae planning on being gallant anymore?"

"I dinnae ken. Ye will have to tell me—after."

"After? After ye bathe?" she asked brightly as he moved to stand before her wearing only his braes.

He ignored that and looked her up and down. "One of us is overdressed."

"Aye, but I will soon mend that."

With a soft laugh she swiftly undid his braes. "Better?"

She giggled as, with a soft growl, he picked her up and tossed her onto the bed. By the time he finished removing her clothes most of her playfulness was taken over by desire. Holding him close and savoring the way his skin felt against hers, she met and returned the hunger of his kiss. Her hands moved over his lean frame with an ill-disguised greed until he caught them in his, stilling them. She met his gaze and caught her breath at the passion revealed there.

"Now, that is better."

"Ah, but is it gallant?"

"Ye can tell me in a minute."

"Only a minute?"

"Ye are feeling pert, arenae ye?"

Rubbing her feet over the back of his legs she smiled and tugged his mouth down to hers. "I have ne'er heard it called that before."

Iain laughed softly, then kissed her. Islaen quickly lost the last of her playfulness as he took them to the sweet oblivion all lovers sought. It was not until her mind cleared and she was holding him close, their sated bodies still intimately joined, that she began to get a little suspicious. She had the sinking feeling that Iain's impetuous lovemaking was spurred on by plans to leave for Muircraig again.

Nuzzling her neck and enjoying the feel of her so intimately close, Iain began to think of a way to gently tell her he would be leaving for Muircraig in a few hours. Making love to her only strengthened his conviction that he had come close to breaking all his rules. Keeping the distance between them that he felt was necessary left him feeling empty and alone. It was a great temptation to end that.

"I must return to Muircraig," he said softly as he kissed her neck and felt her tense briefly.

Not at all pleased to find that she had guessed correctly, Islaen forced herself to relax and asked calmly, "Aye? And when do ye leave?"

"By noon," he replied, and covertly but carefully watched her, not sure she would take the news very well.

Islaen tried very hard not to get angry. She utilized every trick she knew to stop her temper from rising. None of them worked. With a curse, she shoved Iain away, then sat up to glare at him. Clenching her hands, she fought the urge to strike him.

"I see, and ye thought ye best have a quick toss with the wee wife ere ye go," she hissed.

Deciding that it was not a good time to think on her beauty as she sat there naked and fuming, Iain met her glare. "Now, dinnae get into a fit," he began.

"I will show ye a fit."

She tried to push him out of the bed but he was prepared for her move. Try as she would she could not budge him. In frustration she finally hit him. Iain cursed softly and wrestled with her until he got her firmly pinned beneath him.

He supposed she had a right to her anger, and could see that getting her into bed, making love to her, then abruptly leaving was tactless, but he had not expected her to get quite so angry. Hurriedly he searched his mind for the right words

to soothe her yet not reveal the real reasons that he had hesitated to make love to her until the moment before he left. Not
only did he not really like her to be so angry with him, he did
not want to spend what time he had before leaving Caraidland
in argument.

"Islaen, t'was not like that. Ye had a bad time when Fraser
got hold of ye and needed to heal."

"I have been healed for a while."

"So ye say, but e'en now I can see the remnants of his
attack."

"They dinnae hurt."

He eased his hold upon her so that it was more of an embrace than a fettering hold. "Good, for I would hate to think
that, by giving into my needs, I hurt you—which is what I
have feared. I but reached the point today, kenning that I was
to leave, where I was willing to chance it, or, rather, didnae
think on it too much. Islaen," he murmured as he brushed
light kisses over her face, "is it wrong for a husband to want
to have some loving ere he leaves? I but seek a sweet
memory to warm my empty bed at Muircraig. Aye and mayhaps mean to leave ye a wee memory or two."

"Humph, ye mean to sweet talk me out of my anger," she
mumbled as she unsuccessfully fought her rising desires.

"Aye, there is some truth in that but what I said was also
true." He kissed her with a slow greed, then said softly, "I
couldnae leave without a taste of this, lass, not when I ken
t'will be a while ere ye are near enough to reach for again."
He began to toy with her hardened nipples with his tongue,
enjoying the way she moved restlessly against him.

'So dinnae leave or take me with ye,' she thought a little
crossly but bit her lip to hold the words back. She knew it
would be a mistake to press him too hard on the matter. For the
time being, no matter how it hurt and no matter how it de-
stroyed her attempts to build a good marriage, it was best to
open her hands and let him run. Complaints and recriminations

would gain her nothing. She was sure of it just as she was fairly sure that they would cost her more than she was willing to pay.

Closing her eyes, she decided to luxuriate in the passion they shared. She admitted honestly, but only to herself, that she too did not want him to go off to Muircraig without making love to her. There were too many times already when she ached for his loving.

Wantonly, she lay beneath him, nourishing every kiss and caress, greedily soaking up the pleasure he gave her. However, she jerked compulsively when his lips touched the curls adorning her womanhood. Her shock over such intimacy was brief and she soon arched to his kiss. Soon she was shaking with need and tugged on his hair.

"Please, Iain, please, I dinnae want to go alone," she rasped softly and cried out with relief and pleasure when he fiercely joined their bodies, taking them both to desire's apex, their cries of release blending in what Islaen thought was the sweetest of harmonies.

When it was time for him to leave she did her best to hide her anger and frustration. She knew she could not force him to stay just as she could not force him to love her. As soon as he was gone, she went back to her chambers and indulged herself in a furious tantrum, finally collapsing across the bed, a little exhausted after venting so many pent-up feelings.

"Is it safe to come in now?"

"Aye, Storm," she answered with a soft laugh.

Glancing around at the disorder as she entered the room Storm smiled, "Did it feel good?"

"Aye." Sitting up Islaen looked at the strewn clothes and the rest of the mess she had made. "Aye, it did."

"I know." Storm sat next to Islaen. "I have usually enjoyed the ones I finally gave into. Well, until I had to pick up."

"Aye, that will take some of the joy out of it. Still, 'tis better than beating Iain o'er the head with a mallet."

"Mmmm. Husbands find that sort of thing hard to under-stand." Storm joined Islaen in laughing.

"'Tis just that I grow so weary of the game but see no end to it. Aye, and undoubtedly t'will soon take a turn for the worse."

"Why do ye say that?"

"I think that, when next he comes home, I must tell him of the child."

Looking at Islaen's waist which was no longer tiny, Storm sighed and nodded. "I think ye are lucky he has not seen it yet."

"He mentioned that my figure was growing a wee bit fuller but, ere I could fumble with a reply, said he supposed I was just finishing my growing. He sees me as a child, I think."

"Not too much or ye would not be with child."

"There is a blessing. I think too that he sees the years atween us as more than they are." She stood up. "Weel, best I sort out this mess."

"I will help."

"Nay, 'tis my temper that set it all awry."

"Ye can help me next time I have one."

Islaen laughed. "Fair enough." She grew somber as she picked up a gown. "I think t'would nay be so upsetting an I could ken for certain that he doesnae put me from his thoughts as he easily as he puts me from his sight, that may-haps he thinks on us, our marriage and all. Ye ken what I mean, on what we dinnae have and what we could have."

"I feel certain he does."

Smiling faintly Islaen did not reply, but concentrated upon cleaning up the mess she had made. She wished she could have faith in such assurances but she could not. When a man was so determined to keep a distance from a woman, it seemed very reasonable to think that he would learn to put that woman from his thoughts as easily as he did his arms.

* * *

Turning from giving her horse a treat, Islaen watched Wallace, the stablemaster, tend a calf. She had often watched him with the animals and recognized the man's skill. Lately she had found herself thinking a lot about that man's skill and knowledge. The idea she had was a wild one but she had been unable to discard it. She decided she might as well give it a try. There was nothing to lose in trying and, if her wild thoughts and ideas were right, a lot to gain not only for her own sake but for Iain's. As she moved towards the man he suddenly moved to take her by the arm and gently lead her to a seat.

"Ye shouldnae walk about the animals too much, m'lady, not in your condition. Ye set here if ye are of a mind to watch."

"My condition?" she asked calmly.

He frowned at her before turning back to the calf. "Aye the bairn. Didnae ye ken it?"

"Aye, I but wonder how ye did as no one else has, and I have told only Storm and Meg."

"Och, weel, I have seen the look on the mares and all weel enough to ken." He flushed and looked at her nervously. "I didnae mean . . ."

"Dinnae apologize. When a mon loves animals as much as ye do 'tis no insult to be compared to them. Aye and with ones like that chestnut mare of Storm's 'tis a compliment, for they are verra fine indeed." She smiled at him and he briefly smiled back. "Mayhaps ye ken what I wish to talk to ye about then."

"I dinnae ken naught about bairns, m'lady."

"Be it all so different from foals and calves?"

Wallace stared at her for a moment, then sat down by her feet. "Nay, I dinnae think it is. Are ye afraid?"

"I think every woman holds some fear of birth. Wallace, I am going to confide in ye."

"Ye can trust me, m'lady."

"Aye, I ken it. Do ye ken Iain's fear of childbirth?"

"Aye, m'lady, 'tis no secret though he doesnae ken that, I'm thinking."

"Nay, possibly not."

"Is that why ye say naught about the bairn?"

"Aye, that and the fact that, when we were wed, he," she felt herself color but took a deep steadying breath and continued, "made me promise I would do something to make sure I ne'er got with bairn."

"Oh."

"Aye, oh. I didnae do it. I decided the lie was less a sin than what he asked. I also feel sure I can show him that all women need not suffer as his late wife did. That fear he holds must be conquered. If left to fester t'would bring sorrow to both of us. I want bairns and I feel most certain he does too."

"Aye, m'lady. I am sure he does. Ye can see it in the way he is with his brither's bairns."

"Soon I must tell him. There is little hiding it now from a knowledgeable eye. I think Iain remains blind because he thinks me safe from it. I will have lessened the wait a great deal though, and can be thankful for that. What I must do now is try to find a way, any way, to ease the birthing as much as possible."

"Ye cannae think I have the answer, m'lady."

"Aye. Come, Wallace, think. The beasts birth their young so much easier than we."

"But they, weel," he flushed and stared at his hands. "They be larger."

"Oh. Aye." She too flushed but did not falter. "I am fairly certain there are some differences but nay such differences that your knowledge becomes useless. 'Tis the wrong time of the year to watch the birthings but I ken ye can tell me about them." She smiled faintly. "We shall have to learn to control our blushes."

He laughed, then said quietly, "I be a rough mon, m'lady. I am nay sure I can speak on it weel. I mean . . ."

"Dinnae fash yourself, Wallace. I have near a dozen brothers. I doubt ye can say anything I havenae heard or that will truly shock me. I need the knowledge, Wallace. I need to cure my own fears enough to hide them from Iain. I need to ken as much as I can so that I may do my birthing as quietly as some of your beasts do. To hear my pain willnae help Iain. There is a knowledge here, in the ways of these beasts, and I mean to have it. Will ye help me? Will ye share what ye have learned?"

"Aye, m'lady. I just hope it can help ye like ye wish it to."

"So do I, Wallace. So do I. Shall we begin?" He nodded and she smiled, relieved to have him agree, and hoping she would be able to conquer the objections she was sure would come from the others as easily.

"Ye arenae going to the stables again?" Meg exclaimed in horror as Islaen donned her cloak.

Sighing, Islaen nodded. She had become a regular visitor to the stables. Wallace had lost all reticence with her and although she was not certain she had learned much to help her with her birth, she had learned a lot of useful, interesting things.

"Aye and I will keep going 'til the cold or my belly stops me." Islaen started out of her chambers.

"'Tis a dirty place."

"Far cleaner than some keeps I have been in. Wallace takes excellent care of his animals."

"Wallace isnae a mon ye ought to be getting so friendly with."

"Why not? He is a good mon; his work of value."

"I didnae ken ye had such a love of beasts. I tell ye it isnae right for ye to spend so much time there."

"And I say I will." Turning to face Meg, Islaen said firmly, "'Tis important."

"Why?"

"I dinnae think ye will understand but it has to do with the birthing I must soon go through."

"Wallace doesnae ken about bairns, only beasts."

"Who arenae so different from us." She grimaced when Meg gasped in shock. "I didnae think ye would understand. It doesnae matter. Ye willnae turn me in this. I must ken all I am able to about birthing. If naught else I shall find a way to keep my pain a secret from Iain."

"If ye ask me, there be too much kept secret here."

Islaen winced. She did feel caught in a choking net of secrets. The lie she had told Iain still ate at her. It was also hard to hide the fact that she carried his child, something she felt great joy and pride in, yet could not share.

"I am sorry, lass," Meg said softly. "I let my tongue work ere I think. T'was unkind."

"Nay, t'was the truth, pure and simple."

"Mayhaps, but I ken weel ye didnae want it this way, that secrets from your mon arenae what ye like."

"Weel, there is one secret that willnae be one much longer, Meg," she said quietly, her hand resting upon her slightly rounded abdomen.

Watching the group of men riding into Caraidland, Islaen felt her heart leap with delight, then sink, Iain was back. She was pleased to see him but knew this visit would be a troubled one. She was going to have to tell him about the child. Even he could no longer ignore the signs and she felt it was better to tell him than let him find out for himself. It was going to be difficult, however, and she was not looking forward to it at all.

Chapter Seventeen

"Ye are what?" Iain rasped, abruptly sitting down on the bed.

Seeing how pale he had gone, Islaen decided she had been right. He was not going to take it well. She had half-hoped that since it was a fait accompli, he would accept it, but realized that had been a foolish hope. A fear that ran as deep as his was not so easily conquered. She could only be thankful that she had only a little over three months left to wait.

Having followed him from the bailey to their chambers she still had her cloak on, so she removed it. "With child."

With a horrified fascination, Iain's gaze fixed upon her abdomen. The swell there was small but large enough to round the front of her gown. His dazed mind finally made him realize that such rounding took a while.

"How far along are ye?" he asked suspiciously.

"O'er five months."

"And ye didnae tell me?" he yelled.

"Nay and, an I hadnae started to show, I would still be keeping it quiet." She sighed as she saw the anger in his eyes. "Iain, ye didnae want the bairn, didnae want me to get with child at all. I felt t'was news ye wouldnae be anxious to hear so didnae give it to ye until I couldnae hide it any longer. No one likes to tell someone something they dinnae want to hear."

He stood up and began to pace the room.

"So, I am the last to ken it, am I?"

"Weel, I only told Storm and Meg but, aye, ye may be. As ye can see, 'tis most clear now but no one has spoken on it."

"If ye had spoken earlier mayhaps we could have," he began, hating the words even as he spoke them.

"Dinnae say it, Iain," she whispered. "Mayhaps that is another reason I kept silent. I ken that there are ways to take the bairn from a woman's body but I would ne'er do it. 'Tis best we didnae have that confrontation."

"Aye, ye are most like right." He ran a hand through his hair and stared at her stomach. "I ken I wouldnae have made ye either," he whispered, then began to collect his things. "It must have been that night ye came to me. I should be hanged for my lack of control. T'was reckless."

"What are ye doing?" She decided it would be unwise to correct his erroneous conclusion about the time of conception, for then he might start to think about it too much. "Ye arenae going back to Muircraig, are ye?"

"I am going to my own chambers," he announced as he left her chambers, carrying as many of his things as he could.

"These are your chambers. We are wed, so share a room. My being with bairn neednae change that. The bed is big enough for the three of us," she jested weakly but he just ignored her, quietly setting his things down and going back to get more. "Iain, there isnae any need for this," she said a little frantically when he came back into the room.

"Ye are with child."

"So what? I dinnae understand this at all."

"Ye need rest and to be treated gently, to be taken great care of."

"Ye neednae leave our bed to do that." This was a reaction

she had not foreseen, and was at a loss as to what to do about it.

"Islaen, an I share your bed I will make love to you."

"Weel, at least now ye ken that ye willnae get me with child." He ignored that and she began to feel really desperate. "'Tis nay wrong to do so."

"It could endanger ye or the child."

"I have been in this state for months and we have made love often."

"Anither reason why ye should have told me sooner. We are simply fortunate no harm was done."

"Iain, I am certain t'will nay harm me," she said as he gently took her by the arm and led her back to her room.

"I willnae take the chance," he said firmly, then left her standing in the middle of her room.

Stunned, Islaen stared at the door that now separated them. She briefly thought of going after him and continuing the argument, then decided against it. Not only her pride rebelled, but she was sure she would get nowhere while the shock he had suffered was still so fresh. He was in no condition to listen to any argument or reason. It was hard not to race after him and call him an idiot as well as a few other highly unflattering things, but she resisted the urge. She would give him some time to come to his senses. Islaen just hoped she did not grow too round in the meantime, so round that when he did return to her bed she was past caring or he was.

Her hurt feelings about Iain's reaction to her being with child were soothed somewhat by everyone else's reaction when Iain announced it. She had been right in thinking that most everyone had guessed but they were clearly as relieved as she felt to have it openly admitted to.

It was still early when she sought her bed. She knew the others would be up late, but she was not truly in the mood to stay with them. As she settled into her empty bed she mused crossly that she did not really have much to celebrate. Now was a time when she and Iain should be sharing the joy of their coming first child, planning the future. Instead, he was soaking himself in wine and ale and would soon be carried off to his own bed. She had the sad feeling that she would get little support and joy from Iain even if all his kin spoke to him. As she started to drift off to sleep, she hoped, a little vindictively, that his overindulgence this night left him properly sick on the morrow.

Iain groaned and collapsed back onto his bed after only half-sitting up. He heard a noise and opened his eyes a little bit to find a solemn Tavis bending over him. A cool cloth on his forehead eased his discomfort slightly.

"This isnae like ye, Iain," Tavis said quietly as he urged his brother to drink a potion.

Wondering how something that tasted so vile could cure him, Iain rasped, "Getting so fou, ye mean? I have done so before."

"Rarely. I speak more of how ye are acting. Ye left Islaen alone most of the evening. Storm wished me to point out that 'tis cruel of ye to make your fears so clear. Do ye think the lass has none? 'Tis her first bairn. She must have a few."

As guilt swamped him, Iain said a little sulkily, "She kens my feelings in this."

"Aye, but ye need not rub her face in them. And just why are ye here? Why arenae ye in with her?"

"Because she is with bairn and I willnae risk hurting her or the bairn. Nay," he growled when Tavis made to protest, "ye willnae change my thinking on this. She is a wee lass and having a braw rogue like me at her cannae be good."

"Just see if ye can cease looking at her and acting as if she is already in the grave," Tavis snapped and left Iain alone.

It was an effort but Iain tried to follow Tavis's advice. He knew it was wrong to plague Islaen with his fears, so did his best to hide them, but they still ate at him. Although he was tempted to return to Muircraig, he stayed at Caraidland. He felt a need to watch her, to assure himself that, at least for now, she was healthy and safe. Iain thought he was doing very well until one evening when they sat together in the hall, he trying to read a missive from Alexander and Islaen sewing.

Islaen bit her tongue but the words huddled there could no longer be held back. "Will ye cease?"

Looking at his wife in startled curiosity, Iain asked cautiously, "Cease what?"

"Staring at my belly. God's teeth, ye are e'er gazing at it as if ye expect the bairn to burst out."

"That is nonsense," he said, a little weakly, for he strongly suspected that he had been doing exactly what she accused him of.

"Aye, 'tis nonsense," she grumbled as she stood up and collected up her things. "Ye neednae keep watching for it. The bairn isnae going anywhere for a few months anyhow and when it does move it willnae come that way." She hurried away, a little worried that she would say a lot more, too much in fact, if she lingered.

Iain sighed. He again wondered if he should return to Muircraig but could not make himself leave. Although he did make himself stop staring at her so often, he found something else to worry about. Islaen seemed to be spending a great deal of time in the stables talking with Wallace. He was not sure it was good for a woman in her condition to be so close to animals or the stables. He had heard that such things could mark the child although he could not recall exactly how or why that was supposed to happen.

"Islaen?" he ventured as he walked her to her chambers one evening. "Why are ye spending so much time in the stables?"

Pausing just inside her door she stared at him. "To study the animals."

"Oh. Aye. But why?"

"Because I have a bairn coming."

"What has that to do with the stables and the animals?"

She wondered a little crossly why no one seemed to understand what she was doing. "They ken how to birth better than we do. Good sleep, Iain." She abruptly shut her chambers door not really concerned about whether he understood or not.

Although he did not really see what benefit she could get out of it, Iain made no further mention of her visits to the stables. If it eased her mind he felt it was invaluable. He just wished he could find something to ease his.

Finally he left for Muircraig but only stayed away a week. It was late at night when he entered his chambers and he stoutly resisted the urge to go and check on her. That would reassure him as far as his fears for her health went but he knew it would also be a temptation he might not be able to resist. He sighed as he undressed, then washed up and crawled into his too empty bed. Although he felt it best for her health that they sleep apart, he sorely missed her in his bed and ached to hold her. It would be too easy to convince himself that such care was unnecessary.

Islaen lay in her bed and listened to Iain moving around in his chambers. She was a little surprised that his stay at Muircraig had been so short. Then she started to grow angry as time passed and he did not even come to see her. Muttering soft curses, she sat up and started to get out of bed. She decided that the separation he had forced upon them had lasted long enough. Bracing herself for what would undoubtedly be a taxing argument, she started towards his chambers.

Warily Iain watched his wife approach his bed. The thin shift she wore revealed the changes in her lithe shape. Although the clear signs of pregnancy gnawed at his fears, the sight of her stirred his passion.

"Is something wrong, Islaen?" he asked, silently cursing the telltale huskiness in his voice.

"Aye, verra wrong." She crawled into bed at his side, ignoring the way he tensed. "My bed is verra empty. My husband is missing."

"There is a good reason for that." He clenched his hands as he resisted the urge to pull her into his arms.

"Is there? Weel, I havenae heard it yet."

"Islaen, an I share a bed with ye, I will make love to you."

"That is nice to hear." She turned on her side to look at him. "I thought ye might have lost interest because of the changes in me."

"Nay," he rasped and sidled away from her, "but I willnae give into that interest."

"Why not?"

She was beginning to find it all very amusing, despite a stern self-scolding over such ill-timed levity. Nevertheless the way the large muscular Iain was almost running away from his small pregnant wife was amusing. Reaching out and stroking his thigh, she had to bite her lip to keep from giggling when he nearly leapt out of the bed. His extreme skittishness assured her that he did still want her, and it strengthened her determination to end their needless abstinence. She had no intentions of letting him deprive her of his passion, the one thing he gave her freely.

"Islaen, I could hurt ye or the bairn. Ye ken it weel."

"Nay, I dinnae."

"Then ye are being purposely blind."

"Nay, ye are. Did Tavis e'er leave Storm's bed?"

"Weel, nay, but . . ."

"My fither ne'er left my mither's either. I dinnae ken where ye get this notion."

"'Tis a reasonable one. S'truth, physicians have espoused it."

"Aye, they also bleed men with open bleeding wounds, taking more of what the poor soul has already lost too much of. Unless ye mean to toss me about, I cannae see that ye will hurt me. I ken that I might soon grow too full to find pleasure in it, or for ye to want to do it. Seems foolish to waste this time."

In the face of her calm, Iain found it hard to cling to his resistance. It seemed reasonable that she would know better than he did what she could or could not do. Knowing that his own need for her could be clouding his judgment, he struggled to stay firm in his decision on abstinence. He grimaced when she curled up to his side and he made no move to push her away.

"Considering what lovemaking entails, I cannae believe 'tis fully safe," he said and cursed the wavering of his convictions.

"Weel, so long as ye arenae trying to go in whilst the bairn is trying to come out . . ."

"Islaen!" he gasped.

"Wheesht, 'tis true." She sensed his weakening resolve and ran her hand over his chest. "Iain, the troubled time for the bairn is in the first three months, while his hold isnae strong. This bairn is weel set. T'would take more than ye would e'er do to shake him free and ye cannae reach him to harm him."

"Of course I cannae, but . . ." His words strangled to a halt as her tongue flickered over his nipples and, although he told himself to push her away, his hands burrowed into her thick hair.

Islaen smiled faintly sensing his surrender. She knew all she had to do now was convince him of the safety of making love so long as she was comfortable with it, and they did not get too rough. It was important for she knew how easily he could reclaim his former determination to abstain as well as feel both guilt and anger at her for losing it. Her smile widened as she thought of the perfect way to show him that making love could hurt neither her nor the child.

"Iain," she said softly, trailing kisses down to his abdomen as she caressed his hips and arranged herself comfortably between his long legs, "I was with child when Fraser tried to rape me." She decided that was probably true but, even if it was not, it fit in with his opinion of when conception took place.

"Jesu," Iain breathed in shock, briefly distracted from the passion her caresses were stirring. "He was so rough."

"Aye. I was with bairn when MacLennon attacked us. He wounded me too, ye recall, and ye werenae verra gentle getting me to safety." She leisurely kissed her way down one of Iain's strong legs.

It was hard to think when she was firing his blood so, but her words penetrated passion's haze and made sense. "And when Fraser nearly raped ye at the crofter's hut," he murmured huskily, then suddenly sat up. "The blood on your thighs."

Not stopping her attentions she kissed her way up his other leg. "From cuts. Ye saw them yourself." She turned her amorous attentions to his loins and felt him shudder as her tongue slowly stroked him. "And none of that hurt me or the bairn."

He found it impossible to think, let alone speak while her warm mouth and tongue caressed him so intimately, but managed to rasp, "Ye were lucky."

"Aye but I meant for you to see that ye couldnae e'er do worse to me than that. Nay, certainly not by making love."

Closing his eyes as he groaned with pleasure when her mouth engulfed him, he whispered, "Nay, not with that. Ah, God's beard, Islaen, go slow. Go verra, verra slow. I ache to savor the pleasure ye give."

A moment later she sat up to look at him. "Mayhaps we best let ye calm down a wee bit then." When he grinned at her, she knew she had won, that she had succeeded in changing his mind.

Reaching out, he tugged off her shift. "Calm down, eh? I thought ye set out to excite me beyond thinking."

"Weel, not beyond thinking. Ye cannae agree when ye cannae think." Her voice grew huskier as his hands cupped her breasts.

Leaning forward he gently took the taut tip of her breast into his mouth. Islaen cried out softly and, burying her hands in his thick hair, held him close. Iain needed no such urging to savor the sweet bounty of her flesh. Finally, he cupped her face in his hands and brushed his lips over hers until she opened her eyes partway to look at him.

"Do I get a reward for being so agreeable?"

"A reward?" she asked a little dazedly.

"Aye," he said softly. "I have calmed down a wee bit."

He caught his breath when she smiled with a sweet lechery and, with a tantalizing slowness, lay down between his legs. Her gaze never left his as her small tongue flicked out to stroke him and he shuddered. Although she went slowly as he had requested, he knew he would not be able to enjoy her attentions with the same leisure that she gave them. Watching her, seeing in her eyes that she enjoyed pleasuring him so, was shredding what little control he had at an alarming rate. Giving a hoarse cry but moments later, he pulled her up into his arms, sat her astride him and neatly joined their bodies.

"Witch," he rasped as he held her by the hips and slowly moved her against him. "One of these days I shall learn how to enjoy that for longer than a moment or two."

When he put his arm around her and leaned her back a little so that his mouth could play over her breasts, Islaen knew she would not be able to delay her release for very long. The little control she had vanished completely when his hand moved between them. His skilled fingers found that bud beneath the silken curls and, with barely a touch, sent her tumbling into desire's sweet darkness. She clung to him and an instant later his body also shuddered with release. His arms tightened around her as they rocked gently, savoring the remnants of their passion.

Reluctantly, for he enjoyed the way she felt when they were so intimately entwined, Iain eased the closeness of the embrace. Taking her with him, he lay down and tugged the covers over them. Feeling her cuddle up to him, he sighed. It felt good to have her back in his arms.

"I suppose ye are savoring victory," he drawled, idly running his fingers through her hair.

Although she recognized the teasing note in his voice and smiled sleepily, she said seriously, "Nay, not victory. I mean . . ."

He kissed her forehead. "I was but teasing, lass."

"I ken it but in teasing there can lie some truth."

"Mayhaps. I was wrong. I ken it now. I was forcing us to do what neither of us wanted and there wasnae a need to." His hold on her tightened a little. "'Tis just that I . . . Nay I willnae speak on it. Ye probably ken what I meant to say anyhow," he muttered.

Since she did and he knew it, Islaen made no reply, simply held him tightly. When the child within her moved she hoped Iain did not sense it for she did not want his thoughts too much upon what he feared. He tensed and she sighed. Since her belly was pressed against him it had been foolish to think he could miss the movement. Almost shyly his hand came to rest upon her stomach. She waited to see how he would react to the proof of the life within her womb and almost smiled when the child moved and Iain cursed softly, then jerked his hand away. Gently, she took his hand and placed it back upon her stomach.

"The bairn lives, Iain. That is a thing to find only joy in."

"Aye," he whispered hoarsely. "How can ye sleep with such as this going on within your body?"

"Sometimes I cannae." She yawned and nuzzled her face in his neck. "Sometimes e'en that cannae keep me awake."

A moment later he had to smile in soft surprise for, despite the movement he could still feel within her womb, she had fallen asleep. He wondered if she too found it hard to sleep alone. It was pleasant to think that she did, even if it stirred a feeling of guilt for he knew he made her sleep alone much too often. If an empty bed gave her sleepless nights, he was fully to blame.

Long into the night he lay awake, his hand upon her stomach. Every sign of life he felt left him torn between wondrous joy and terror. He indulged in a great many prayers before he finally went to sleep, his fears briefly obliterated by exhaustion.

The weather turned bad the next day giving the land a brief taste of the swiftly approaching winter. Islaen did not mind it for it held Iain at Caraidland for a while.

The night the weather finally broke, Iain made fierce love to her and Islaen knew that he would be leaving her again. She was not at all surprised when, as they lay sated in each other's arms, he told her he would be leaving in the morning. Islaen wished she could see into his mind, see if he was hurrying away because something she had done or said had touched him, for then she would keep doing it.

"Muircraig willnae be ready for us this winter," she said only half-questioning the fact.

"Nay, and e'en an it was I think we should stay here."

"Until the bairn is born."

"Aye. There is help for ye here and I cannae take it all to Muircraig."

"Ye dinnae mean to winter at Muircraig, do ye?" she asked softly, unable to keep all of her fear out of her voice as that possibility suddenly assailed her.

"Nay." He held her tightly. "I will be with ye when your time comes."

She knew that would be hard for him just as she knew she would keep him as uninvolved as she could but she was glad he would be near. If nothing else she wanted him close at hand to hear her confession about the deceit she had employed so that if anything went wrong he could not blame himself. In some ways it would be easier for her if he was not near but she also knew she would do all she could to see that he was close by.

Chapter Eighteen

Rubbing his hands together in a vain attempt to warm them, Iain searched the ground for some sign that a man had recently passed through the area. Phelan had seen signs and the youth's skill in such matters was not to be questioned. Iain felt sure it was MacLennon and there was an eagerness with him to confront the man. He wanted the final confrontation over even though it could mean that he would never know if Islaen survived childbirth or see the child she gave him. His eagerness to face his foe came from a weariness that reached to his soul. Iain was simply tired of living half a life, of always waiting for the man to strike.

As he dismounted to check something a little more closely, he admitted that this was another reason he spent so much time at Muircraig. He wanted to draw MacLennon away from Islaen. Caraidland was well guarded, but MacLennon had already showed how little that mattered. The man's main target was still him. By being at Muircraig while Islaen was in Caraidland, he divided the man's targets and felt sure that MacLennon would come to him first.

"Ye willnae find me there, MacLagan," mocked a voice that chilled Iain's blood.

A little surprised that the man was showing himself, Iain

slowly turned to face his enemy. He felt sure that MacLennon knew about his men that searched for signs nearby. Iain wondered if constant failure was finally driving the man to act carelessly. If so, it could prove a boon. 'That is, if I escape this meeting,' he thought wryly as he swiftly drew his sword.

"Ye grow verra tiresome, MacLennon."

"I will see that ye are soon beyond caring. Today ye die, MacLagan."

"So ye continue to boast but ye ne'er accomplish your aim." He saw fury flare in the man's eyes and knew he was right, that MacLennon grew frustrated by his continued failure. "Come, try again why dinnae ye? Or, do ye grow weary of failing?"

With a bellow of rage Iain was certain would reach the ears of his men, MacLennon attacked. Iain was staggered by the force of the man's strike. It was hard to believe the smaller, slender man was stronger. Iain could only presume that the man's madness gave him such strength. Having enraged him had simply added to that strength. With a thrill of alarm Iain also recognized that the cold had slowed him, stiffening him and robbing him of some of his agility. It could prove to be a fatal handicap.

The sound of approaching horsemen drove MacLennon to make one final, furious assault upon Iain before fleeing. Iain was stunned by the ferocity of the attack. He neatly blocked a sword strike but felt a sharp pain in his side. In dismay he saw that MacLennon held a now bloodied dagger in his other hand. The giggle that escaped MacLennon as Iain staggered, clutching his side, made Iain feel slightly ill. He readied himself as well as he could to face another attack but MacLennon was gone. He caught a faint glimpse of the man disappearing into the wood just as Phelan, Murdo and Robert arrived.

"After him. He went that way," Iain rasped even as he sat down heavily, suddenly overcome by dizziness.

Robert dismounted and hurried to his side as Phelan and

Murdo raced after MacLennon. "Wheesht, Iain, he came close to skewering ye weel this time," Robert muttered as he hurried to staunch the flow of blood. "'Tis nay fatal though."

"I didnae see him draw his knife. Must be growing slow in my declining years," he jested weakly.

"What troubles me is that we didnae see him," Robert grumbled after smiling briefly. "We should have seen him, Iain."

"We ne'er see him, do we. I begin to think we deal with a specter. He leaves but a faint trail yet, e'en when we find it, we ne'er find him." Iain suddenly collapsed against Robert, no longer able to fight off unconciousness.

"God's beard, did MacLennon win then?" Phelan asked in horror when he and Murdo returned.

"Nay, he has but swooned. Ye lost the mon," replied Robert.

"Aye. Curse him."

"I think we best take Iain to Caraidland."

"Aye, there will be better care for him there."

Islaen frowned, her attention diverted from some frolicking puppies she played with in the stables. Wallace stood looking out at the bailey and she waited for him to tell her what was causing the mild disturbance out there. When he glanced her way rather worriedly, she felt her heart lurch with fear and rose. He hesitantly moved as if to stop her and her alarm grew.

Slipping around him she looked out and swayed as she saw Iain being lifted off of a litter. "Nay," she whispered then cried, "Iain," as she started to run towards her husband only to be caught by Robert before she reached Iain's side.

"He isnae dead, lass. Just cut a wee bit." He held her close when she slumped against him. "Calm yourself and then I will take ye to him."

"MacLennon?" she asked as she fought to calm herself as he had commanded.

"Aye but we lost him."

"God's tears, not again."

"Aye, again. Better now?"

"Better. T'was just seeing him carried in like that."

"Weel, I think t'was a lot of things that sent him into a swoon. Come, we will go and see him now." He took her hand and started towards the keep. "It wouldnae have done him much good to see ye so pale and upset. He would most like feel he had caused some harm to ye and the bairn by giving ye a bad turn. This will end his work on Muircraig 'til spring, I think."

Later, as she sat by his bed and waited for Iain to wake Islaen decided Robert was probably right. So long as infection or fever did not set in the wound was not fatal. It was deep, however, requiring a couple of stitches, so it would be a while before he could move much without the threat of breaking open his wound. By the time he was healed enough to do any real work, Islaen felt sure that winter would have begun in earnest. There would be no working at Muircraig then nor any time until the spring.

"So, husband," she murmured, "ye will have to stay near your wife for a change. Nary a place to run to."

"Islaen," Iain groaned as he fought his way to consciousness and thought he heard his wife's voice.

Praying that he had been too groggy to understand her words, she smiled at him when he opened his eyes. Carefully helping him to sit up a little bit she gave him a drink of water. She decided that he was too pale and hoped that that would soon pass.

"How did I get here?" Iain rasped as he laid back down.

"Robert, Phelan and Murdo brought ye here. They felt it better for ye."

"'Tis bad?" He gingerly touched the bandaging at his side.

"Nay, 'tis deep though, and ye must rest to heal right. Rest and be still so that ye dinnae pull out the stitches. Ye have lost enough blood. No need to start any more flowing out of ye."

"Ah, Jesu, we nearly had him, Islaen." He gripped her hand when she took hold of his in a gesture of sympathy. "I grow so verra weary of this game."

"So do I, Iain, and I havenae played it near as long as ye have. Are ye sure the mon isnae a sorcerer?"

"Or some ghostie, eh?" He smiled faintly. "Nay, though I oft find myself wondering. Howbeit, if we cut him, he bleeds. I think only living flesh does that," he drawled. "They were careful bringing me in, were they? Ye cannae afford a bad turn now, lass."

"Robert was quick to catch me ere I really had time to think the worst. He was watching for me."

"Good," he murmured weakly, feeling strongly inclined to go to sleep again. "Ye get some rest, Islaen; I will be fine."

"I ken it, Iain." She leaned forward and kissed his cheek. "I will just sit here until ye are asleep again. I but needed to see ye wake once to ease my worries. Do ye need anything? Want anything?"

"MacLennon's head on a salver," he jested sleepily then grasped Islaen's hand more tightly. "Dinnae think ye can do it."

She smiled and held his hand between hers, bringing it up to her lips. "I swear I shall be a verra good lass."

"Swear it?" he asked, opening his eyes enough to look at her with tired sternness. "Ye have ne'er done anything so reckless whilst I have been with ye, but I have this feeling ye might give some wild idea a thought."

"Mayhaps an I didnae have twa lives to consider each time I do anything."

"Ah, of course. Of course," he murmured, falling asleep almost as soon as he had finished speaking.

She sat beside him for a long while simply watching him

sleep. Occasionally she reached out to brush the hair off of his forehead and gently test for any signs of fever. Islaen had a feeling that it was not simply his wound that made him sleep so deeply. There were signs of exhaustion upon his face. She hoped his weariness would not weaken him too much thus furthering the chances of infection and fever. It was not until Storm nearly forced her from his side that Islaen gave up her vigil, leaving Tavis to watch over Iain for a while.

Islaen glared at her husband and seriously considered hitting him with the tray she held. He was nearly healed enough to have his stitching removed but she was sorely tempted to give him a few new wounds. She decided he was worse than even her brother Colin who made the most miserable patient of all her kin and told him so.

"Weel, why dinnae ye lay about in a bed all day after cursed day and see how ye like it," he grumbled.

"I dinnae like it and I suspicion I wasnae a verra good patient when I had to, but I do think I at least tried not to make life miserable for everyone."

Iain watched her as she moved angrily around the room, tidying it up. Slowly his temper faded. He knew he was being miserable but could not help himself. Glancing at her ever-rounding belly, he decided it was far past time for him to exercise a little more control of his temper. She could not afford such upsets at this time.

"Forgive me," he said softly, smiling crookedly when she turned to look at him. "'Tis just that I cannae abide this lying about."

She sat down on the edge of the bed and took his hand in hers. "Ye neednae apologize, Iain. I understand your anger." Smiling faintly, she said, "Ye will be up and about soon and then ye can curse your weakness instead of me."

"Impudent wench."

"Aye, most like." She got the salve from the bedside table and rubbed a little upon his wound to ease the itching she knew came with the healing. "These can be removed soon. The wound has closed weel."

Her light, gentle touch enflamed him. He had been too long without her. Wounded or not he was determined to ease that need. Grasping her around the waist as she put the salve away, he tugged her into his arms.

"Iain," she gasped, "be careful. Your wound . . ."

"'Tis not only my wound that tries my temper, lass," he interrupted.

One look into his eyes told her what he was thinking about but she looked at him innocently. "Ye dinnae like the salve."

"Verra amusing." He slid her hand down his body until it rested upon his manhood.

"Ye want me to put salve on that?"

"Islaen," he growled, "it isnae wise to taunt a desperate mon."

"Are ye desperate, Iain?" she murmured as she stroked him.

"Aye, witch."

He kissed her hungrily even as his hand sought the warmth between her thighs. Islaen felt her somewhat neglected desires flare to life. Nevertheless, when he finally released her mouth to spread warm kisses over her throat, she fought to recall his wound.

"I am nay sure ye ought to do this, Iain."

"I am." He undid her gown enough to free her breasts.

"Are ye sure we can do this without hurting your side?"

"I am about to show ye that we can and verra nicely too."

Islaen said no more until she lay sated in his arms. "Aye, that was verra nice." She giggled when the baby kicked her and Iain grunted. "Ye should feel it from this side."

"Nay, I think I can live content to a ripe old age without kenning it."

Moving off him, Islaen straightened her clothes. "Where did ye put my braes?"

"Tossed 'em aside."

"How uncivilized."

Crossing his arms behind his head, he grinned at her. "Aye, ye should learn to control yourself."

"My, we are feeling better, arenae we," she drawled as she got off of the bed and started to look for her braes.

"There are some potions that cannae be matched."

Finding her braes all the way across the room, Islaen turned her back to him and put them on. "Ye didnae toss them; ye hurled them."

"Why bother putting them back on?"

"I feel naked without them. Just keep feeling as if something will show. I have gotten accustomed to wearing them. Truth tell, I begin to think the women that dinnae wear them be the odd ones." She returned to sit on the edge of the bed. "Do ye want anything else?" she asked pertly.

Iain was about to make an outrageous reply when Islaen gasped and put her hands over her stomach. "Islaen?"

"Aye, just a moment," she gasped as she hurriedly lay down by his side and grasped his hand in what she could see was a vain attempt to ease his worry. "The bairn dances," she said breathlessly.

Almost timidly he put his hands on her swollen abdomen. His eyes slowly widened as he felt the prodigious activity within. It was little surprise that it offset her. He wondered how she could tolerate it.

"Does it hurt?" he whispered.

"Nay, not truly, but 'tis not comfortable either," she replied with an increasing calm as the activity within her womb eased a little and she was less startled by it.

"Mayhaps a physician."

"To leech me or cup me? He will think it something in my blood so take some out, mayhaps too much. Aye, he will still the activity. A dead bairn cannae move too muckle much. Dinnae bring one of those corbies near me, Iain. Swear it."

"I swear it. Calm yourself, Islaen," he soothed, then jested weakly, "ye will have the bairn kicking his way out in fright."

"Feels so, doesnae it. 'Tis just that I dinnae like physicians."

"That was easy to see. Why not?"

She shrugged. "I dinnae ken really save that I have seen their work and it turns my stomach. I could say t'was because of what was done to my cousin, a youth named Ninian, save that I had already begun to distrust the breed by then."

"What happened to Ninian?" He relaxed a little as he sensed the growing calm in her and the child in her womb.

"He was hurt in a raid. His kin brought in a physician. The mon was near at hand after all. I was there for my fither and brithers were part of the raid. Poor Ninian was already weak and wan with the loss of blood but that carrion and his assistant wanted more. Ninian's fither was nearly swayed to believe their cries that t'was needed. He e'en went so far as to let them put the leeches on. Ninian didnae have the blood to spare, Iain. Any fool could see that."

"Did he die?" Ian asked softly.

"Nay," she muttered, not sure she wanted to finish the tale.

"What happened? Come, ye cannae stop in the midst of the tale."

"Och, weel, they left, the physician, his aides and Ninian's fither too. They sought a drink and the privacy to speak. Nathan and I took the leeches off while Robert fetched a calf. When the men returned they found fat leeches, ones so bloated they had fallen off. Ninian's father took one look at the creatures, thought on all the blood they had taken from a youth who had already lost so much and sent the physician away. Ninian still hasnae told his fither the truth. He doesnae like physicians either.

"They could have killed him, Iain, and would have an it

had been Ninian's blood in those leeches, blood Ninan couldnae spare."

"Letting blood is an accepted practice," he said calmly although he silently admitted that he had little liking for it.

"Iain, when a person gets a wound they seek to stop the
blood flowing out of it. Losing blood makes ye weak. Losing
too much can kill ye. Most everyone kens that. Ye will ne'er
get me to believe 'tis wise to purposely draw it out. If God
didnae want what's in there to stay in there He wouldnae have
put it in there to begin with."

"I have oft thought the same." He brought her hand to his
lips and kissed it. "Are ye feeling, better?"

"I didnae feel poorly. 'Tis just that I feel it best to lie down
when the bairn jumps and reels so. It can make me feel a wee
bit unsteady on my feet. I dinnae wish to fall."

He nodded slowly, chilled by even the thought of such oc-
currence. She seemed to be rounding out at an alarming rate.
He did not dare to say anything, however, for he knew his fear
would taint his words and possibly infect her as well. Iain did
wish there was someone he could talk to about the matter and
greeted his brother almost hopefully when Tavis arrived.

"Does she look large to ye, Tavis?" he asked almost the
moment Islaen had left.

"She is starting to round out, isnae she."

"That I can see for myself," Iain drawled. "What I asked
was if ye think she has rounded out too much."

"Nay. Dinnae look for trouble, Iain."

"The movement of the bairn makes her seek a bed. That
cannae be right."

"An it isnae then Storm has erred with each of our bairns.
Storm told me that she didnae have to lie down, just felt a wee
bit safer if she did so for the movement made her feel unsteady."

"So Islaen said."

"Then heed her. She kens what she does or doesnae feel,

can feel better than ye can if there is aught wrong. Truth tell, I think a woman kens her body, the weaknesses, strengths and ills of it, better than a mon does his. I think they need to."

"Mayhaps. 'Tis just the way it feels," he whispered. "An I can feel it so strongly, I cannae help but worry o'er how it makes her feel. She says the bairn dances and, God's beard, 'tis what it feels like."

"Aye, I was oft astounded o'er the feel of it. I shouldnae like to bear it. Dinnae let her see how ye fret, Iain."

"She kens it."

"No doubt, but there is no need to flaunt it afore her eyes. She does all she should, Iain. Rests, eats weel, doesnae let herself grow too weary."

"Catalina stayed abed."

"Catalina was a fool. Aye, and mayhaps 'tis why she is dead. After months of doing naught but lying in bed what strength did she have to birth a bairn with? Dinnae think on her. Islaen isnae Catalina. There is naught to compare between them. We best leave the matter, Iain, for I have little patience with your worries, understand them though I do, and ye cannae shake them.

"Heed this, though. Islaen may be a wee lass but she isnae a weak one. Ye have seen that. She is of a line of women who have large healthy broods and fare none the worse for it. Her brother Robert loves her dearly but he seems little worried. She does all she should to keep herself strong and in good health. The bairn she carries shows life, strong vigorous life. She has been through a lot, yet is still hale and still carries the bairn. She is neither growing wan nor grows sickly.

"Heed all these things, Iain. Keep them in your mind. Use them to hold your fears back. Aye, she seems content and shows no fear but the fears are there. Every woman has them. Dinnae make them worse by feeding them with yours."

Iain nodded, solemnly recognizing the truth in Tavis's words. He had already seen the need to hide his fear as much as he could but it did strengthen his resolve to hear another point it out. Although he knew nothing could fully still his fears, he was determined to remember every good thing Tavis had mentioned. He could easily see how they could give him strength.

The day his stitches were removed, he tested his strength to stand and walk but found little there. As he cursed his weakness he suddenly recalled Islaen saying he would. Glancing her way he saw her fighting a smile and started to laugh. It was the only time he found any humor in the situation. He found the rate at which his strength returned far too slow a one.

Islaen watched her husband sleep and smiled crookedly. It seemed a little unfair that her method of soothing him had not seemed to work as well for her. She was wide awake. However, the current activity in her womb was undoubtedly the real reason she could not sleep despite the warm, pleasant feeling of sated desires. She wished the child would suit his schedule of being active and inactive to suit hers a little better but suspected few women had such luck.

Deciding to get up for a little while, she rose and donned her robe. She moved to the window, opened the shutter and looked out. The hint of winter was definitely in the air. Just as she wondered if Wallace had been wrong in predicting snow she saw the first flakes fall. Winter could bring with it a lot of ills, not the least of which were hunger and sickness. For once, however, she was glad to see it arrive. It signaled the end of all work upon Muircraig.

"Islaen?"

"By the window, Iain."

"Are you mad?" he grumbled as he rose and hurriedly donned his robe against the chill before moving towards her. "'Tis cold. Ye could catch a chill."

"Just a moment longer, Iain. Look. 'Tis snowing. It has just started but Wallace says t'will be a strong storm."

"Do ye like the snow, Islaen?" he asked as he came up behind her and slipped his arms around her.

"Oh, aye, Iain."

"'Tis pretty but it means winter is here to stay for a while."

'Aye,' she mused silently, 'and so are you, husband.'

Chapter Nineteen

Biting her lip, Islaen fought against crying out when a strong contraction gripped her. It had been fairly easy so far but she realized it would soon be impossible to hide the fact that she was in labor, and had been since the very early morning. She could only hope that there were not many hours left. It was important to keep Iain from knowing for as long as possible. A glance towards her husband told Islaen that that might not be so easy. He was staring at her and paying little attention to what his brother and father were saying.

He had stared at her a lot lately and she knew it was not all from a fascination with how big she had grown during the last stages of her pregnancy. Her impish sense of humour had reared its head too often, but she had consistently beaten down the urge to do something silly, pull some prank. Iain was in no state of mind to find it funny. He would never understand that his staring had prompted her, would probably think her cruel beyond words.

Another was watching her closely and Meg leaned nearer to mutter, "Will ye nay seek your bed now, lass?"

Smiling faintly, Islaen shook her head. Meg helped in every way she could and Islaen was grateful to her. Without Meg's help, many of the minor troubles and ills of pregnancy could never have been hidden from Iain. In the past few months Islaen had come to see, more clearly than ever before, that Meg cared for her. It had been a great source of comfort, especially as she had adjusted to new kin, new surroundings and the loss of her large, boisterous family.

"Nay," Islaen replied softly. "An I maun, I will have the bairn upon this cursed settle rather than make Iain wait through a minute of labor."

"'Tis mad ye are," Meg grumbled, her keen eyes seeing another contraction grip Islaen. "Keep that bit o' cloth ye are making a muckle great mess of o'er your belly. 'Tis easy tae see that the bairn tries to get out."

Islaen smiled. "I suspicioned that it might be. If Wallace is right, I still have time left me."

Meg made a rude noise but softly. "Ye are a woman, nay a cow or a mare nor a cursed ewe."

"I ken ye dinnae like to hear it said but their way of birthing is as ours save quieter. I learned a lot."

"T'was no place for a lady, mucking about in the stables. Those pains are coming muckle close togither now, lass."

"Aye, but not close enough yet. Ye ken that as weel as I do, Meg. Dinnae pinch at me so."

"When will ye confess your trickery, lass?"

"I plan to tell him when I hand him a healthy, squalling bairn."

That confession worried her more than the ordeal she faced. In truth, she did not really need to make it. Having forgotten the one time she had had her menses, Iain still felt that their first night together had seeded the child. He had not the slightest suspicion that she had not kept her promise. It was sorely tempting to let matters stand that way but she knew she could not.

Lying was foreign to her although she could never claim to be free of that sin. Lying to Iain had caused her a lot of anguish. She had to confess even if she feared how he would react. The lie was becoming a slow poison to her and she wanted it out of her blood. She could only pray that Iain would understand and forgive her.

She continued to fight the revealing of her labor. The needlework she pretended to work on progressed not at all, but it served to hide the rippling of her contracting belly and gave her something to stare at in the hope that none could read what was happening in her face. She almost welcomed the increased ferocity of the pains and their growing proximity to each other for it meant that her time of birthing drew nearer.

Not all men were ignorant of the various intricacies of birth. Tavis may have missed the birth of his firstborn, but he had more than made up for that with his other children. Although he could not say exactly what made him suspect, he felt more confident with each glance that his brother's tiny wife was in labor. The moment he could do so without stirring Iain's curiosity, Tavis left the table and strolled to where Storm struggled to teach Aingeal needlework. His little daughter was easily sent off for she had little liking for the lessons.

"She will ne'er learn e'en a modest ability if ye keep releasing her from the lessons."

"I ken I will be forgiven this time. Try not to be too obvious about it but have a good look at wee Islaen."

It was not easy to be subtle when her curiosity had been stirred to a fever pitch but Storm managed. What was even harder was to hide her shock as her keen eyes noted all the signs of advanced labor. That she had to look closely to see it made her mentally shake her head in wonder. She knew well how the pains of birth could wrack the body at such a late stage of labor.

"The little fool. What do ye wish me to do?"

"There must be some way to get her up to her chambers without alerting Iain. If she excuses herself, he will be after her and fretting like an old woman. Mayhaps if ye take her off he willnae think on it. The mon's in a verra sad state."

"Aye, poor man. I ken t'would kill him an aught happened to Islaen for I am certain that he loves her, though he is as loathe to admit it as ye e'er were."

Grinning, Tavis kissed his wife's pert nose but then he grew serious. "This wee lass owns his soul though I doubt she kens it and, an Iain does, he isnae saying. Enough of this talk. Get the wee lass up to her bed ere Iain's firstborn comes forth upon that settle."

Islaen silently thanked Storm with her eyes when the woman got them out of the hall on the excuse of looking over some infant clothes and necessities. Once out of the hall, Storm and Meg took turns scolding her as they helped her up the stairs. They were just outside of her chambers door when her waters broke. A terse word from Storm was all that was needed to make the maids share in the secrecy.

The back stairs were used to bring whatever was needed. So too were the back stairs used to take word to Wallace, a circumstance that caused many to wonder, but less so than when Wallace called for a bath. Robert was secretly sent on his way to the MacRoths by the same manner.

The help and support of Storm and Meg was greatly appreciated by Islaen. She was too far gone in her labor to do much for herself when they reached her chambers. The two women efficiently undressed her, helped her into a loose shift and did their best to make her as comfortable as they could, not an easy chore when her body was wracked by pain and she needed all her strength to keep calm and quiet.

For a moment, Islaen found herself angry with Iain. She needed him, his strength and support. Quite naturally, she had her own fears but he was too caught up in his to notice or to aid her in easing them. She had to fight that battle all alone and she was tired of the fight.

Then she silently scolded herself for that brief weakness.

Managing it on her own was necessary. Iain was not to blame for his fears. She told herself to accept the lack of his support as the penance for her lie and turned her attention to Storm.

"I have sent word to the men that we have retired for the night," Storm said after a few hours had passed. "T'will hold them for a while."

"Ah, good," Islaen gasped as a pain subsided. "Would it not be wondrous to be all done ere Iain seeks his bed?" She tried to flow with it as another pain ripped through her. "I thought that the breaking of the waters was a sign that t'was soon."

Storm sighed as she bathed Islaen's sweat-beaded forehead. The girl was on her knees gripping the bedpost and Storm could well recall her own labors, bearing the children in such a position. All signs pointed to imminent arrival but nothing happened. Despite the pain so clearly etched upon Islaen's face, she made no sound save for an occasional moan and a great deal of panting. Storm could not help but admire the girl's strength and marvel at the depth of her love for Iain, both of which kept her from the very natural reaction of crying out from the pain that gripped her whole body. Even though she admired it, it was somewhat eerie. Screaming was a part of labor.

"It can be but not all women are the same. The first always comes the hardest and takes the longest."

"Could ye send for Wallace? T'would ease my mind an he would check me. He can tell by touch whether the bairn is turned wrong."

That was a thing that Storm feared but hid it, saying soothingly, "There's naught to fear. It has not been that long that we need to worry."

"I dinnae fear it, Storm, but an it is holding matters up I wish to ken that. My mither had several bairns enter the world feet first."

Without any further word and, ignoring Meg's sputterings, Storm sent for Wallace. The man arrived but moments later having been seated in the kitchens awaiting any possible request for him. A faint color touched his cheeks as he entered the exclusively female domain, but one look at Islaen erased his discomfort. Talking to her much as if she were one of his treasured stock, he ran his knowledgeable hands over her belly.

"Aye, ye kenned it richt, m'lady. The bairn's wrong way round. Needs turning."

"Turning?" squeaked Meg. "Ye cannae turn a bairn in the womb like ye do some foal."

"Why can ye not?" asked Storm, quite taken with the idea.

"She is just a wee lass, not some cursed great mare. How can ye, weel," Meg flushed, "gie at the bairn?"

"Like ye do a foal, ye silly auld coo. If the bairn can gie out, then a hand can gie in." He looked at Storm. "Ye hae wee hands, m'lady. Can ye do it? I will talk ye through it. Aye, the lass could bring the bairn oot as it lies but 'tis verra dangerous. A bit o' pain now can save a muckle lot later. I ken ye helped with a foaling last spring."

"That I did. I cannot say I will enjoy this but an I maun, I maun, as ye heathens say."

She grinned briefly as she moved to wash her hands and the three Scots grinned back at her although Islaen's turned into a gritting of teeth. Wallace stood with his broad back turned to where Storm knelt between Islaen's legs. Meg bathed Islaen's face as Storm eased her hand up the birth canal and said nothing to the instructing Wallace when he soothed Islaen with strokes and murmurs as if she were some animal. All three of them tensed when a soft but audible gasp escaped Storm.

For one brief moment, Islaen felt terrified. With a concerted effort she forced her fears away. Fear would weaken her and she needed all her strength now especially if something was not right.

"I am sorry, so very sorry. I did not mean to afright you.

That gasp was not because of a fault. There is more than one babe in here and t'was a shock to find a head near the back of the babe I was trying to turn. Ye are to bear twins as I did."

"Me mither had twa pairs," ground out Islaen. "I ken I need something to bite on ere I shorten my tongue."

"Here, sweeting," Meg soothed as she placed a thick piece of leather between Islaen's teeth.

"When ye get the bairn's head where it should be, make sure the cord's clear o' the wee neck," Wallace instructed.

"Aye. 'Tis clear of both wee necks. That all, Wallace?" When the man nodded, Storm removed her hand and went to wash.

"Weel, I will just gie back tae the kitchens," Wallace said with a definite touch of regret.

"Ye dinnae have to, Wallace. I ken ye would like to be in on the birthing of a bairn. Ye have been such a help so ye maun stay if ye wish it." Islaen's voice was strained and broken by pain. "We may have need of ye yet."

There was no need to further persuade him. Wallace was eager to see the birth he had spent so much time discussing with Master Iain's tiny wife. Islaen was glad for it was the only way she could think of to repay him for all he had done. She also found his methods of soothing her very effective and was not at all perturbed by the fact that she had seen him treat his precious animals just so. Islaen hoped she would yet be done before Iain sought their chambers.

Knowing it was what Islaen wanted, Tavis tried valiantly to keep Iain in the hall but failed. Iain knew he would not sleep much at all for he had not since he had discovered he was to be a father, but he could not keep away from Islaen for any length of time. Although Islaen, with her astonishingly large belly, was the source of his agitation and nightmares he could not stay away from her nor find any ease of mind if he did. He lay beside her at night, his eyes and often his hands exploring the swell of her abdomen, fascination and terror warring with each other as he felt the prodigious activity within.

It was not in him to accept the death of any young woman easily, but he had never felt so terrified of it when Catalina had faced it as he did with Islaen. Guilt concerning his need for her, a need that had brought her to this, nearly choked him. It was only recently that he had finally left her alone. The thought that he could lose her ate away at him day and night. Catalina's death had affected him mostly through guilt, the knowledge that he had used her as had others. Islaen's would touch him in every way.

Briefly he indulged in cursing her for putting him into such a state. He had neither wanted nor needed to feel so about any woman. Despite all his efforts to keep a distance between them, Islaen had pulled him ever closer, subtly pulling him deeper beneath the spell she wove so effortlessly.

As he started to their chambers, he told himself not to be so unfair. Islaen plied no tricks nor played any games. Islaen was simply Islaen. The web he found himself tangled in was one he had walked into with a full knowledge of his fate. He had seen the danger and simply lacked the strength to fight it.

"Iain," Tavis called as he followed his brother up the stairs, Colin watching with curious concern from the hall.

"What is it?" Iain asked in a taut voice as a cold feeling seeped through him.

Gripping Iain by the shoulders in a gesture meant to comfort, Tavis said, "The bairn is on its way."

Iain felt as if he had been dealt a powerful blow to the stomach. He swayed slightly beneath the shock of Tavis's quiet announcement. Although he had been expecting Islaen to deliver the child at any moment he had expected some warning of the event when it came. There had been none. Or at least none that he had seen or been told about, he thought suddenly, and looked at Tavis with growing suspicion.

"Ye kenned and said naught?" Iain hissed, the cold in

him turning to sheer ice as Tavis's words continued to sear his brain.

"She didnae want ye to ken it was time. Aye, she was in labor as we dined but I didnae guess it 'til later."

"Oh God," Iain groaned as he broke from Tavis's light grip and bounded up the stairs, his father and his brother at his heels.

There was no real sound to be heard when he stopped outside of the door of his chambers, a circumstance that chilled his heart. A low moan and the soft murmur of a man's voice reached his ears and his fist wreaked havoc upon the closed door. It did not gain him the entry he desired. Instead, he found himself facing Meg, who planted herself firmly between him and the reshut door.

"Ye cannae go in there. 'Tis nay a place for a mon."

"There is a mon in there now. I can hear him."

"'Tis Wallace. He has a way of soothing the lass like one of his beasts and is as guid as any midwife. Ye will stay out here."

"God's beard, ye old corbie, I want to see my wife."

"I ken ye arenae intending to sweet talk yer way in. Ye arenae going in. Ye are in a sorry state and thinking on death. It willnae do the lass any guid to have such a dowie face keeking at her. Stay here or gie tae the hall to get drunk but ye arenae going in to fret o'er her." She slipped back into the room, slammed and bolted the door.

"I will set right here, witch," he bellowed but then began to pace the hall in agitation.

Colin slipped away and returned a few moments later with some whiskey. Flanked by his brother and father, Iain sat directly opposite the door. Although Tavis and Colin managed to get a dram or two, it was Iain who did most of the drinking. The lack of noise usually associated with a woman in labor began to bother them as well. Somehow it seemed ominous not to be assailed with the vocal expressions of the pain they knew she had to be in. A hearty scream would almost be welcome.

Islaen was sorely tempted to give a scream that would bring down Caraidland's sturdy walls. With the entrance of her son into the world she felt as if she were being torn in two. Her teeth nearly met through the leather she bit on. The worst of it was that it was not over. Her exhausted body hardly took a breath but it was straining yet again to eject another babe. Despite that she smiled when the lusty cries of her firstborn filled the room followed immediately by Iain's pounding fist on the still-bolted door.

For someone who was so terrified of childbirth, Iain seemed very eager to come and see, she thought with a weak smile. His obvious concern was support of a sort and she found a source of renewed strength in that. He might not be right beside her but he was near and clearly concerned and that was good enough.

"Let me in," Iain belowed. "Now!"

"Nay," Meg bellowed right back, "ye cannae come in yet. There's things that be left tae be done. Ye'd be surprised if ye kenned," she muttered.

"Islaen," called Iain, thrilled by the sound of a living child but still terrified for his wife, "are ye all right?"

It was not easy but Islaen answered him. "Aye. I go along fine, Iain. Be patient. T'will not be long now."

"There," Tavis soothed as he pulled Iain back from the door, "doesnae that ease your mind? The bairn lives as does Islaen."

"Wee Islaen would say she goes along fine if she had to use her dying breath to do it. I wish to see with my own eyes that she does."

"They will be cleaning up and all," said Colin. "Then ye can go in and look all ye care to. The worst is o'er now, laddie."

It was not true and they both knew it. Now came the danger

that, as with Catalina, the bleeding would continue until the life drained from the woman's body or a fever took her within days of the birth. A live baby would mean little to him if it cost him Islaen. Iain wanted to be with her as if by the sheer strength of his will and presence he could keep her from slipping away from him.

Each minute the door remained closed to him, denying him the sight of a living Islaen, was a torture to Iain. He saw all too clearly all the ways she could die, envisioned every horror that could visit a childbed. As he waited for what seemed a lifetime he took little notice of a second and third wail.

"Mark the first-born," gasped Islaen as her second son loudly proclaimed that he lived and she wondered why her body still strained. "I want no doubt as to which has what rights. Ye three will be witnesses to it. As my fither had done, Meg."

Begging forgiveness for hurting such a harmless creature, Meg cut the baby's right palm then tended the wound in a way that would leave a scar. It would be a lasting mark that would ever denote the boy as the first to have left his mother's womb. Less important was the way it would ever make the twins easy to tell apart. MacRoth had dubbed it the Heritage Scar for it told without question how the line of succession went. Meg then turned her mind to Islaen and fought to hide her fear and worry.

"What is it, Wallace? Can ye tell why the poor child still labors as if there is yet a bairn to be born?"

After his knowledgeable hands moved over Islaen's still swollen, contracting belly, Wallace said, "Seems there still is a bairn to come."

"Oh God," Islaen moaned softly, "am I to bear a litter like some bitch?"

"Nay, 'tis the last but dinnae hope too much for it tae live, lassie," he said softly. "T'would be a miracle an it did."

Islaen knew that would bring her pain later. The exhaustion

and pain that gripped her so firmly at the moment kept Wallace's soft, grim prediction from delivering much of a blow. She simply wanted to be done. To be finished with her labors and get some rest was all important to her.

The girl that emerged from her mother's womb was tiny, its cry but a mew. To the women's amazement, Wallace ordered them to see to Islaen as he took the baby. They had barely bathed Islaen and put a clean gown on her when Wallace scooped her up in his arms. He laid her down next to the washed, tightly swathed girl he had placed before the freshly stoked fire.

"Gie her the first suckle, lass. Then ye maun get a wet nurse for the bairn. She'll need milk aplenty if she is tae hae a chance and ye'll be sore tried tae feed her brithers. Grizel what married the blacksmith will do. She be clean and loving and heavy with milk for her bairn died but hours after it were born."

A little blindly, Islaen stared at the child Wallace had pressed into her hold. The little girl was very tiny and looked weak. Islaen felt grief stir beneath her exhaustion but it was unable to gain the strength needed to bother her much. Later she would face the loss of the babe she had nurtured within her body for so many months. She was glad of the protection her weariness gave her against that pain.

Wallace told her all he would do and have done to keep the child alive as Islaen let each boy know where nourishment was to be found. When her bed was clean and all signs of blood erased, he carried her to her bed. He was sent to fetch Grizel and a priest to baptize the babes. As he stepped out of the room he was nearly knocked down by Iain rushing to his wife.

Through exhaustion-glazed eyes, Islaen stared at her husband. He looked as bad as she felt and she almost smiled but then she remembered that she had to tell him about her lie. For the first time since uttering the lie she was not afraid of confessing it to him. She was simply too tired. Fearing her weariness would pull her into sleep's firm hold before she could speak she hurried to get the words out.

"Are ye weel?" he asked her as he sat on the bed and clasped her hands in his.

He thought she looked small and pale. Her eyes looked bruised, their color weakened. It looked as if whatever strength she had had been completely sapped. Her hands were limp in his.

Valiantly he struggled to still his fears. If things had not gone well or took a turn for the worse, she would need him calm and require his strength. With all his will, he dredged up what he could but was not sure it would be enough to keep him from crumbling if something was wrong.

"Aye, just weary. Look at your bairns, Iain."

"M'God," he breathed, staring at the three bundles with as much shock as his brother and father. "Three?"

His mind refused to accept what his eyes told him. Living twins were a miracle in most people's eyes. He himself often considered them such. That a woman, especially one as small as Islaen, could bear three children at one throw was more than his frantic mind could comprehend. It helped little at all that his father, brother, Storm and Meg seemed to see it as fact. Deciding he would deal with that confusion later he turned his full attention back to a heavy-eyed Islaen. In truth, she was all that mattered to him at the moment.

"We fear the lass willnae live, Iain. I am sorry. Wallace is getting a wet nurse for her and a priest. I maun tell ye something," she said with sleepy urgency.

"Ye can tell me later, sweeting."

"Nay, now. I lied to ye, Iain. I ne'er used those things. Forgive me?"

"Aye," he said in a choked voice, "I forgive ye."

Her eyes closed as sleep conquered her. "Thank ye. I was

tired of feeling wicked but I had to show you that I could do it."

"Oh, aye, ye showed me right enough," he whispered and, unmindful of his audience, clasped his sleeping wife to his breast and wept into her hair with a mixture of joy and relief.

Chapter Twenty

Smiling, Islaen watched her father coo at her sons. He and six of her brothers had arrived at Caraidland three days after the birth. They too feared for the little girl, named Liusadh, and shared her grief. Despite that lingering possibility of sadness, no one, not even herself, could hide their delight in the boys, Morogh and Padruig. Such healthy babies were a blessing that could not be ignored. Neither could anyone feel it right to deprive them of any love through a grief that they could not understand.

"How fares the lass today, sweeting?" Alaistair asked as he handed Islaen a restless Morogh.

Putting her son to her breast, she replied softly, "She still lives, Fither. Grizel says her appetite grows as does her voice."

"Both good signs but dinnae let your hopes rise too high," he said gently. "I wish I could save ye from that pain."

"No one can. We all pray daily for her and none could work so hard to keep her alive as Grizel does. 'Tis in God's hands now."

Alaistair nodded, then smiled at Padruig who patiently waited his turn. "Here's a sweet bairn. Good natured."

"Aye, seems to be." She let Morogh clutch her finger. "I think this is the lad with the devil in him."

"Mayhaps. 'Tis best an he is the stronger, since he is the heir. Do ye ken, lass, I think if wee Liusadh survives, she will be the real devil of the three. Any lass who can live when all says she shouldnae has a strength and a spirit that promises to put muckle a white hair upon her parents' heads."

"Ye may just be right."

"And how fares your marriage, lass? Other than fruitful," he added with a slow grin. "The lad o'er his fears now, is he?"

Glad she had told her father of Iain's demands and her deceit, she nodded. "Aye, I believe so but dinnae expect anither grandchild too soon. We mean to be careful." She watched him closely and saw him nod with approval.

"Good. Your mither and I were. 'Tis said to be a sin but I cannae believe it. God couldnae have meant for us to kill our women with childbearing, wearing them into the grave by filling their bellies every year. 'Tis a sin to waste the life God gave and that is what constant childbearing does, wastes life. Your mither proved ye can be both fruitful and careful."

As her father took Morogh and gave her Padruig she smiled at him. "I am glad ye came."

"So am I, lass." He kissed her cheek. "Ye arenae really happy yet, though, are ye?"

"Iain is a good mon. 'Tis early yet and I cannae expect a return for my feelings simply because I feel them. Ye need not fash yourself o'er me. Truly. I have more than many women find and I will seek my happiness in that."

She wished she was as confident as she tried to appear to her father. When Iain joined her later, bringing her a meal they would share in the privacy of their chambers, she did not feel confident at all. It did not really help that they had not really talked since the children were born. She had heard him say he forgave her, but as the days slipped by and he said no more on the matter, she began to doubt what she had heard.

Once the meal was done, she took a deep drink of wine and decided to bluntly ask him how he felt.

"Iain?"

Taking his gaze from his sleeping sons, he looked at her with mild curiosity. "What is it, love?"

He still found it all very hard to believe. Not only had his tiny wife given two sons but, if God was merciful, a daughter too. So too was Islaen alive, was in fact healed enough already to grow impatient with the lying in bed that was forced upon her. To look at her one would find it hard to believe she had been through the ordeal of birth so recently. Considering the torment he had been through, he could almost resent her good health.

"Iain," she began hesitantly and reached out to take hold of his hand, "Do ye truly forgive me for my deceit?"

Moving to sit beside her on the bed, he took her into his arms.

"I told ye I did, lass," he said softly, pressing a kiss to her hair. "Right after the birth I told ye that I forgave you."

"And I heard ye say it, yet ye have ne'er said any more on it and I grew afraid."

"There seemed no more to say. There is no way to thank ye for the bairns."

"Liusadh . . ."

He put his finger over her lips to silence her. "Nay, dinnae speak on it. If God means for her to live then she will. If not then we must find joy in the bairns we have and the ones to come."

"Ye want more then, Iain?"

"Aye, but only when and if ye feel strong enough to nurture my seed. I will ne'er insist that ye get with child."

"I want more bairns, but I wouldnae trick ye again, Iain."

"I believe ye, Islaen. Ye arenae one to lie and I should ask forgiveness for forcing ye to do so."

"Ye had good reason, Iain."

"Selfish reasons."

"Nay."

"Aye. Selfish. I didnae want to suffer that guilt again."

"Iain, t'was not your fault. 'Tis not a thing ye can tell until too late."

"I ken that now. Ye are e'en smaller than Catalina, yet ye came through fine. So too does Storm. There was naught to see in Catalina to tell me she wouldnae give me a bairn as easily as Storm gives Tavis bairns. T'was because she didnae want my touch that I blamed myself. T'was as though I had cursed her."

"That is nonsense."

"Aye, I can see that now. Although," he shook away his somber thoughts and leered at her playfully, "mayhaps not seeing as ye like the touching weel."

"Iain," she groaned, coloring with embarrassment.

He laughed softly and hugged her. "I cannae say I willnae have fears and worries when ye get with child but 'tis less. Tavis says he still tastes the fear each time Storm gets with child. There is always a danger but," he glanced at his sons, "the rewards are great and if ye are willing to take the risks then so am I." He grasped her by the shoulders and said firmly, "Ne'er forget though, Islaen, that I will ne'er make ye face those risks. If ye said this once was enough, I would be content with that."

She nodded. "I ken it, Iain. I will ken too when I wish to stop. Storm does. One more, she thinks, mayhaps two, but then she is done an only because she wants to see them all grow while she is young and strong enough to enjoy it." She tried to smother a yawn.

"That sounds verra reasonable. And," he quickly kissed her, "what else is reasonable is leaving ye to rest." He climbed out of bed and collected the tray, then said carefully, "Alexander sends love and good wishes. He says he will come soon."

"Iain, if ye dinnae want him about ye need but say so."

"He is a friend."

"Aye, Iain, he is. I think ye would find it hard to find any better."

"Aye, I would." He bent to quickly kiss her. "Rest, Islaen. Ye can get out of bed for a wee while tomorrow."

"That will be verra nice," she murmured even as her eyes closed. "Good sleep, Iain."

"Good sleep, Islaen," he said quietly but doubted he would have one for he found his bed too empty, the nights too long.

Islaen almost regretted her first meal in the hall. Her family took it as a sign of her complete recovery, as it was, and announced their departure. With Iain close by her side, watching to see that she did not grow too weary, she followed her family around as they prepared to leave. Iain made no complaint until she started to go outside with her father.

"I am not sure 'tis wise for her to take the air yet."

"Wheesht, lad, 'tis a fine day and she is bundled up weel," Alaistair said as he put an arm around Islaen's shoulders and took her out with him. "A drop of fresh air will do her good."

"'T'will soon be spring," Islaen murmured as she took a deep breath of the clean, crisp air and savored it.

"Aye, 'tis near. That will be good for your wee lass. If she can make it through 'til the weather turns finer, warmer, I will feel she has a good chance. 'Tis the cold that is the greatest danger to the weak ones. I will pray long and hard for an early spring and a warm one." He hugged Islaen and kissed her. "I wish I could stay until her fate is more certain."

"Ye cannae and I ken it. We thought her fate certain when she left my womb, yet a fortnight has passed. Nay, ye go as ye must. We will send ye word when we feel certain and that could be weeks yet." She sighed. "I do hate the waiting."

After clasping her shoulder briefly in sympathetic understanding, Alaistair left her to say farewell to her brothers.

"Now, ye have watched them ride away so ye can get back inside," Iain said sternly even as he turned her around and urged her back inside.

Glancing at him, she drawled, "Oh, and I thought we might have us a wee gallop."

"Ye are mad."

"Weel, I may soon be an I must keep to my chambers much longer. T'would nay hurt an I sat about in a different room."

He looked at her for a moment, then nodded. It was easy to understand her feelings. The few times he had been confined to his bed by wounds or illness he had felt much the same. Too much confinement bred a dangerous recklessness that prompted one to do things too soon. She was healed enough now to start suffering from that and he intended to try and curtail it.

Islaen felt her patience grow weaker as her body grew stronger. Telling Iain that she knew what she could and could not do as well as anyone did not stop his close watch over her. She noticed that even Storm tended to mother her, and finally decided enough was enough. When, after a month, Storm still insisted on picking up the babies for her, Islaen looked at her dear friend sternly.

"Ye need not do that anymore, ye ken. I didnae break my arms during the birthing."

Startled by the tartness in Islaen's voice, Storm first gaped. Then her eyes slowly widened as she thought on what Islaen had said. Finally, she laughed, shook her head and sat down next to Islaen on the bed.

"I am sorry, Islaen. I e'er hated it when I was treated thus, yet here I do it to you."

"Nay, I am sorry." Islaen smiled crookedly as she began to nurse Morogh. "I shouldnae snap at you. Ye but meant to help."

"I was cosseting you and well I know it. Do not apologize," Storm said with a smile as she let a hungry but patient Padruig suck on her finger. "I am sure ye have more than enough of it. Ye held back your annoyance longer than I e'er could."

"'Tis not easy but I keep reminding myself that ye all mean weel, that 'tis because ye care. Aye, e'en Iain, I think."

"Ye think? Surely some of your fears have been eased by the way he has acted these last months? Ye can see how he cares."

"Aye, about the mother of his bairns." She smiled slightly when Storm grimaced. "I daren't see too much in his actions."

"Nay, I recall feeling so when I carried Tavis's first babe, well, babes. Of course when I first told him I was with child, I had caught him with his old mistress in his arms. It may have shaded my feelings some," she drawled.

"Oh, aye, a wee bit." Islaen laughed softly. "When I saw Iain with another in his arms, I wept."

"Ye do not carry a knife, 'tis all. A very quiet babe is Padruig."

"Considering the blood in his veins, 'tis a surprise, eh?"

"Quite."

"Robert is quiet. We call him the peacemaker. He is slow to anger but when he does," she grimaced. "'Tis a sight to behold."

"From a distance."

"Quite a long distance. Iain is quiet."

"Aye, and ye are patient."

"I have no choice."

"Aye, your heart gives you none. Do not totally disregard how Iain acts now, Islaen."

"Nay, I willnae but neither will I forget that it could be the bairns. Most men treat a woman with child, in her belly or at her breast, kindly. E'en more so if 'tis his bairn. Iain wanted children though he tried to deny himself and that desire could guide how he acts. T'would be foolish to ignore that. I would

be asking for a hurt and one he didnae intend to give. I will
find joy in his forgiveness."

"Of course he forgave you. T'was not a malicious deceit. I
should like to call you fool and tell you to value Iain's actions
now, yet I understand your reluctance. I think I would have
the same. 'Tis so hard to know for certain. Ye daren't let your
heart lead you."

"It leads me enough as it is. Dinnae fash yourself o'er me,
Storm. I have it better than most." She smiled crookedly.
"T'would be a wee bit easier an I didnae have ye and Tavis
to show me what I dinnae have and thus make me taste envy
and dissatisfaction."

"That was hard won. T'was o'er a year ere we e'er sorted
ourselves out. Love shared rarely comes easy or fast."

"So long as it comes," Islaen whispered, "be it one year or
five. I but ask God for the patience to wait for it and not lose
faith." She grimaced. "That would be easier an Iain didnae
pull back each time I see a sign of softening, a hope to gain
his heart."

"He cannot run forever."

Islaen was not so sure of that as the days went by. She was
ready to have him come back to her bed, ached for him to
hold her in the night, but he made no move to do so. Although
she told herself he might still be giving her time to heal,
might think she needed more time than she did, her fears
began to grow with each night that he left her to sleep alone.
He seemed oblivious to her hints and unmoved by her subtle,
shy attempts at seduction. The man seemed to have lost all interest in the passion they could share. When she kissed him
good night, he would leave with every appearance of calm
while she was left breathless and frustrated.

Iain closed the door between his bedchamber and Islaen's
and leaned against it. He was astounded that he could continue to walk away when every inch of him ached with the
need to make love to her. Seeing the want in her fine eyes

only made it all the harder. She would certainly not complain if he rejoined her in her bed, if he gave into the hunger knotting his insides.

Moving to get ready for bed and yet another sleepless night, he thought about leaving. The weather had cleared enough for work to begin on Muircraig again. Perhaps if he were not so near to her it would be easier, he mused. It would at least mean that he did not have to see her willingness, would not be pulled at by the desire in her eyes.

Watching as Iain directed his men in preparing to leave, Islaen sighed and struggled to hide her hurt. He had Muircraig to retreat to again. She had had all winter to reach him but had failed. It was difficult not to wonder if she reached for the unattainable.

"Come, Islaen, dinnae look so dowie. He doesnae go to war, only to Muircraig," Robert said quietly as he put an arm around her.

"Aye, to Muircraig. I grow to hate that place."

"At least 'tis not a woman."

"Nay, but it may as weel be."

"I wish I kenned what to tell ye, how to make it better."

She smiled at him. "So do I. Och, weel, dinnae fash yourself. This is what I wanted. If 'tis not all I want or need 'tis my worry. No one can mend it for me. I must do that myself or learn to live with what I have. When all is said and done, I have more than many anither. I fear I am just greedy."

"Nay, not greedy. Ye reach for what we all do. Dinnae cease to reach, Islaen. Someday ye shall look to find it in your grasp." He kissed her cheek. "Patience, dearling. He is a good mon and I ken he ne'er means to hurt you. 'Tis all that keeps me from beating him."

She laughed softly, then frowned. "Just why do ye travel to Muircraig, Robert?"

"Many reasons, my wee suspicious sister. The sure way to keep you happy is to keep Iain alive so I go to protect him. I also go to have something to do other than lurking about keeping watch. There is work at Muircraig. And, finally, I go to see that, while he sorts himself out, he doesnae get tempted into erring against you. That Maura and Lady Mary lurk nearby. I dinnae think the first is any threat for she is newly betrothed and sounds a woman wise enough to take what is certain and discard the gamble. Lady Mary is different. I dinnae trust the wench. Iain I trust but he is but a mon, a troubled mon."

"Aye, weel, take care, Robert." She did not want to think about Lady Mary, who may not have been fully deterred by Iain's rejection at court, so she turned her attention to her husband as he approached her and Robert discreetly left. "Ye have fine weather."

"Verra fine. I pray it holds. 'Tis good weather to work in."

"Ye will be careful, Iain?" she said softly, grasping his hand.

Taking her hand to his lips, he smiled faintly. "I take as many warriors as workers and craftsmen. Dinnae fash yourself loving."

"'Tis easier said than done. Will ye stay away long?" she asked quietly, then cursed herself for the weakness that prompted the question.

"There is much work to be done. I dinnae wish to be left with work to do when winter returns again."

"Nay, of course not."

"Ye take care, Islaen." He lightly kissed her. "I will pray for our wee lass," he added softly, then abruptly left her.

Islaen watched until Iain could no longer be seen, then, with a heavy sigh, turned to go back into the keep. She found herself wishing that Alexander had not made such a fleeting visit, then cursed herself. Her friends and kin could not be made to fill the place her husband left empty in her life. It was wrong and, in Alexander's case, perhaps a little cruel. There were other ways to fill the days without making demands upon friends and kin. The emptiness Iain left was not something they could ever fill anyway. They could only deter the pain it caused and it was past time that she learned to manage that on her own.

She made her way to the nursery to find Grizel and Liusadh. At first she had been reluctant, almost afraid, to see her little daughter. Islaen realized she did not want to grow too fond of the baby when the child's life was still so uncertain. Once she faced that, she stopped trying to protect herself. She knew little would ease the loss of a child, even one considered doomed from birth, just as she knew she would deeply regret not coming to know her child for however long God decided to let the baby survive.

Smiling crookedly, Islaen watched Grizel take the baby from the blanket sling Liusadh rarely left. She might come to know her daughter, but Islaen doubted Liusadh would take much notice of her. It hurt a little but, if Grizel's constant care and love let the child live, it would be worth it. Indeed, not having Liusadh's full love seemed a small sacrifice if Liusadh gained a full life.

"She is verra tiny," Islaen said softly as she gazed down at the child she held. "'Tis as if she is but newborn."

"Och, weel, after holding those two bonnie laddies I suspicion she would feel so, but she's agrowing, m'lady."

"Strange, is it not, that she doesnae look as the lads do? In truth she is just the opposite. They have my hair but Iain's eyes and she has Iain's hair but my eyes. Ye would think they would each resemble the other." She gently touched Liusadh's dark curls.

"M'lord Tavis's twins dinnae look exact alike. They too are mixed about. Yet, when they are side by side there is a sameness. She will be a bonnie lass, m'lady. Do ye," Grizel cleared her throat. "Do ye wish to have the care of her now?"

"Nay, I still cannae give her all she needs. We are verra fortunate to have ye, Grizel. A bairn like this needs constant warmth and food. She would ne'er survive if she had to fight her brothers for it. I but hope she will understand when she grows."

"Aye, she will, m'lady. I will be sure she does. And grow she will, m'lady," Grizel vowed softly but vehemently.

"I begin to believe she will. Best ye take her back. There is still the bite of cold to the air, the threat of a chill." As she watched her daughter disappear into the sling across Grizel's ample bosom, Islaen whispered, "Another month and my fears for her will ease."

Outside of the nursery she met Storm who immediately asked, "How fares Liusadh? All is well?"

"Aye," Islaen replied as she started towards her chambers. "If ye see worry upon my face tis but the fear that that will change."

Slipping her arm through Islaen's, Storm said, "Each day she lives gives us reason to hope. She has already lived longer than most thought she would. Find strength in that, Islaen. Why, she does not e'en sicken but grows stronger each day."

"But so slowly. When I hold her my heart tightens with fear for she is so verra tiny."

"She began life very tiny. T'will be a while e'er she gains much weight. Mayhaps she but gains now what she was unable to gain in the womb."

"Aye, I am certain the lads took much of the nourishment."

"She will probably ne'er be very big, certainly not like her brothers."

"Nay, of course not. I ken that but 'tis hard to recall it when I hold her. There is so much she must fight, yet with so little."

"But fight she does, Islaen, so ye know there is strength there."

"Aye, I do, but I think I will increase my prayers too." She smiled crookedly as she heard Morogh's angry squawl come from her chambers as she stopped before her door. "Weel, I think her brothers will see that I delay e'en praying for their wee sister. I hope she has a chance to pay them back for their greediness."

Storm stayed to help change the boys and to entertain Padruig while Islaen fed Morogh. As soon as Morogh was satisfied, Storm left Islaen with her children.

For a while she played with her increasingly active sons, putting aside her fears for their sister. Despite her pleasure in them she could not fully stop herself from comparing their plump, active bodies to Liusadh's tiny, too quiet one. It did seem a little unfair that they should get so much and Liusadh so little. The division of health and strength had not been very equal.

Placing her sons in their bed, she knelt by the crib. Singing softly she rocked them, watching them as they fell asleep. At times she wished to see them grow swiftly so that she could know the men they would become, but at other times she wished them to stay babies so that she could hold them in her arms.

Kneeling by the cradle that held her healthy sleeping sons, she clasped her hands. Her thoughts were fully upon Liusadh now, the tiny girl that clung so tenaciously to life, and she began to pray.

"Lord, Ye must be verra weary of me but I beg Ye to heed me. I thank Ye for my sons but my mother's heart cries out for more. If 'tis greed, I beg Ye to forgive me but I pray for Liusadh, for my third bairn. God, please, I ken the value of all Ye have given me but, please, let the bairn live. Grant me but one small miracle."

Chapter Twenty-one

One small miracle was efficiently stopped from pulling on her brother Morogh's hair by Grizel, the woman Islaen felt almost fully responsible for her small daughter's survival, God and Wallace taking the rest of the credit. Liusadh was still tiny but she was very much alive, striving as hard as her brothers to throw off the dependency of infancy. Islaen was so pleased to have her daughter alive and growing that she felt little jealousy about the way Liusadh turned so often to Grizel rather than her mother.

Grizel had followed Wallace's instructions for plenty of warmth and food with a vengeance. Islaen often mused that, until just recently, Liusadh had seemed permanently attached to Grizel's ample bosom. Not only had Grizel carried the child next to her warmth with a blanket sling all day, but she had slept with the child at night to further thwart the damp and the chill. Islaen felt Grizel's grief over her own dead child had turned into an iron determination that Liusadh would live.

Islaen scowled out the window thinking of Iain. She knew full well that Muircraig was no ruin, yet Iain was working long enough hours to have built it from the first stone up.

Either that or she would find herself moved into a place fit for a king.

"Does he not plan to return here this night?" asked Storm, breaking into Islaen's less than kind thoughts about her beloved husband.

"Aye, he will return to eat a hearty meal, quaff a few tankards of ale, then collapse upon his bed to snore the night away."

"His bed? He still sleeps apart from ye?" Storm's voice echoed the incredulity written upon her face.

"Quite apart," Islaen said mournfully. "An his own chambers are too close, he runs to that cursed keep." She looked down at her figure, then at Storm. "I cannae see that I have changed since having the bairns."

"Nay, ye were back to yourself long ago."

"Then what is it? There must be some reason."

"Mayhaps he fears ye will get with child again too soon."

"That isnae it, for I plan to use those things. I dinnae want to bear a bairn a year. If they come I willnae pine but I cannae see any wrong in resting a wee bit." Islaen grimaced. "Especially an I am to bear three at a time."

"Does Iain know you feel so?"

"Aye. I told him that. An I had born naught but a girl I might have tried again quickly for a son, but there isnae any need for that. In one sitting I have given him an heir and anither son as surety. Nay, Iain cannae be afeard of that."

After a moment of deep mutual thought Storm saw Islaen pale suddenly. "What ails ye, Islaen?"

"Ye dinnae think he has a woman, do ye? Mayhaps at Muircraig even?"

"Nay," Storm replied confidently. "These MacLagan men have their faults but they are faithful. As long as the wife warms the bed they will not stray or, at least, not willingly. They are not the sort to keep a mistress. Ye have not turned Iain from your bed?"

"He turns himself from it. I am willing near to shameless-
ness. Ye forget, though, that he didnae want to wed me."

"T'was not ye but any woman and well you know it. He did
not wish to bury another wife. Ye have eased his fear there.
Nay, I will not believe it of Iain, an only because he ne'er was
the wencher his brothers were and are. If Tavis can be faithful, then Iain certainly can."

Islaen's fears were not so easily put to rest. "I disobeyed
him. It could turn him away."

"He understood that, Islaen. I heard him forgive ye with
my own ears. Ye need not worry on that count."

She did not want to worry that there was another woman
for it tied her stomach into agonizing knots but neither could
she put the thought completely aside. Word had come through
the usual extensive chain of gossip that Mary was indeed at
home and still unwed.

Telling herself that it was wrong to distrust him did not
help. He had loved Mary. Though it hurt to admit it, he did
not love her. One turning away from Mary's freely offered
charms did not mean that he would consistently reject the
woman. His sense of honor would surely weaken in favor of
his heart's dictates.

Recalling his disillusionment that night did not help either.
That could fade. The memory of a love shared could make
him doubt his opinion. Mary was one who could make full
and quick use of that doubt. The woman was one of those
who could easily appear innocent no matter how guilty she
was. She was also a woman who learned from her errors and
would be careful to hold her temper so as not to expose her
real nature and aims to Iain a second time. Mary was also one
of those women who could sorely tempt a man no matter how
he felt about her and Iain had been nearly six months without
a woman, if he had been faithful.

"Which isnae my fault," Islaen thought angrily. She had
been more than willing to share his bed again. Once healed

from the birth of their children she had gently hinted such to Iain. He seemed oblivious to hints.

She tried to put those thoughts out of her head but it proved impossible. As she lay awake in her lonely bed she found herself wondering if Iain's was as lonely. It seemed impossible that a man as lusty as Iain could go so long without a woman. She was finding it painfully difficult to go so long without him. For a week she tortured herself with thoughts of Iain having a lover, then sought out Storm for advice. There had to be something she could do.

Finding Storm working in her garden, Islaen sat down on one of the rough benches Storm had had placed there. The flowers were blooming and their sweet scent was refreshing. Islaen could see why even the men no longer teased Storm for planting what many thought was frivolous. It was peaceful and soothing to sit among nature's beauty.

"I have a problem, Storm," she said abruptly, not wanting to be wooed by the garden into forgetting her purpose for coming.

"I did wonder. Ye are looking wan as if something preys upon your mind."

"Aye, Iain."

"That hardly surprises me. Ye still do not think he has a woman, do ye?"

"Aye, I fear I do. Part of me scolds me for being so mistrustful but that doesnae stop the wondering. He is no wencher, as ye said, and he is a mon that holds dear his vows but he is also a mon that has been months without a woman."

"And ye have been months without a man."

"Aye, and as I think on how I feel the doubts grow stronger. A mon isnae bound by the same rules we are."

"Mayhaps if ye go to his bed, let him know ye are ready and willing."

"I thought on that. I did it when he took to sleeping apart from me after I told him I was with child. When he does come to sleep at Caraidland, however, his sleep is of the dead. I dinnae think I could rouse him. Also, why should I always be the one? 'Tis pride that makes me say that, I ken it, but, truly, does there ne'er come a time when I should cease running after him, pulling him back to me?"

Sitting back on her heels, Storm looked at Islaen for a moment. "Aye, and I fear I should have reached it ere now."

"Nay." Islaen smiled faintly. "Ye suffered a lot to win Tavis's love."

"Aye but he ne'er stayed out of my bed. 'Tis why I have trouble knowing what to say to help you. Aye, Tavis and I had many troubles but they were not the same. Had I been a Scot, Tavis would have wed me soon after I came here. All I had to do was make him love me, make him see that he did. Ye could get that from Iain and still have troubles. I do not know what to tell you."

"Tell me what ye would do in my position. I have many an idea, I but need some direction."

"Well, I would swallow my anger and give him one more chance. He will come here soon that is certain."

"Aye, whate'er he feels for me, he cannae stay away from the babes too long."

"I think 'tis ye he comes to see too," Storm said softly and Islaen shrugged. "One more chance. Iain's fears about childbirth ran deep and strong. He may see now that he was wrong but that does not mean he has ceased to view childbirth as a greater trial than mayhaps it is. Ye had three babes, Islaen. Three. Many still find that hard to believe, do not understand how ye could do that and heal as ye did. Iain may feel the same. He may be giving ye extra time to heal."

"Twa months a bairn? 'Tis a muckle long time indeed," Islaen said dryly.

"Aye, too long but ye must remember his fears, remember that he looks upon childbirth differently than we do."

"True. Ye are right. He could think such a birth needs a far longer time of healing than an I had but one bairn. Why he cannae see with his own eyes that I am fine, I cannae say. I think 'tis wrong that men keep apart from childbirth as much as they do. 'Tis what makes them get such strange ideas. 'Tis no more dangerous than the battles they are e'er fighting."

"Tavis faces it much as he does a battle." Storm laughed softly. "Ah, but we puzzle them as much as they do us."

"'Tis just." Islaen exchanged a grin with Storm, then grew serious. "So, I give him another chance. Then what? He could do as he has done since the birthing, naught but sleep like the dead, and then run back to Muircraig."

"Ye could hobble him until he comes to his senses."

"'Tis passingly tempting," Islaen drawled.

"Well, then ye must chase him again I fear. 'Tis all I can think of."

"I thought of packing up and going home but I fear he wouldnae stop me nor come for me."

"That would be your last ploy, the one born of desperation."

"Aye, tell him what I think, that I have no marriage so might as weel return to being my fither's wee lass."

"Exactly, but first go after him one last time, just once and not so blatantly as putting yourself in his bed."

"Ah, ye mean tempt him and see if he takes the bait, come at him from behind and gently, ye mean."

Storm nodded. "Ye must reach him when he is awake, alert and has not prepared himself for seeing you."

"He is ne'er like that when he is here. To catch him like that I must needs reach him at Muircraig."

"I fear so. 'Tis a longish ride but do ye not think t'would be worth it an it works? Ye would have him back."

"As much as he would let me, aye. 'Tis a thought, better than most of mine. What excuse would I give for going?"

"Take him a meal. What excuse do ye need? Ye are his wife and ye see him little."

"Or mayhaps I but wish to see how near to done he is, what Muircraig looks like."

"Quite so. 'Tis to be your home. He would ne'er think it strange that ye wish to look upon it."

"So, then, when I draw him off to be alone with me, I seduce him."

"Aye."

"I am nay sure I ken how."

"It should not be hard to do. I would think a man having been without for so long should be easy game."

"Aye, an he has any passion left for me," Islaen whispered, voicing her fears. "T'was all I had and I fear I may have lost e'en that."

"I do not believe that but I know the fears that plague you and only Iain can cure them." Storm reached out and took Islaen's hand in hers in a gesture of sympathy. "'Tis hard to love yet not know if that love is returned. I know that well. I dare not tell ye that he loves you but I do feel certain that he cares, he cares a lot. The way he has acted each time ye have been in danger shows it."

Islaen tried to remember that as the days crept by. She tried to use it to lift her sagging spirits and quell her fears. Unfortunately, she knew that the man Iain was could account for how he had acted when she had been in peril. He was a man who would always stand to protect those smaller and weaker than himself.

It was a week after her talk with Storm that Islaen woke in the middle of the night. A noise in the chamber next to hers told her what had woken her up. Iain had returned. She lay tensely in her bed, but was not really surprised when all went quiet and he did not show.

Silently she slipped from her bed and crept into his chambers. She simply had to look at him. It felt as if it had been years since she had caught even a glimpse of the man she called husband.

Staring at him she felt worry twist her heart. She felt guilty too for she found herself a little glad that the way their lives were at the moment was not doing him much good. He looked haggard and worn. He certainly did not look a man content with his life for even in his sleep he looked troubled, the lines of worry not fading with sleep's relaxing hold.

She wished he would confide in her even as she feared the knowledge of what troubled him. MacLennon was still a threat but she could not believe that was all of it. Something else preyed upon him and she felt frustrated that he gave her no clue as to what that was. It left her prey to her own fears and she had the feeling that they were worse than the real problem. Sighing, she clenched her hands into fists to resist the urge to touch him and crept back to her own bed.

In the morning she found Iain in the nursery. She ruthlessly quelled an attack of jealousy over how he sought out the children yet worked so hard to avoid her. No matter what happened between herself and Iain she knew she should be glad that he loved the children. Children needed a parent's love and, from what she had seen, too few gave it.

Inwardly bracing herself she entered the nursery. She had vowed that he would find no reason in her words or actions to justify his neglect and she intended to stick to that vow. It was getting a lot harder to do, she mused. The urge to beat him soundly with a heavy, blunt object was harder to resist, she admitted to herself as she sat down across from him.

"They seem to have grown apace each time I see them. They will soon be walking."

'Probably by the next time ye decide to grace your family with your presence,' she thought crossly, then took a deep breath to cool her anger before answering, "Aye, Morogh can pull himself to his feet e'en now."

He laughed and gently ruffled Morogh's wine-red curls. "He will be a devil, I am thinking."

"Aye, Padruig is much quieter. My fither feels 'tis Liusadh

we must watch, though. He said that e'en before we kenned
that she would survive. Fither felt that a wee lass who could
hold off death whilst still a bairn was one who would be a
right devil."

For an hour they spoke of and played with the children.
Then the boys began to fret, wanting their meal. Without
thought, unused to Iain's presence, Islaen began to nurse
Morogh. She blushed when she caught him staring at her. For
one moment she met his gaze, then he hastily left. She was
almost certain she had seen wanting in his eyes, that blaze of
passion that had been so long absent, yet, she mused, an he
felt so why did he do nothing about it? Sighing, she forced
her full attention to her children as Grizel hurried in to see
to Liusadh's feeding. She was growing weary of trying to understand her husband. It only gave her a headache in the end.

Once away from Islaen, Iain hurried to his chambers. He
splashed cold water on his face several times but it did no
good. With a groan, he sprawled on his bed and indulged in a
lengthy, colorful bout of cursing.

When Islaen had put their son to her breast Iain had felt
every lustful inclination he had worked so hard to subdue
spring to life. He had come very close to taking her, there on
the floor in the midst of their children. Before he actually succumbed to such a rash urge he had fled the room. Fleeing had
not stilled his urge for her, however. He briefly wondered if
he should just give in and return to her bed.

It was not easy but he shook away that temptation. He had
to keep on as he had been. It was best for both of them. He
had seen that he could not walk any middle ground with
Islaen. It was all or nothing. Although it twisted his heart he
had decided that it would be nothing and would stay with that
decision. After seeing how weak he was in the nursery, he decided that he had better make this visit a short one, that he
had not yet gained the strength he sought. When he greeted
a guest to Caraidland a little later he wavered in that decision.

* * *

"Alex," Islaen cried with delight when she entered the hall that evening and he rose to meet her. "When did ye come?"

"Only a short while ago." He kissed her hand. "Ye look as lovely as ever."

"Flattery. How is your daughter? Weel?"

"Aye and I am anxious to see how your brood has grown. I ken weel how swiftly bairns change o'er the days."

Although she told herself to be careful, for Alexander still looked at her with wanting, Islaen enjoyed his company as they dined. He could make her laugh and feel womanly, neither of which Iain had done in a long while. When she caught Iain sending dark looks at her and Alexander she paid him no heed. If he did not like Alexander talking to her, then he could keep her company himself, she thought crossly. He did not want anything to do with her but it seemed he wanted no one else to either.

When Islaen retired for the night, Alexander turned his attentions to Iain. "I can see how pleased ye are to see me."

"Ye have a way of quickly wearing your welcome thin."

"Why? Because I pay heed to your wee wife as ye ne'er do?"

"Ye enter into what isnae your concern."

"Ye are a fool, Iain MacLagan. Ye turn aside that which many a mon craves."

"I must. There is an axe hanging o'er my neck. She could be made a widow at any time, but I will at least leave her heart free."

"What heart is left after ye toss it about. We all have an axe hanging o'er our necks, my friend."

"Aye, but we dinnae all ken when it will drop nor who will wield it. I do. T'will be soon and t'will be MacLennon."

"How can ye be sure t'will be soon?"

"Because the mon lurks near as he ne'er has before. He is hunted as he ne'er has been before too, and is pressed to move fast. My allies draw ever nearer to him. Aye, he has to strike soon for he is but a step ahead of a sword himself."

"That doesnae mean ye will die."

"'Tis a great possibility and weel ye ken it. At least I can save Islaen from too much grief."

"But is that your decision to make? 'Tis her heart. She might feel the chance is worth taking."

"'Tis my place as her husband to protect her from hurt. I am doing so."

"Are ye? Or, are ye protecting yourself? Do ye ken what I think ye do?"

"Nay, but I ken ye will tell me for all that."

"Aye, I will for I feel ye ought to think on it. 'Tis not just her grief ye try to prevent but your own. Ye hold her away because ye dinnae want to ken what ye can have with her, thus what ye can lose if ye lose her or ye die."

"Really?" Iain said tightly. "Say ye are right. What would ye, in all your great wisdom, suggest I do?"

Ignoring that sarcasm, Alexander replied, "Stop this game. Ye have no marriage. If God means to take ye, He will. Ye cannae stop that. Do ye mean to waste the time ye have? 'Tis what ye do now. And Islaen's. Ye keep her locked in a barren marriage thinking to protect her, yet, if ye but asked, ye would ken weel that isnae what she wants. She wants to enjoy what she can while she lives, not shut herself away from life and love because she might die tomorrow. 'Tis what ye should do."

Alexander's words struck deep and Iain could find no response. Uttering a harsh curse, he left Alexander, left the hall and retreated to his chambers. He did not want to think on all Alexander had said, wanted to deny it and forget it, but the man's words pounded in his brain demanding attention. With a soft curse, he decided it would be a long night.

* * *

Balancing Morogh on her hip, Islaen watched Iain prepare to leave, checking the cinches on his saddle. Her brother went with him and Alexander had been asked but had refused. She supposed she ought to be glad that Iain was always so well protected but she really wished that someone would stop him from leaving at all. If he were to be made to stay home they might just be able to lessen the chasm that now seemed to yawn between them.

"Muircraig must be near done," she murmured when he stopped before her to give her a kiss much like the ones he bestowed upon the children, a cool kiss upon her cheek.

"Nearly. We will winter there, I am thinking."

'And then I shall truly be alone,' she mused silently but said, "Weel, take care, Iain."

"Aye and ye." He found it difficult to turn from her but hurried away from her before he weakened and stayed.

Islaen sighed, waving half-heartedly as Iain and the others rode away. It would be good for them to go to Muircraig but she also knew it could be disastrous. If he found a way to avoid her there, a way to cut her out of his life, she would truly be alone. At least at Caraidland she had friends, people who honestly cared about her. They could never make up for the neglect of the man she loved but they did help to ease the loneliness.

Taking Padruig from Grizel because Liusadh was tormenting him, Islaen started toward the nursery where she knew she would find Storm. She was a little dismayed to find Alexander there too. When she managed to get Storm away from the children, Alexander followed. She finally decided that it did not matter if he heard what she had to say. The man knew what troubles she had so there was little point in being secretive. She often felt that all of Caraidland knew.

"I have given Iain his chance, Storm," she said as they retreated to a deserted corner of the hall.

"Aye, ye did." Storm sat down on a chest next to Alexander.

"And ye saw what he did with that chance."

"Aye, I fear I did," Storm said with a sigh.

"So now I try your plan."

"When?"

"In a week's time. I will give him a week."

"To lessen his guard?"

"Aye, to grow nicely unsuspecting." She looked at Alexander and was suddenly glad that she had not excluded him for she suddenly had an idea of how he could be very useful indeed. "Alexander," she purred.

"Uh-oh. I have a feeling I may regret being here."

"Nay, I but need ye to share with me your skill in one particular thing."

"And what is that?" he asked suspiciously.

"I want ye to tell me all about seduction." She smiled slowly as Alexander began to laugh.

Chapter Tweny-two

"He will, of course, immediately suspect me of having a hand in this," Alexander said as he and Islaen neared Muir-craig.

"An all goes weel, that shouldnae be any great burden to bear. I hope this works," she muttered, beginning to feel nervous.

"Islaen, if ye but get him alone and employ but some of what I taught you, his capitulation is assured."

She giggled. "What vanity. Ah, but Alex, I am nay as pretty as you, nor do I have such a fine, seductive voice."

"I find your voice most seductive," he murmured, reaching out to capture her hand in his and kiss it.

"Behave yourself, ye rogue. Beltraine will be jealous." She patted her mount's strong neck and stared at Muircraig.

To her eyes the keep looked more than ready to be lived in. That opinion changed little the nearer they got. It looked strong enough to protect those who lived within from both hostile armies and hostile weather. She felt the pinch of hurt and insult and ruefully admitted that she had hoped to find some visual reason for Iain's neglect. If the keep had been in ruins, she would have had something to excuse him with, thus soothing her feelings. Instead, she found a place that the most exacting could find pride in.

As she rode through the gates she briefly felt an urge to turn around and return to Caraidland. Standing close to Iain was a woman Islaen had hoped never to see again. For a moment, all her fears swamped her but then she found her courage. She was not about to run away as if she was in the wrong. If he was using Muircraig as a trysting spot, then he was the one in the wrong.

"Easy now, lass. That she-wolf's presence doesnae mean there had been aught going on," Alexander said softly.

Islaen was not so sure of that. Iain looked rather guilty to her. She fought for calm as she approached her husband, telling herself that Robert would not have allowed anything to happen. A small voice in her mind asked her just what Robert could have done to stop it and she ruthlessly shut it up. She would do Iain the courtesy of believing him innocent until he was proven otherwise. Fixing Lady Mary with a cold look, Islaen decided that she owed that woman no courtesy at all.

Iain stared at his wife in near horror. She had never come to Muircraig of her own accord before. He felt it was the worst piece of luck that she should come now. His mind went blank as he tried to think of an explanation for Lady Mary's presence. He could all too easily guess what his wife thought, especially when he saw how hard her usually soft eyes had gone. Forcibly, he shook himself free of his shock. It was an awkard situation but there was nothing for him to feel guilty about.

"Islaen," he murmured and kissed her cheek, fighting to hide how stirred he was by the fresh, clean scent of her, "What has brought ye to Muircraig?"

"I but wished to see what has been done. Greetings, Lady Mary. Ye look weel."

"As do ye, m'lady." Mary struggled to hide her fury over this interruption. "I hear ye are now a mother."

"Aye, m'lady. I dropped the litter near six months past," Islaen drawled, then grinned when Alexander choked on a laugh.

"How witty," Mary murmured, then tucked her arm through Iain's. "Iain was just about to show me Muircraig."

"Ye can see it verra weel from here," Iain muttered as he extracted himself from Lady Mary's hold, "or mayhaps Robert will escort ye about." He looked at Islaen's grinning brother who did nothing to hide a grimace of distaste at the suggestion.

"But, Iain," Lady Mary pouted, "I came so far just to see you."

"So did my wife, m'lady."

The anger Lady Mary could not hide almost made Islaen smile but she scolded herself for such pettiness. She also reminded herself that the ease with which Iain was pushing Lady Mary aside was not really proof of anything. The woman was still a threat and, until she was more secure in her marriage, Islaen felt she would be a fool not to recognize that threat.

She found it difficult not to bombard Iain with questions as he took her around Muircraig. The presence of Lady Mary at Muircraig was but one of the many things she wanted explained. Islaen sensed, however, that direct questioning was not the way to get any answers from Iain. If he wished her to know, he would tell her in his own good time.

"Ye are right, Iain. We should be able to winter in this place," she said as they returned to the bailey. "Are ye sure 'tis not ready now?" She felt sure it was and that he knew it but was curious about what answer he would give.

"There are still a few things that must be done ere I feel it secure enough for ye and the bairns."

'Verra weel said,' she thought wryly. Iain had clearly learned a lot from the courtiers who sought favor at court. He was pushing her away again, refusing her, yet made it seem as if it were all for her own good. She wished that she had such a skill with words.

Glancing down at his wife, Iain caught a look in her eyes that nearly made him wince. She did not believe him. He could not really blame her. Muircraig was secure and it would be comfortable. The work he did now was but extra strengthening of the defenses and a few slight additions to the living quarters to add to their comfort, ideas he had gathered in France and from foreign visitors to court. They were things that could be done while they lived there with little or no lessening of comfort or safety. He was hiding at Muircraig and he had the distressing feeling that she suspected as much even if she did not know why. He wondered why she did not question him about it for she was usually most forthright.

"'Tis time to eat," he murmured as he saw the men start to put down their tools. "I fear all we have to offer ye is camp fare."

"Ye ken weel that I have no complaint about that. Howbeit, mayhaps such a thing will make ye more amiable to what I had planned."

She was looking at him in a coy, teasing way that made him ache to kiss her even as he wondered when and where she had learned such a trick. "And what is your plan?"

"I have in that pannier ye can see upon Beltraine a fine meal. All the best delicacies of Caraidland and some verra fine wine."

"There is a feast," he exclaimed with open anticipation. "Far better than what sets in that pot all the men gather round."

"Aye, so t'would be almost unkind to dine upon such right afore their eyes. I havenae brought enough to share with all here."

"We could dine within Muircraig," he said thoughtfully as

he tried to shake the feeling that he was being gently drawn into a trap.

"On such a fine day? 'Tis not often we have such sun and warmth to enjoy, Iain. I have brought a blanket to spread upon the ground and but a short distance from here is a muckle fine spot with clear water and a carpet of flowers."

"We shouldnae be off alone," he murmured, hesitant to refuse her such a treat yet not sure he could resist all the temptations of being alone with her. "MacLennon still lives and but awaits a chance at me, at us."

Tugging him closer to her horse she pointed out the horn that hung from her saddle. "To call for aid if 'tis needed. The place I saw is near enough to Muircraig that one blast upon this will be heard clearly here yet we will be private."

"Aye, t'would work an he gives us time."

"An he falls upon us so quickly and quietly, then all the men here wouldnae be enough protection. Ah, Iain, t'would be so fine. I havenae much time now to enjoy the few fine days the summer brings."

He sighed for he knew he would go. She was tied to home and hearth by the babes. Somehow she had managed a few hours of freedom and he did not have the heart to deny her simply because he had a fear that he would weaken in his resolve to leave her alone. When he saw Lady Mary moving their way he decided there was another good reason to go. He would rather chance breaking his vows of restraint with Islaen than stay within the reach of the persistent and increasingly annoying Lady Mary.

"Iain, where do ye go?" Lady Mary demanded as he called for his horse to be saddled.

"To dine quietly and privately with my wife, m'lady."

"But what of me? I am your guest," she almost hissed.

"There are many here to see to your needs, m'lady. Ones such as Robert, Alexander or Phelan, wherever Phelan has hied to." He was a little startled when Murdo brought his mount over. "That was quick."

"Weel, sir, Sir MacDubh said ye'd be wanting him saddled so I had done it afore ye asked."

Looking at Alexander who simply smiled sweetly, Iain murmured, "I see."

As Iain helped her mount, Islaen fervently hoped that he did not see. If he did, she was sure he would either stay at Muircraig or thwart all her attempts to put an end to the abstinence that was making her nights much too long. She breathed a sigh of relief when he mounted, then looked at her expectantly. If this plan failed she had but one move left to make and she was loathe to employ such drastic action. With a little smile she led him out of Muircraig.

Islaen spread out the blanket and watched Iain tether the horses. She wondered a little crossly why she had to love that particular man past all reason. If hers had been as so many other marriages were, she would probably find his aloofness and constant absences a blessing. She would find her happiness in running the household and making the greatest use of whatever prestige her marriage had brought her. Instead, she constantly tried to reach his heart and did not seem to know how to stop even though she seemed no closer to him despite so many months of marriage. A person with some sense, she thought crossly, would have given up by now.

Sighing a little as she set out the food she tried to ignore the fact that what she planned would probably solve very little. It might bring him back to her bed but a man in her bed did not make a marriage, not the sort she craved. She needed his love and she was beginning to wonder if everyone was wrong, if perhaps Iain MacLagan simply had no love to give. It was a thought that chilled her for it made the years that stretched ahead of them look frighteningly barren.

"Did ye leave something behind?" Iain asked as he sat down. "Ye looked mightily upset for a moment."

"Nay, 'tis all here." She smiled at him. "I feel certain I have brought all ye favor."

"Aye, and more than enough of it too. I think ye have some grand ideas about the size of my appetite."

"Weel, if there is much left o'er," she murmured as she served him, "ye can keep it at Muircraig to add to your camp fare."

"An I do, I shall need to keep it weel hid for such as this would tempt the most honest of men to thievery."

He asked about the children, which did not surprise her but she had to bite back a sigh. It was good that he had such an interest in his offspring but it seemed as if they had little else in common.

She forced away such dismal thoughts. It would be impossible to enact her plan if she grew sad or angry.

Struggling to recall all that Alexander had told her she began to seduce Iain or so she hoped. At any moment she expected him to guess her game and hurry them back to Muircraig. She also worried that he would be totally unmoved, that she would see all too clearly that she had lost his passion. If that was true then she knew she had irrevocably lost.

There was also a look in his eyes on occasion that made her wonder if she was doing it right and it caused her to hesitate a moment to try to recall Alexander's instructions. As the meal progressed and she seemed to stir little more than confusion in him she grew frustrated. According to Alexander, Iain's lengthy celibacy should have made him highly susceptible to seduction and success should have come quickly, yet they had already finished the meal and were enjoying the sweet but he had not even kissed her. The only person she seemed to have seduced was herself for she was certainly feeling very warm and eager.

Iain watched his wife closely as she broke off a piece of sweetmeat and fed it to him. It was very nice to lie in the sun and be so waited upon but he felt sure she was up to something. She was constantly touching him, found every opportunity to lean close and brush her body against his. So too was she acting strangely flirtatious. Occasionally, she would hesitate and a cross look would swiftly pass over her face, but then she would renew her apparently unconscious assault upon his starved senses.

He crossed his arms beneath his head to keep himself from grabbing her. The resolve to leave her alone was crumbling swiftly. An urge to hurl her to the blanket and thoroughly ravish her was becoming too much to resist. 'An I didnae ken her better,' he mused idly, 'I would think she was trying to seduce me.'

That idle thought stuck firmly in his mind. She was still innocent, still somewhat unpracticed in the arts of love, yet she had put herself in his bed the last time he had kept himself away from her. The more he watched her the more certain he became that she was trying to seduce him. It was subtle, even hesitant, but it was definitely a seduction.

For a moment he thought about hurriedly collecting up their things and returning to Muircraig, then hastily sending her on her way back to Caraidland. Then Alexander's words spun through his mind. Since the birth of their children he and Islaen had been little more than strangers. The fact that she would go to such lengths to draw him back to her if only in passion showed him how little she liked the situation between them. He admitted to himself that he did not like it either.

As she took far too long to clean away what meager crumbs might have stuck to his face, he came to a decision. He had wasted months of their lives and would waste no more. Neither of them gained anything from his faltering attempts to protect them from pain. He was past protecting and she was obviously miserable, caught in a marriage that was really not much of a marriage. All he could do was hope that he was not letting his starved body do his thinking for him.

"Islaen," he murmured as she gently wiped his mouth, "are ye trying to seduce me?" He smiled when she blushed.

She thought that if he laughed she would definitely strike him. "'Tis so obvious?" she asked softly.

"Nay, I wasnae quite sure at first." He studied the small face so close to his and ached to kiss her.

"Weel, I was trying not to be too obvious. I wanted ye to think that t'was your idea."

He laughed softly. "So what do ye do now?"

"I am nay too sure. I have used all of Alexander's suggestions."

"Alexander?"

"Aye. I felt t'was only wise to seek advice from an expert."

"So long as his advice was but words and not actions."

"He behaved himself most gallantly except that he kept laughing." She smiled faintly when Iain laughed.

"Aye, he would. So ye have come to a sticking point, eh?"

"Ye were supposed to have succumbed by now."

She felt her heart skipping at an alarming rate. He was not stopping the game, not making any move to return to Muircraig. There was a soft, warm look in his eyes that raised her hopes. He seemed willing to fall in with her game but she could not be sure.

"Aye, I have succumbed."

"Ye look more relaxed than I had expected ye to. Are ye certain?"

"The question should be—are ye certain, Islaen. T'was a hard birthing ye suffered," he murmured, frowning in concern as he recalled it.

"'T'was six months ago, Iain," she said a little angrily. "I didnae need twa months a bairn to recover. Mayhaps a wee bit more than other women but nay six months."

"I thought we should wait until they were talking," he drawled, then laughed at her horrified look.

"Wretch," she grumbled and half-heartedly struck him on the arm. "Ye shouldnae tease me so at such a time."

"Nervous, sweeting?" He began to unpin her hair.

"Weel, aye. I wasnae sure I was doing it right."

"Ye were doing it right but before I grant ye your victory, is there naught ye wish to ask me?"

"Ask ye?" She found it a little difficult to think when what she had ached for for so many months was finally close at hand. "What do I want to ask you?"

"About Lady Mary?"

"Oh. I was just trusting you, Iain."

He traced the shape of her mouth with his finger and felt her tremble slightly. "'Tis verra good of you, little one. Lady Mary has been only a nuisance. I was trying to think of ways to make this her last visit. I will be honest with you, lass. A time or twa I thought on using her as the whore she is to ease the aching my abstinence caused me."

"I ne'er asked it of you," she whispered.

"Nay, I forced it down our throats and t'was kenning that t'was my choice that kept me from Mary, that and the knowledge that she couldnae give me what I need."

"And what do ye need?" She clutched his shoulders when his lips lightly brushed over hers for she was so starved for him that that light touch was all she needed to set her aflame, her barely tethered desire leaping to full life.

"I need ye, lass."

"Ye are verra slow to show it."

"Ah, loving, the need is so strong I fear to hurt you. My urge is to ravish not make love slow and gentle as ye deserve."

He kissed her, a slow, gentle kiss as if he leisurely savored the taste of her. That leisureliness was belied by the way he held her. His arms gripped her tightly as he dragged her atop of him and pressed his hips against hers, both of them crying out at the contact. Almost frantically they moved against each other, their need for each other making them desperate to join.

"Islaen, my wee wife," Iain rasped as he turned so that she was sprawled beneath him and his shaking hand burrowed beneath her skirts to clumsily remove her braes, "have ye e'er had your skirts tossed up like some crofter's wench and been taken with no finesse by a lust-crazed fool of a mon?"

She laughed softly. "Nay and weel ye ken it. 'Tis fun?"

"Ye can tell me the answer in a wee while."

A cry of pleasure tinged with relief escaped Islaen when Iain joined their bodies with one fierce thrust. It was fast and furious, their release coming with a shattering unity. Their need for each other was too great to allow any gentleness or any lingering at the edge of desire's chasm.

Still not quite steady, Iain raised himself up on his elbows to look at Islaen. She lay beneath him, her eyes closed and her long dark lashes forming a thick arc upon her flushed cheeks. Although she seemed to be all right he frowned worriedly as he gently brushed the hair from her face. He had been rough, taking her fiercely. She was so tiny and delicate that he feared he might have hurt her with his lack of control.

"Islaen, are ye all right?"

"Aye." She opened her eyes partway and smiled slowly as she put her arms around his neck.

"Are ye sure I didnae hurt ye?"

"Nay, ye didnae hurt me. I am nay so delicate as ye think Iain." She started to unlace his tunic.

"Weel, 'tis not right to take your wife like some peasant slut."

"E'en if that wife quite enjoyed herself?"

"Did she now?"

"Aye, tell me, if that is how ye tumble some crofter's wench, how do ye tumble a tavern wench?"

He grinned as he eased the intimacy of their embrace so

that he could help her remove his tunic. "Sometimes right upon the table."

"Ye could get splinters." She grinned when he laughed. "Weel, we havenae got a table here."

"A shame," he murmured as he watched her tug off his boots. "I would ne'er have a sweeter meal set out for me."

She blushed and busied herself unbuckling his sword. "I dinnae think I wish to chance splinters in my backside."

"I should put down a cloth of the finest linen to protect that sweet tail. Nay, dinnae put it too far away," he commanded softly when she set his sword aside. "Mayhaps e'en a pillow."

"There is gallantry. What of the miller's wife?"

"On the sacks of grain, of course."

"Of course. Weel, we havenae got those either."

"No matter. They tend to shift about beneath ye and ye cannae keep a steady gait, can e'en be tossed out of the saddle."

Even though she blushed slightly she giggled at the image he painted. "'Tis a most absurd conversation we are having."

"Aye. Ask me about the blacksmith's daughter."

Eyeing him suspiciously as she removed the last of his clothes, she asked, "And how would ye tumble the blacksmith's daughter?"

"On the anvil."

She giggled and drawled, "Nay on the forge."

"No mon wishes to get that warm."

"Weel, we dinnae have an anvil, either." She ran her hand over his strong thigh and saw his eyes darken with desire.

"We have a blanket."

"Aye. That we do."

She watched her hand move over his abdomen and was deeply stirred by the sight of his lean naked form. There was a playfulness about him, nearly a carefree air, that she had not seen in a long time. She felt her hopes rise. It could be that he had decided to put an end to much more than his abstinence, that perhaps he was ready to make their marriage a full one.

"This fine blanket is the perfect place for a mon to tumble his wife."

"Why, I think ye may be right," she said, biting back a smile as she knelt by his side.

"There is a wee problem though."

"Aye? And what is that?"

"Just that the husband is lying here as naked as the day he was born . . ."

"And a verra fine sight it is, an I may say so."

"Ye may," he said haughtily, smiling when she laughed. "As I was saying, the husband is naked and," he glanced down at himself, "quite ready but the wife is still clothed. What do ye think ought to be done?"

"Someone best undress her then," Islaen said softly but her words ended on a shocked gasp.

Suddenly there was a sword point at Iain's throat. She stared at it in horror then cried out as a hand painfully grabbed her by the hair and yanked her to her feet.

Islaen felt her blood turn cold as a smooth voice murmured, "Oh, please, allow me to do the honors."

Chapter Twenty-three

"MacLennon."

Iain felt as if all his worst nightmares had come true. Both the horn to signal for aid and his sword were in reach. Because of Islaen's struggles MacLennon's sword was not so steady against his throat. He felt he had a chance but, just as he tensed to move, deciding to grab for his sword, MacLennon's sword suddenly left his throat. Iain watched in horror as MacLennon's sword came to rest against Islaen's throat, pricking her smooth skin enough to cause blood to well up and slowly trail down her slim neck.

"Move and she dies now, MacLagan."

Islaen froze when the chill of the blade touched her throat. When Iain also froze she realized they could well be in a trap there was no escape from.

"Now, toss the sword and the horn into the trees."

"Nay, Iain," Islaen cried, then gasped when MacLennon's sword pressed more firmly against her throat, pricking her skin yet again.

"Let her go, MacLennon," Iain said as he tossed away his sword and the horn. "'Tis me ye want."

"Aye, 'tis ye I want but I want you to suffer and I think I hold the rack to stretch you upon, MacLagan. Such a wee, pretty rack she is too." Abruptly shoving Islaen onto Iain, MacLennon took a coil of rope off of his shoulder and tossed it at them. "Tie him up."

"Nay, I cannae. I willnae," Islaen protested even as MacLennon's sword drew nearer to her.

"Do it, Islaen," Iain ordered, praying that, if he could just keep them alive for a while, someone would come.

"Aye, do it, Islaen," MacLennon mocked. "Be a good wee wife and do as your husband commands. Kneel, Iain, and put your hands behind you. Now, wee Islaen, ye will tie him exactly as I tell ye to."

"Iain, I cannae."

"Do it, Islaen. Do just as he says."

Shaking with the fear that she was only preparing her husband for the slaughter, Islaen began to tie him up, following MacLennon's instructions exactly. The way Iain had looked at her made her think he tried to tell her something, tried to relay some message. She could only assume that he meant for her to go carefully, to garner as much time as she could. As she continued to tie him up she got the horrified feeling that time was something they had little of. The way she was tying Iain would mean that he could not move without strangling to death. She gasped and immediately stopped.

"Nay, I cannae. T'will be a torture."

"Now, m'lady, do ye mean to be disobediant?" MacLennon drawled as he moved to stand facing Iain. "Shall I cut him to make ye obey? Mayhaps a scar upon the other cheek. Ah, then there is this proud fellow."

Paling when he prodded Iain's loins with his sword, Islaen finished tying Iain up. "'Tis done. Ye may cease your tormenting now."

"Ah, but me dear lady, I have but begun." He stood up and smiled coldly at Iain. "I shall let ye keep the wee fellow a while longer."

He laughed and pushed Iain over causing a strain to be

put on the rope. Islaen gasped, then rushed at the man, infuriated by his cruelty. She did not even land one blow. Almost casually he swung at her sending her sprawling. She stared up at him and knew that, although they may have gained some time, that time would be a torture filled with whatever horror MacLennon's twisted mind could conceive. Somehow he knew that the chance of anyone coming to their rescue was slim and he intended to play with them.

"Come now, m'lady, I believe ye were about to remove your clothes. Dinnae let me stop you."

For one brief panicked moment Iain thought of shouting for help but he ruthlessly quelled the urge. The chances that anyone would hear were small. So too would it insure a quick death for himself and Islaen. What rescuers might arrive would only find their dead bodies. He had to try to be strong, to let MacLennon play his mad games, for there was always the chance that someone would see signs that MacLennon was near or simply worry that he and Islaen had been gone too long and come looking for them. Knowing what MacLennon planned for Islaen, however, made Iain fear he would lack that strength. He really did not think he could silently watch her raped even for the chance to save their lives.

As he faced the very real prospect of their deaths, Alexander's words haunted him. God had given him the joy of Islaen and he had wasted every day of their short time together. Beside his fear for her and his helpless anger was a grief for time lost.

"Islaen, I am sorry," he said, the taut rope around his neck making his voice raspy.

"For what? Because this mad fool thinks our pain can end his? Because he thinks our deaths can resurrect the long-dead Catalina?"

"Be quiet and undress," MacLennon hissed. "Catalina's death must be paid for."

"Then speak to God, fool. He is the one who took her. She died on childbed."

"Bearing his child," MacLennon screamed.

"Aye, just as she would have died had ye wed her and got her with bairn. What would ye have done then? Taken revenge upon yourself?" she sneered. "Fallen upon your sword at her graveside, mayhaps?" She cried out when he struck her sending her sprawling.

He hesitated as he stood over her, his sword raised to strike. "Nay, nay, ye willnae make me kill you. Nay, not yet. Get up."

As she slowly got to her feet, Islaen wondered if that was what she was doing, trying to make him kill her. With an inner shake of her head she rejected that idea. She had no wish at all to die, not even knowing what he planned to do to her. Anger born of fear and frustration prompted her words. She was simply enraged that this madman could play his vengeful games, threaten Iain's life and her own, and she seemed helpless to stop him. Inside she raged at the injustice of it all and that spilled out in bitter, stinging words. She did wonder, however, if she could make him angry enough to make that one error in judgment that would give her and Iain a chance.

"Get undressed," he hissed. "Ye cannae stop me in this. I mean to make him watch me take his woman as he took mine."

Although her heart seemed to be in her throat, Islaen shrugged and began to unlace her gown. "Are ye sure ye can? Are ye sure ye didnae bury your manhood with Catalina as weel as your mind?" She inwardly tensed for the blow when he raised his fist but, with a visible effort, he controlled himself.

"Ye have a sharp tongue, m'lady. Ye best be wary that someone doesnae cut it off."

"Ye do seem to have a taste for chopping off bits of people."

Out of the corner of her eye she saw a stout piece of wood and, as she held out her tunic and let it drop, she began to make a plan. She ceased taunting him and began to concentrate on removing her clothing as slowly as possible, deliberately holding each piece out to let it drop. When she bent to roll down her hose she saw the look upon his face that she had been waiting for. MacLennon might be mad but he still suffered a man's lusts. She could use that against him if she was both careful and clever.

Gasping for air, his compulsive move to aid Islaen tightening the rope about his neck, Iain lay still. For a moment he feared MacLennon was right, that Islaen tried to drive the man to kill her quickly. He discarded that idea although he was not sure why, only sensed that Islaen would not do that.

Then he grew confused for her anger seemed to fade. As he watched her undress it seemed as if she were trying to seduce MacLennon and, by the look upon the man's face, it was working. He could not understand why she should do such a thing. When her plan revealed itself he was both proud of her because of her courage and terrified that her risk would bring her further pain, enraging the madman so that he increased whatever torment he dealt her.

Slipping off her petticoat, Islaen held it out as if to drop it as she had all her other clothes. When MacLennon's gaze briefly flickered to her bared legs, she flung her petticoat at him. It covered his head and, as he struggled to pull it free, she grabbed up the wood she had spotted. He was just tossing aside the petticoat when she swung her rough club with all her might and hit him in the stomach. When he doubled over she swung again hitting him on the head. He sprawled on the ground and she stared at him in amazement for a moment, surprised that she had done what she had and that it had worked.

Hurriedly shaking free of that shock she briefly thought of taking his sword to cut Iain free but discarded the idea as she rushed to Iain's side. She could never wield a sword well enough to cut Iain's bonds without cutting him. Trying to stay calm so that she did not fumble too long over the knots, she began to loosen Iain's bonds.

Once the rope loosened around his neck, Iain rasped, "Ye could have gotten killed, lass."

"Seeing as he was planning on murdering me anyhow I cannae see what your complaint is. Dead is dead."

"Get the horn and call for the others."

"I will get ye free first so that ye can at least move out of the way of his sword." She undid the last knot and heard Iain groan. "Are you hurt?"

"My muscles have knotted 'tis all."

"I will get his sword. I should have done that but only thought of getting ye free and I coudnae use it for that."

"Look out, Islaen," Iain tried to shout but his voice was little more than a hoarse cry and he could not move to save her.

Islaen had taken one step towards MacLennon when suddenly the man was on his feet and racing towards her. She turned to flee but he caught her by the hair, using it to pull her around to face him. He backhanded her across the face sending her sprawling on the ground, then leapt upon her. For one brief moment Islaen feared he was still intending to rape her and Iain would not recover from being so painfully trussed up in time to save her. Then she experienced real terror as his hands closed around her throat and no amount of tearing at his hands could loosen his grip for he was too enraged, too crazed to even feel the pain she was inflicting.

She tried to buck him off but he only laughed. Her body did not have the strength to throw his weight over even when strengthened by the fear of death. Then, suddenly, an arm snaked around MacLennon's neck and he was the one fighting for air. For just a moment he kept his grip upon her throat and Islaen felt near to blacking out. Then he let go to turn all his efforts to breaking Iain's hold upon his neck. Islaen turned on her side, her hand to her abused throat, and gasped for air. For a short while getting air back into her body was all important.

Iain felt relief fill him when he saw Islaen move. He had feared that it had taken him too long to make his cramped muscles move. All he had been able to think of as he had struggled to save her was how small Islaen's neck was, its slenderness encircled by the strong hands of a madman who tried to kill her.

"Islaen, get to the horses," he yelled hoarsely, then cried out as MacLennon broke free and sent him sprawling.

Nodding, Islaen stumbled to her feet. She felt weak and light-headed but fought it. Thinking a little hysterically that Iain was going to be exceedingly cross, she headed not for the horses but towards where he had thrown the horn. She had no intention of running for her life at the cost of his, knew she would never be able to live with herself if she did.

With his attention torn between his wife and MacLennon, Iain was able to do little more than keep out of MacLennon's reach. "Islaen, I told ye to go to the horses! Get out of here!"

"In a moment," she replied but doubted he could hear her for her voice was little more than a raspy whisper.

When he realized where she was headed he managed to turn his full attention upon MacLennon. He knew she looked for the horn and did not think it would be too hard to find. Once she blew upon that help would arrive in minutes.

Desperately, on her hands and knees, Islaen searched for the horn. She almost wept when she found it for it meant rescue from the nightmare they were caught in. Her relief turned to despair when her first attempt to blow it brought forth a sickly tone that would fail to travel a yard. Praying for strength, she took several deep breaths though they hurt her and tried again. The sound was louder, clearer, but it stole what strength she had. Collapsing upon the ground, she prayed it had been enough to bring the help they so desperately needed.

Alexander looked up from the dice game he played with Robert when Phelan rode into Muircraig. "Where have ye been?"

"About."

"Verra informative. Ye just missed Lady Mary. She rode out of here but moments ago in no good a temper, I might add."

"No need. I saw the slattern. Where is Iain?" Phelan asked as he dismounted. "I think ye are losing, Robert. 'Tis best not to play with Alexander."

"Ye should have told me that ere I lost near all I own. Iain isnae here."

"Where did he go?"

"Off with Islaen if ye must ask," Alexander replied. "She planned to seduce him. Must have worked or they would have returned by now."

"Oh, then t'would most like be awkward to seek him out," Phelan murmured, frowning slightly.

"Why should ye wish to?"

"Well, Alex, I saw signs whilst I was out riding."

"MacLennon?"

"I fear it might be. There was an effort made to hide the signs and I can think of no other man who wouldst be trying so hard to creep about here without being seen."

"There is none." Alexander stood up, tensed yet hesitant. "Howbeit, Iain is alert to the danger. They went prepared."

"How alert can a man be," Robert asked as he too stood up, "when he is enjoying what he hasnae tasted for o'er six months."

"Not verra alert at all."

"Still, he may not appreciate any interruption," Phelan said, "especially when I have no proof."

"And I cannae say I wish to be privy to my sister tussling with her mon," Robert drawled.

"An all ye fear is to catch them at it, then we can announce our approach loudly and clearly," Alex said.

"Ye think 'tis worth warning him," Phelan murmured.

"Aye, I do. As we have agreed, who else could it be but MacLennon?"

"None," Robert muttered. "Best we go then. Hold!" Although Robert grasped only Alexander's arm everyone in Muircraig stilled as the single clear note cut through the air.

"Aye," Alexander hissed, "I heard it." He raced for his horse. "The bastard has found them."

"M'lord," Murdo cried as he hurried forward buckling on his sword.

"Follow as ye can, man. We cannot hesitate," Phelan yelled as he vaulted onto his horse. "Do ye know the way, Alex?"

"Aye," he answered as Robert mounted behind him. "We can be there in but minutes."

"Pray God He allows us those minutes," Robert said as they galloped out of Muircraig.

Islaen fought the blackness that threatened to engulf her and struggled to her feet. She had no time for the luxury of pandering to her hurts. Looking toward Iain and MacLennon she wondered frantically what she could do to help.

She cried out in dismay when MacLennon picked up the wood she had used as a club. Even while she tried to keep a close watch on the fight she searched the area for Iain's sword but could see no sign of it. Then MacLennon struck Iain and she forgot all about the sword. Iain was staggered by the blow, truly helpless, and MacLennon was going for his sword. Trying not to make a sound, Islaen moved towards the rough club MacLennon had tossed aside. She grasped it even as MacLennon, sword in hand, turned towards Iain and smiled gloatingly.

Iain fought to stay conscious. The blow to his head had staggered him. It had also cut him, sending blood streaming into his eyes and blinding him. He was helpless, unable to avoid the blow MacLennon was sure to give him. He prayed Islaen had fled once she had given the signal to bring help. MacLennon did not seem to realize what she had done and Iain hoped that this time the man would die.

As if through a fog he saw MacLennon lunge at him. He stumbled out of the way but felt the tip of MacLennon's sword score his side. The way the man laughed told Iain that the man played with him and he cursed viciously, wishing he had his sword. Naked and rendered helpless, then taunted by a madman seemed a poor way to meet one's end. There was little glory in it.

For the first time in her life Islaen tasted pure hate as she watched MacLennon taunt Iain. It was cruel beyond words to play so with a man. Iain was helpless, could barely see where his foe stood and could not fight back, not even if he had held a sword. Her love had to know that the death stroke would come, had probably braced for it, yet MacLennon tormented him by holding back. It was good that MacLennon sought such a twisted pleasure, for it allowed her time to creep near enough to strike at him, but she loathed the man for it.

When MacLennon stepped back after scoring Iain's thigh, Islaen struck. The man was a lot taller than she but her club was long enough that she could reach his head well enough for a sound blow and that was what she aimed for. Putting all her strength and fury behind her swing, she struck him. Despite the hatred she felt for him, her stomach churned at the sound made when her club struck his skull.

Her dismay faded abruptly when he ceased to stagger and turned towards her. Shock caused her to drop her club when she saw the damage she had done. With such a wound in his head the man should not be standing, she thought, yet he advanced on her. He gave a cry that made her shudder, then hit her. Islaen felt her head explode with pain. She seemed to fly backwards, then landed hard upon the ground. There was another burst of pain in her head and the last thing she was aware of was a scream that sounded as if it was torn from the throat of something less than human.

Despite wiping frantically at his eyes, Iain was unable to fully clear his vision or help after Islaen struck MacLennon and the man turned on her. Hearing the sound of a blow, he echoed Islaen's cry of pain. He took one step towards her, barely able to make out her crumpled form, when he froze. MacLennon seemed to clutch his head, then screamed in a way that chilled Iain's blood. For an instant MacLennon wavered, then collapsed. The ensuing silence was something Iain found as chilling as MacLennon's inhuman cry.

Moving towards the two sprawled forms, Iain stumbled and fell to his knees. After trying several times to get up, he started to crawl towards Islaen. Despite his growing fear for her he paused by MacLennon. He knew he should make sure that the man could not rise up to threaten them again.

Looking closely at MacLennon Iain knew the man was dead even before he checked for a heartbeat. He did not need perfect vision to know that such a head wound had to be fatal. Iain was amazed that the man had not immediately died or at least collapsed.

"Islaen," he rasped as he reached her side and her stillness began to terrify him. "Islaen, can ye hear me?"

Never had he felt so helpless. He could barely see and he knew he was very close to blacking out. Islaen needed his help but he could not even keep himself upright. All he could do was pray that she was alive, that someone had heard her call for aid and would be there to keep her alive.

When his shaking hand could locate no pulse he nearly

wept. In trying to put an ear to her chest to find a heartbeat he collapsed on top of her. Beneath his ear, however, he heard the steady beat of her heart. With a deep sigh of relief he gave into unconsciousness knowing that, even if Muircraig had not heard the call, someone would come when they were absent for too long.

"Sweet Jesu," Alexander breathed as he came upon the scene. "They are all dead."

"Nay," Robert cried as he dismounted and raced over to his sister.

He gently moved Iain off of Islaen. She was bruised on her face and her shift was splattered with blood. Once he was sure that she was alive it took him several moments before he was sure that her only wound was a bad bump on the back of her head.

"Iain lives as weel," Alexander reported, "but he has a bad head wound."

"So does Islaen," Robert said as he moved to get the blanket so that he could wrap her in it.

"How fares MacLennon?" Alexander asked Phelan.

"Quite dead." Phelan rose from where he knelt by the man. "Someone caved in his head."

"Good. The bastard has been a plague for too long. Help me get Iain's braes on. I am certain he wouldnae wish to be taken back home naked."

Alexander and Phelan had just finished covering Iain's nakedness when the men from Muircraig arrived. While Phelan and Murdo bathed Iain's wounds, Alexander saw to the making of a litter for Iain. Islaen could easily be carried safely by a man on a horse but Iain would be far too great a burden. Once satisfied that matters were seen to, he knelt by Robert who sat holding Islaen, gently pressing a cool damp cloth to her forehead and vainly trying to rouse her.

"What do we do with MacLennon's body? Do we leave it to the carrion?"

"T'would please me to do so," Robert growled.

"Me as weel," Alexander said coldly, "but we best take him with us."

"Why? The mon deserves no Christian rights. He was mad and tormented twa people that had done him no wrong."

"Aye, Robert, but he has haunted Iain for o'er twa years." Alexander sighed and ran a hand through his hair. "I cannae say for such has ne'er happened to me but in his place I think I should like to ken that my tormenter is indeed dead."

"He killed the mon. He must ken that he is dead."

"Aye, he killed the mon but he may have fallen himself ere he was certain that the mon was dead. Best we take the body so there can be no doubt in Iain's mind that he has finally won."

Looking from his unconscious sister to the equally unconscious Iain, Robert met Alexander's worried gaze and asked softly, "But has he?"

Chapter Twenty-four

"Islaen," Iain cried and tried to sit up only to be held in place by one strong hand upon his chest. For one panicked moment he had feared to find himself still in the wood and MacLennon still alive, still threatening him and Islaen.

"Where is Islaen?" he rasped. "I must see Islaen."

"Islaen lives. Now, drink this."

After painfully swallowing the soothing herbal potion Alexander helped him drink, Iain demanded, "Where is she?"

"In her chambers with Meg and Storm holding court over her. She hasnae woken up yet," he said softly.

"How long?"

"Since yesterday." Alexander held Iain still again when he tried to rise.

"I must see her."

"Ye must stay in this bed, friend. Ye would only fall flat on your face if ye tried to rise and I have toted ye about enough."

Iain knew Alexander was right. He could feel the weakness of his body. So too had he suffered some dizziness simply raising himself slightly with Alexander's help. To stand up would get him nowhere but sprawled upon the floor. He ached to see Islaen, however, and cursed his helplessness viciously.

"Come, she lives. Let that be enough for now."

"Would ye?"

"Nay, but ye have e'er had more sense."

"I have had no sense at all since I set eyes on her. Mac-Lennon?"

"Dead. Do ye recall bashing his head in?"

"Nay, for t'was not I that did so but Islaen."

"Islaen?" Alexander gasped.

"Aye, she . . ."

"Wait. Let me fetch your kin. They have awaited your great awakening. If ye had but waited an hour, t'would have been Tavis setting here."

"Ere ye fetch them get me a chamberpot," Iain said with a sigh, disgusted to be needing help with even that.

Alexander helped him as he emptied his bladder, then hurried away to find the MacLagans. Iain found that he needed the few moments it would take to fetch his kin to recover from the simple chore of relieving himself. By the time they arrived, he was able to tell them all that had happened. Recalling the nightmare of that time left him weak and he knew most of that was because he could not yet see Islaen. Each memory only made him more aware of all she had endured.

"I still cannae believe Islaen struck him down," Alexander murmured and shook his head. "She is such a wee lass."

"Ah, the lasses can surprise ye, laddie," Colin said with a nod. "If they were trained as lads are, they could probably wield a sword."

"She should have been riding away, fleeing as I had ordered her to," Iain muttered.

"Ye had about as much chance of her heeding that order as I would have had with Storm an it had been us in that trouble. Ye were still in danger, weaponless, and she couldnae leave ye. We wouldnae leave them. 'Tis no surprise they feel the same."

"Aye, I ken it, Tavis, but that madman nearly killed her

once. I wanted her out of his reach. Ye are certain he is dead? I recall deciding he was."

"Verra dead," Colin assured him. "We have his body. Put it in a vat of brine. Thought ye might need to see to be sure."

"Nay. I saw him. I just wanted someone to agree with what I thought I had seen. Confused as I was, my head reeling, I still knew dead when I saw it. Just wasnae sure whether to believe it or nay. This has gone on for so long."

"'Tis o'er now," Tavis said. "Now that ye have roused I think ye will soon be up and about."

"But will Islaen?"

"She isnae a muckle great beast like you. T'will take her longer. An it will ease your mind, I will ask Storm to come speak with you."

"Aye, please. An I ken all that I may about how she fares I may rest easier."

When his kin left and Alexander took up his seat by the bed again, Iain closed his eyes. The visit had worn him out. He wanted to wait to see Storm but soon drifted off to sleep again. Twice more he woke, then dozed before waking to find Storm entering the room with a tray. He grimaced with distaste when she helped him sit up and placed the tray before him.

"Gruel."

"Just for today, I think," Storm said as she sat down near the bed. "Now, ye eat and I will tell ye what I can about Islaen."

"What do you mean—what ye can?" he growled as he started to eat and discovered that he was hungry enough to enjoy even gruel.

"I am no physician, Iain."

"Praise God. Those fools would bleed her and she doesnae need that."

"Nay, she does not. Iain, it has not been that long yet. From what I was told I know t'was a terrible ordeal. Some of this sleep may be due to that. All that she suffered wore her out, exhausted her. That could lengthen the sleep the knock on the head sent her into."

"Ye dinnae sound too sure of that."

"What you hear is ignorance. I do not know much of head wounds. No one does."

"Ye havenae eased my worries much, lass. Can ye tell me naught that is good?"

"She lives, Iain. Aye, the lump on the head is large but neither Meg, myself nor e'en Wallace can feel any damage done beneath the skin. The cut left by the blow was but a small one. She does not sleep the sleep of the dead. Several times she has stirred and cried out. That is a good sign, I believe. T'would seem to show that she has not pulled too far away from us."

He nodded, then sighed. "I wish to see her."

"That must wait, Iain, but not for much longer. Mayhaps e'en on the morrow."

When Storm rose and reached for the tray, he grasped her hand. "Thank ye for tending her so weel."

"I tend her because I care for her. We have become dear friends while ye were so much away."

Smiling crookedly, he murmured, "I deserve the condemnation I can hear in your voice."

"Nay, Iain, I . . ."

"Dinnae lie to soothe me. I begin to think I have been too much soothed."

"Your fears were very real, Iain."

"Aye, but I let them rule me, force me to hide away like some craven dog. Alexander didnae soothe me."

"Alexander meddles," Storm muttered, fearing the man had hurt Iain.

"He does but I cannae fault him this time. He was right and, in speaking blunt, in trying to make me think about what I was doing, he gave up something—the chance to claim Islaen."

Storm grimaced. "I had wondered if ye had noticed that."

"Aye, I had noticed and Alexander told me himself."

"There has been naught but friendship between them, Iain."

"I ken it. Islaen says t'will truly be that and no more especially an he finds a lass that can look beyond his bonnie face. There is more beyond it than e'en I kenned. He saw what I did and made me see it. Aye, I was trying to protect Islaen, trying to be certain she wouldnae be left grieving or with child if MacLennon won, but I was protecting myself too and I was failing at it. Do ye ken what I mean?"

"Aye. Ye did not wish to care for her," Storm said softly. "I am not the one ye should be telling this to," she continued.

"I ken it but I feel a need to test my words. Do ye think she can understand and forgive me?"

Storm decided it was not her place to tell him how easily Islaen could do that. "I should think so especially if ye have some sweet words for her as weel."

"Oh, I think I can manage a few," he drawled, then sighed. "I pray I havenae lost my chance."

"Nay," she picked up the tray, "I just do not feel that is so. Rest, Iain, and might I make a suggestion?"

"Aye, what?"

"Be sure ye have her where ye can talk all this out without interruption and mayhaps where ye can have a few days to prove to her that ye mean it. That might not come for a few days. There will be people about and she will need time to heal."

Iain sighed and nodded, recognizing the wisdom of what she said. He had many months of foolishness and neglect to atone for. There would be wounds to be soothed and he could not do that in a few snatched moments. Since Robert had sent word to the MacRoths, he suspected that a few snatched moments would be all he would get for a while.

When he woke up next it was with a start. He bolted

upright in bed and suffered a moment's confusion, then knew what had awakened him. Islaen was crying out his name. He started to get out of bed and suddenly Alex was there.

"At least put your braes on e'er ye stumble in there," Alex said even as he helped Iain do so.

"Where did ye come from?"

"A pallet in the corner. T'was thought t'would be wise to watch ye close a while longer."

Even as he stood up Iain realized he would need the supporting arm Alexander put around him. The ache in his head had lessened considerably but he was by no means healed. As they started towards Islaen's chambers, Iain cursed his weakness for it slowed them down.

With the slow return of consciousness, Islaen was assaulted by the memories of the ordeal with MacLennon. The most tormenting of all the visions was Iain standing helpless before an armed MacLennon. She grew more and more afraid as she realized that she did not know what had happened after she had been knocked down by MacLennon. The thought that Iain was dead made her scream his name. She sat up only to cry out as her head throbbed with pain. Clutching her head she still struggled to leave the bed, driven by her need to see Iain, but Storm and Meg hurried over to stop her.

"Lass, ye cannae just sit up and dash off," Meg cried as she struggled to make Islaen lie back down.

"I must see Iain," Islaen protested but found that she was much too weak to fight Meg and Storm and was soon tucked back into bed.

"Ye cannot see Iain," Storm said firmly.

"He is dead then, isnae he," Islaen said in a flat lifeless voice. "MacLennon killed him."

"Weel, an he did, lass, he did a muckle poor job of it," Iain drawled, arriving in time to hear her words.

Her head ached so badly she found it hard to see clearly as she turned towards the voice. "Iain?"

"Weel," he slipped into bed beside her, "'tisnae Alexander climbing into your bed."

"Och, weel, mayhaps next time," she jested, her joy at finding that he lived raising her spirits despite the pain in her head.

"Islaen," he growled and glared fleetingly at Alexander who chuckled merrily.

She gripped his hand tightly. "I feared ye were dead, Iain. I couldnae recall how matters stood after MacLennon struck me. I must have been knocked out."

"Aye, for twa days."

"How did ye escape him?"

"He fell right after he struck you."

"That was the scream I heard."

"Aye. Your blow to his head took a moment to work but work it did."

"He is dead then?"

"Quite dead, Islaen."

"I should be glad of it and, in part, I am but I wish it could have been otherwise."

"It had to be, Islaen. He ne'er would have let us be. His madness demanded that he keep on until one of us was dead."

She nodded but carefully, in deference to her aching head. He was right. MacLennon had left them with no other choice. The only way to stop his madness was to kill him. She just wished she had not been the one to strike the killing blow. Despite all the man had done and had planned to do, something inside of her drew back in horror over the violence she had committed.

"Come, Islaen, ye maun drink this potion," Meg urged as she stood by the bed and held out a goblet.

Islaen made a childish grimace and turned away, curling up at Iain's side. "Nay, I willnae drink it."

Although he sympathized with her feelings, having had to put down a few potions in his time, Iain said a little sternly, "Be this any way for a grown woman and mither to act?"

"Aye," Islaen muttered, "and ye would act the same had ye drunk any of Meg's vile potions."

"I havenae killed ye yet, lass," Meg said crossly.

"It has been a near thing a time or twa."

"Islaen," Iain said with quiet firmness though he felt an urge to laugh.

"Oh, verra weel." She tried to sit up but started to feel dizzy. "Wheesht, I am weak."

Supporting her, Iain nodded. "Aye, so am I still but I can feel my strength returning e'en now. Ye were unconscious longer than I. T'will be a while ere ye can run about, lass. What is the potion for, Meg?"

"Murder," Islaen grumbled.

Meg ignored her. "To ease her pain. I ken weel that her head hurts." Meg nodded in approval when Islaen downed it and ignored the girl's grimaces. "I made it weak for ye."

"Will it make me sleep?" Islaen asked making no protest when Iain settled her comfortably in his arms.

"I dinnae need to give ye aught for that. Ye will sleep a muckle lot for a day or so, child."

"But I only just awoke."

"She is right, Islaen. I did the same." Iain sighed and shook his head. "I couldnae stay awake long at all e'en when I tried."

"Weel, now that ye have seen how she fares, sir," Meg said to Iain, "ye can go back to your own bed."

Resisting the urge to hold tighter to him, Islaen murmured, "Aye, ye neednae stay here, Iain, if ye dinnae wish to."

"I wish to. I am staying here." He settled himself more comfortably in the bed as if to add strength to his firm pronouncement.

"But I maun tend to the lass and all."

"Meg, Islaen and I are wed. I dinnae think I will see aught I havenae seen before."

"So gently put, my friend," Alexander murmured as Meg gasped and Islaen groaned softly in embarrassment.

For only a moment was Islaen concernèd about a need for some privacy. She needed Iain more. Her fear that he had been killed still left a bitter taste in her mouth.

"I think t'would be best an Islaen got some rest now," Iain said softly as he felt his wife go lax in his hold. "An her kin travel here as swiftly as they did after the bairns came they will be here on the morrow. She will need rest to see them."

Meg frowned but nodded in agreement. "Aye and they will insist upon seeing the lass too. I will sit for now, m'lady," she said to Storm. "'Tis your turn to rest. Aye, and Master Iain's right. The MacRoths will come soon and there will be a muckle lot of work."

Islaen woke with a start partly because Iain had and partly because of a loud crash. Peering over the shoulder of a softly cursing Iain, she smiled. The still shuddering door explained the crash.

"Greetings, Fither. Have ye nay learned to knock yet?"

"Ye wouldnae have heard me," Alaistair growled as he strode to the bed and studied his daughter, scowling at the bruises on her face. "Put up a good fight, did ye, lass?"

"Weel, I wouldnae say being slapped around was much of a fight, Fither. Er, Fither, do ye think ye could wait but a moment for this visit? There is one or twa things I need to do ere I sit and talk."

At that moment Storm nudged her way through Islaen's brothers who were gathered in the doorway. She efficiently moved everyone out into the hallway except for Alaistair. Islaen nearly laughed as she watched her father nearly carry a startled Iain into the other room to see to his needs while

Storm quickly helped her see to hers. Iain was still looking bemused when Alaistair brought him back and bundled him back into bed at her side.

"I will fetch ye some food to break your fast," Storm said as she started to leave. "Do not frown so, Iain. T'will not be gruel." She opened the door and stared at the group of large MacRoth men. "I will bring ye a lot of food," she drawled.

"God's toenails, has everyone come then?" Islaen asked weakly as her brothers filed into the room. "Nay, the big twins arenae here."

"Nay," Conan said as he moved forward to kiss Islaen in greeting, "and we left that lad, Gamel, behind as weel. He was carrying on some about having failed ye. William plans to take him for a wee swim an he doesnae hush soon."

"Oh dear, poor Gamel. Weel, I had hoped ye would make him see things a wee bit less dreamily."

"He is a good lad, dearling," her father said as he sat down by the bed, "and beneath all that hair is some wit when ye can get him to cease talking nonsense. Now, introduce your mon to Angus and Conan, then ye can tell me all that happened."

Even though she was certain Robert had told her father most everything, she dutifully obeyed. Storm and Meg arrived with food about halfway through the telling. Islaen ate and gave over most of the telling to Iain for she found that the memories of that horrifying time were still too fresh and disturbing to speak of calmly. By the time the tale was done, all questions answered, she was feeling weary. Her head did not ache half as much as it had but it still drained her strength. Leaning against Iain she felt his arm slip around her shoulders to hold her more comfortably against him.

"Ye did yourself proud, lass," her father said quietly.

"She should have fled when I told her to," Iain murmured.

"That wouldnae have been Islaen. Ye needed help. Now I can see how ye think, lad, and the lass ought to obey her mon but I can see clear why she didnae. Aye, and approve of it. Ah, the bairns," he expained joyfully as Meg, Storm and Grizel entered to deposit the children upon the bed.

Islaen suddenly became aware of the fact that she felt no need to feed her children and looked at Storm with consternation as the woman handed her Padruig. "Storm, I dinnae think I can," she whispered.

"They have been fed. I had suspected that your milk had dried up and was prepared. The shock of your attack and your injury," Storm shrugged. "They have begun to need more than milk anyways and they take well to goat's milk. Grizel has had no trouble keeping them all fed although she has had to enlist the aid of a young girl for they all seem to become demanding at the same time. 'Tis not such a tragedy, Islaen," she added softly.

Although she nodded, Islaen was not quite sure she agreed. She felt a keen sense of loss. The time while she had held her sons close as she nursed them had been a pleasing time. There was also a small sense of jealousy concerning Grizel which she knew was wrong but was unable to fully subdue.

"Here, lass," Alaistair murmured as he bent forward in his seat to pat Padruig affectionately, "dinnae look so dowie."

Seeing Storm, Grizel and Meg slip out of the door, she smiled weakly at her father. "'Tis but foolish jealousy. I feel as though I lose them."

"Nay, ye cannae lass. E'en Liusadh will soon turn to ye more once her belly isnae her first and only concern, though the maid will e'er be dear to her. Many fine ladies dinnae feed their bairns, but if they wish their love 'tis there for them. Ye can feed them the goat's milk and gruel so ye arenae missing out completely from their feeding time. Ye held them in your body for near nine months and the lads to your breast for six. The mark is upon them.

"Here, lass, think on fithers. They ne'er carry the child in a womb nor feed it but there are few bairns that dinnae feel some bond to the mon whose seed made them."

"Aye, ye are right, Fither." She kissed his cheek. "'Tis a loss I wasnae prepared for and felt it too deeply for a moment." She glanced towards Iain who was smiling rather foolishly at his tiny giggling daughter. "Liusadh kens her fither weel already and beguiles him."

When his granddaughter turned her wide-eyed gaze his way, Alaistair smiled with a touch of sadness. "She has your mither's eyes. Shame she got your rogue of a husband's dark hair but she will be a beauty for all that," he drawled, then looked at Iain and grinned. "Aye, that is a lass that will cause ye a time and more once she becomes more woman than child."

It was not long before Alaistair put an end to the visit. Islaen smiled sleepily as she watched her children carried out by their doting uncles. It gave her a very good feeling to know that, no matter what occurred in the future, her children would never lack for love. Yawning, she snuggled up to Iain and knew she would soon be asleep.

"I dinnae think I like the way your fither grins so when he talks on the trouble Liusadh will be in a few years," Iain drawled.

Even though she laughed, she said, "She will give it to him too. Fither feels about each of his grandchildren as if they are his very own children. If Liusadh makes ye pace the floor, Fither will be keeping step at your side. If ye could see him with the others, ye would ken it."

"Islaen, are ye still upset about your milk drying up?"

Due to his extended absences she was not accustomed to discussing the matter with him and felt herself blush slightly. "'Tis already passing. T'was unexpected. Aye, and I found myself prey to fears and jealousies. I feel as if Liusadh will ne'er be really mine and feared to lose the lads as weel. But, Fither is right. 'Tis but a small part of the bairn's lives and I can find muckle another way to tend to them and love them. Fither wasnae there for me as a mither or nurse was but I

couldnae love the mon more. When I kenned that I was
greatly soothed." She yawned widely.

"Get some rest, Islaen."

"If ye dinnae want to sleep, Iain, ye neednae stay with me."

"I am staying."

There was a tone to his voice that both puzzled her and
raised her hopes. He had sounded almost as if he made a vow.
Before MacLennon had come she had thought there had been
a change in Iain's feelings but was afraid to hope. She wished
she were not so sleepy for she would like to try and have a serious talk with him. It was time for them to stop hiding how
they felt or thought, to stop trying to guess each other's heart
and mind, and be open with each other. However, that sort
of discussion required that she have all her wits about her and
they were hopelessly dulled at the moment. As sleep conquered her, she told herself firmly that if all she had accomplished was to bring him back to bed that would be enough
for now.

Chapter Twenty-five

Iain muttered and cursed as he and Alexander took a chest out to one of the waiting carts. It had been over a week since the MacRoths had arrived and they showed no signs of leaving. By the time he got any time alone with Islaen she was too tired to have any serious discussion. He was getting no closer to sorting out the troubles he had bred in his marriage.

"Do ye feel inclined to tell me why ye are in such a dark mood? Are ye regretting leaving Caraidland?"

Looking at Alexander as they hefted the chest into the back of a wagon, Iain managed to growl, "MacRoths, curse them."

"They are a great help. Ye will be moved to Muircraig in but one journey."

"Aye, that is true." Iain sighed and leaned against the cart. "'Tis just that I am fore'er tripping o'er them and have no time with Islaen. When she and I reach our chambers of a night she can do naught but sleep."

"Surely if ye can maintain an abstinence of six months, ye can last but a fortnight," Alexander drawled, his lack of sympathy obvious.

"There is that but that wasnae what I was referring to. Ye see, Alex, I did think on all ye said about wasting time and all.

The curse of it is, I decided ye were right on the day MacLennon attacked us."

"Ah, and ye have had no chance to speak to Islaen yet."

"None. Storm felt t'would be best done when there is time and privacy to do it verra weel, to say what I must and make her believe it."

"Aye, she may have doubts. T'will seem almost a full turnabout."

Iain nodded. "I willnae blame her if she does doubt." He shook his head and grimaced. "I begin to think t'will be anither year e'er I get the chance, though."

"I doubt that."

"Have ye no suggestions about how I might be rid of the MacRoths yet not cause any offense?"

"I dinnae meddle."

The scathing comment Iain meant as a response to that haughtily delivered lie was smothered by the arrival of two of Islaen's brothers. By the time he had directed them in placing the chest they carried, Alexander had slipped away. Iain did not spot the man again until they were ready to leave Caraidland. Alexander was in the midst of the MacRoths and Iain frowned slightly, then told himself not to be so suspicious before looking around for Islaen.

Islaen hugged Storm and fought an urge to cry. She wanted to start her own home, yet hated to leave Caraidland. Although Iain stayed in her bed, he had not made love to her yet and they seemed no closer to any sort of communication. She feared the loneliness she might suffer if that distance in their marriage continued even at Muircraig.

"Come, Islaen," Storm said, giving a trembling smile, "we will not be so far apart. 'Tis best that ye finally go to live in your own home with Iain and no longer share that of others."

"Is it? I am nay too certain of that." Islaen hooked her arm through Storm's and they stepped out into the bailey.

"Is there still trouble between you?"

"Nay, no trouble, but little of anything else either. MacLennon is dead and I ken weel that, though mayhaps nothing can fully ease Iain's fear of childbirth, I have lessened it some, yet we move no nearer to any real bond. He shares my bed but he has yet to make love to me and we share naught else."

Storm had to bite her tongue to keep from revealing all Iain had told her in order to take the sadness from her friend's eyes. "Give it time, Islaen. Mayhaps he but does not know how to start. As concerns the lack of lovemaking, well, ye have been very tired of late. I do not think ye were healed enough to bear the strain, joyous though it may be, of having so many kin visiting."

"Aye, I have been quick to fall asleep. I but hope ye are right. Muircraig will be no home an I have no marriage, have but a mon who sometimes uses my body and treats me weel but no more."

"T'will not be so dismal. I feel that in my heart. Now, come, Iain searches for you. 'Tis time to leave."

Sitting in a cart with the children, Meg and Grizel, Islaen watched Iain ride with the men, occasionally moving along the line of carts to see that all went smoothly. Her heart ached for he seemed as out of reach as ever. She was not sure she had the strength or patience to continue to fight for some place in his affections. Her love for him was as strong as ever but a strange lack of initiative had overcome her lately. After so many long months she was weary of the battle.

Once at Muircraig, she busied herself directing the placement of all they had brought. Several times she saw Alexander in deep conversation with her kin but her suspicion that he might be up to something was fleeting, for she was far too busy to worry about it. If Alexander was meddling again she was sure she would find out later.

"Things still arenae right," Alaistair muttered as he stood by Alexander and watched his daughter and her husband.

"They will be soon."

Smiling crookedly, Alaistair eyed the young man with a little sternness. "Ye ken too much of what is between those two."

"They are both my friends and I act out of caring for them, wishing their happiness, which I strongly feel can only be found within the marriage they were both pushed into."

"They have had months to find it, yet it still eludes them."

"Aye, it has. It was changing ere MacLennon died. Unfortunately MacLennon struck ere Iain could speak to Islaen of this change of heart."

"The attack came o'er a week ago. Has the lad lost his urge to speak?"

"Nay. Iain must have time," he looked at Alaistair and smiled crookedly, "and privacy to say his piece and then prove his words."

"Then privacy he shall have for I am fair sick of watching the wee lass trying to act as if naught is amiss." He immediately sought out his sons to tell them that, as soon as everything was unpacked, they would leave.

"But, Fither," Islaen protested when he told her that they were leaving, that the last item was unpacked and put away, "we brought food enough for all of ye. Would ye not rather wait until the morning?"

"Nay. We stayed this long for we wished to aid ye in moving. We will hie back to Caraidland to pack our goods, then go from there at dawn. Now, let me see the bairns once again ere I go. T'will most like be months ere I see them again."

"Before the winter comes again," Iain said quietly as he slipped an arm around her shoulders and watched her family and Alexander ride away, "we shall go to visit them. Bairns and all. I think the bairns will be old enough to bear the journey weel."

"Aye, I think so and their aunts and cousins are eager to see them. Shall I have our meal readied?"

"Aye, I should like to retire early." He looked at her. "Verra early."

Feeling herself blush, Islaen softly cursed and hurried away to see to their meal. He did not have to mean anything other than he wished to go to bed early, she told herself crossly. He had certainly not indicated a desire for anything other than sleep just lately. She told herself not to think anything but she knew that she would. Just lately she could think of little else save of making love. She had often awakened in the morning cursing herself for fallng asleep so soundly and quickly and Iain for not trying to rouse her. Finally, she told herself that, no matter how anxious she grew for his touch, she would not be the first one to act. 'This time Iain can,' she thought angrily. 'He can beg for it first. Weel, ask nicely.' By the time she joined him for their meal she had decided that just some indication from him that he was feeling inclined would be enough, then chided herself for her weakness.

Iain maintained an amiable chatter throughout the meal. He also made certain, subtly, that Islaen did not have too many sips of wine. It was going to be an effort to say all he thought he ought to, what he wanted to say despite his sudden attack of cowardice, and he did not want to have to repeat it all because she was too dulled by wine. He let her go to their chambers first as well, so that he could have a little time to prepare himself and stiffen his suddenly weak backbone. Ruefully, he admitted that he feared rejection or simple disinterest. He feared he had waited too long to come to his senses, that he had killed whatever feelings she had held for him with his constant pushing her away. Finishing his wine, he started toward their chambers deciding it was best to get it over with.

When Iain entered their chambers, Islaen watched him covertly. She had hurriedly undressed, washed and gotten into

bed but had decided that it was useless to even try to feign
sleep. Iain had been acting somewhat strange since her kin
had left, almost flirtatious at times, and he had seemed to be
constantly watching her. It made her nervous.

"Islaen, we must talk," he said softly as he got into bed and
reached for her.

Talking was not what Islaen felt inclined to do when he
held her so close, but she did not voice her real wishes. She
was also afraid of what he might say. If she could see their
marriage as a failure he could also but, unlike her, he was not
urged by love to keep trying to mend things. The longer he
hesitated to speak, the more certain she was that he was about
to suggest that they live apart, perhaps even seek a way to
have the marriage ended.

"I can stay with my fither," she blurted out.

Abruptly distracted from trying to think of a proper way to
open the discussion, Iain stared at her. "What?"

"My fither will take me in, an I claim it as my decision.
There should be no real difficulty." She was surprised that she
could speak of something so painful with such relative calm.

"What are ye babbling about?"

"Ye sending me away."

He held her tighter. "God's beard, 'tis the last thing I want.
Why should I do such a thing?"

Her brief conviction faltered alarmingly and she said
weakly, "Because this marriage hasnae worked e'en after so
long."

"'Tis barely eighteen months since we wed. 'Tis not so
verra long. And, if this marriage hasnae worked, 'tis only
myself to blame. I wouldnae let it work. I told myself t'was
best an it didnae."

Hardly daring to breathe for fear of stopping a conversation that held the promise of at least explaining a few things,
Islaen whispered, "Why didnae ye, Iain?"

"Have ye no idea?"

"A few but I cannae feel certain."

"Aye, 'tis impossible to read a person's thoughts or heart and I told ye naught. I thought to save ye from grief. I thought to protect ye from the pain of it, Islaen."

"Did ye ne'er think that grief could come from a live but cold husband, from e'er being kept at a distance?"

"Aye, but I thought t'would be a lesser grief. Ye would still have the heart left to find another, to love and wed."

"Or mayhaps I wouldnae wish to chance failing again. After giving all to ye and gaining naught mayhaps I would-nae have the heart nor the strength to try again. Some find failure as deeply bitter as grief, Iain," she said as he looked at her with some surprise. "Are ye telling me that ye arenae going to be running away from me any longer, that mayhaps we have a chance to make our marriage a good one and Muir-craig a real home?" She ran her hand over his hip and felt him tremble slightly.

"Would ye like that, Islaen?" He told himself to behave, that they still had a lot to talk about, but continued to unlace her shift.

"Aye. Verra much. 'Tis what I have always wanted. Iain, kiss me," she whispered.

"We arenae done talking," he said with equal softness even as he brushed his lips over hers.

"I ken it, but once ye stilled some of my fears I got to thinking on other things. It has been so verra long, Iain."

"Aye, too long," he growled and then kissed her, moving so that she lay beneath him. "God's beard, how I have missed your sweetness," he rasped as his lips followed the descent of her shift as he eased it off of her body.

Her hands clenching in his hair as he paused to suckle the aching tips of her breasts, she found her voice thick and husky with passion when she was finally able to speak. "Yet ye stayed away for so long."

"I had to." He finished removing her shift, then crouched

over her, the sight of her lithe, naked form all the foreplay he needed. "T'was a torture, sweeting. I dinnae think there was a moment I didnae ache for ye."

Curling her fingers around his shaft, she urged him to join their bodies. "I ken the torment weel, Iain. End it now, husband."

What little control he had ended the moment he joined their bodies. Islaen held him close as the hunger in his kiss matched the fierce thrusts of his body. She welcomed the fury of his passion and met it, wanting to savor each movement of his body within hers but unable to control her starved desires. Vaguely she was aware of him watching her when her passion crested but, as she fell into passion's abyss, she knew he was with her, felt him drive deep within her and heard him cry out her name.

Feeling satisfaction turn to renewed desire, Iain set aside the cloth he had washed them with and rejoined Islaen in their bed. Lying on his side next to her, he gently brushed the tangled hair from her face and smiled into her sleepy gaze. He still held her passion and that gave him hope, gave him the strength to finish talking.

"Now, where was I ere ye interrupted me?" He idly drew circles around her nipples with his finger and watched them slowly harden.

"Iain, if ye mean to have a talk, I dinnae think ye should do that," she murmured but made no move to halt him, lying quiescently beneath his idle yet sensuous attentions. "I might get distracted again."

"Weel, if ye keep lying verra still ye may be able to let me finish most all of what I have left to say."

Feeling decidedly wanton, she just smiled. There was something exciting about just lying there letting him do as he pleased and feeling renewed desire seep through her veins. She was a little curious as to how long she could do so before having to touch him. Concentrating on his words would slow passion's control over her and she exerted herself to do just that.

"Weel, what else did ye have to say? That wasnae all of it?"

"Nay. I ken I dinnae really have to say it all but I will. I want all cleared between us."

"A fresh start."

"Aye, a fresh start. Islaen, t'was not only ye I ran from. I ran from myself, from all ye could make me feel. After losing Mary, then Catalina's death, I shut myself away, locked up my feelings. I put my heart in armor as strong as any warrior's. I didnae want to feel and I didnae want anyone to make me feel. From the moment we met, Islaen, ye chipped away at that wall. I think the hardest thing to fight was the way ye could make me smile. Passion, ye ken, doesnae need to touch the heart and, e'en though t'was the fiercest and best I have e'er tasted, I oft felt I could control that. A mon has many years to learn to keep his lusts free of any other feelings. Och, 'tis so hard to explain."

"Ye dinnae need to be too exact, Iain," she said softly and trembled when he stroked her thigh.

"I dinnae think I can be." He leaned down to tease at her hardened nipples with his tongue. "Ye moved."

Clenching her hands which had begun to reach for him, she muttered huskily, "'Tis harder than I thought. Iain, when did ye decide to stop running? It wasnae just today was it?" She fought to keep her mind on the conversation and not on the hand caressing her thighs and legs and making her ache. "Was it when MacLennon was killed?" She moaned softly when he began to suckle gently.

"Nay, before that. When ye were taken by Fraser I thought my reasons for keeping a distance justified. If ye could feel but a part of the pain that seared me when I thought ye dead, then t'was my duty to protect ye from it. E'en then I think I kenned I hoped to protect myself too, to pull back some. T'was myself I feared for as much as ye." After savoring the view of her breasts damp and swollen from his attentions, he turned his amorous skills upon her midriff. "Ye are squirming, lass."

"I will make ye pay for this, Iain MacLagan."

"I will consider that a promise," he murmured, moving so that he was sprawled between her thighs. "Now, I was going to tell ye what changed my mind." He encircled her navel with kisses as his hands gently stroked her hips.

"I think ye best hurry, Iain."

"But, sweeting, I was meaning to go slow with ye. 'Tis all I have thought on these last months."

"I meant hurry and finish talking," she rasped as he scattered kisses down her leg.

"Alexander changed my mind."

"Alexander?" she croaked as he held her foot and slowly kissed each toe.

"Aye. He got me to thinking on how only God can decide when someone will die, that I didnae have to be killed by MacLennon. He got me thinking on how I was depriving both of us, wasting the precious time God had given us." He started up her other leg. "His words swam around in my mind for days but took firm hold when ye came to Muircraig, when ye seduced me. That ye would do that told me ye werenae happy with the way things were and I wasnae either. I also finally admitted to myself that I sought to protect myself as much as ye. I had wasted so many months of both our lives." He kissed the top of each inner thigh, then placed his lips upon the soft, heated warmth between them. "I will waste no more."

Very quickly Islaen gave up all attempts to be still. She arched to his intimate caress, then tried to pull him into her embrace. A soft cry of frustrated need escaped her when he slowly made his way back up her body, then joined their bodies with an equal leisureliness, seemingly oblivious to her near frantic need. Her eyes closed with pleasure as she felt the union of their bodies but flew open again when he did not move but lay still, cupping her face in his hands.

"Aye keep those lovely eyes open," he rasped, his control nearly breaking as he strained to move within her eager body with a slow, measured stroke. "I want to see your pleasure. I want to see how black your eyes grow making the gold shine as if polished." He brushed his lips over hers. "I want ye to see my pleasure, dearling, to see what ye do to me." Seeing how close she was to her release, sensing it and wanting to be there with her, his thrusts grew fiercer. "Aye, sweet Islaen, look deep. I want ye to see my love," he rasped softly even as she cried out with her release.

Holding her tightly he let her drag him into desire's abyss with her, groaning his delight over the way her body drank of his. When he felt recovered enough, he propped himself up on his elbows and stared down at her. Lightly kissing her still-flushed face he deemed her lovely beyond compare. He felt a strong pleasure, even pride, in the fact that he could bring her such happiness, a fact she had never tried to hide from him. Iain hoped that that was a sign that his feelings were or soon could be returned in full. He admitted that he needed her to love him, needed it badly.

Islaen was almost afraid to open her eyes. She could hear his passion-roughened voice speaking of love, but feared it had been a dream, a delusion inspired by her own desires. So many times had she prayed to hear those words that she found it easy to disbelieve her own ears. She also feared that she might give into the strong temptation to ask him if she had heard right and thereby embarrass herself, making her own hopes clear, or completely destroy this new blossoming openness Iain was revealing by pushing too hard.

"Ah, ye cannae go to sleep yet, wee Islaen." He touched his lips to hers.

"I wasnae asleep." She opened her eyes slowly.

"T'will be different now, Islaen. I swear it to ye. I ken I will need time to prove myself to ye . . ."

"Nay, Iain."

"Lass, I havenae been a good husband. I havenae given ye what I ken ye needed."

"Ye ne'er promised me anything, Iain, save to say that ye were no wencher nor wife beater. Ye havenae e'er lied to me either. If ye say things will be different now, then I believe ye. I may be a bit slow to believe, but only because change takes getting used to, and because I have wanted it so badly I may fear I have fooled myself into thinking I have it."

He lightly traced the delicate lines of her face. "I dinnae deserve ye, Islaen. Ye have had a lot of patience with this fool."

"Ye arenae a fool, Iain. Ye did what ye felt was right and kind. Just because we didnae all agree with it doesnae mean ye are a fool. I also have no choice." She ran her fingers through his hair and smiled a little sadly, knowing she could no longer hold back the words that filled her heart, yet still afraid of the reception such a declaration would get. "Aye, I was angry at times, e'en bitter, but I couldnae stop, couldnae turn from the path I was on, not since I first set eyes upon ye."

There was a look in her eyes that had him tense, almost breathless. "Why couldnae ye, Islaen? Why?"

So intense was his gaze that she found she could not look away even though she wanted to. "Because I love ye," she whispered and not only found herself the recipient of a very fierce kiss but felt him harden within her. "Weel," she gasped when his mouth finally freed hers and he held her tightly, his face pressed against her neck, "that wasnae what I expected to happen."

"Why not?" he asked huskily as he looked at her, his hand moving slowly over her curves. "Shouldnae a mon be delighted, nay, overjoyed, to discover his love returned e'en though he's done his best to kill all chance of it?"

"His love returned?"

"Aye, Islaen, didnae ye hear me or had pleasure deafened ye?" he teased.

"I wasnae sure. I have wanted ye to say the words for so long that I feared I was now making myself hear them, dreaming them if ye will."

"Nay, dearling, ye werenae dreaming. I love ye." He laughed-softly when she hugged him tightly. "Ye neednae squeeze the words out of me. They will come freely and often now."

"I pray so for I will ne'er tire of hearing them. Och, Iain, I have loved ye for so long and I was so afraid I would ne'er find it returned, that I wasnae the one ye could love."

"Ah, Islaen, 'tis ye I love and I kenned it coming from the start. Ye bewitched me," he murmured as he turned so that she was sprawled on top of him. "I will love away all your doubts."

Propping herself up so that she could see him, she started to say that she had none, that her heart and her eyes told her he spoke the truth, but then she smiled slowly. "Weel, I think I feel a wee doubt coming on."

Seeing the mischief in her face, he grinned. "Then I best love it away. Do ye think ye will need proof of my love often?"

"Oh, aye," she breathed as she bent to kiss him, "in this life and beyond."

"T'will be no trouble as long as ye love me back, Islaen."

"Oh, I intend to."

"In this life and beyond."

"Aye, in this life and beyond."

New York Times *bestselling author Hannah Howell*
returns to the breathtaking Scottish Highlands
with the unforgettable Murray clan and the
stunning Annora MacKay, who cannot resist
the desire an alluring stranger offers . . .

Annora MacKay senses a disturbing evil in
Dunncraig Keep, the estate acquired by her cousin, a cruel
and ruthless man. Only her affection for the tiny girl he claims
is his daughter stops her from fleeing. Then a mysterious
woodcarver arrives at the castle, and she cannot stop
thinking—or longing—for him . . .

James Drummond, once a laird now an outcast, wants what
was stolen from him—his good name,
his lands, and his child. His disguise for getting
into Dunncraig is step one of his plan, but the
enticing raven-haired woman who cares for
his daughter is an unwelcome surprise. For he
has come seeking justice, not love . . .

**Please turn the page for an exciting sneak peek of
Hannah Howell's**
Highland Wolf,
coming in December 2007!

"Still, he... ... appreciate any interruption," Phelan

Prologue

Scotland
Spring, 1477

Sir James Drummond, once laird of Dunncraig, once a husband and a loving father, crawled out of his hiding place deep in the Highlands' most remote mountains and slowly stood up. He felt the hint of spring in the air, the promise of warmth in the moist dawn breeze, and took a deep, slow breath. He felt like some beast waking from a long winter's sleep, only his had lasted for three long hard years. He was ragged, filthy, and hungry, but he was determined not to spend another season slipping from hollow to hollow, afraid to venture near friends or kinsmen because he had death at his heels and afraid to pass even the most fleeting of greetings with another person because they might be the one who would recognize and kill him. It was time to stop running.

He clenched his hands into tight fists as he thought on his enemy, Sir Donnell MacKay. Even though he had never liked or fully trusted Donnell, he had allowed the man to come and go from Dunncraig as he pleased, for he was Mary's kinsman. That simple act of courtesy and his wife Mary's own sweet innocence, the sort that never saw evil in anyone, had cost her

her life. James had barely finished burying his wife and was thinking how he could prove that Donnell had killed her when the man had made his next move. James had found himself declared guilty of murdering his wife; soon after that he was declared an outlaw; and then Donnell had claimed both Dunncraig and little Margaret, James's only child. The few people who had tried to help him had been killed and that was when James had begun to run, to hide, and to keep himself as far away from those he cared about as possible.

Today the running stopped. James collected the sack holding his few meager belongings and started down the rocky slope. As he had struggled to survive the winter, living no better than the beasts he had hunted for food, James had come up with a plan. He needed to get back to Dunncraig and find enough proof to hang Donnell MacKay and free himself. There was still one man at Dunncraig that James felt he could trust with his life, and he would need that man's aid in beginning his search for the truth and the justice he craved. He would either succeed and then reclaim his good name, his lands, and his child—or he would lose it all, including his life. Either way, at least he would not be running anymore.

At the base of the hill, he paused and stared off in the direction of Dunncraig. It was a long, arduous journey, one that would take him weeks because he had no horse; but he could see it clearly in his mind's eye. He could also see his little Meggie with her fat blond curls and big brown eyes, eyes so like her mother's. Meggie would be five now, he realized, and felt his anger swell as he thought of all he had missed of his child's growing because of Donnell's greed. He also felt the stab of guilt born from how he had thought mostly of saving his own life and not what his daughter might be suffering under Donnell's rule.

"Dinnae fret, my Meggie, I will come home soon and free us both," he whispered into the breeze. James straightened his shoulders and began the long walk home.

Chapter One

"Pat the dirt o'er the seed verra gently, Meggie."

Annora smiled as the little girl patted the dirt as slowly and carefully as she patted her cat, Sunny. Margaret, who stoutly preferred to be called Meggie, was all that kept Annora at Dunncraig. Her cousin Donnell had wanted someone to care for the child and her family had sent her. That was no surprise for she was poor and illegitimate, a burden every kinsman and kinswoman she had was quick to shake off whenever they could. At first she had been resigned; but then she had met little Meggie, a child of only two with huge brown eyes and thick golden curls. Despite the fact that Annora thought Donnell was a brutish man, even feared him a little, she had some doubts about his rights to claim Dunncraig. Three years later she was still at Dunncraig and not simply because she had no better place to go. She stayed for little Meggie, a child who had stolen her heart almost from the very first day.

"Seeds are precious," said Meggie.

"Aye, verra precious," Annora agreed. "Some plants just grow again every spring all by themselves," she began.

"Cursed stinking weeds."

Bending her head to hide a grin, Annora quietly said, "Young ladies shouldnae say *cursed*." Neither should ladies of four-and-twenty, she mused, fully aware of where Meggie had heard those words. "But, aye, weeds grow all by themselves in places where ye dinnae want them. Some plants, however, cannae survive the winter and we must collect the seeds or roots, storing them away so that we can plant them when it is warm again."

"'Tisnae warm yet."

Annora looked up to find Meggie scowling at the sky. "Warm enough to plants seeds, love."

"Are ye certain we shouldnae wrap them in a wee plaid first?"

"The earth is their plaid."

"Annora! The laird wants ye to go to the village and see how good that new mon makes a goblet!"

Even as Annora turned to respond to young Ian's bellow the youth was already heading back into the keep. She sighed and carefully collected up all the little bags of seeds she had intended to plant this afternoon. Ian was probably already telling Donnell that Annora was going to the village and, of course, she would. *One did not say nay to Donnell.* Taking Meggie by the hand, Annora hurried them both into the keep so that they could wash up before leaving for the village.

It was as they were about to leave that Donnell strode out of the great hall to intercept them. Annora tensed and she felt Meggie press hard against her skirts. She fought the urge to apologize for not having raced to the village without hesitation and met his dark scowl with a faint, questioning smile.

My cousin is a very handsome man, Annora thought. He had thick dark hair and fine dark eyes. His features were manly but not harsh. He even had good skin and no visible scars. Yet Donnell constantly wore such a sour or angry expression that his handsomeness was obscured. It was as if all that was bad inside of the man left some irrevocable mark upon his looks. The way Donnell looked now, Annora could not see how any woman could find him attractive.

"Why arenae ye going to the village?" he snapped.

"We are going right now, Cousin," she said, doing her best to sound sweet and obedient. "We but needed to wash the dirt of the garden off our hands."

"Ye shouldnae be working in the gardens like some common slut. Ye may be a bastard, but ye come from good blood. And ye shouldnae be teaching Margaret such things, either."

"Some day she will be the mistress of some demesne or keep with a household to rule. She will rule it much better if she kens just how much work is needed when she orders something to be done."

The way Donnell's eyes narrowed told Annora that he was trying to decide if she had just criticized him in some way. She had, all too aware of how little Donnell knew or cared about the work he ordered people to do. He never gave a thought as to how all his needs and comforts were met, except to savagely punish the ones he deemed responsible if they failed in some way. Annora kept her gaze as innocent as possible as she met his look of suspicion, breathing a silent sigh of relief when he had obviously decided that she was not clever enough to be so subtle.

"Get ye gone then," he said. "I have been hearing a great deal about what fine work this new mon does and I seek a goblet or the like so that I may see his skill with my own eyes."

Annora nodded and hurried past him, little Meggie keeping step close by her side. If the fool was so interested in this man's skill she wondered why he did not go and have a look for himself. It was the fear of saying that thought aloud that made her scurry. Donnell's response to such words would be a hard fist and she preferred to avoid those whenever possible.

"Why does the laird need a goblet?" asked Meggie the moment Annora slowed their fast pace to an almost lazy stroll.

"He wants to see if the mon who carves them is as good at what he does as everyone says he is," replied Annora.

"He doesnae believe everyone?"

"Weel, nay, I suspicion he doesnae."

"Then why will he believe us?"

"A verra good question, love. I dinnae ken why he should if he doesnae heed anyone else's word, but 'tis best if we just do as he asks."

Meggie nodded, her expression surprisingly solemn for one so young. "Aye, or he will hit ye again, and I dinnae want him to do that."

Neither did Annora. Her cousin had come close to breaking her jaw and a few other bones the last time he had beaten her. She knew she ought to be grateful that Donnell's second-in-command Egan had stopped him from continuing to punch her, but she was not. Egan did not usually care who Donnell beat or how badly he did so, was in truth just as brutish as Donnell was. The fact that the man did not want her beaten, at least not too severely, made her very nervous. So did the way he always watched her. Annora did not want to owe that man anything.

"Neither do I, love," she finally murmured and quickly distracted Meggie from such dark thoughts by pointing out the cattle grazing on the hillside.

All the way to the village Annora kept Meggie entertained by drawing her attention to every animal, person, or plant they passed. She exchanged a few greetings with a few people, yet again regretting how closely watched and confined Donnell kept her and Meggie. Although she would have preferred choosing the times and reasons she traveled to the

village, Annora enjoyed the pretense of freedom, able to
ignore the guards she knew were right behind her. She only
wished she would be given enough time and freedom to come
to the village more often and get to know the people of Dunncraig better.

Annora sighed and inwardly shook her head. She had not
been given any chance to become a true part of Dunncraig,
but that was only part of her regret about not getting to know
the people as well as she would like. Something was not right
about Donnell's place as laird, about his claim to these lands
and to Meggie. Annora had sensed that wrongness from the
start, but after three years, she had not uncovered any truth to
give some weight to her suspicions. She knew someone at
Dunncraig knew the answers to all the questions she had, but
she had not yet found a way around Donnell's guard long
enough to ask any of them.

Approaching the cooper's home and shop, Annora felt her
spirits lighten just a little. Edmund the cooper's wife Ida might
be at home and Annora knew the woman would readily sate her
need to talk to another woman. Her pace grew a little faster in
anticipation. She dearly loved Meggie but the child simply
could not satisfy the need for a good, long woman-to-woman
talk.

"Rolf, she is coming."

This time James did not hesitate to look up from his work
when Edward called him by his assumed name. It had taken
James longer than he had liked to become accustomed to being
called Rolf. He hated to admit it but Edmund had been right
when he had counseled patience, had warned him that he
would need time to fully assume the guise of Rolf Larousse
Lavengeance.

Then what Edmund had just said fully settled into James's
mind. "Meggie?"

"Aye, but to ye she must be Lady Margaret," Edmund reminded him.

"Ah, of course. I shallnae forget. Who comes with her?"

"Mistress Annora and, a few yards behind, two of Donnell's men."

James cursed. "Does the mon think there is some danger to the woman or Meggie here?"

"Only to him, I am thinking. MacKay doesnae allow the woman to talk much with anyone. Nor the bairn. Some folk think the lass thinks herself too good for us and is teaching the bairn to be the same, but I think Mistress Annora is forced to keep to herself. E'en when she has a chance to talk to someone, there are always some of MacKay's men close at hand to try to hear all that is said."

"'Tis his own guilt making him think everyone is eager to decry him."

"I think that may be it. My Ida says the lass is clever and quick. MacKay may fear she has the wit to put a few things together and see the truth. 'Tis a big lie he is living, and it has to weigh on the mon."

"I hope it breaks his cursed back," James muttered as he tried to clean himself up just a little. "Better still, I want it to hang him."

"So does most everyone at Dunncraig," said Edmund.

James nodded. He had quickly seen how cowed his people were. Donnell was a harsh, cruel laird. He was also unskilled in the knowledge needed to keep the lands and the stock thriving. There were all too many signs that the man glutted himself on the riches of Dunncraig with little thought to how his people might survive or the fact that care must be taken to ensure that there was food in the future. The people might be afraid of the man seated in the laird's chair but they did not hold silent when they were amongst themselves, and James had heard a lot. Donnell was bleeding the lands dry to fill his belly and his purse.

Ida stuck her head into the room. "The lass says the laird sent her. He is wanting a goblet made by Rolf."

Before he could say anything, Ida was gone. For a moment James simply sat at his work table and breathed slowly and evenly to calm his excitement and anticipation. This was the first step. He had to be careful not to stumble on it. He knew Donnell spent a lot to make Dunncraig keep as fine as some French king's palace. That required a skilled woodworker and he wanted to be the one who was hired.

"That one," said Edmund, pointing toward a tall, richly carved goblet.

"Aye, I think ye have chosen the perfect one, old friend," James said and smiled.

"I havenae seen that expression for a while."

"'Tis anticipation."

"Aye. I can fair feel it in the air. The mon is a vain swine who spends far too much of your coin on things he doesnae need, things he thinks make him look important. Ye guessed his weakness right. Do ye really think the mon would leave some proof of his guilt around though?"

It was a question Edmund had asked before and James still was not confident of his feeling that the truth was inside the keep. "I cannae be sure but I think there has to be something. He cannae be rid of all proof. Mayhap I will but hear something that will aid me." He shrugged. "I cannae say. All I do ken is that I must be inside Dunncraig if I am to have any chance of getting the truth."

"Weel, then, let us get ye in there then."

Annora looked up as Edmund and another man stepped out of the workrooms in the back of the little shop. She stared at the man with Edmund, wondering why he so captivated her attention. He was tall and lean, even looked as if he could use a few good scrath meals. His hair was light brown and it hung past his broad shoulders. There was a scar on his right cheek, and he wore a patch over his left eye. The right eye was such a beautiful green she felt a pang of sorrow for the loss of its mate. His features were handsome, cleanly carved yet sharpened a little by the signs of hunger and trouble. This man had known hardship and she felt a surprising tug of deep sympathy for him. Since she had no idea what sort of trouble may have put that harshness on his handsome face, she did not understand why she wanted to smooth those lines away. The way his slightly full lips made her feel a little warm alarmed her somewhat. The man was having a very strange effect upon her and she did not think she liked it.

Then she saw his gaze rest on Meggie and put her arm around the child's shoulders. There was such an intensity in his look that she wondered why it did not make her afraid. A moment later, Annora realized that the intensity held no hint of a threat or dislike. There was a hunger there, a need and a grieving; and she wondered if he had lost a child. Again she felt a need to soothe him and that need began to make her very nervous.

She looked at the goblet he held in his elegant long-fingered hands and gasped softly. "Is that the one ye wish to sell to the laird?" she asked.

"Aye," the man replied. "I am Rolf, Rolf Larousse Lavengeance."

Annora blinked and had to bite her lip not to say anything. It was a very strange name. It roughly translated to wolf, red-head, and vengeance. It was also strange for a poor working man to have such an elaborate name. There had to be a story behind it and her curiosity stirred, but she beat it down. It was not her place to question the man about his name. As a bastard, she was also all too aware of the hurt and shame that could come from such questioning; and she would never inflict that upon anyone else.

"It is verra beautiful, Master Lavengeance," she said and held her hand out. "Might I have a look?"

"Aye."

As she took the goblet into her hands, she decided the man had been in Scotland long enough to lose much of his French accent and pick up a word or two of their language. If Donnell hired the man to do some work at the keep that would make life a great deal easier. Donnell had absolutely no knowledge of French and could easily become enraged by a worker who had difficulty understanding what he said. And, looking at the beautiful carvings of a hunt on the goblet, she suspected Donnell would be very eager to have the man come and work at Dunncraig keep. The thought that she might have to see a lot of the man in order to translate orders for him made her feel a little too eager and Annora felt a sudden need to get away from this man.

"I believe this will please my cousin weel," she said. "Your work is beautiful, Master Lavengeance. The stag on this goblet looks so real one almost expects to see him toss his proud head."

James just nodded and named his price. The woman named Annora did not even blink, but paid for it and hurried Meggie out of the shop. Moving quickly to look out the door, James watched her lead his child back to the keep, two of Donnell's men in step a few yards behind them. He felt a hand rub his arm and looked to find Ida standing at his side, her blue eyes full of sympathy.

"Annora loves the wee lass," Ida said.

"Does she? Or is she but a good nursemaid?" James asked.

"Oh, aye, she loves the lass. 'Tis Lady Margaret who holds Mistress Annora at Dunncraig and naught else. The child has been loved and weel cared for whilst ye have been gone, Laird."

James nodded but he was not sure he fully believed that. Meggie had looked healthy and happy, but she had said nothing. There was also a solemnity to the child that had not been there before. Meggie had been as sweet and innocent as her mother but had had a liveliness that Mary had never pos-

sessed. There had been no sign of that liveliness, and he wondered what had smothered it. He would not lay the blame for
that change at the feet of Mistress Annora yet, but he would
watch the woman closely.

He inwardly grimaced, knowing he would find it no hardship to watch the woman. Mistress Annora was beautiful.
Slender yet full-curved, her body caught—and held—a
man's gaze. Her thick raven hair made her fair skin look an
even purer shade of cream, and her wide midnight-blue eyes
drew in a man like a moth to a flame. After three years alone
he knew he had to be careful not to let his starved senses lead
him astray, but he was definitely eager to further his acquaintance with Mistress Annora.

Suddenly he wondered if Mistress Annora was Donnell's
lover; and then wondered why that possiblity enraged him.
James told himself it was because he did not want such a
woman caring for his child. It might be unfair to think her
anything more than she seemed, but her beauty made it all
too easy to think that Donnell would not be able to leave her
alone. Mistress Annora's true place in Dunncraig keep was
just another question needing an answer.

Stepping more fully into the open doorway of Edmund's
shop, he stared up at the keep that had once been his home. He
would be back there soon. He would enter the keep as a
worker, but he meant to stay as the laird. For all her beauty, if
Mistress Annora had any part in Donnell's schemes, she would
find that her beauty did not buy her any mercy from him.

About the Author

Hannah Howell is an award-winning author who lives with her family in Massachusetts. She is the author of twenty-three Zebra historical romances, and is currently working on a new Highland historical romance, *Highland Wolf*, to be released in December 2007! Hannah loves hearing from readers, and you may visit her Web site: www.hannahhowell.com.

Discover the Romances of
Hannah Howell